OBABAKOAK

BERNARDO ATXAGA

OBABAKOAK

A NOVEL

Translated by
MARGARET JULL COSTA

PANTHEON BOOKS, NEW YORK

All rights reserved under International and Pan-American
Copyright Conventions. Published in the United States by
Pantheon Books, a division of Random House, Inc., New York.
Originally published in Basque by Editorial Erein in 1988.
This English translation was originally published in Great Britain
by Hutchinson, London in 1992 and is based on the author's own
Spanish version published by Ediciones B, Barcelona in 1989.
Copyright © 1989 by Bernardo Atxaga.

Library of Congress Cataloging-in-Publication Data

Atxaga, Bernardo.
    [Obabakoak. English]
    Obabakoak / Bernardo Atxaga ; translated by
    Margaret Jull Costa.
        p.   cm.
    ISBN 0-679-42404-0
    I. Title.
PH5339.A802313   1993
899'.923—dc20   92-50774
                                           CIP

Manufactured in the United States of America
First American Edition
9 8 7 6 5 4 3 2 1

CONTENTS

CONTENTS

TRANSLATOR'S NOTE

Obabakoak was originally written in Basque and published by Editorial Erein in 1988. This English translation is based on the author's own Spanish version, published by Ediciones B in 1989.

I would like to take the opportunity to thank Bernardo Atxaga, Neil Belton, Annella McDermott, Faye Carney and Philip Polack for all their help and advice.

THE GAME OF THE GOOSE

The Game of the Goose (*el juego de la oca*) (first mentioned on p. 153) is still played in other parts of Europe (for example, *le jeu de l'oie* in France, *il gioco dell'oca* in Italy). It is played on a circular board of sixty-three squares, the sixty-third being occupied by Mother Goose. The first person to reach square sixty-three wins. Geese also appear on other squares and if you land on one of these, you jump forward to the next goose and get another throw of the dice. If you land on less fortunate squares such as the maze, the prison or the square symbolising death (a skull or skeleton) you must either wait for another player to take your place, go back several squares or return to square one.

PROLOGUE

(The author speaks of his language, *euskera*)

I write in a strange language. Its verbs,
the structure of its relative clauses,
the words it uses to designate ancient things
– rivers, plants, birds –
have no sisters anywhere on Earth.
A house is *etxe*, a bee *erle*, death *heriotz*.
The sun of the long winters we call *eguzki* or *eki*;
the sun of the sweet, rainy springs is also
– as you'd expect – called *eguzki* or *eki*
(it's a strange language but not that strange).

Born, they say, in the megalithic age,
it survived, this stubborn language, by withdrawing,
by hiding away like a hedgehog in a place,
which, thanks to the traces it left behind there,
the world named the Basque Country or *Euskal Herria*.
Yet its isolation could never have been absolute
– cat is *katu*, pipe is *pipa*, logic is *lojika* –
rather, as the prince of detectives would have said,
the hedgehog, my dear Watson, crept out of its hiding place
(to visit, above all, Rome and all its progeny).

The language of a tiny nation, so small
you cannot even find it on the map,
it never strolled in the gardens of the Court
or past the marble statues of government buildings;
in four centuries it produced only a hundred books . . .
the first in 1545; the most important in 1643;
the Calvinist New Testament in 1571;

the complete Catholic Bible around 1860.
Its sleep was long, its bibliography brief
(but in the twentieth century the hedgehog awoke).

Obabakoak, this book published now in this city,
the city of Dickens, of Wilkie Collins and of so many others,
is one of the latest books to join the Basque bibliography.
It was written in several houses and in several countries,
and its subject is simply life in general.
And *Obaba* is just Obaba: a place, a setting;
ko means 'of'; *a* is a determiner; *k* the plural.
The literal translation: *The People* or *Things of Obaba*;
a less literal translation: *Stories from Obaba*
(and with that I conclude this prologue).

CHILDHOODS

ESTEBAN WERFELL

ESTEBAN WERFELL'S books, mostly leather-bound and ranged in serried ranks along the shelves, covered almost every inch of the room's four walls. Those ten or twelve thousand volumes were the summation of two lives, his own and his father's, and when he sat down amongst them to write, as he did on that February day, they created a warm enclave, a high protecting wall separating him off from the outside world. Like many of the books, the old oak table at which he wrote was another reminder of his father; when still very young, he'd had it brought there from the family home in Obaba.

There was, however, one chink in that wall of paper, pages and words, a window through which, while he wrote, Esteban Werfell could see the sky, the willows, the lake and the little house built there for the swans in the city's main park. Without really impinging on his solitude, the window made an inroad into the darkness of the books and mitigated that other darkness which often creates phantoms in the hearts of men who have never quite learned how to live alone.

For some minutes Esteban Werfell contemplated the cloudy, greyish-white sky of that February day. Then, looking away, he opened one of the drawers in his desk and took out a notebook with stiff covers, bearing the number twelve, identical down to the last detail with the other eleven notebooks he had already filled and that contained his personal journal.

They were nice those notebooks with their stiff covers, he liked them. He often used to wonder whether he didn't misuse them, whether the stories and reflections he noted down in them did not perhaps turn them from the proper destiny that might otherwise await a notebook, especially one with stiff covers.

Perhaps it was foolish to think that way about something like a notebook. It probably was. But he couldn't help it, still less when he was about to start a new one, as he was then. Why was he always thinking about things he didn't want to think about? Once his father had said to him: 'It isn't the fact that you've got a few batty ideas that worries me, it's just that they're always the same batty ideas.' It was true, but he'd never understood why he was so drawn to such ideas.

Whatever the reason, the force propelling him towards them was very strong, and Esteban Werfell couldn't resist the temptation to look up at the shelf where he kept the other eleven notebooks. There, half hidden amongst various geographical treatises, were the pages that bore witness to his life, the pages that contained all its most beautiful moments, its most important events. Not that they were a treasure. They'd lost any brilliance they once had. Re-reading them was like perusing papers smeared with ashes; re-reading them he felt ashamed and saw how the desire for sleep and oblivion still grew within him.

'Notebooks full of dead letters,' he murmured to himself. Even that expression wasn't new.

But he couldn't allow such thoughts to distract him from the task he'd sat down at the table to perform, nor, as had happened on countless other occasions, allow them to carry him from one sad memory to another, deeper and deeper down, to a land which, long ago – ever since his days as a student of geography – he'd named the Cape of Despair. He was a grown man now, able to fight against his own compulsions and fight he would, by filling that new notebook.

Esteban Werfell picked up his pen – the one with the wooden shaft that he used only when writing his diary – and dipped it in the inkwell.

'17th February 1958,' he began. He wrote in a beautiful, neat hand.

Outside the window the sky had turned completely grey and a fine, invisible rain was darkening the ivy that covered the swans'

4

house. The sight of it made him sigh. He would have preferred a different kind of weather. He didn't like the park being empty.

He sighed once more, then dipped his pen in the ink again and bent over the notebook.

I have returned from Hamburg – he wrote – with the intention of writing a memoir of my life. But I will not do so in the ordered and exhaustive manner of one who, perhaps quite rightly, holds himself to be the mirror of an age or a society. That, of course, is not my case and that is not how I will proceed. I will restrict myself to recounting what happened one afternoon long ago, when, to be exact, I was fourteen years old, and the important consequences that afternoon had for me. For a man already in the autumn of his life a few short hours may not seem a matter of much significance, but it is all I have to tell, indeed it is the only thing worth telling. And perhaps, given the life I have led, it is not such a small thing. After all, I dedicated myself to teaching and a life spent sitting at a teacher's desk is a surer recipe for constipation than it is for adventure.

He sat back in his chair to wait for the ink to dry. The day was still grey, but the rain was much heavier than it had been a few minutes earlier and the sound it made, the dull murmur of rain on grass, was clearly audible in the room. And there was a change too around the lake: the swans had come out of their house now and were beating their wings with unusual vigour. He'd never seen the swans like that before. Did they enjoy getting wet? Or was it the lack of spectators that cheered them? He didn't know, and it really wasn't worth wasting time on such stupid questions, time better spent going over what he'd just written.

He never got off to a good start. The words refused to give faithful expression to what was demanded of them, as if they were lazy, or as if they lacked the energy to do so. His father used to say: 'Thought is like sand and when we try to grasp a fistful of it, most of the grains trickle out between our fingers.' And it was true. For example, here he was proposing to write a memoir, but it would have been more exact to describe it as a meditation, because that in fact was what he wanted to write: a fine meditation on the events of one afternoon in his adolescence. And that wasn't the only blunder, there were others.

He could, of course, cross out what he'd written and start again, but he didn't want to. It was against his rules. He liked his pages to look immaculate, his as well as other people's, and he felt proud that his scrupulousness had led his students to nickname him after a well-known brand of soap. Anyway, why worry about finding a good beginning? He'd make mistakes on the second attempt too. There would always be mistakes. It was better to press on, getting it right as he went along, gradually making amends for his poor beginning.

He looked out at the park again. There were no swans on the lake now, they'd retreated to their house. No, they didn't like the February rain either.

However – he wrote – any attempt to select out special moments of our life may prove a grave mistake. It may be that a life can only be judged as a whole, *in extenso*, and not by its parts, not by taking one day and rejecting another, not by separating out the years like the pieces of a jigsaw puzzle, in order to conclude that this bit was very good and this very bad. The fact is that everything that lives is like a river, with no shortcuts and no halts along the way.

But, whilst that is true, it is equally true that memory tends to behave quite differently. Like all good witnesses, memory takes pleasure in the concrete, in selected details. If I had to compare it with anything, I'd say it was like an eye. I would never, on the other hand, compare it to a book-keeper who specialises in taking inventories.

For example, right now I can see the swans' house, covered

from ground to roof with ivy, which is by its nature dark and darker still on rainy days like today. I see it but, strictly speaking, I never see it. Each time I look up, my gaze slides over the monotonous green and black of the leaves, and doesn't stop until it finds the reddish stain on one of the corners of the roof. I don't even know what it is. Perhaps it's a scrap of paper or a primula that's chosen to bloom there or a single tile that the ivy has left uncovered. As far as my eyes are concerned, it doesn't matter, for they shun the dark and unerringly seek out that one point of light.

Esteban Werfell stared out at the reddish stain, but still failed to assuage his doubts. It could as easily be a primula as a scrap of paper or a tile. In the end, though, such a detail was of no matter. What did matter was what he had just written about memory. To say that memory took pleasure in the concrete was inexact. It was a question of necessity, not pleasure.

That is how the eye behaves – he went on – and, if my idea is correct, memory does too. It disregards the ordinary and instead seeks out remarkable days, intense moments; in my own case, it seeks out one particular far-off afternoon of my life.
But enough of this. It's time to begin the story itself.

Once he'd ruled a line to bring to a close that first page of his notebook, Esteban Werfell felt relieved. There it was, he had managed to outline an introduction to what he wanted to say. He didn't know quite why he went about things that way, with all those detours and delays, but it was certainly very typical of him, it always had been. He never wrote or spoke directly, he never dealt frankly with the people around him. After all these years, he accepted his timidity, his cowardice, as a character defect, but the opportunities he had let slip by because of it still hurt him. His whole life had been one of silence, passivity, withdrawal.

But he was getting sidetracked again. It wasn't a question now of how he lived his life, but of how he wrote, and it was a matter of indifference whether he took a circuitous route to get there or not. No one would ever read his personal journal. He did occasionally allow himself to fantasise about some imaginary future reader – sitting at that same table after his death – poring over his notebooks, but he could never really bring himself to believe in him or her. No, there would be no such reader. There was, therefore, something slightly ridiculous about his preoccupation with style.

As he dipped his pen in the inkwell, he looked across at the park. In the rain, without the usual walkers, the area round the lake looked more solitary than ever. The little streams that sprang up amongst the grass rippled as they flowed over the pebbles.

Hic incipit – he wrote – here begins the story of the afternoon when, for the first time in my life, I was taken to church. I was fourteen years old and I lived with my father in a place called Obaba.

It was Sunday and I'd arranged to meet up with some schoolfriends and go to the cinema that had been built some three miles from Obaba near the railway. But for the first time, and contrary to the rules governing our friendship, my friends turned up at the house long before the agreed hour and, as soon as I opened the door to them, made a most unexpected request. 'Come to church with us this evening,' they said, 'come and sing in the choir. Ask Mr Werfell to let you come. You can tell him it's just a matter of singing some psalms, you don't have to believe in anything.'

Such behaviour was odd in them. Such boldness, I mean. And the word 'boldness' is apt on this occasion, since in Obaba paying social visits – insofar as that implied seeing the interior of someone else's house – was considered to be in distinctly bad taste, in the same league as turning round to stare when someone was getting undressed. Moreover, my father was a foreigner, a stranger and an enemy and everyone knew how much he hated the church and religion in general.

Looking back, I have no doubt that the person behind that proposal was the canon of Obaba, a Jesuit. In his eyes I must have seemed a soul in mortal danger, a child who, lacking a mother – she had died when I was born – was at the mercy of a hateful man, a man who would not hesitate to drag his own son into the abyss in which he himself lived. The canon must have thought there could be no better way of attracting me than through my friendship with my schoolfellows.

The hatred between the canon and my father was not, so to speak, purely intellectual. It had its roots in something other than the iconoclastic approach adopted by my father from the moment he was put in charge of the mines at Obaba. That something was my existence. To use the words I heard on the lips of the schoolmaster one day, I was not the 'legitimate fruit of a marriage'. And I wasn't, for the simple reason that my parents had joined together in free union, without recourse to the church, a fact which at that time and in that place was deemed inadmissible. But that's another story and has no place in this notebook.

The park was still deserted and the trees, oblivious of the coming spring, seemed listless. Not even the swans gave any sign of life.

He looked away from the window and re-read what he'd written. No, his parents' story had no place in that notebook, perhaps in the next notebook, the thirteenth. It would, above all, be the story of a young woman who chose to live with a foreigner and, because of that, was slandered and condemned to be ostracised. 'Your mother would sleep with anyone. Your mother didn't wear any knickers. Your mother died young because of all the wicked things she did.'

The words heard during playtime at the school in Obaba still wounded him. He wasn't sure whether he would write that thirteenth notebook or not but, if he did, he knew how difficult it would be. But he would face that when he came to it. The task in hand was the story he had brought back with him from the trip to Hamburg.

Esteban Werfell bent over his notebook again. His schoolfriends' unexpected visit once more filled his imagination.

Seeing my astonishment, my friends proceeded, rather clumsily, to argue their case, studiously avoiding all mention of the canon. According to them, it was wrong that they and I should have to go our separate ways on Sundays. It was a sheer waste of time, because sometimes they finished their singing ten or fifteen minutes earlier than usual, minutes which could prove vital if we were to get to the cinema on time, minutes which, in fact, were never put to good use; all because of me, of course, because I was their friend and they had no alternative but to wait for me.

Summing up, one of them said: 'We always arrive after the film's started, and it seems stupid to me to cycle three miles only to miss half the plot. It would make much better sense to stick together.'

Their arguments were, as I said, rather clumsy; in fact the service tended to finish later rather than earlier. I said nothing to contradict them, though. Deep down I wanted to go to church. Not just because it was forbidden territory, and therefore desirable, but also because of the need I felt to be a normal child, to be one of the boys. Apart from my father, I was the only person in Obaba who had never set foot in that building and, naturally – I was after all only fourteen – I didn't like being marked out as different.

Their proposal was in line with my own desires, therefore, and I didn't argue with what they said. I simply indicated the door of the library, where my father was working. It was his permission they required. No, I didn't dare to ask him, it was best that they should do so. Not that I thought he would agree. I expected my father to dismiss them in a loud voice, declaring that he had no intention of going against the principles of a lifetime on that or any other Sunday.

Instead I heard him say: 'If he wants to go, let him.' I felt first surprised, then frightened; it was as if every pane of glass in the window had suddenly shattered. Why did he say yes? I couldn't even begin to imagine why.

A swan stood at the door of its house making loud honking noises, as if to reproach the continuing rain. It rained on and on, flattening the grass and forming puddles that grew ever deeper. Soon the whole park would be awash.

Esteban Werfell clasped his hands and rested them on the notebook. No, at fourteen he couldn't possibly have understood his father, because at that age, he saw him not with his own eyes, but through the eyes of others, through the eyes of those who, he later realised, were his father's declared enemies. In Obaba it was said that Engineer Werfell was a proud, intractable man and that's what he thought too. It was said – a little girl who played with him in the square told him this – that he was so cruel he beat the mineworkers; and Esteban would simply smile and nod. Indeed he accepted that image because he had no other. What was his father? Just that, his father. And beyond that? Beyond that, nothing. Well, apart from being a mining engineer.

But that time had passed. He was a grown man, not a rather unsympathetic adolescent. He thought now that he understood why his father had accepted his schoolfriends' proposal.

'Sheer weariness,' he sighed. He was beginning to enjoy the rain. It was helping him to remember.

Engineer Werfell had indeed grown weary, he regretted having left his native city of Hamburg to move to a place where all his ideas seemed ridiculous. At first, he dreamed of returning. 'We'll go back, Esteban, and you can study at the same university

I went to.' Those words ran like a refrain throughout his childhood.

But then the bad news began to arrive. One day it was the mine closing down; the next it was the failure of the bonds he'd bought on the Stock Exchange, leaving him almost penniless; then came the letter from his best friend, Theodor Steiner, telling him that the association to which both belonged – the Eichendorff Club – had been banned in Germany and that his ideas were now outlawed even in the country of his birth.

By the time Esteban was fourteen, his father had given up hope. He would die in Obaba, he would never return to Germany. His son would never study at a German university. It was logical then, given the circumstances, that he no longer had the strength to fight for his son's education. What did it matter? 'If he wants to go, let him.' The battle was lost anyway.

The swan standing at the door of his house honked again, this time managing to get all the other swans inside to join him. The din distracted him from his memories.

'Be quiet!' he shouted and went on to wonder: Why was he so proud? He didn't want to cut the thread at that moment joining him and his father.

If he'd been more humble, Engineer Werfell would have been better able to accept life in Obaba. If he'd been more intelligent too. Yes, that was what real intelligence was, the ability to adapt to any situation. A man able to adapt would never know that descent into hell. On the contrary, he would achieve happiness. What use had all his books, reading and ideas been to his father? In the end he'd been defeated. 'Only the mean of spirit adapt to life,' his father used to say. But he didn't agree with him any more. Nor did he agree with the old maxim coupling knowledge and suffering, or with the one that says the more a man knows, the more he suffers. As he used to say to his students, that unfortunate consequence came only after climbing the first rungs up the ladder of knowledge. As a man climbed higher, he had to learn to triumph over suffering.

The swans seemed to have quietened down. Esteban Werfell dipped his pen in the inkwell and covered the first lines of a new page with his neat writing. He was determined to note down these reflections in his journal.

Even in the most difficult situations there comes a moment when giving up the struggle becomes something desirable, even pleasant. Thus, for example, the victim of a shipwreck ultimately becomes reconciled to the sea, even someone who has sweated blood trying to save his ship and has spent the whole night beneath the stars, encircled by fishes, in the most utter solitude, defying the waves. It doesn't matter what he's done, or how dearly he clings to life, the end is always sweet. He sees that he can do no more, that no one is coming to his rescue, that no coast is in sight, and then he accepts the situation, he rests, he gives himself up to the sea like a child wanting only to sleep.

But my father was too proud. True his ship had foundered and he had no option but to submit, but he wouldn't accept that, he didn't want the final pleasure of defeat. He replied brusquely: 'If he wants to go, let him', and shut himself up in his library, the 'only place in Obaba that he liked'. When I knocked to ask him for money to go to the cinema, he didn't answer. He simply slipped a coin under the door. Now, I think, I regret the joy I showed then.

For as soon as I had the money, we all rushed off, pushing and shoving, the way we did when the teacher let us out at break time. Then we wheeled our bikes up the hill known in Obaba as Canons' Hill.

It was a spring day of unsettled weather, with almost continual showers and squally winds, and the ditches by the roadside were full of water. Where they'd overflowed, the fallen apple blossom carried along by the current almost covered the ground. We trod on it as we passed, and it was like treading on carpets of white.

We walked briskly along, pushing the bikes which as Andrés, one of my friends, quite rightly remarked, seemed much heavier going uphill. At the end of the road, on the brow of the hill, stood the imposing spire of the church.

We all felt really cheerful. We laughed for no reason and rang our bicycle bells to compare the different sounds they made. 'Are you happy, Esteban?' I told them I was, that it was an event of real importance for me, that I was bursting with curiosity. 'Aren't you a bit nervous too?' I told them I wasn't. But I was and my nervousness was growing minute by minute. The time was approaching. As my father would have put it, I would soon be on the Other Side.

A moment later I was entering the church for the first time.

The massive door was extremely heavy. I had to lean the whole weight of my body against it before it yielded.

Andrés said to me: 'Before going in you have to make the sign of the cross.'

I told him I didn't know how to. So he wetted my fingers with his and guided my hand in its movements.

'It's so dark!' I exclaimed as soon as I went in. I was blinded by the contrast between the brightness outside and the shadowy depths inside. I couldn't see a thing, not even the central aisle immediately in front. 'Don't talk so loud,' said my companions going in ahead of me.

Far away, where I imagined the end of the aisle to be, a large candle was burning. It was the only point of light in the whole building. I took a few steps in that direction, only to stop again. I didn't know which way to go and my friends seemed to have disappeared.

My eyes remained fixed on the flame at the other end of the aisle but gradually I began to make out a few other things. I noticed the stained-glass windows, which were blue, and the golden reflections on a column near the candle. But still I didn't dare to move. Then I heard a voice behind me say: 'Don't be frightened, Esteban. It's only me,' and, despite the warning, I jumped.

Before I had time to recover, a long, bony arm had encircled my neck. It was the canon. Bringing his face closer to mine, he said:

'Come now, Esteban. Don't be frightened.'

His clothes smelled very strange to me.

'The flame of that candle never goes out, Esteban,' he whispered, pointing ahead with his free hand. 'When we have to light a new candle, we always light it from the dying flame of the old one. Just think what that means, Esteban. What do *you* think it means?'

I was so scared I was incapable of thought and I felt ashamed every time the canon said my name. I kept silent.

'It means,' he began, 'that the light we see today is the same light seen by our grandparents and our great-grandparents; it's the same light our ancestors gazed upon. For hundreds of years, this house has united us all, those alive now and those who lived before us. That's what the church is, Esteban, a community that transcends time.'

This argument clearly took no account of the circumstances of my own life. The Church not only united, it also divided; the fact of my being there was but one example of that. I said nothing, however, to contradict the canon. In fact, I felt humbled, as if my exclusion from that community were a personal defect or stain. I broke out in a cold sweat.

Smiling, the canon remarked that since there were still some minutes before the service was due to begin, I should take the opportunity to have a look at the altar and to visit other parts of the building. And, leaving me alone, he moved off towards a side door that led to the choir loft. I heard the rustle of his clothes even after he was out of sight.

We tend to think that things are in themselves either big or small, failing to realise that what we call size is in fact always relative. They are only big or small in relation to other things and that is why I can still say now, in all honesty, that I have never again seen anywhere as big as the church at Obaba. It was a hundred times the size of the school, a thousand times bigger than my bedroom. What's more the shadows blurred the edges of walls and columns and made the bosses and the ribs of the vault seem even more remote. Everything seemed larger than it really was.

One of the picture books I used to read at the time recounted the adventures of an expedition that had become trapped inside a hollow mountain and I associated the pictures in that book with the place I saw before me. Not only because of the obvious physical resemblance but also because of the asphyxia that was beginning to afflict me as it had the characters in the story. I continued on up the aisle but with the growing conviction that I would surely suffocate before I reached the flame burning on the altar. Then I noticed an old lady dressed in black approach the foot of the altar and lift a lever. Immediately the whole church was filled with light.

That change from darkness to light made me feel better and I began to breathe more easily. With some relief I thought: it isn't a hollow mountain, it's more like a theatre, like the ones my father used to go to in Hamburg, like the places where they put on operas.

Most of my father's memories revolved around the theatre and I knew by heart the plots and choreography of everything he had seen at the opera house on Buschstrasse or at the Schauspielhaus, as well as many stories about the actors and actresses of the time. Comparisons between what I'd imagined in those conversations with my father and what I saw then seemed unavoidable. Yes, the church was a theatre with a large central stage, images of bearded men, and seats and benches for the audience. And everything was golden, everything shone.

A deep, almost tremulous sound ran through the whole

church and when I turned my head towards the choir loft, I noticed some twenty women kneeling at their pews. They were moving their lips and staring at me.

Oppressed by so many eyes, I ran towards the door the canon had entered and a moment later I was taking the stairs two by two up to where my companions would be waiting.

Esteban Werfell laid his pen down wearily on the table and raised his eyes to the window, though without seeing anything in particular, without even noticing the din the swans by the lake were making. One of his 'batty ideas' had just flitted across his mind, interrupting him, obliging him to consider the meaning of that twelfth notebook. What point was there in remembering? Wouldn't it be better to leave the past well alone, rather than stir it all up?

'Only the young really enjoy looking back,' he thought. But when they talked about the past, they were really talking about the future, about the fears and desires they had about that future, about what they wanted from life. Moreover, they never did so alone, as he did. He didn't really understand his urge to remember. Perhaps it was a bad sign, a sign that everything was over once and for all, that he was tired of life.

He shook his head to drive away such thoughts and finally noticed what was going on outside. By the side of the swans' house someone had stopped to shelter from the rain and to throw pieces of bread into the lake. The swans were swimming back and forth honking like mad things. 'Their first visitor of the day,' he thought, 'they must be hungry.' Then to himself he said: 'Back to the choir loft.'

The moment I entered the choir loft, the canon got up from his seat at the organ and stretched out his arms. Almost sweetly, he said:

17

'Young Werfell is finally amongst us. Let us all rejoice and give thanks.'

Putting his hands together he began to pray out loud and all my companions followed suit.

'Welcome, Esteban,' he said afterwards, assuring me that: 'From now on you will belong to our community, you will be one of the chosen.' My companions stared at me as if they were seeing me for the first time. Andrés was in charge of distributing the books of psalms. The copy he handed me was almost brand new.

'Don't worry, Esteban. A few more Sundays and you'll be as good as us. You'll probably end up being the best of all,' he whispered.

The pages of the book were very thin and had gilded edges. A red ribbon marked the psalms for that day.

When the canon asked me to sit at his side, the gaze of my companions became even more fixed. I hung back. I realised that it was an honour to be asked, but feared the physical proximity of the canon. The disagreeable smell emanating from his clothes was still fresh in my memory.

'Don't be frightened, Esteban. Come and sit up here with me,' said the canon, as he began to play. The floorboards of the choir loft vibrated.

I was puzzled to see that the organ had two keyboards and that in order to play it, one had to move one's feet. Sometimes the melody grew unpredictable with abrupt highs and lows and the canon seemed to be dancing sitting down, rocking back and forth on the bench and bumping up against me. I found it difficult to follow the melody of the psalms we sang, I couldn't concentrate.

By the third psalm, I had closed the book and simply sat looking at the scene before me. There were my companions opening and closing their mouths and down below were the kneeling women; a little farther off, the candle flame burned, giving off orange lights.

Suddenly the flame began to rise into the air. At first it seemed to be moving of its own accord, as if propelled forward by something at its base. But then, when it was already hovering above the altar steps, I saw that this was not the case, that the flame was not travelling forwards on its own but was held in the hand of a young girl with fair hair. She was the one hovering there, gently, unhesitatingly.

'She's coming towards me,' I thought. The light from the flame was blinding me now.

The young girl flew across the whole length of the church and came to a halt in front of me. She hovered in the air, about a yard above the floor of the choir loft. The organ had fallen silent.

'Do you know what love is, Esteban?' she asked sweetly.

I replied with a nod and tried to get up from the bench in order to see her face. But the candle flame kept me riveted to the spot.

'Could you love me?' she asked and for a moment I glimpsed her nose, her half-open lips.

'Yes,' I said. It seemed the only possible answer.

'Then come and find me, Esteban. Come to Hamburg,' she said. 'My address is Maria Vockel, 2 Johamesholfstrasse, Hamburg.'

Having said that, she turned and began to move off towards the altar. I cried out that yes, I would come to Hamburg and find her, but asked her not to go just yet, to stay a little longer. Then I heard someone say: 'It's all right, Esteban, it's all right. Calm down.' I was lying on the floor of the choir loft with the canon bending over me. Andrés was fanning me with the pages of a score.

'Maria Vockel!' I exclaimed.

'Calm down, Esteban. You must have fainted.'

There was a gentle edge to the canon's voice. He helped me to my feet and asked Andrés to take me outside to get some air.

'You'd best not go to the cinema, Esteban. Better safe than sorry,' the canon advised me as we said goodbye. 'You won't go now, will you?'

But the image of the fair-haired young girl still filled my mind and I did not feel strong enough to reply.

Andrés answered for me, reassuring the canon: 'Don't worry, father, he won't go and neither will I. I'll stay with him, just in case.'

The canon said that would be fine and returned to the organ bench. The service had to go on.

I felt better as soon as I got outside and my mind grew clearer. Very soon the image of the young girl with fair hair began to grow tenuous, to disappear, the way dreams do, the way specks of dust vanish the instant the ray of sun illuminating them moves on. But by my side was my schoolfriend, Andrés, to ensure that the scene I'd witnessed in the choir loft was not entirely lost. He was two or three years older than me and much preoccupied by affairs of the heart; he would never forget a woman's name.

'Who's Maria Vockel?' he asked at last.

It was then, when I heard her name again, that the image returned to me. Again I saw her flying from one part of the church to the other and remembered her questions. Hesitantly, I told Andrés all that had happened.

'It's a shame you didn't see her face,' he commented when I had finished. He seemed very interested in that missing detail of the girl's portrait.

'No, just her nose and her lips. But I'm sure she's prettier than any of the girls in Obaba.' I spoke as I thought, with the slightly ridiculous vehemence of my fourteen years.

'She can't be prettier than the girl who works in the bar,' he replied gravely.

'Sorry, I didn't mean to be rude,' I said.

I had forgotten how touchy Andrés could be on the subject of female beauty. From his point of view – which even then, at the height of my adolescence, struck me as slightly absurd – no woman could compare with the waitress he was pursuing. He spent every free moment scrounging enough money to enable him to spend Saturday evenings drinking at a corner of the bar where she worked. Drinking and suffering, of course, because she, the prettiest girl in the world, spoke to everyone but him.

'You do forgive me, don't you?' I urged. I didn't want him to go, I needed someone to talk to.

'All right,' he said.

'Do you fancy a stroll?' I suggested. I didn't want to go straight home, I needed time to sort out the feelings at that moment thronging my mind.

'We could cycle.'

'I'd prefer to walk, really. I've got a lot to think about.'

We set off along a path which, starting from the church, encircled the valley where Obaba's three small rivers met. It was narrow and somewhat ill-suited to two walkers like us with bikes to push, but I felt very drawn to the landscape you could see from there. It was green and undulating, with a scattering of white houses, the sort of landscape that appears in every adolescent's first attempts at poetry.

'It looks like a toy valley,' I said.

'Yes, I suppose it does,' replied Andrés, rather unconvinced.

'It looks like those cribs you make at Christmas time,' I added, stopping for a better look. I was starting to feel euphoric. The strange vision I'd had in the choir of the church had made my heart drunk.

It had stopped raining at last and the swans were taking advantage of the lull to seek out scraps of food along the edges of the lake. The friendly passer-by who had been throwing them bread was now walking away towards the city along the main path of the park, his empty white bag folded beneath one arm.

Attracted by the new turn the day was taking, Esteban Werfell left his notebook and went over to the window. 'I was so young then!' he sighed, recalling the conversation he'd had with Andrés.

Yes, very young, and tormented by the remarks made about Engineer Werfell and about his own mother, tormented and confused, seeking in picture books the affection and security he failed to find at school or in the streets of Obaba. His heart then had been like a small Cape of Despair, fertile soil for a fantasy figure like Maria Vockel. He wanted to believe in the reality of that fair-haired young girl, he wanted to believe in her words. The way in which she had appeared to him was, after all, not so very different from the methods employed by the heroines in the novels he read.

Even after all these years, Esteban Werfell still felt it right to consider Maria Vockel his first love. Walking along the path encircling the little valley, he grew melancholy, dreamy, just like Andrés. For the first time in his life, he felt he understood how his companion suffered over his waitress.

'At least you can see her. I'll never see mine.'

He remembered his words now with a smile. They were ridiculous, like most of the words recorded in his personal journal of the time. But to deny the past was mere foolishness.

'Why don't you go to Hamburg? That's where your father's from, isn't it?' reasoned Andrés. He was concerned with details, but not with the apparition in itself, nor with the likelihood of such an occurrence. On the contrary, it seemed quite reasonable to him. He knew of lovers who had communicated in much stranger ways than that. By becoming owls, for example. Maria Vockel must have had some reason for choosing that particular method.

Leaving his memories for a moment, Esteban Werfell opened the window and leaned out over the park. The sky was growing steadily bluer and late evening visitors were out walking their dogs or throwing bread to the swans. On the other side of the lake, a group of some twenty children were playing football.

'Anyway,' he thought, leaning on the windowsill and returning to his memories. 'Andrés was no exception. People in Obaba had no difficulty in accepting even the strangest events. My father used to make fun of them.'

'They have crude minds, Esteban,' his father would say. And he always came up with some humorous anecdote to illustrate that point of view. But he had disliked the anecdotes and it seemed to him that his father was unfair to the people of Obaba, that he was wrong to despise them.

'I was a true Werfell for all that, though,' he thought, closing the window and returning to the table. 'However much I wanted to believe in that apparition, my mind refused to do so. This was real life, not a novel. It seemed ridiculous to accept even the possibility that what had happened was real. No, Maria Vockel could not be real, she could not possibly live at 2 Johamesholfstrasse.'

Esteban Werfell closed his eyes and saw the fourteen-year-old Esteban on his way home, full of doubts, telling himself that his head was full of stories about Hamburg, full of women's names, the names of singers and actresses, and that they must be the source of the words he had heard in the choir.

Before continuing, he counted the number of blank pages left in the notebook. There were quite a few left, enough for him to be gripped by a desire to finish that last part of the story as quickly as possible. If he finished early, he would still have time to go out into the park and watch a bit of the football match the children were playing. But the desire lasted only a moment. He must tell the story with all its details just as he had decided to do before returning home from his visit to Hamburg.

He dipped his pen in the inkwell. A final glance at the park revealed a small boy wagging an umbrella threateningly at the swans.

'What are you doing home so early?' my father asked as soon as I opened the front door.

'I didn't go to the cinema after all.'

'Why not?'

'Because I fainted in church,' I confessed, shamefaced.

I saw that he was alarmed and quickly explained that nothing untoward had happened. The darkness in the church and the flickering candle flame had been to blame. I shouldn't have stared so hard at it.

Sighing, my father gestured towards the library.

'Esteban, if it's spirit you want, you'll find it in those books in there not in the darkness of a church,' he said. After a silence, I stammered: 'Can I ask you something?' I couldn't go on talking to him and still keep my secret. I needed to know what he thought about the Maria Vockel incident.

'Of course.'

He sat down in an armchair and indicated that I do likewise. He appeared nervous and it seemed to me that he no longer saw me as a child but as an adult, capable of making my own decisions.

I described everything that had happened from the moment I entered the church: the conversation during the fainting fit, my feelings at the time and my subsequent doubts. He listened attentively, without interrupting. When he saw that my story was over, he got up and began to pace about the room. He stopped by the window, plunged in thought. 'Now he'll go to the library and look up some book that will explain it all away,' I thought. But he didn't move.

'Could something like that really happen?' I asked. 'Is there any chance Maria Vockel might be real?'

'There's only one way to find out, Esteban. By writing to that address,' he said, smiling. I was glad to find him so understanding. 'I'll help you write the letter,' he added, still smiling. 'I haven't quite lost my grasp of my own language yet.'

Despite their friendly tone, his words made me lower my gaze. My father had not been successful in his attempts to teach me German. Even at home, I preferred to speak as I did with my friends and I grew angry when he refused to use 'the language we both knew'. But that Sunday everything was different. Repenting of my earlier attitude, I promised myself that I would make up for lost time, that I would not offend him like that again.

But my father was happy, as if the events of the afternoon had revived pleasant memories. He put his hand under my chin and made me look up. Then, spreading out an old map of Hamburg on the table, he started to look for Johamesholfstrasse.

'Look, there it is. In the St Georg district,' he said pointing to it on the map, adding: 'Shall we write the letter now?'

'Yes, I'd like that,' I replied, laughing.

Now, after all these years, I realise that the letter marked the end of an era in my life. I, who had never been like the other children in Obaba, was about to become, from that moment on, a complete foreigner, a worthy successor to Engineer Werfell. I would no longer go around with my schoolfriends and I would never again return to the church. Furthermore, I would begin to study, to prepare myself to go to university.

The sending of the letter was followed by a period riven by doubt. One day I'd be certain that a reply could not be long in coming, the next I'd think such a possibility ridiculous and grow angry with myself for cherishing such hopes.

That state of uncertainty ended one Friday, when my father came running into the room where I was reading and showed me a cream-coloured envelope.

'Maria Vockel!' I shouted, getting up from my chair.

'Maria Vockel, 2 Johamesholfstrasse, Hamburg,' replied my father, reading out the sender's address.

A shiver ran down my spine. It seemed impossible that such a thing could happen. But there was the proof that it had. The cream-coloured envelope was real, as were the two handwritten sheets it contained. 'Ask me anything you don't understand,' said my father before leaving the room. I picked up the dictionary he'd given me for my birthday and began to read the letter.

Outside the window, the sun, having failed to make any impression on the clouds, was burning out like a faint fire and a dark mantle was falling across the whole park, across the grass, the trees and the lake. Only the swans seemed whiter and more luminous than before.

Esteban Werfell switched on the lamp and took out Maria Vockel's letter from one of the drawers in the table. Then, with great care, he began to transcribe it into his notebook.

Dear Esteban,

We shouldn't be frightened of things we don't understand, at least not when, as in our case, what is incomprehensible is also so delightful. That Sunday of which you speak, I was in bed with a slight sore throat and feeling very bored, when suddenly I felt like reading a book. But, as it happened, an electrical fault had plunged the whole house into darkness and I couldn't start reading without first going to look for a candle. So I got up and went to the kitchen to find one.

The event in which we were both involved occurred shortly afterwards, as I was returning to my room holding the lit candle in my hand. First, I heard the sound of an organ and then I saw a dark-haired boy sitting next to the old man who was playing the instrument, breathing heavily as he did so and swaying about over the keyboard. Then I heard the same words you did and I felt very happy, as if it had been a dream, a very nice dream. Is that what happened to you? Did you feel happy too? I hope so.

Afterwards I told my mother about it. But she took no notice of me and sent me back to bed saying I must be feverish. But *we* know what happened to us. The same thing happened to us both and there must be some reason for that.

Then Maria Vockel went on to tell him about her life in Hamburg, so very different from the life he led in Obaba, so much more interesting. She learned languages, she went skating and sailing.

She also went to the cinema, but not to see silent films; silent films it seemed, were now old hat.

The letter ended with a request. She would like a photo of him. Would he be kind enough to send one? She would reciprocate by sending hers. 'I'm much blonder than you imagined,' she declared.

Esteban Werfell smiled when he read that and returned the letter to the drawer. He had to go on writing and as fast as he could, for it was growing dark. The park had filled with shadows and the swans were asleep now in their house.

Maria Vockel's letter cheered me up so much that for the first time in my life I began to feel superior to the people of Obaba. Something astonishing had happened to me, not the sort of thing that would happen to just anyone, something that truly made me one of 'the chosen'. Henceforward, I would be a strong person and not allow myself to be intimidated by the other 'chosen ones' who used to point their fingers at me.

For some time I continued going around with my schoolfriends. I needed their company, in part because my relationship with Maria Vockel was too great a novelty to be kept a secret. And when, like the adolescents we were, we met up to exchange confidences, I tended to be the most talkative of all, even more than Andrés.

But they didn't like that girl from Hamburg. They said she was probably ugly and wore glasses and was bound to be boring, why else would she talk so much about books and reading.

'Doesn't she ever mention "it"?' they would ask, laughing and making obscene gestures.

I defended myself by showing them the photo of a young girl, fair-haired and without glasses, her lips curved in a smile, and chided them for their coarseness. But they would just start laughing again and cast doubt on the authenticity of the photo.

Relations between us soon began to cool. I refused to show them the letters that arrived regularly now from Hamburg and only joined them to go to the cinema. And when, following the example of Andrés, they stopped going and instead took to hanging around in bars, the rupture between us was complete. I preferred to stay at home studying German and reading the books in my father's library. I wanted to prepare myself, I wanted to be good enough for Maria Vockel.

My father couldn't conceal his joy at my withdrawal from everything to do with Obaba. On Sunday afternoons he would ask, a shade apprehensively:

'Aren't you going out with your friends?'

'No, I'm fine here at home.'

My reply, which was always the same, made him happy.

When I was seventeen, I left Obaba and went to university. By that time more than a hundred letters had passed between Maria and myself and not a single topic remained undiscussed. Together they would have served as an illuminating book on the problems of adolescence.

The letters also spoke about the future of our relationship. I asked her to wait for me, told her that it would not be long now before I came to Hamburg. Reading between the lines, that request was a promise of marriage.

Life, however, had a different future in mind for us. Our relationship, so intense up until my first day at university, fell off sharply from the moment I entered the lecture halls there. It was as if someone had given a signal and, so to speak, all the music had suddenly stopped.

Maria Vockel took longer and longer to reply and the tone of her letters was no longer enthusiastic; sometimes she was merely polite. For my part the change disconcerted me, filled me with uncertainty. How should I react? By demanding explanations? By repeating my promises? In fact I simply let the days drift by, unable to bring myself to act.

When I returned to Obaba for the Christmas holidays, I saw a cream-coloured envelope on the table in my bedroom. I knew at once it was her letter of farewell.

'Bad news?' my father asked over lunch.

Crestfallen, I replied: 'Maria's finished with me.' However foreseeable, the news had affected me deeply.

My father gave an amused smile.

'Don't worry, Esteban,' he said. 'The pain of love is like toothache. Intense but never serious.'

Sure enough, my dejection lasted only a short time. I was angry at first, to the point of sending Maria a fairly sharp riposte, and then, almost without realising, I forgot all about it. By the time I'd finished my studies, the relationship I'd had with her seemed something very remote and I was glad it was over.

When my studies were completed, I worked as a geography teacher. I married one of my colleagues at work and the cream-coloured envelopes remained buried and forgotten. By then my father lay beneath the earth of Obaba.

Esteban Werfell stopped writing and began to re-read the pages of the notebook. On the first page he read: 'I have returned from Hamburg with the intention of writing a memoir of my life.'

He sighed, relieved. The memoir was nearly complete. All that remained was to describe what happened on the trip to Hamburg.

Bending over his work again, he hesitated as to whether or not to write the word 'epilogue' at the beginning of the new page. He chose instead to rule a line separating off that final part of the story.

Outside it was now completely dark. The park was lit by the sodium light of the streetlamps. Beneath the line he wrote:

And, were it not for the trip I have just made to Hamburg, that would have been the end of this review of my life from that particular Sunday afternoon onwards. But what I found there obliges me to make a leap in time and continue the story.

When I left for Hamburg, my main aim was to get to know my father's city, something which for many years I had been prevented from doing by the political situation and, in particular, by the war. I wanted to visit the places he used to go to before he left for Obaba and thus pay homage to his memory. I would go to Buschstrasse, I would buy tickets to the opera at the Schauspielhaus and I would walk by the shores of the Binnenalster lake.

I had a secondary aim too: 'If I have time,' I thought, 'I'll go to 2 Johamesholfstrasse. Maybe Maria Vockel still lives there.'

But, after ten days in the city, when I felt I had achieved my primary objective, the idea of visiting my 'first love' – something which until then I had considered perfectly natural – began to trouble me. I told myself I would gain nothing from my curiosity, that, whatever happened on such a visit, all the fond memories I had of Maria Vockel would be undone. Basically, I was afraid of taking that step.

For several days I remained undecided, growing more and more agitated. I didn't even leave the hotel but spent my time at the window gazing out at the St Georg district of Hamburg. There lay the street whose name I'd first heard pronounced in the choir loft in the church; there were the houses represented by the dot my father had marked on the map of the city.

Only a few hours before I was due to catch the train home, I suddenly tore myself away from the window, ran down the stairs and hailed a taxi. 'If you don't do it, you'll regret it for ever after,' I said to myself.

I was invaded by the memory of Maria Vockel, plunged into another time, a time outside the one in which I actually found myself. In a way, it was like being fourteen again.

The taxi dropped me opposite 2 Johamesholfstrasse. It was an old, rather grand house with three balconies.

'So this is where she wrote all those letters to me,' I thought, letting my eyes take it all in. Then I went up to the door and rang the bell. My heart was beating so hard my whole body shook.

An old man of about eighty appeared at the door. He was very thin and his face was deeply lined.

'Can I help you?' he said.

The question brought me abruptly back to real time and I was overcome by a feeling that what I was doing was utterly ridiculous. I was left speechless. At last I managed to stammer out:

'I wondered if Maria Vockel still lived in this house.'

'Maria Vockel?' said the old man, puzzled. Then, pointing at me and opening his eyes very wide like someone suddenly recalling some remarkable fact, he exclaimed: 'Werfell!' and burst out laughing. I was stunned.

'My name's Esteban Werfell actually,' I said. Still laughing, the old man invited me in.

'Werfell! Mein Kamerad!' he cried, embracing me. Then he introduced himself and it was my turn to be wide-eyed.

The old man was Theodor Steiner, my father's old friend, his comrade from the Eichendorff Club.

'I thought you'd never come!' he exclaimed as we climbed the stairs.

When we went into the library, Herr Steiner asked me to sit down and he began searching the bookshelves for something.

'Here it is!' he said, picking up a copy of Joseph Eichendorff's *Gedichte*. A cream-coloured envelope protruded from between the pages.

'Señor Werfell, the Maria Vockel you thought you knew was only an invention of your father's. There was an actress by that name in the Hamburg opera, of course, but she never lived in this house.'

Herr Steiner looked at me very gravely.

'May I read my father's letter?' I said.

'Please do. It's been waiting here for you for thirty years.' He sighed, then disappeared down the corridor.

His father's letter still lay between the pages of the Eichendorff book and both now lay on the table. Esteban Werfell opened the cream-coloured envelope and began to transcribe the text which would complete his twelfth notebook.

My dear son,

Forgive me for having deceived you. I am nearly at the end of my life but I still don't know if what I did on that Sunday was right or not. I feel afraid. Sometimes I think I'm just a foolish old man.

I'd like to call you to my side and explain myself to you frankly, without having to resort to this letter, but I dare not. If some day you go in search of Maria Vockel, Theodor will hand you this letter and you will know the truth. If not, it will remain a secret. Whatever happens, I ask your forgiveness once more, a thousand times more.

In fact, everything happened purely by chance, with no premeditation on my part at all. When you told me what you had seen and heard when you fainted, I realised at once that the whole scene was made up of snippets of conversations you'd had with me. 2 Johamesholfstrasse, for example, was the address of the one friend who still wrote to me with news of my country; Maria Vockel, on the other hand, was the name of one of my favourite opera singers.

Then I had an idea. It suddenly occurred to me that *I* could become Maria Vockel and influence your life that way. You may not remember now, Esteban, but at the time you had grown away from me and your view of life had become more like that of the people of Obaba than mine. In my eyes, as you well know, that was the end, the very worst thing that could happen. I didn't want you to become one of them and I thought it my duty to prevent that happening.

I wrote to Theodor asking for his help and we came to an arrangement. The system was very simple. I would write the letters here at home and send them to my friend Theodor. He then had them copied out by a girl the same age as you –

everything had to look as authentic as possible – and sent them back to Obaba.

The game lasted until I saw that you were safe, until you went off to university. Once you'd tasted university life, you would never choose to return to live amongst these mountains again. Still less after the education I had given you through the letters. I had made you learn my language, I had made you read . . .

The letter continued, but the words his father used to conclude his explanation were so personal, so full of love, he felt unable to transcribe them.

'Here ends this memoir', he wrote. Then he switched off the light and was left in the dark, feeling happy and at peace.

An exposition of
Canon Lizardi's letter

THE LETTER in question covers eleven sheets of quarto paper, parts of which have been rendered illegible by the many years it lay forgotten in a damp cellar, for it was never sent. The first sheet, the one in direct contact with the floor, is in a particularly parlous state and so badly stained that one can scarcely make out the canon's opening words at all. The rest, with the exception of one or two lines on the upper part of each sheet, is in an excellent state of preservation.

Although undated, we can deduce that the letter was written in 1903 since, in the closing words that immediately precede the signature, the author states that he has been in Obaba for three years and, at least according to the cleric who now holds the post, everything seems to indicate that Canon Lizardi took over the rectorship of the place around the turn of the century.

He was clearly a cultivated man, judging by the elegant, baroque calligraphy and the periphrastic style laden with similes and citations he uses to broach the delicate matter that first caused him to take up his pen. The most likely hypothesis is that he was a Jesuit who, having left his order, opted for ordinary parish work.

As regards the addressee, he was doubtless an old friend or acquaintance, even though, as mentioned earlier, the poor condition of the first page does not permit us to ascertain that person's name and circumstances. Nonetheless, we feel justified in assuming that he was a person of considerable ecclesiastical authority, capable of acting as guide or even teacher in the very difficult situation prevailing in Obaba at the time, if one is to believe the events described in the letter. One should not forget either that Lizardi is writing to him in a spirit of confession and his tone

34

throughout is that of a frightened man in need of the somewhat sad consolation of a superior.

On the first page, according to the little that one can read at the bottom, Lizardi writes of the 'grief' paralysing him at that moment and describes himself as feeling 'unfitted to the test'. Those few scant words allow us to place in context the story that the canon unfolds over the subsequent ten pages and prevent us being misled by the circuitous, circumlocutory style. Let us look now at the form the test referred to at the very start of the letter might have taken. This is what Lizardi writes on the second page, which I transcribe word for word:

. . . but first, dear friend, allow me to speak briefly of the stars, for it is in astronomy books that one finds the best descriptions of this daily wandering, this mysterious process of living which no metaphor can adequately encompass. According to the followers of Laplace our universe was born out of the destruction of a vast ball or nucleus drifting through space, drifting alone, moreover, with only the Creator for company, the Creator who made everything and is in the origin of all things; and out of that destruction, they say, came stars, planets and asteroids, all fragments of that one lump of matter, all expelled from their first home and doomed ever after to distance and separation.

Those, like myself, who are sufficiently advanced in years to be able to discern that dark frontier of which Solinus speaks, feel cast down by the description science so coldly sets before us. For, looking back, we cannot see the world that once enwrapped us like a cloak about a newborn babe. That world is no longer with us and because of that we are bereft of all the beloved people who helped us take our first steps. At least I am. My mother died fifteen years ago and two years ago the sister who shared my house with me died too. And of my only brother, who left to travel overseas whilst still only an adolescent, I know nothing.

And you, dear friend, you yourself are far away; at a time when I need you so, you too are far away.

This paragraph is followed by a few barely legible lines which, as far as I can make out, refer to the psalm in which the Hebrews in exile from Zion bemoan their fate. Then, on the third page, the canon concludes his long introduction and embarks on the central theme of his letter:

. . . for, you know as well as I, that life pounds us with the relentlessness and force of the ocean wave upon the rocks. But I'm straying from my subject and I can imagine you growing impatient and asking yourself what is it exactly that troubles me, what lies behind all these complaints and preambles of mine. For I well remember how restless and passionate you were and how you hated procrastination. But remember too my weakness for rhetoric and forgive me: I will now explain the events that have led to my writing this letter. I hope with all my heart that you will listen to what I have to say with an open mind and ponder as you do so the lament in Ecclesiastes: 'Vae soli!' Yes, the fate of a man alone is a most bitter one, even more so if that man, like the last mosquitoes of summer, can barely stagger to his feet and can only totter through what little remains of his life. But enough of my ills; I will turn my attention to the events I promised to recount to you.

Nine months ago last January, an eleven-year-old boy disappeared into the Obaba woods, for ever, as we now know. At first, no one was much concerned by his absence, since Javier – that was the boy's name, that of our most beloved martyr – had been in the habit of running away from home and remaining in the woods for days on end. In that sense he was special and his escapes bore no resemblance to the tantrums that, at some point in their lives, drive all boys to run away from home; like that time you and I, in protest at an unjust punishment at school, escaped the watchful eyes of our parents and spent the night out in the open, hidden in a maize field . . . but, as I said, this was not the case with Javier.

I should at this point explain that Javier was of unknown parentage or, to use the mocking phrase so often used here to describe him, 'born on the wrong side of the blanket'. For that reason he lived at the inn in Obaba, where he was fed and clothed in exchange for the silver coins furnished to the innkeepers – *vox populi dixit* – by his true progenitors.

It is not my intention in this letter to clear up the mystery of the poor boy's continual flights but I am sure Javier's behaviour was ruled by the same instinct that drives a dying dog to flee its masters and head for the snowy mountain slopes. It is there, sharing as he does the same origins as the wolves, that he will find his real brothers, his true family. In just the same way, I believe, Javier went off to the woods in search of the love his guardians failed to give him at home, and I have some reason to think that it was then, when he was walking alone amongst the trees and the ferns, that he felt happiest.

Hardly anyone noticed Javier's absences, hardly anyone sighed or suffered over them, not even the people who looked after him. With the cruelty one tends to find amongst the ill-read, they washed their hands of him saying that 'he would come back when he was good and hungry'. In fact, only I and one other person bothered to search for him, that other person being Matías, an old man who, having been born outside of Obaba, also lived at the inn.

The last time Javier disappeared was different, though, for so fierce was my insistence that they look for him, a whole gang of men got together to form a search party. But, as I said before, nine months have now passed and poor Javier has still not reappeared. There is, therefore, no hope now of him returning.

Consider, dear friend, the tender hearts of children and the innocence in which, being beloved of God, they always act. For that is how our children are in Obaba and it gives one joy to see them always together, always running around, indeed, running around the church itself, for they are convinced that if they run round it eleven times in succession the gargoyle on the tower will burst into song. And when they see that, despite all their efforts, it still refuses to sing, they do not lose hope but attribute the failure to an error in their counting or to the speed with which they ran, and they persevere in their enterprise.

Javier, however, never joined in, neither then nor at any other time. He lived alongside them, but apart. The reasons for his avoidance of them lay perhaps in his character, too serious and silent for his age. Perhaps too it was his fear of their mockery, for a purple stain covered half his face, considerably disfiguring him. Whatever the reason, the conclusion . . .

The third page ends there. Unfortunately the top of the following page, page four, is badly affected by mould and none of my efforts to clean it up have met with much success. I have only been able to salvage a couple of lines.

Reading them, one has the impression that Canon Lizardi has once more abandoned the story and returned to the sad reflections of the beginning of the letter. At least so I deduce from the presence there of a word like 'santateresa', the local word for the praying mantis, an insect which, according to the nature guide I consulted, is unique in the natural world for the way in which it torments its victims. The author of the guide comments: 'It devours them slowly, taking care not to let them die at once, as if its real hunger were for torture not for food.'

Was Lizardi comparing the behaviour of that insect with the way life had treated the boy? For my part, I believe he was. But let us leave these lucubrations and look at what Lizardi did in fact write in the legible part of that fourth page.

. . . do not think, dear friend, that I ever abandoned or neglected him. I visited him often, always with a kind word on my lips. All in vain.

I was still caught up in these thoughts when, at the beginning of February, one month after Javier had run away, a pure white boar appeared in the main street of Obaba. To the great amazement of those watching, it did not withdraw before the presence of people, but trotted in front of them with such calm and gentleness that it seemed more like an angelic being than a wild beast. It stopped in the square and stayed there for a while, quite still, watching a group of children playing with what remained of the previous night's fall of snow.

The upper part of the fifth page is also damaged but not as badly as the page I have just transcribed. The dampness only affects the first three lines. It goes on:

. . . but you know what our people are like. They feel no love for animals, not even for the smallest which, being too weak to defend themselves, deserve their care and attention. In respect of this, I recall an incident that occurred shortly after my arrival in Obaba. A brilliantly coloured bird alighted on the church tower and I was looking up at it and rejoicing to think that it was our Father Himself who, in His infinite kindness, had sent me that most beautiful of His creatures as a sign of welcome, when, lo and behold, three men arrived with rifles on their shoulders . . . they had shot the poor bird down before I had a chance to stop them. Such is the coldness of our people's hearts, which in no way resemble that of our good St Francis.

They reacted in just the same way towards the white boar. They began shooting at it from windows, the braver amongst them from the square itself, and the racket they made so startled me that I came running out of the church where I happened to be at the time. They only managed to wound the animal, however, and in the midst of loud squeals, it fled back to the woods.

Since it was a white boar, and therefore most unusual, the hunters were in a state of high excitement; they could already imagine it as a trophy. But that was not to be, at least not that day. They returned empty-handed and, faint with exhaustion, they all ended up at the inn, drinking and laughing and with great hopes for the next day. And it was then, on that first day of the hunt, that Matías confronted them with these grim words: 'What you're doing is wrong. He came here with no intention of harming anyone yet you greet him with bullets. You'd be well advised to consider the consequences of your actions.'

As you will recall from the beginning of the letter, Matías was the old man who loved the boy best and was so grieved by his disappearance that many feared he might lose his mind. And there in the inn, hearing those words and what he went on to say, no one doubted that this was exactly what had happened. For in his view, the white boar was none other than our lost boy, none other than Javier, who, because of the sad life he had led as a human being, had changed his very nature. It seems he argued his case as follows:

'Didn't you see the way he stopped in the square to watch the boys playing in the snow? Isn't that just what Javier used to do? And, again just like Javier, didn't the boar have a purple stain around its snout?'

Those who were present say that the old man's speech was followed by a heated discussion, with some hunters denying that the boar had any such stain and others passionately affirming that it had. Now tell me, dear friend, can you imagine anything more foolish? What kind of a person is it who raises not the slightest objection to the idea of the boy's metamorphosis and believes, therefore, that it was indeed Javier hiding beneath the boar's rough coat, and yet grows irate and argumentative over the incidental detail of a birthmark. But, as you well know, superstition still lingers in places like Obaba and just as the stars continue to shine long after they are dead, the old beliefs . . .

The first ten lines of the sixth page are completely illegible and we can learn nothing of what happened in the days following the boar's first appearance. We can, on the other hand, find out what happened later, since the latter part of page six and the whole of page seven are perfectly conserved.

. . . but one night the boar returned to Obaba and, gliding through the shadows, made its way to a solitary house situated some five hundred yards from the square. Once outside the house, it began to beat and gnaw at the door, emitting such furious grunts that the people who had been sleeping inside were dumbstruck and unable to call for help, so great was the terror that gripped them.

I should not say that the animal acted with criminal intent for I know it is wrong to attribute to animals faculties that are proper only to men. And yet I am sorely tempted to do so. How else explain its determination to enter the house? How else explain the damage it caused to the livestock when it saw that it could not break down the door? . . . for I should tell you that, before disappearing back into the woods, the boar killed a horse and an ox kept by the inhabitants in a nearby outhouse. But I am not proud and I know that only our Father can know the true reasons behind such behaviour.

After what had happened, the hunters' anger was roused and many who until then had remained calm decided to throw in their lot with the hunting parties that had already been established. And, as ever, old Matías was the one dissenting voice. He went out into the streets and pleaded with those setting off for the woods:

'Leave the boar in peace! You'll only enrage him by doing this! Javier will recognise you!'

41

The hunters responded with violence, forgetting it was an old man they were dealing with, an old man speaking to them, moreover, out of his delirium. Then they continued on their way. But you should not judge their rudeness and their intemperance too harshly. For, as I explained, they were quite beside themselves with terror. They feared the boar would continue to attack their livestock, livestock which is on the whole of the poorest quality, so poor it barely provides enough to feed and clothe them. But Matías had his reasons too:

'Javier has nothing against you! He only attacks those who did him harm before!'

Unfortunately for everyone concerned, what the old man said was not pure madness. For the family the boar had attacked was the least Christian in Obaba, its members having for generations been much given to cruelty, a propensity they gave full rein to during the last war. Often, when they got drunk at the inn, they had made Javier the butt of their cruelty, mocking and even beating him, for evil always vents itself on the weak. But was there a connection between the two facts? Should I entirely disregard what the old man said? These were the questions I asked myself, the questions that tormented me.

Mothers in Obaba tell their children a story in which a daughter asks her wicked father if he believes he will ever die. The father tells her that this is most unlikely because, as he explains: 'I have a brother who is a lion and lives in the mountains and inside that lion is a hare and inside that hare is a dove. That dove has an egg. If someone finds that egg and breaks it on my forehead, then and only then will I die.' However, the person listening to the story knows that the little servant of the house will discover the connection between all those things and that the father, who is in fact a demon, will die. But I lacked the little servant's ingenuity and was unable to answer my own questions. Perhaps I was slow; perhaps the thread that led from the boar to Javier was more difficult to find than that linking the father's life to the dove's egg.

However, subsequently, things happened so quickly that there was little time for reflection. For on the third day of the hunt, the boar pursued and wounded a straggler from one of the hunting parties.

The letter continues on the eighth page of which the top half is well preserved, the sheet having been placed the other way up from the preceding pages. Of the lower part, however, about eight lines remain illegible.

The man's companions considered that the white boar had again acted with prudence and discernment, waiting amongst the leaves and watching the party until one of them, the man whom he later wounded, was alone and defenceless. Old Matías summed up the thoughts of all of them:

'It would be best if from now on you cover your faces. Especially those of you who did Javier wrong. It's clear he wants vengeance.'

It was on one such day that I suddenly realised that spring was upon us and that the fields were fragrant and full of the lovely flowers the Creator provides us with. But for me and for the other inhabitants of Obaba that whole garden of flowers bloomed in vain; no flower could perform its true function there, no flower could serve as a balm to our spirits. The pinks and lilies in the woods were born alone and died alone because no one, not the children or the women or even the most hardened of the men, dared go near them; the same fate awaited the mountain gentians, the thickets of rhododendrons, the roses and the irises. The white boar was sole master of the land on which they grew. One of the broadsheets published in your own town put it well: 'A wild animal is terrorising the small village of Obaba.' And do you know how many nights it came down to visit us only to . . .

The eighth page stops here. Fortunately the next two pages are perfectly legible. In this final part of the letter, Canon Lizardi's handwriting becomes very small.

. . . what Matías had foretold came to pass with the exactitude of a prophecy. Night after night, without cease, with the resolve of one who has drawn up a plan and does not hesitate to carry it out, the white boar continued to attack the houses of those who were members of the hunting parties. Then, when panic had filled every heart, the old man came to see me at the rectory. The moment he came in, he said: 'I've come to ask you a question and the sooner I have your answer the better. I want to know if I can kill the white boar?'

His words filled me with fear and not just because of the brusque manner in which he spoke. For, since in his eyes there was no difference between the boy he had known and the boar currently plundering our valley, what the old man really wanted was for me to give my blessing to a crime. I must confess that I myself had my doubts on the matter. I was wrong, you will say; a simple priest has no right to doubt what has been proven by so many theologians and other wise men. But I am just an ordinary man, a small tree that has always grown in the utmost darkness, and that animal, which in its actions seemed to exhibit both understanding and free will, had me in its power.

For all those reasons, I wanted to avoid a direct answer. I said:

'There's no point even trying, Matías. You're an old man. You'll never catch an animal like that, one that has made fools of our best hunters.'

'It will be easy for me,' he replied, raising his voice and not without a certain arrogance, 'because I know Javier's habits.' Then he added: 'Anyway that's my affair. What I want to know is whether or not I can kill the boar. You have a duty to answer me.'

'But is it necessary? Why kill an animal which, sooner or later, will leave Obaba? Provided that . . .'

44

'Of course it's necessary!' he broke in, almost shouting now. 'Have you no pity for him? Don't you feel sorry for Javier?'

'Matías, I wouldn't want to . . .'

But again he would not let me finish. He sat up in his chair and, after scrabbling in the bag he had with him, placed a filthy handkerchief on my table. Do you know what it contained? No, how could you? It was the bloody foot of a boar. It was a ghastly sight and I stepped back, horrified.

'Javier is in terrible pain,' the old man began.

I remained silent, unable to utter a word.

'The people of Obaba are cowards,' he continued after a pause. 'They don't want to meet him face to face and so they resort to snares and traps and poison. What do they care if he dies a slow and painful death? No good hunter would do that.'

'It's only natural that they should be afraid, Matías. You're wrong to despise them for that.'

But I wasn't convinced by what I said and it was an effort to get the words out. The old man was not listening anyway; he seemed to be in mid-soliloquy.

'When a boar falls into a snare, it frees itself by gnawing off the trapped limb. That is the law it lives by.'

He spoke hesitantly, breathing hard.

'Don't you think Javier's learned fast?' he asked then, looking into my eyes. The smile he gave me was that of a father proud of his son's achievements. I nodded and thought to myself how utterly justified his feelings were and that on the last day, God our Father would not have the least hesitation in bestowing on him the paternity he claimed. Yes, Matías was Javier's true father; not the one who abandoned him at birth, nor the other one who, having taken him in, treated him only with contempt.

'Can I kill him?' the old man asked me. He had grown sombre again. As you know, dear friend, pity is an extreme form of love, the form that touches us most deeply and most strongly impels us towards goodness. And there was no doubt that Matías was

45

speaking to me in the name of pity. He could not bear the boy's suffering to continue. It must be ended as soon as possible.

'Yes, you can,' I said. 'Killing the boar would not be a sin.'

Well done, you will say. However, bearing in mind what happened afterwards . . .

The tenth page stops at that point. The first four lines are missing on the next and last page; the rest, including the signature, is perfectly preserved.

. . . on the outskirts of Obaba, not far from this house, there is a thickly wooded gully in the form of an inverted pyramid, and at one end there is a cave that seems to penetrate deep into the earth. That was where Matías sensed the white boar was hiding. Why, you will ask, on what did he base such a supposition, a supposition that later – I will tell you now – was to prove correct? Because he knew that was what Javier used to do when he ran away from the inn. He would hide there in the cave, poor boy, with only the salamanders for company.

But, as I said, I only knew all this when it was too late. Had I known before, I would not have given my consent to Matías. No, you can't go into that cave, I would have told him. No hunter would wait for a boar in a place like that. It's too dangerous. You'll be committing a grave sin by going there and placing your own life in mortal danger.

But God chose not to enlighten me. I made a mistake when confronted by a question whose rights or wrongs I could not hope to fathom and, later, there was no time to remedy the situation. The events I will now recount happened all in a rush, the way boulders, once their support has gone, hurtle headlong down hillsides. In fact, it was all over in a matter of hours.

When Matías left, I went into the church and it was there that I heard what, at the time and to my great astonishment, sounded like an explosion. At first I could not establish the origin of such a loud noise, so unusual in Obaba. It was certainly not from a rifle, I thought.

'Unless the shot were fired in a cave!' I exclaimed. I knew at once that I was right. With God's help, I had guessed what had happened.

Matías was already dead when I reached the gully. He was lying face down at the entrance to the cave itself, his rifle still in his hand. A few yards away, further inside the cave, lay the white boar, panting and losing blood from a wound in its neck.

Then, amidst the panting, I thought I heard a voice. I listened more carefully and what do you think I heard? The word that any boy would have cried out at such a moment: 'Mother!' Before my very eyes, the boar lay there groaning and whimpering and saying over and over: 'Mother, mother' . . . pure illusion, you will say, the imaginings of a weary, overwrought man; and that is what I tell myself when I remember all I have read in science books or when I recall what faith requires us to believe. Nevertheless, I cannot forget what I saw and heard in that cave. Because then, dear God, I had to pick up a stone and finish him off. I could not leave him there to bleed to death, to suffer; I had to act as honourably as the old man would have done.

I can go no further and I will end here. I am, as you see, a broken man. You would be doing me the greatest favour by coming here to visit me! I have spent three years in Obaba. Is that not enough solitude for any man?

With that question – and the signature that follows it – both letter and exposition end. I would not, however, wish to conclude my work without reference to a fact which, after several conversations with the present inhabitants of Obaba, seems to me significant. It concerns the matter of Lizardi's paternity. Many of those who spoke to me state that Javier was, without a doubt, his son, a belief which, in my view, a second reading of the document certainly tends to substantiate. That fact would also explain why the letter never left the rectory where it was written. A canon like Lizardi would never dare send a confession from which, in the end, he had omitted the one essential detail.

Post tenebras
spero lucem

THE farthest-flung quarter of Obaba was called Albania and it possessed neither a main road nor its own school building. So, since there was nothing better to be had, the local children learned their alphabet and their punctuation – as well as where Denmark and Pakistan could be found or how much forty-six plus twenty-seven came to – in what had been a meeting room on the first floor of the local boarding house.

All together there were thirty-two students of whom seventeen were girls and fifteen were boys and every morning – having pushed passed the leather bottles containing wine and oil that cluttered the doorway – they would line up in single file behind the schoolmistress and go up eight, then ten, then five steps to reach the last – if my sums are correct – of the twenty-three stairs. And once in the improvised classroom, they would sit down at the desks in order of seniority: the youngest in the front rows and right at the back the fourteen-year-old adolescents who had to grapple with Dalmau Carles' very comprehensive, very difficult encyclopaedia-cum-textbook.

They would finish their work at five o'clock and then – in great disorder and making a tremendous racket – go down first five, then ten, then eight steps, twenty-three steps in all, and go off home in search of an afternoon snack of bread and chocolate or else go and play in the wash house with their cork boats and little glass bottles.

Thus at five o'clock, the schoolmistress would be left alone in front of the blackboard, bent over her long table; and because she was both very young and very new to that mountainous region, she preferred to stay at school marking her pupils' exercises than to go back to the grey and white house she'd been assigned on the outskirts of Albania, for she still did not feel at home there, she felt very foreign and alone.

To the schoolmistress the days in Albania seemed endless and she spent most of her spare time writing letters. She wrote, above all, to the man she called (capitalising the first letter of each word) Her Best Friend. In her first letter she told him:

> Since there's no main road, I live here as if under siege, with all escape routes blocked. The first Sunday after my arrival, I went down to the village, to the streets of Obaba, I mean; but there was nothing there for me, except bars, the kind women aren't supposed to go into. To be honest, it's an uphill struggle living here without the walks we used to take along the seafront, the whole gang – María, David, Carlos, Cristina, Ignacio, you and I. Here, when it's misty or drizzling, I spend the afternoons lying on my bed going over in my mind the talks we had on the beach. As you see, my memories of the summer are my only consolation. Not that it's always like that, sometimes it's sunny and then I take the children out catching butterflies. The other day, for example, we caught a huge *Nymphalis antiopa*, the biggest I've ever seen.

In almost all her letters she made a point of mentioning butterflies, always giving them their correct Latin names, because she knew how much her friends admired her knowledge of the subject. But, contrary to all her expectations, eight days passed, then twelve, then seventeen; in fact, if my sums are correct, one whole month and a week passed and not a single letter was delivered to her letterbox, not even the one she awaited most keenly, the letter from Her Best Friend.

'I never thought they'd forget me that quickly. They're a complete washout as friends and I'm never going to write to them again,' she decided.

It was a firm decision and as such was written down in the notebook she used as a diary.

Meanwhile, autumn came to an end and as the days passed so the butterflies disappeared. Now they could find only the red admirals that feed on nettles and live near the shadowy deeps of rivers. As for the swallows, they were already lined up along the telegraph wires: one hundred and twenty swallows on one wire and one hundred and forty on the other, two hundred and sixty swallows in all. At any moment they would take flight and set off on their great journey south.

'The swallows have gone, winter has arrived,' the school-mistress wrote in her notebook when the air in Albania – minus two hundred and sixty swallows – seemed suddenly empty.

The thoughts she confided to her diary gave the school-mistress an outlet for her feelings and provided her life with the consolation shared confidences always bring. They restored to her some sense of calm and Her Confused Heart (again duly capitalised) regained its normal rhythm. However, her Heart was not the only problem. Other impulses stirred within her inner being, other forces that no notebook could encompass and it was those impulses – secret but nonetheless powerful and which occasionally obliged her to sleep entirely naked – that brought to mind Her Best Friend and then it was as if he were by her side once more and was kissing her as he had on that June night when they'd broken away from their other friends and got lost among the dunes.

But she was stubborn and didn't want to go back on the decision she had taken. She wouldn't write him another letter until he replied to hers. And so she used her pen only on official matters or transactions, usually to write to the schools inspector. In one such letter she wrote:

I believe, Inspector, that teaching is always difficult, but the truth is that in cases such as my own it can become an almost

impossible task. The roof leaks. The desks are falling to bits.
Two of the windows have no glass in them. Bearing in mind that
winter is nearly upon us, repairs, especially to the roof, seem to
me absolutely essential. I am not exactly well supplied with
teaching materials either. For example, I have no maps of Asia
and Africa and when I have to talk to the children about these
continents, I am forced to improvise maps by tracing them in
sawdust.

She was proud of how well Africa and Asia had turned out, with
their main geographical features and cities scattered amongst the
sawdust, and it seemed to her that such a brilliant idea could only
have occurred to someone who had spent many hours playing with
sand on the beach. That was the real reason for bringing the
deficiency to the inspector's attention. The lack of maps did not in
fact worry her that much.

The inspector's reply arrived with great promptness.

I fully understand what you say in your letter but, unfortunately,
we do not dispose of the necessary funds to refurbish all our
establishments. Nevertheless, I will visit you there on 17th
November and we can talk about it then. I need to see the school
before I can make any decisions.

The letter broke the monotony of fifty endless days in Albania and
receiving it provoked in the schoolmistress a joy of almost
extravagant proportions, far in excess of what might be expected
from someone in receipt of what was, after all, only an official note.
But her heart, which was still confused, reacted with equal
vehemence to all stimuli, whether false or genuine.

'The inspector will come on the seventeenth,' she wrote in her
diary. Then she went over to the calendar she'd hung in her kitchen
and circled the date in red. Even the arrival of Her Best Friend
would not have merited so many notes and underlinings.

When the seventeenth of November arrived, the school-mistress spent the whole day looking out of the school window. But no inspector appeared in Albania.

Back home again, she wrote at the top of a sheet of paper: 'I am most upset that you failed to keep your promise.' But then, deciding not to continue the letter, she lay down on the bed and stayed there, her eyes open, staring into the darkness. And when, at last, she did manage to fall asleep, she was besieged all night by dreams of spiders and snakes that crawled out from her own heart.

The barking of the local dogs announced the dawning of a new day and it seemed to her they had been barking for all eternity and would go on barking for ever, that they would never be silent. And her illusion gained substance when she got up and looked out of the window, for on the other side of the glass panes winter had laid its imperious hand over everything, as if it were the only possible season.

'The fields were like this when I first arrived,' she thought, 'all frozen and white.' She was still thinking like a sleepwalker.

The hermitage clock told her it was now eight in the morning, but what the position of its hands actually meant was beyond her comprehension. She felt exactly the same about the number eighteen that appeared on the calendar, right next to the number circled in red. What was the eighteenth of November? A day. And if you added that day to another twenty-nine or thirty days they made a month, one month which, when added to another eleven months, made up a year. But that probably only happened in other places, not in Albania.

'I'm not ill. It's just that I haven't been to the beach,' she said when she looked at herself in the bathroom mirror and noticed how pale she was. But the fear of illness kept nagging at her while she washed.

Later, sitting at the kitchen table and looking at the butterflies she kept displayed in the glass-fronted dresser, she wrote in her notebook: 'I'm a *Melanargia russiae*, pinned to a piece of cork, slowly bleeding to death.'

But the moment she re-read those words, indeed for the first time since she'd arrived in Albania, Her Confused Heart rebelled. The comparison was too extravagant. In its reference to blood, it could even be taken as a clumsy description of her own physical state, for her period had finally started, fifteen days late.

She pursed her lips, crossed out what she had written and added a new thought to her diary:

I must do something: move about, go for a walk, find new friends, anything. If I don't, this cold Albania will be the death of me.

She didn't quite know what steps she should take to achieve these aims; but what mattered, after all, was her new resolve.

Shortly afterwards, just when the clock was striking half past eight, a knock at the door startled her properly awake. She gave a satisfied smile: she knew it would be her favourite pupil, the young servant boy from the Mugats house. He had come, as he did every day at that hour, to pick up the schoolroom key.

'Time hasn't quite stopped. And here's the proof,' she thought as she hurried down the passage.

'It's very cold today, Manuel. Would you like a hot drink?' she said, on greeting him.

In response to the unexpected invitation, the servant boy hesitated, half-perplexed and half-distrustful, then advanced slowly along the passage, not saying anything, eyes firmly fixed on the floor.

'Go into the kitchen, Manuel. Don't be shy. Would you like a bowl of milk and some biscuits?'

The schoolmistress was deeply grateful for this visit because it shook her out of the gloomy introspection into which she had sunk the moment she'd got out of bed. Her cheerfulness was beginning to return.

'I wouldn't mind a cup of coffee,' he said solemnly. Then he immediately took a cigarette from his pocket and offered it to the schoolmistress:

'Would you like one?' he asked.

'I don't smoke, Manuel. And you'd do well to follow my example. You're much too young to be smoking.'

'But you're a woman and you can't compare men and women. Women are much weaker physically than men. Everyone knows that.'

The servant boy's manners and behaviour were not what one would expect in a child of twelve. There was something ancient about him and, when he spoke, he did so gravely in the forthright tones of one who has always lived in the open air, in the woods, amongst the rocks on the mountains, beneath the stars. Compared with the other pupils at school, he seemed more adult, from another era, yes, that was it, from another era entirely.

'He hasn't really had a childhood,' thought the schoolmistress as she handed him the cup of coffee. 'He started work so young and he's never really had anyone of his own age to play with.' Her heart – free now from her dark dawn thoughts – aroused feelings of tenderness in her.

'The stove's working well, don't you think?' she asked, for the servant boy was the only pupil with the sole right and responsibility to keep the school at a pleasant temperature.

'Seems to be. At any rate we haven't been cold in school up till now.'

And when he said that, he smiled for the first time since he'd entered the house.

'He has a very nice smile,' thought the schoolmistress, at the same time congratulating herself on her excellent judgement in putting him in charge of maintenance of the stove. The job gave him a position in the school, gave him an authority which, behind as he was in his studies, he would never have achieved on his own.

'When did you start going to school, Manuel?' she asked.

The servant boy might well have been surprised by the

schoolmistress's friendliness and her sudden curiosity about the details of his life, but if he was, he didn't show it. He expressed himself with growing confidence.

'I started when I was nine. Before that, from when I was six, I worked as a shepherd up in the mountains. It wasn't a bad job. Better than the job I've got now at any rate,' he replied, then gulped down in one what coffee remained in his cup.

'Is your present boss a bad man then?'

'He's a pig.'

His boss only let him go to school in the mornings, not in the afternoons, and the schoolmistress assumed it was that prohibition that had merited him the name of pig. But the boy saw things quite differently.

'He drinks, you see,' he began, by way of explanation. 'And, as you know, when someone drinks, they haven't the energy to do anything else. I usually have to cope with all the work on my own. Today, for example, I've been up since five. Apart from that, he's a good bloke. I really like him.'

By now there was only a quarter of an hour before class was due to start and he was shifting restlessly on his chair.

'I'll get you the key now,' said the schoolmistress when she noticed his nervousness.

'I'll have to hurry if the school's to be warm for when the lesson starts,' explained the servant boy, getting up. Then as soon as he had the key, and without even a goodbye, he had slammed the door and was off down the street.

'He takes it so seriously!' sighed the schoolmistress, smiling.

To get from the grey and white house to the school he had to take one hundred and thirty steps, then forty, then eighty, that is, he had to take a total – if my sums are correct – of two hundred and fifty steps. The servant boy made some calculations and worked out that if he hurried and covered three steps in one, then it would take him only half a minute to reach the stove, instead of the minute and a half it usually took him. Then, forgetting all about arithmetic, he ran off towards the school.

But his calculations did not come out quite as he expected, for when he'd covered only half the distance, he tripped over a tool left by the workers repairing the drains in Albania and, as ill luck would have it, in the sudden movement he made to keep his balance and not fall over, the key slipped out of his hand and fell into the bottom of a trench.

'Don't worry, son, it won't fall any further,' said a fat man who was working in the trench.

'Could you give me the key, please,' Manuel asked, his face serious.

'Something tells me you're going to have to get it yourself. I do hate getting my hands dirty.'

The fat man scooped up the key on his spade and sent it flying into one of the puddles in the trench. He smiled mockingly.

'Give me the key, you pig!'

The servant boy disliked practical jokers and had even less time for good-for-nothings always on the lookout for an excuse to stop work. They made the blood rush to his head.

'Come down here and I'll give it to you,' teased the fat man, still smiling.

'Mind how you go, lad,' warned one of the other labourers working in the trench.

The servant boy was very keen on wrestling and once, the most glorious day of his life, he'd been present at the bout in which the champion, Ochoa, had defeated every one of his opponents using his innovative back heel trip and ever since then, up in the mountains, with the animals and trees, Manuel's one ambition had been to train himself up and learn how to execute that move properly.

'He's too sure of himself, this one,' he thought and a moment later the fat man was lying flat on his back in the trench. The other labourers laughed as Manuel ran off down the street with the key firmly grasped in his hand.

'I did that almost as well as Ochoa himself,' he thought proudly, opening the door to the school.

During the three years he'd spent up in the mountains as a shepherd, with only the animals for company, the servant boy had learned how to entertain himself and he felt at ease as soon as he entered the meeting room that served as a school. He designated that empty area the Great Space where he and his dog Moro – and no one else – could play at being what they were not. Had the schoolmistress ever seen the plays they put on there, she would never have thought that, in comparison with the rest of the pupils, Manuel was the most grown-up. On the contrary, she would have thought him the most childish.

His plays always took as their backdrop the lands of Asia and Africa, which the schoolmistress had drawn in sawdust, and in those plays Moro acted as his adjutant, that is as the adjutant of Hannibal, the mighty king of Carthage, in Manuel's opinion the only truly valiant man in the whole encyclopaedia.

That day he began the play thus: 'Asia has turned traitor, Moro, and joined forces with the Romans. I have, therefore, decided to punish them. I'm going to burn down one of their cities.'

Then, reading the names the schoolmistress had written on little flags placed on the map, he added:

'Which city shall we burn down, Moro? Peking, Nanking, Chungking?'

'I don't mind which you choose, as long as it's not Chungking. It would be a pity to destroy a city with such a funny-sounding name,' Moro informed him.

'What about Peking?'

'No, not Peking either, Hannibal. It's such a nice name for a dog. I myself would like to have been called Peking, so I'm afraid . . .'

'You refuse me everything today, Moro.'

'How about those mountains to the left of China? Why don't we burn them?'

'I'll have to think about it. Wait just a moment.'

He had to confess that, since that mountainous region bore neither flag nor name, his adjutant's suggestion was really very sensible. It was always easier to condemn complete strangers.

Beneath his gaze the whole of China lay humbled at his feet: Peking, Nanking, Chungking, Canton, Hong Kong, Shanghai, Taiwan; and in all of those places he saw hordes of tiny people raising supplicant eyes to him. 'Don't do it, Hannibal,' they said, 'have pity and do not burn our cities. We will never again be the vassals of Rome. We swear it!'

At last, picking up a few handfuls of sawdust and wrapping them in a piece of paper, he pronounced: 'So be it, I will burn those mountains instead! For Carthage can never forgive!' Shortly afterwards, a large section of the Himalayas was burning in the stove.

'That's a good blaze you've got going, Manuel!' said the schoolmistress as soon as she opened the door, raising her voice above the hubbub emerging from twenty-four (thirty-one minus seven, who had gone down with flu) childish Albanian throats. By then, he'd already sat down at his own desk, the one nearest to the stove.

'It's nothing special. At least it didn't smoke, that's the main thing,' he replied, with a gesture dismissing the importance of his achievement. His tone had grown serious again.

The young servant spent the morning looking through the stove's inspection window, keeping an eye on the fire. Because, needless to say, the fire was always ready to surprise you and the worst thing you could do was to trust it. One minute it could be blazing away merrily and the next have burned so low it looked as if it might die down altogether. If you didn't watch it all the time, the fire could easily just burn itself out.

'Turn to the arithmetic section in your encyclopaedias,' the schoolmistress said, having left the younger ones practising their handwriting.

The servant pulled a face. He disliked arithmetic anyway and felt a special hatred for the problems they were set at the end of each lesson; he found them totally incomprehensible.

But the schoolmistress was already reading out the problem they had to solve that day and he tried to look as if he were really paying attention.

'A man had six horses. He sold three of them for 1,500 pesetas each. He sold another two for 1,300 pesetas each. The last horse, on the other hand, broke a leg and had to be slaughtered. Question: Bearing in mind that he received a total of 7,300 pesetas, how much money did the butcher give him for the sixth horse?'

'How did the horse come to break its leg in the first place?' wondered the servant boy. That stupid encyclopaedia always left out the most important bits.

Then he heard a voice ask: 'How much money did the butcher give him, Manuel?' The blood rushed to his face. He liked the fact that the schoolmistress said his name out loud in front of everyone but he didn't like what that fact implied. Having to answer caused him intense embarrassment.

'We don't eat horse meat in these parts, Miss,' he blurted out. The pupils in the back row burst out laughing and the schoolmistress had to threaten them with the ruler to silence them.

'Now come on, Manuel. How much money did he give him?' she asked again.

'I don't know. About seventy-five pesetas I should think!'

'Two hundred pesetas!' shouted a girl with her hair in a plait.

The schoolmistress nodded.

'Did anyone else get that answer?'

Everyone in the back row put their hands up. But the servant boy didn't agree.

'What do they know?' he declared to himself, looking at the others with scorn. 'You try going to a butcher with a clapped-out old horse and see if he gives you two hundred pesetas for it. Not a chance!'

Then he got up to get firewood for the stove and, as he passed the schoolmate who had laughed loudest at his reply, he crouched down and said: 'If I catch you on the way out from school, I'll kill you.'

The boy who had laughed so heartily went pale. He knew all too well that no one had yet managed to better the servant boy in a fight. He could beat everyone, even boys twice his age.

*

Post tenebras spero lucem: at six in the evening it was already dark in Albania and so, all the lights on the boarding-house stairs had fused, with the banister for support, the schoolmistress had to feel her way down the twenty-three stairs – five plus ten plus eight – that led to the hallway cluttered with the leather bottles of wine and oil.

But, as well as that outer darkness, there was the other darkness lodged in Her Confused Heart and which was, without a doubt, the darker of the two, a darkness that obliged her to stop and stand still when, after the first fifteen stairs, she had reached the main landing. From there she could clearly hear the conversations of the labourers drinking and laughing in the boarding house immediately below her. To begin with, that pause had simply been a rest, then an innocent entertainment, then suddenly, when midwinter was upon them, a habit she didn't even dare confess to her diary.

'They're always so cheerful and yet they've spent the whole day working in that trench,' she thought.

At first, Her Confused Heart listened with equal interest to all the men (masculine plural). But as soon as she was able to distinguish the different voices, her interest in their plurality abruptly disappeared. She wasn't interested in the ten or twelve labourers gathered around the bar, nor even in half of them, nor even in half of that half. She was only interested in one. She saw him every morning, working near the wash house; he was a dark man with curly hair ar l a tattoo on his right arm. Some nights, those nights when she slept in the nude, that tattoo – in the form of a ship – even penetrated into her dreams.

Sometimes she felt like inventing an excuse to go into the bar, for example, going in and asking for a volunteer to help move the blackboard, or for a glass of water, or for advice on the leaking roof. But instead she always walked on towards her house on the outskirts of Albania. And it wasn't just a matter of shyness, it was also because the tattoo reminded her of a real ship: the blue and red ship Her Best Friend worked on.

The night before her twenty-third birthday – it was the second of December, a Friday – she remained standing on the stairs for longer than usual. The place seemed to be packed and, above the customers' chattering and whistling, she could hear the strains of a harmonica playing.

'I expect they're dancing,' she thought, recalling a scene she had witnessed shortly after her arrival in Albania, where it was not unusual for the men to dance together.

Then she heard someone say: 'Right, I'm going to do it!' The doorway lit up and the man with the tattoo came out, followed by two friends. They were all laughing and his friends kept tugging at his shirt.

The schoolmistress swallowed hard when the man began to unbutton his flies. It occurred to her that she might be discovered there.

'Come on, mate, cut it out, we believe you!' pleaded his two friends. She couldn't take her eyes off the opening in his trousers. She saw a lump of swollen flesh and the liquid that flowed from it formed small black streams amongst the flagstones.

'God, you're a pig!' his friends said, laughing, and she had to hold hard to the banister rail to keep her balance.

Plunged into darkness again, the schoolmistress continued slowly on down the final eight steps to the main door. Once there, her foot sought out one of the streams still wet on the flagstones and then, very deliberately, she stepped in it. She reached her grey and white house feeling light and strong and, as she changed her clothes, she almost danced, swaying her body and her arms. An intense joy flooded her heart.

Had the schoolmistress been a mature, experienced woman, the scene she'd witnessed from the landing would have passed into her life as a trivial anecdote one only recalls later at some get-together, to amuse one's friends. But she'd only just left her city on the coast and – as far as that aspect of life was concerned and apart from her night-time fantasies – she had only the brief experience of that one night in June, the night Her Best Friend had invited her to walk with him in the dunes. She thought, therefore, that she'd done something of great significance. The wet sole of her shoe symbolised, beyond all doubt, that she had passed the Great Test set for her in Albania.

After supper, galvanised by that new state of mind, the desire to write to Her Best Friend was reborn in her. She looked for her writing pad, pale blue in colour, and opened it resolutely. A cup of coffee steamed on the table.

Have you all forgotten about me? – she began with a steady hand – Well, frankly, I think it's pretty bad. Awful, in fact. It doesn't surprise me in the others, but in you it does. Surely it wouldn't be such an effort to write me a few lines. But perhaps I'd better change the subject, I'll only get angry otherwise. Of course, knowing nothing of your life, what you do, how you're finding things on the ship, or indeed anything at all, it's a little difficult to know what to write about. In fact, I have no option but to write to you about the winter which in these godforsaken regions is extremely cold, hard and persistent. If it's foggy one day, then it stays foggy for the whole week. The same with the rain. So there's no chance of going for a walk or going out to find Clysandra or Falena caterpillars. So you can imagine what fun life is here. Sunday's the only day when there's something to do, that's when the young people in the village hire a blind accordionist to play for them. But I never go to the dance. And you know perfectly well why not. Although, on reflection, I'm almost sure you don't, because you seem to be as blind as that accordionist. But now I've started saying things I shouldn't again and so I'll end the letter here.

'And here it will stay if I get no word from you tomorrow,' she thought, mentally addressing Her Best Friend.

'I do hope you haven't forgotten my birthday!' she sighed.

That night she slept more peacefully than she had for some time.

The following day – it was Saturday and her work at the school finished at midday – she didn't feel like going straight home to have lunch and decided to take a long detour before returning to her grey and white house, taking seven hundred steps to the cemetery, then three hundred to the hermitage and finally five hundred to the door of her house; and once that distance was travelled, one thousand five hundred steps in all, she looked up and saw the letter the postman had left stuck in a crack in the door.

It was a postcard covered with signatures. Her parents and brothers and sisters wished her a happy birthday and sent their love.

She decided then that she still didn't feel like eating and continued walking, as far as the mountain this time, and took seven thousand steps all in one go to the source of the river, then another five thousand to the hill from where one could look down onto the church and the streets of Obaba and, later, back in her own part of the village, the same number of steps again plus two thousand more. At last when – if my sums are correct – she had taken twenty-six thousand steps, she went into her kitchen, exhausted and hungry, and began preparing a special meal.

Making the cream sponge took her the longest, but once she'd put it in the oven, she picked up her notebook and sat down to write.

Third of December. Twenty-three years old. My family sent me a birthday card. It's been a very noisy day here in Albania. In the morning skeins of geese flew over, tracing numbers in the sky and because the strong winds force them to fly very low, there are hunters everywhere. There's been the sound of rifleshots all day. And, excited by all the fuss around them, the dogs haven't stopped barking either. I'm writing these lines keeping one eye on tonight's cake. Judging by the smell coming from the oven, it should be a good one.

She went across to the window and wondered if she should add something more to that paragraph. But she didn't feel like going over the feelings provoked by Her Best Friend's neglect. She didn't want to wallow in despair.

At last she wrote: 'The moon is playing hide and seek in the sky.'

She was just about to take the cake out of the oven when she heard someone knocking at the door.

'Manuel, what are you doing here?' she exclaimed, surprised to find the little servant boy there.

'I'm very worried about something, Miss,' replied the boy, keeping his eyes on the ground.

Once in the kitchen, the schoolmistress noticed his bruised, swollen lip and thought she understood the meaning of what he'd just said.

'What happened to your mouth, Manuel?' she said, alarmed.

'It's nothing, Miss. I just had a fight with a pig weighing 130 pounds more than me. You probably know him. He's one of the men working on the drains.'

'The one with a tattoo on his arm?'

'No, not the dark one. One of the others, a much fatter bloke.' The schoolmistress felt relieved to hear that.

'But why were you fighting?'

'Because the other day he tried to take the school key away from me and I kicked him. And of course this morning he came to get his own back. But he didn't stand a chance with me.'

'He didn't stand a chance with you, eh?' laughed the school-mistress. The boy's confidence in himself amused her.

'He's a coward that fat bloke. At first I fought clean, then I had to back off because the brute was just too heavy for me. But because he'd hurt my mouth, I picked up a stone and bashed him one right on the head. You should have seen his face, Miss!'

Now it was the servant boy's turn to laugh.

'And,' he went on, 'I told him that he'd better not come near me again, if he does he'll pay for it. I know you shouldn't really use stones but there's a huge weight difference between us. What do you think, Miss?'

'I think you did very well,' replied the schoolmistress with a broad smile. She felt proud of the way the boy had acquitted himself.

'But I didn't come here to tell tales, Miss. Like I said, there's something I'm worried about.'

'Wait a minute, Manuel. First, I'm going to ask you a question. Have you had your supper?'

The boy shook his head.

'And have you noticed the good smell coming from the oven today?'

This time he nodded. It was impossible not to notice.

'There's a cake in there. Have you ever had cake?'

'Twice.'

'Well, today will be the third time. But first we're going to eat some other nice things. To start with, croquettes. Do you know what they are?'

'I think so,' said the servant, his eyes widening a little. Then he put his hand in his pocket and pulled out a fistful of cigarettes. 'Would you like one?'

She was going to refuse, but the despair lodged in her heart rebelled against the negative. She was fed up with being what her mother called 'a nice girl'. There was no point in being a nice girl. And she was, after all, celebrating her birthday and Manuel was keeping her company at the only party she was likely to have.

'I will have one, but after supper. First things first. And while we eat you can tell me what you're worried about.'

'Well,' the boy began, not even touching the croquettes she set before him, 'the thing is that next week I won't be able to come to school because we've got masses of work to do at home. And I'm worried about the stove, because no one else knows how to light the fire and the school will just fill up with smoke, I know it will.'

'We'll find a way round it, Manuel. Now eat up!'

But the servant boy didn't move.

'Who'll be in charge of lighting the fire while I'm away?' he asked, lowering his gaze. He was clearly afraid of losing his job.

'I'll take charge of it myself in your absence, Manuel,' said the schoolmistress. At last she'd discovered the real source of the boy's concern.

'What do you think?' she asked.

'Great! I think that's a great idea!' he exclaimed, reaching out for his first croquette. Then, while they ate supper, he regaled the schoolmistress with stories of his life, talking with the candour, confidence and joy of someone who sees their future as entirely unclouded. Where were his parents? No longer in this world, of course; they'd died when he was only three. And did he have any brothers? Yes, he had two brothers, much older than him, but he never saw them, they'd gone to America. What about sisters? No, no sisters, nor any need of them. What did he like doing? What he most liked doing in the world was wrestling, that and working as a shepherd with his dog. But more than anything else he liked wrestling. That was why, as soon as he could, he'd leave Albania and go somewhere where he could train seriously and get to be as good a wrestler as Ochoa.

'Where will you go, Manuel?' asked the schoolmistress, getting up to see to the cake.

'I don't know yet, America probably, where my brothers are.'

Through the kitchen window they could see the moon submerged amongst the clouds. The sky had a reddish tinge to it.

'It's started to rain,' said the young servant.

'I don't like the rain. I like the snow,' she remarked, sniffing the cake and placing it on the table. It had turned out perfectly.

'Well, you'll have to wait another two weeks for that. There won't be any snow until then.' The boy spoke with the confidence of one who has often slept out in the open.

'I've got a little sherry, Manuel. Shall we have some with the cake?'

'If you like, Miss . . .'

'And don't call me "Miss", Manuel. Forget I'm your teacher,' she said, going off in search of the bottle.

They ate their cake and sherry as if performing a ceremony, in silence and very slowly, only occasionally laughing. Outside the wind and the rain joined forces to beat insistently at her window. But she and Manuel didn't listen; they were aware only of the good cake and the good wine. The warmth of the kitchen protected them from all enemies.

'It'll be Christmas soon, Manuel. Why don't we sing a carol?' said the schoolmistress when they'd finished. The servant nodded.

They sang for a long time and then smoked and later drank some more. When the hermitage clock struck midnight, they were exhausted, especially the servant boy.

'I'm sorry, Miss, but I really must be going,' he said to the schoolmistress, forgetting what they'd decided earlier about forms of address. 'I've been up since really early this morning and I can barely keep my eyes open.' He'd just given a few demonstrations of Ochoa's famous back heel trip.

The schoolmistress – her third cigarette of the night in her hand – went over to the window before replying. The wind and the rain were still out there.

'You'll have to stay here, Manuel. It's a filthy night.'

The servant boy didn't reply. He was falling asleep in his chair.

'I know what we'll do. Do you see that mattress?'

'Why've you got a mattress in the kitchen?' asked the servant boy, opening his eyes.

'When it's very cold I usually sleep in here. And that's what you're going to do tonight. It's lovely sleeping in this kitchen. Come on now, don't be silly, lie down.' The servant obeyed like an automaton.

As soon as the boy had lain down and closed his eyes, the schoolmistress's Confused Heart began to protest. She was acting unwisely, or rather, she already had, by letting the party go on so long, by encouraging the boy to drink and by drinking and smoking herself. She shouldn't stand there looking down at that mattress, she should withdraw, go out and take a walk beneath the cold December rain and think it all through properly. But it was pointless. The voice with which the other forces of her inner self spoke was much stronger, more persuasive. She must not be a coward. The world was a long way from that kitchen. What did Albania matter, or her city by the coast, or anything? Anyway what was her hand doing? And was that hand perhaps wiser than Her Confused Heart?

The schoolmistress closed her eyes and took a deep breath. Then she went to her room.

'Settle down to sleep now, Manuel. I'll be in to put out the light in a minute,' she shouted from the passage. The servant boy didn't reply.

Standing in front of the big mirror in her room, the schoolmistress unzipped her skirt and let it fall to the floor. She liked her thighs. They were twenty-three years old today as well. They were strong and smooth, not flabby like her girlfriends' thighs. When she walked along the beach lots of people turned to look at them.

Slowly, every part of her body was paraded before the mirror. Then, wearing only a summer nightdress, she tiptoed into the kitchen.

'Manuel, you've gone to sleep with your clothes on,' she said half-sitting, half-lying down by his side.

*

The day after her birthday, the fourth of December, the school-mistress's feelings had changed. The confusion that had filled her since her arrival in Albania had disappeared completely to be replaced by fear. She was no longer the woman of the Confused Heart; she was the woman of the Frightened Heart.

More than anything else that change affected the way she moved about Albania, because she no longer dared take her usual route home from school, instead – in order to avoid people's eyes – she took the long way round: one hundred and twenty steps, then eighty, then seventy-five and finally twenty-two, making – if my sums are correct – a total of two hundred and ninety-seven steps.

Once inside the house, she turned again and again to her diary and gave expression there to the thoughts Her Frightened Heart needed to think if she were not to become even more frightened and thus lose control of her life. They were long passages, filling whole pages:

> I read once that one needed only two things in order to be happy: the first was self-respect and the second was to give no importance whatsoever to what other people might think of you. I used to believe that I fulfilled both those conditions, that I was different from my family and my friends. But it isn't true, I fulfill neither of them. Especially not the second one. I live in fear, I'm frightened of the local people and the gossip that might be circulating about me and I'm obsessed with what they might and might not know. Sometimes I get the feeling that they know what happened; well, what happened and what didn't happen but that they imagine happened; and I see malicious smiles in the street, in the shop, in the boarding house, everywhere. The day before yesterday, for example, when I was just about to go into the shop, I distinctly heard someone say 'it looks like even she needs someone to cuddle up to' and I turned round and came

home. Anyway, I'm trying to dismiss all these conjectures; and I want to believe that they are only imaginings on my part, that the whole quarter cannot possibly be concerned with what I might or might not have done. But I feel uneasy. Time will tell.

But Time seemed disinclined to clarify matters, at least not immediately, choosing instead to remain silent for several days, limiting itself to bringing the first snows, just as the boy had predicted. Nevertheless, the third Sunday in December arrived and when night had fallen, shortly after the blind accordionist had stopped playing, the schoolmistress did feel that Time was speaking directly to her, that, in response to her invocation, Time had chosen to speak to her through the mouths of two young men it had previously plied with alcohol. 'Miss!' they called, having planted themselves outside her house.

She didn't dare open the door to them, but she watched the two boys from the window. They were standing beneath the lamppost by the roadside, their arms around each other's shoulders. All about them was utter whiteness.

'Open up, Miss!' they called.

Then gathering snow from the ground, they began throwing snowballs at her door.

'What's wrong? Don't you like little boys anymore? We are only little, honest!'

'It's true. At any rate his is!'

Convulsed with laughter, the two boys lurched off.

They were the first messengers, but not the only ones, for throughout that night, as if wanting to make its reply absolutely clear, Time kept sending her drunken young men: eight of them around eleven o'clock; three more at midnight; one half an hour later; making – including the first two – a total of fourteen messengers.

It was the last messenger, at half past midnight, who troubled Her Frightened Heart most though. Unlike the others, he didn't shout or make a racket, he came in silence; and then he called very gently at the window, whispering: 'Open up, it's me, the one with the ship tattooed on his arm.'

The man with the tattoo repeated his plea every ten minutes. He seemed prepared to spend the whole night there in that vigil, in the midst of the darkness and the snow that the frost was gradually hardening.

I've been very stupid. I've done everything wrong – the school-mistress wrote that night, when it was already two in the morning. At that moment she needed her notebook more than ever. These reflections were her only way out. – The attitude I adopted from the moment I arrived in Albania, that of not talking to anyone, of keeping my distance and trusting no one, has worked against me. Because my arrival, naturally enough, provoked a mood of expectation amongst the local people. They wanted to know about this girl coming from outside, what her story was, and my attitude only increased their curiosity. But now, at last, they have something to get their teeth into; I myself provided them with the long-awaited story; and there they all are licking and biting their way through it and who knows how long it will take before they've had enough. Of course, it can't be said that my situation has improved much. Before I couldn't leave Albania. Now I can't leave my house. And who knows what the future will bring. There's still time for things to get even worse than they are already.

But there's one person who would like to get his teeth into me, not just into the story – she wrote, after going to the window and coming back. – The man with the tattoo on his arm is outside my house right now, watching me. But he'll wait in vain, because I've no intention of opening the door to him. I'm not stupid enough to do that. The worst thing would be if he were to stay there until morning. I wouldn't be surprised if he did, because these people seem completely impervious to the cold; maybe it's all the alcohol they drink or something.

But it was freezing hard now and even that final messenger gave up in the end. By three in the morning he had gone, had disappeared into the shadows of Albania.

The schoolmistress assumed that her conversation with Time was now at an end and decided her only option was to be patient and to hold out against the siege. Sooner or later they would tire of licking and biting at her story. Besides, the Christmas holidays were nearly upon her. Just a little longer and she would be back in her city by the sea, in her true home.

But Time was still there and had not yet done with her. It wanted to press home its answer, to continue the conversation. And so it was that on that same Monday, it sent two more messengers to the schoolmistress: the first of them at half past eight in the morning and the second at one o'clock in the afternoon.

The first announced himself with loud bangs on the door. And when the schoolmistress opened up, startled by such insistence, the messenger hurried into the house and went to sit down in the kitchen, with no show of good manners, neglecting even to say good morning.

'I've come for the key,' he said, lighting a cigarette.

'What do you mean by this, Manuel? Is that any way to come into someone's house?' She was still half-asleep and found it hard to find the right words.

'I wouldn't say it was the right way, but you kept me out there knocking on the door for a quarter of an hour and that's not right either.'

'I had a bad night and I've got a headache. And that's quite enough of your cheek!' the schoolmistress said angrily.

'Well I've been working in the woods all week and I haven't got a thing!'

Just for a moment, she thought a smile of complicity flickered across the servant boy's lips and considered that perhaps he was just playing, just putting on that swaggering air. But Her Frightened Heart, which required a Guilty Party, told her not to be so sentimental, that she should disregard her memories. After all, who was it who had revealed her secret, who had fuelled the exaggerated tales currently doing the rounds of Albania? It could only have been the boy sitting there before her. Who else if not him?

'Ah, now I understand,' began the schoolmistress levelling a finger at him. 'You're the one who's been spreading all these lies.'

'All what lies?' exclaimed the boy, growing serious.

'It makes no difference whether you admit it or not. As I said, I understand it all now,' said the schoolmistress with a scornful look. Then, seeing that it was growing late, she gave him the key and told him to get out of the house.

'See you later, love,' she heard him say as the door closed.

The boy's attitude remained the same all morning or at least so it seemed to the schoolmistress when she went over what happened in the classroom. He was continually talking, moving about amongst the desks and finally, when they were about to leave, he had had the nerve to wink at her.

Back home, she reached for her notebook and added a few lines to the previous night's entry:

> First consequence of what happened: Manuel will no longer be in charge of lighting the stove. He has lost his post, out of sheer stupidity.

Some time later, when she was having her lunch, she heard someone tapping on the kitchen window. It was the local postman, Time's second messenger of the day, the one o'clock messenger.

'Excuse me, Miss, but I've got three letters for you,' he said when she opened the door to him.

'Three letters?'

'Yes, three of them. They must have got lost because look . . .'

The postman showed her the letters one by one. Not one of them bore the name 'Obaba'.

'That's why they've taken so long to reach you. Because they didn't put the name of the village, only the name of the quarter.'

The schoolmistress nodded her agreement, stunned, unable to utter a single word. She'd recognised the writing on the envelopes. There was no doubt about it, it was that of Her Best Friend.

They've opened a new restaurant by the beach. It would be nice if we could have supper there during the holidays. If you'd like to, of course, and haven't any other plans. It would be my treat. Seriously, though, I'd love to have supper with you, but just the two of us, and not as it used to be, with all our other friends around. That way I can find out how much you've changed since your departure for the end of the world.

That paragraph, the final one of the third letter, merited five or six readings and, like the grain of mustard seed in the parable, it put down roots in the schoolmistress's heart ready to grow into a great, leafy tree. But, in fact, every line written by Her Best Friend was important, not just that one paragraph; every line comforted her, contributed something to the joy which from then on would constitute her strength. After reading those three letters, the notes and thoughts she'd written down in her diary seemed mediocre and insubstantial.

'They're not going to beat me,' she thought, remembering the events of recent days. 'I won't allow their calumnies to continue. I'll make them respect me.'

The people of Albania didn't frighten her any more.

Before going back to school, she selected a postcard with a *Nymphalis antiopa* on the front and scribbled a few lines in reply to Her Best Friend:

Your invitation is accepted. Supper at the new restaurant it is. On one condition: it will be *my* treat. I haven't even touched my first wage packet yet. I was so pleased to get your letters, so pleased.

75

You know why. See you soon. PS I only got your letters yesterday. I'll explain why later.

'I hope this letter doesn't get lost as well! Try and make sure it arrives before I do!' she said to the postman when she went to deliver it.

She spent the afternoon teaching the children Christmas carols and singing along with them. Afterwards, while she was putting away the school things, she considered her new situation, promising herself that she wouldn't let this opportunity pass her by, that she would hang on with all her might to this happiness that had appeared in her life just when she'd least expected it. In other words, the tree that had put down roots in her heart was not going to let any weeds or bushes grow up around it.

The next day, the Tuesday before Christmas, dawned clear and cold in Albania, with a blue sky and a brilliant sun and the schoolmistress waited at her window for the arrival of the servant boy. Immediately opposite her, in the distance, rose seven white mountains – two plus three plus two.

The boy arrived a little before half past eight.

'You stay right there,' the schoolmistress ordered when he made to come into the house. 'I presume you want the key,' she said. And without giving him time to reply went on: 'Well, I'll give it to you today, but this is the last time.'

The boy looked down and had to swallow hard before he could say anything.

'But why?' he managed to stammer out in a dull voice.

'Do I really need to tell you why?' answered the schoolmistress pushing the door to.

'You could leave the key outside and then I wouldn't have to bother you.'

'No, Manuel. You've lost the job.'

The door of the grey and white house closed.

The boy took the two hundred and fifty steps required to reach the school and once there, he started slowly up the stairs as if he were very tired, stopping first on the sixth stair, then on the tenth, then on the seventeenth and so on until he reached the last of the twenty-three steps. But, once inside the school, he seemed suddenly to recover all his energy and in a matter of seconds, almost without realising what he was doing, he had trampled into nothingness a large part of the lands of Africa and Asia.

'Why take it out on Egypt, Hannibal?' Moro asked accusingly, for that was the country that had suffered the fiercest attack, adding: 'Now what are they going to do, with the Nile in ruins?'

He had to admit his adjutant was right and he was doing his best to repair that longest of rivers when he heard the hermitage clock strike nine and he fled to his house, to the mountains, abandoning the Egyptians to their fate.

If I could,
I'd go out for a stroll
every night

I. *Katharina's statement*

IF I could, I'd go out for a stroll every night, except that I don't
dare, I'm too frightened. Sometimes, when I'm feeling braver,
I go down to the front door of my house and I walk as far as the
station telling myself over and over: Katharina, don't be silly, it
doesn't matter if the streets are empty, just walk quietly along and
don't think about all those things they write about in the papers,
because the newspapers exaggerate everything, they almost seem
to enjoy talking about murdered women and all that. But I've
barely finished thinking this than I've turned round and I'm back
home.

The other thing is that I feel a bit embarrassed going out for a
stroll on my own. A neighbour told me I should buy a dog and that
way when someone said to me: 'What are you doing out for a stroll
at this time of night?' I could reply: 'It's the dog, you see, I can't let
this lazy lump just lie around all day and get fat and ugly.' And the
dog would act as protection too, because when it came to buying
one I'd choose one of those specially trained dogs, the ones that go
straight for the throat, a Doberman, or something like that.

If it didn't rain so much in this city, that's the solution I'd opt
for, the dog I mean. I'd call it Clark and it would want for nothing,
it would have rice and meat to eat and a comfortable place to sleep
in. But the days here tend to be rainy and cold and it's impossible to
keep pets, and I don't want to buy a dog only to have it fall ill for
lack of exercise.

So I have no alternative but to forget about going for a walk and go to bed instead, but not to sleep, just to lie quietly and enjoy the last breath of the day from there. In fact I have my time very well organised. First I correct the exercises from the private maths lessons I give the children. Then I turn on the radio and I read one of those magazines that tell you all about the love life of the Aga Khan and things like that. Daft magazines, I know, and terribly superficial but just the thing when you don't want to think about anything serious. Later on, at about two o'clock, I start knitting a sweater, knitting it or unknitting it, because I'm one of those indecisive types and I find it very hard to stick with whatever colour or size I've chosen.

Even when the radio programmes finish, I still find lots to do, I get on with my own things, with my knitting or whatever, in no hurry to go to sleep because, since I give private lessons in the afternoons, I don't have to get up early. And anyway there's the train, above all there's the train.

I often deny it to myself but, if I'm being honest, it's true, I am usually waiting for the train and in the end I do what I do because of the train, that's why I don't sleep and all that.

The train passes through the city at twenty-five to four. Up to that moment I'm usually on the alert, listening to the noises of the night, the voices and sounds that have grown familiar through repetition. So, for example, the last bus stops on the corner shortly after three and its one passenger gets off, a man, it seems, who loves to whistle and sometimes he whistles the same tune all week. Then, at about three fifteen, the street sweepers arrive. At half past three it's the turn of the man I call Fangio, because he usually speeds by about then and the noise his car engine makes is first like a roar and then later, when he's far off, like the moan of an animal that's wounded or in pain. Then, at last, after a few more minutes, the train arrives.

The iron bridge warns me of its arrival. Up to that moment I can't be completely sure, because you can be mistaken and confuse the train with the sound of the wind or with something else. But the iron bridge never lies, it acts like a loudspeaker and, besides, the train makes a loud hammering noise when it crosses it.

Mostly it arrives on time, at twenty-five to four. But there are days when it's late and then I can't help but get nervous. I start counting every second, I listen as hard as I can, and even get up to look out of the window. One day it didn't turn up until eight in the morning and I was in tears and everything because I felt sure there'd been an accident. Later I learned that the delay had been caused by nothing more serious than a landslip, or so I read in the paper.

The train usually has about twenty carriages and its destination is Hamburg. I don't know if it always carries the same cargo but the day I travelled on it, it was carrying horses. I was told they were bound for America and that was why they were unloading them at the port. What will have become of those horses? I don't know and the truth is I'd rather not. It might be that after that long journey all that awaited them was the butcher.

The train reduces speed when it crosses the bridge and that's the most important moment of the night. That's when I light the cigarette I usually keep on the bedside table; and that's when I start imagining.

First I imagine the two drivers at the engine. I imagine them both silent, each one immersed in his own thoughts. At first, when they started working together, I'm sure they had loads of things to tell each other, but once that first stage was over, after they'd talked about their family and their friends, they'd find it difficult to come up with new topics of conversation. Of course they could talk about football and stupid things like that, but I don't think so. People do talk about those things but not at four o'clock in the morning, not when they've been working for five hours.

I imagine, then, that they're both silent, watching the lights on the control panel or looking ahead at the rails. Especially looking at the rails. Or at least that's what I did that day. The horses in the wagons kept neighing and neighing, they were frightened and the truth is so was I until I got used to the speed, because it seemed to me that at any moment the rails were going to fly apart. But when I got over my fear I kept looking straight ahead, because the same thing happened to me as when I go to the sea, I was sort of hypnotised, I couldn't take my eyes off those rails continually coming together and moving apart, because that's what happens when you travel in a train at a hundred miles an hour, that's what the railway lines do.

And the rails aren't the only frightening thing when you travel in the engine of a train, because you suddenly realise that another train could emerge out of the darkness, coming from the opposite direction, I mean, and crash into you. But engine drivers aren't like me. They're not afraid. Perhaps they were on their first journey, but not now, now they're used to it, and I imagine them feeling bored, looking indifferently out at the villages that appear along the way.

Each of them immersed in his own thoughts, that's how I imagine them. One of them is married and has two children and thinks of them whenever he sees the lighted windows of a house because he assumes there must be some child in the house who's ill or who won't go to sleep. And then he feels like phoning his wife to find out how his children are because, of course, they too could be ill or have trouble sleeping and he probably will do that, phone home I mean, as soon as he gets to Hamburg, and even if he doesn't it won't matter, at least he thought of it.

And I stop thinking about the first driver and I start imagining what the second one, Sebastián, is doing, what's going on inside his head. And then I imagine that he's thinking of me, that he'd like to come to this room where I lie smoking my cigarette, and that it grieves him not to have his wish.

But in imagining these things, I'm only fooling myself. Sebastián's forgotten about me. If he hadn't he'd blow the train whistle three times, two short blasts followed by one long one, as soon as he crossed the iron bridge, the way he used to do night after night for the forty-four days that followed our journey together with the horses.

IF I COULD,
I'D GO OUT FOR A STROLL
EVERY NIGHT

II. *Marie's statement*

IF I could, I'd go out for a stroll every night because the night is
so lovely, just like the last hour of evening, which is lovely too,
and that's what the four of us used to do, grandfather, Toby,
Kent and me, we'd finish our work just before the sun went down
and set off for the valley to go for a walk. Grandfather would ride
Kent and I'd carry the miniature white walking stick they give all
the children at the village fiesta every year and Toby would be
running and leaping about and, because he's pretty stupid, he'd
keep barking at the swallows, but the swallows would make fun of
him by flying right past his nose at full pelt, screaming as they
went, because, as you know, when evening comes the swallows do
scream when they're out hunting for mosquitoes. They catch the
mosquitoes and store them in their wings and amongst their
feathers and they work really hard, especially in the spring, for
their young, I mean, because they usually have families to keep,
and whenever it was that time of year, grandfather used to help the
pair that lived in our stable, he'd open the babies' beaks and feed
them bread-crumbs soaked in milk because that particular couple
had a lot of mouths to feed, five babies in all, quite a responsibility,
anyway that's what they always say in my house, that life's
expensive and that our farm, for example, will never make us rich,
and that I won't be able to go on to college, even though I'm an
only child, but I don't really mind that much and anyway I'm only
eleven and it's years yet before I'd go.

So that's what we'd do, leave the farm when the swallows came out and set off very slowly towards the valley and grandfather would take with him the tape measure my mother uses for sewing because my mother's a seamstress and from time to time makes dresses and once she made a bright red one for the village schoolmistress and I really, really liked it but that idiot Vincent didn't, Vincent made fun of the dress and said the teacher had bought it because she was in love and that she looked like a tomato in glasses, and he even made a drawing on the blackboard and then the teacher punished the whole class.

But, as I was saying, grandfather would take this tape measure with him and use it to measure the plants to see how they were growing and one day we'd measure the alfalfa, another day we'd measure the clover and, because grandfather's very old, I was the one who would kneel down and put the zero on the tape measure right on the ground and then grandfather would make his calculations and say: 'No need to worry about this plant, Marie. It's grown two and three quarter inches since yesterday. That means the world's still alive.'

It made me really happy to hear grandfather say those words, in fact I'd often feel like laughing, and there was one particular day when I laughed a lot because the four of us were in a field of that lovely plant fenugreek, doing our measuring as usual and suddenly Kent stretched out his neck and ate a whole clump of the stuff, the very clump we'd marked with white thread because, naturally, each time we measured a plant we'd then tie a piece of white thread round it, as a marker, so that we'd know which plant we should look for the next day. And grandfather got annoyed with Kent and told him it was high time he showed a little respect for his work and that if he didn't, we'd pull all his teeth out. But he wasn't angry for long because Kent was a very good horse, as good as gold, and whenever we told him off he'd get very, very sad and look at you with his big eyes and then we'd forgive him everything.

Measuring a plant here and a plant there, we would eventually arrive at the bridge where a bat called Gordon lived and grandfather always used to say that Gordon was a very indecisive creature and that was why he flew the way he did, always zigzagging, always changing direction, only to end up exactly where he'd started, and that grandmother was just like Gordon, very indecisive that is, and that's why she never went out, not even to the church which is only a mile from our farm. And there was a bird that lived near the bridge, he was called Arthur and Arthur was always late, he'd hang around in the fields and come flying back home at the last minute, hurrying along so that night wouldn't find him out of his tree and we could scarcely see him when he flew over us but grandfather would look up and scold him:

'Late again, Arthur! You just like giving the folks at home something to worry about, don't you!'

I liked Arthur more than Gordon but I liked Gordon too, or at least I didn't dislike him, but that idiot Vincent did, bats bothered Vincent, and one day he caught one and took it to school and put a lit cigarette in its mouth. And because bats don't know how to exhale the smoke, it got bigger and bigger and finally its stomach exploded and it died. And because it was just like Gordon, I burst out crying and then that creep Vincent made fun of me.

After crossing the bridge we'd go up a hill from where you could see the village lights and the railway and then grandfather would open the supper basket and I'd eat a hard boiled egg, then white bread and salt pork and an apple for dessert. We used to eat in silence, sitting quietly, and both Toby and Kent would lie down in the grass, and we all felt contented, really happy, and it was even better when the summer arrived and the paths would fill with people and there'd be a south wind blowing. And in the summer we'd take longer walks, sometimes going as far as the railway tracks and one day we met the schoolmistress there and because it was night grandfather and she talked about the stars and how hot it was and grandfather warned her to watch out for snakes.

Grandfather was very afraid of snakes and that was why on

very sultry days there'd be five of us, the usual four plus Frankie the chicken; but there was a problem because Frankie didn't like walking in front and so couldn't kill any snakes that might threaten us.

'Frankie! Get in front!' grandfather would shout.

But Frankie was a very stubborn chicken and wouldn't obey him and grandfather would get furious.

'Frankie!' he would yell at the chicken, 'I didn't bring an expert with me in order to have him bringing up the rear.'

That's what grandfather thought, that snakes are evil things that kill birds, frighten horses and steal the milk from cows, but that they'll having nothing to do with chickens, because chickens are experts at killing snakes.

And so that last summer, the five of us went for our walks, with grandfather riding Kent and me with the little white walking stick I'd been given at the fiesta, and then the autumn came and it was just the four of us again, because there was no longer any danger of snakes and Frankie stayed at home, and we went on walking and walking until the day the teacher took us to the station.

That day we spent the whole morning doing arithmetic and we were all very good, even Vincent behaved himself, and the schoolmistress was very pleased and she said that, as a reward, we wouldn't have the last class but instead we'd go to the station to see the horses.

So we went and I'd never seen so many horses all together, there were at least two hundred of them and as it was fairly cold they were all steaming and now and then one of them would whinny. I looked hard at them all, first at one and then at another, comparing them with Kent and it seemed to me that there wasn't one horse there handsomer than Kent.

Then, of course, Vincent came over to me, as usual, because he's a pest and won't leave me alone, not at school nor anywhere else, and it was just the same that day, he came over and started talking nonsense, things about the schoolmistress, that he knew who she was in love with, that it was the engine driver, the one that was going to take away all these horses, that he knew this was true because he'd seen them kissing, and all of a sudden I forgot I was angry with him and I asked him a question:

'Where are they taking these horses?'

'They're taking them to Hamburg,' he replied, laughing.

'Why Hamburg?'

'To put them on a ship and send them to America.'

'To America?' I asked, puzzled. I just couldn't understand why they should do that.

And Vincent told me not to frown, that I wasn't so pretty when I frowned. And after that stupid remark, he looked over at the horses and said:

'Yes, America. Americans really go for horse meat.'

That was when I realised that those horses were going to the abattoir and that they were going to make that whole journey and then be killed and I felt very sad and didn't want to stay there any longer. I went back to school to pick up my schoolbag and then I walked very slowly back to the farm, stopping here and there to pick up dry leaves because, it being autumn, the path was covered with them.

An hour later I reached the farm and I saw my grandfather sitting at the door and he saw me, and then he did an odd thing, he lowered his head, he didn't even greet me, just lowered his head, and suddenly I remembered Kent and I remembered the horses at the station and what Vincent had told me and I flung my schoolbag down and went running to the stable: there was Toby, there was Frankie but no Kent.

'You've sold Kent!' I shouted and grandfather shouted back and so did my father. And just then I heard that loud whistle the trains give when they're about to leave the station.

That's why I don't go out for a stroll at night any more because we no longer have Kent and because grandfather's too old to go walking without Kent and since he stays at home, so do I, I don't even go to school anymore, because something else happened too, the schoolmistress ran off with the engine driver and hasn't come back yet, and now every night we have supper in the kitchen and I no longer know how the plants are growing, how Gordon and Arthur are, and I feel very sad when I think that, by now, Kent will have been eaten by some American.

NINE WORDS IN HONOUR OF THE VILLAGE OF VILLAMEDIANA

ONE autumn, when I was nine years old, I was staying with my aunt and uncle for a few days and a man came to their house. He walked straight into the kitchen and, without even a word of greeting, leaned against the wall and began to talk. With some astonishment, I realised that his main topic of conversation was none other than myself; the man was talking about me, about the very first time he'd seen me and about the clothes I was wearing then. He was possessed, he said, of a phenomenal memory and could remember absolutely everything, right down to the colour of the sweater I wore at the time and then, crouching down, he asked if it hadn't been a red one with white stars on it.

'How do you expect the child to know that? He can only have been a baby then, surely you can see that,' my uncle said and, in an attempt to change the subject, began talking about the weather and the south wind that was blowing. However, the man took no notice of him and just went on talking about me, about where and with whom I was playing that first time he saw me and how much I used to enjoy playing games, especially football.

'That much you're right about,' said my aunt, butting in. And, grabbing my arm, she led me out of the kitchen and told me to go and play, saying I'd be better off out in the street.

I remember that day very well, the air was unusually clear and warmed by a gentle sun, and I wandered about the square until it was evening, by which time I'd completely forgotten about the man who'd turned up at my aunt and uncle's house just after lunch.

But when I went back to the house, he was still there, still talking and still with his back to the wall but with his arms outstretched on either side, so that he looked, as my aunt remarked later, rather like Christ on the cross at Calvary. He was making absolutely no sense at all now; his conversation was like one long, weary exhalation and my aunt, so preoccupied that she didn't even notice I was back, was saying: 'If he doesn't shut up, the poor man will choke' and trying to get him to drink a glass of water. But the man was aware of nothing; behind their thick glasses his blue eyes seemed fixed on some point beyond the kitchen. He was dribbling now too, his face was bright red and the roots of his curly hair were beaded with sweat.

'Please, be quiet. Calm yourself. Let's all just sit down at the table and have supper together,' my uncle suggested, going over to him, smiling. But it was useless. The man, terrified, stood on tiptoe, pressing himself even closer to the wall, as if he were on the edge of a precipice and in grave danger of plunging into it.

'I'm going to call the doctor,' my aunt said decisively and, taking off her apron, she ran down to the inn to use their telephone.

The doctor, who was a well-built chap, did his best to prise the man off the wall, but without success, because the man began to scream the moment he felt anyone touching him.

'Bring me a bucket of water,' ordered the doctor and my aunt and uncle rushed out to the fountain opposite the house, where the water was coldest. The man, meanwhile, kept laughing, and his only discernible words were: 'Now you really are a swine.'

They threw the bucket of water over him and drops spattered the whole kitchen. The house fell suddenly silent and I realised that the man was about to fall headlong, that his knees were buckling under him. But the doctor and my uncle caught him in time and carried him to a dry corner of the room.

'Is he dead?' I asked.

'No, he's just asleep,' my aunt said to reassure me.

But my fear wouldn't go away and I stayed in the kitchen listening intently to the ensuing conversation. That's why I still remember the term the doctor used, a term that struck terror into my heart even then, when I barely knew what a hospital was. The term he used was 'electric shock treatment'.

'The trouble with him is that he remembers too much,'

remarked my uncle when the three of us were left alone again.

'Plus the fact that he lives on his own and spends months in the woods without talking to a soul,' added my aunt, wiping the kitchen floor dry with a cloth.

And that's both the end of the first story and the beginning of the second, which took place twenty-five years later.

One cold winter afternoon, after toiling up a long hill, I reached the gateway to a mansion built by a rich Spanish emigrant on his return from South America. Enclosed by a stone wall and surrounded by a large garden, the mansion was, at first sight, what most people would term 'beautiful', but there was something about it that aroused my immediate dislike. It was too green, too lush.

But, for all its lush greenness, it would have been just another melancholy, gloomy spot were it not for the fact that it had been permanently sullied. For the builder's original aim had been altered and one glance at the entrance was enough to understand the nature of that change: an ugly, new, steel door filled the presumptuous Chinese arch which, indulging a caprice, the rich emigrant had had built there. To one side of the door there was a small notice that read: Psychiatric Hospital.

The arrival of a porter wearing a blue overcoat over his white uniform tore me away from my musings about the arch. I told him I had a friend there and had come with the intention of visiting him, that I had with me an authorisation from his family, signed by my friend's mother. But it was too cold to bother with formalities and so he led me straight through the garden and into the building. As I passed, I noticed the rose gardens, the tennis courts and the artificial streams flowing through caves carved out of rock, all utterly abandoned, overgrown by brambles and nettles. The house itself – mock-country house in style – had been better maintained, but there was a monstrous addition to the green shutters in the form of thick, black iron bars. At first I assumed they'd been placed there to stop the inmates escaping. But then it dawned on me that they served another far more dreadful purpose: they were there to stop the inmates hurling themselves out.

'I'm afraid your trip may have been in vain. Your friend's in a very bad way,' the director told me when I explained the reason for my visit. He was an oldish man, gentle and softly spoken.

'But can I see him?'

'I don't suppose we'll lose anything by trying,' muttered the director as if to himself. And he took me to the upper floor. 'I'll go in first. And, please, when you come in, don't make any sudden movements,' he said when we came to the last room on the corridor. The door was bolted from outside.

The room had padded walls and through the crack left open by the director I could see my friend sitting on the bed in his pyjamas. When he realised he had a visitor he looked up and put his hands to his glasses. It was not a gesture I recognised. It was new in him and seemed more the gesture of a troubled child than of a thirty-year-old man.

When the director told me to go in, I approached my friend slowly. Again he put his hands up to his glasses.

'Martín, how are you?' I asked, feigning joy and walking towards him in expectation of an embrace. We were old friends and for a long time had shared a house together.

Suddenly, crouched in one corner of the room, Martín began to cry and so intense was his desire to hide that he pressed his face to the wall, crushing his glasses. Then his crying became a shout. And, like that previous gesture of raising his hands to his glasses, both the crying and the shouting seemed the actions of a child of two.

The director led me out into the corridor then went back into the room. For a quarter of an hour I listened to him talking affectionately to my friend, even singing to him now and then.

'What's wrong with him?' I asked when he came out. I was sweating by this time.

'He didn't recognise you,' said the director.

Astonished, I asked how that was possible.

'He's lost his memory and he's very frightened. Up until about two months ago your name would have meant something to him. Now it means nothing.' He seemed as concerned as I was. Then he said: 'How about a cup of coffee?'

We walked over to a summerhouse set in one part of the garden, a sort of restroom for the doctors working at the centre. With its woodlined walls and ceilings, it was the only place that seemed to preserve the ambience of a past era.

'Everything in Martín's head has been wiped clean, as if it were a tape. The worst thing is that he can't record anything new on it either,' he explained as we drank our coffee.

'But there's a chance he'll recover.' Martín's mother had told me that there was.

'I don't think so,' he said and that struck me as an opportune moment to change the subject.

'When I was a child I met another man whose mind was unhinged. But he went mad because he remembered too much,' I began. And I told him about what had happened at my aunt and uncle's house.

'I think of the memory as being rather like a dam,' he said, after a pause for thought. 'It irrigates and gives life to our whole spirit. But, like a dam, it needs overflow channels if it's not to burst its banks. Because if it ever does overflow or burst, its waters will destroy everything in their path.'

'And, on the other hand, once it's emptied out, it will dry up forever,' I added. He nodded, a little wearily. 'I find it hard to believe that anyone could descend into such a hell,' I said, mainly to ease my own fears. And I told him what my own experience had been. I even said that, for me, the past consisted of only a few images. That when I looked back I found no guiding thread, no neatly constructed landscape, but a void scattered with islands, with memories. A sea of nothingness broken up by a few islands, that was how I pictured my past.

What I said clearly struck the director as odd. He smiled wanly and patted me on the back.

'You're right, of course, but memory can be a tricky thing. Memory, how can I put it? . . . Memory, like the heart, is a bit antiquated. It pays little heed to logic.'

'So how much should you remember?' I asked, half-joking, as I got up from my armchair to indicate that it was time for me to go.

'Neither too much nor too little.'

'But how many words, say?'

'Nine,' he said, laughing, and I didn't ask him to explain further because I thought it must be some kind of private joke and that the number had some special significance for him.

We said goodbye at the door of the summerhouse. He went back to the house and I to the Chinese arch.

And that brings to an end both the second story and the introduction with which I wanted to preface my memories of the village of Villamediana, an introduction which, illustrating as it does two examples of faulty memory, should act as a lucky charm and ensure a successful end to my work. However, even with that protection, I feel afraid, I fear the dangerous places through which I will inevitably have to pass. I will, therefore, follow the advice given me by the hospital director. I will speak of Villamediana, but neither too much nor too little. Nine words will suffice for me to sum up my long stay there.

1.   LOOKING back on my life, I come across an island by the name of Villamediana. If I were asked to choose five words from the dictionary and use them to form a kind of instant description of the village or to give some sense of what it was like, I would have to choose, first and foremost, the word 'sun'. For I saw it almost every day: streaming in through the cracks in the shutters when I woke, fixed like a golden nail in the centre of the blue sky when I went out into the street and setting the brushwood aflame and

painting the adobe walls blood-red as evening fell. The second word I'd choose would be 'wheatfield' and then I'd have to describe its colours, first green and then yellow, a yellow which, in summer, extended from the very edge of the village as far as the eye could see and beyond. The last three words would have to be 'empty', 'crow' and 'sheep', for most of the houses in Villamediana were empty and crows and sheep were frequently the only creatures enlivening the landscape.

Whilst those five words would, on the one hand, be enough to give an impression of that island I call Villamediana, even perhaps of the whole of Castile, on the other hand, such a description is no more adequate than a simple schoolboy composition or the visions of poets who, judging by what one sees and reads, only go there for their holidays. Many details of my experiences there would of necessity be omitted, for example, what happened on my arrival in the village. For I arrived in Villamediana, not when the village was awash with sun and girdled by wheatfields, but on a dark winter's day.

2. SOME people proudly claim that their mood doesn't depend on what kind of day it is outside. My happiness, they say, doesn't depend on the colour of the sky, I have my own inner climatology.

Unfortunately, I can make no such proud boast. If it's true that we retain within us the memory of all existence and that a vestige of primeval time lives on in our cells, then I'm convinced that the ferns and mosses of the beginnings of life wield a powerful influence over my changes in mood. My spirit is essentially the same as that of plants: it revives with the good weather and is cast down by the rain or the cold. A pleasant enough dependency, of course, when I find myself in sunny climes, but most unpleasant if the forces of winter militate against me, as happened on my first encounter with Villamediana.

For, as I said, I arrived in Villamediana on a dark winter's day.

By noon the mist had closed in completely and when, after sorting out my things, I went to look out of the window, the village appeared to me as if wrapped, rather ineptly, in a length of ice-cold, off-white linen that left only fragments of landscape uncovered: a rooftop here, the bare crown of an elm there, the rounded belltower of the church near the centre. They were dim shadows, chilly ghosts hanging in the air, more intimidating than the mist itself.

It was a disappointing landscape for someone, like myself, who has allowed himself to be seduced by the sort of mirage that always accompanies a change of address. Before undertaking the journey I was convinced that the simple fact of arriving at this new place would mean that I could jettison a whole section of my past life like so much ballast; henceforward everything would be easy, luminous, different. When I imagined myself living there, the only thing I had difficulty in picturing with any exactitude was the landscape: how many roads there would be, how many houses, what those houses would be like and if the bleak plateaux really would look like squat trapeziums. But, as regards the sky, I had no doubts. For in the sky, as if daubed there by a naive painter, I always placed the sun, the symbol of my new life. It would be a weak sun, as befitted winter, but strong enough nonetheless to cheer even a spirit such as mine, overgrown with ferns and mosses. But there was no sun, no light. I was greeted instead by that dank, rather grubby mist.

My first walks around the village did nothing to improve that first impression. There wasn't a soul to talk to in the eternally empty streets and the silence that wrapped about them forced me back in time to confront again one of the nightmares of my infancy, that of being an abandoned child in a dead city. The only sound to be heard was that of the drips the mist formed along the gutters beneath the rooftops as it condensed; for the drips became threads of water and the threads became streams that fell at last onto the cement surface of the pavements producing an echo of applause that reverberated faintly out towards the church, the main road and the plateaux. But that was all. No other sign of life penetrated the mist.

After only a couple of days in Villamediana, the mirage that had led me there started to fade. The old world, the one I had so longed to leave behind, began to seem attractive to me again. To my surprise I found myself lying in bed and missing the cinemas, the cafés, the noise. But I had to put up with it. For various reasons, my immediate return to the city was impossible. Furthermore I knew, from the agency that had rented me the house, that the village had two hundred inhabitants. Sooner or later, they would appear and I would meet them and speak with them.

One afternoon, it must have been on my third day there, I heard a noise other than the applause of falling water. It was the sound of music, of a strident song issuing from a radio in a house not very far from mine.

'Someone's alive out there,' I thought, going out into the street in search of the source of that one sign of life. Then I noticed a small house with all its windows lit tucked away in the upper part of the village. That was where the music was coming from. A record player – not a radio – was playing at full blast and a series of voices, mostly female, were singing along as if to outdo it in volume. There was no doubt about it. There were people in Villamediana, real live people.

From then on the route of my daily walks changed. I circled the house, again and again, morning and evening. And there was always music playing, the windows were always lit. Such evidence of joy was in itself astonishing but it was proof too that not everyone's spirit was overgrown with ferns and mosses. No, mood wasn't necessarily dependent on climate.

Some time later, when I'd been in the village for over a week, the mist lifted. The falls of applauding water ceased, the gutters began to dry up, the drop of water which, ever since my arrival, had hung from the clothesline on my balcony – in my letters I'd described it as resembling a 'glass pea' – fell to earth for good. There were patches of blue in the sky, the plants stood tall again and the square filled up with old people and children.

'It seems the worst is over,' I wrote to my friends.

My life flowed now along normal channels. I found out where people gathered to play cards or to drink and that was where I went to meet and talk a little with my new neighbours. Nonetheless, my curiosity remained centred on the house with the record player and the lighted windows. The chance nature of that first contact had forged a link between it and me. Who lived there? What lay behind that display of happiness? But I had decided to be discreet and to avoid asking any direct questions. I had to be patient and wait for someone to tell me.

I didn't have to wait long and the answer was handed to me, so to speak, by one of the shopkeepers in Villamediana. She was a plump woman and friendly in the way all shopkeepers are when a new customer presents himself, and she was very interested in my reasons for being in the village. She couldn't get it into her head that I had come simply to 'be there'.

'I don't believe it. You're hiding something,' she said to me one day.

By then, after four or five visits, the ice was broken and we talked to each other with a certain intimacy.

'I wish I was, but I'm not. I'm here because I like the place,' I replied.

'Forgive my saying so, but I find that extremely hard to believe. There isn't a sadder, more boring village to be found.'

'Well, I can't see what's sad about it,' I lied. 'On the contrary, it seems to me that people here live very happily.'

She smiled mockingly, making it clear that she still did not believe me, that thank you for the compliment but no, she wasn't deceived. I hurriedly explained about the house in which I'd observed that zest for life.

'Oh, you mean the shepherds! That's the shepherds' house!'

she said, laughing and adding, with the expression of one unwilling to reveal everything she knew: 'I know it takes all sorts, but those shepherds, how can I put it . . . they'd much rather spend their money on treats for their children than on buying them books. Look,' she said pointing out at the square where some children were playing, 'they don't even send them to school. At this hour theirs are the only children you'll find still playing out in the streets.'

So it was the shepherds' house. And more by her look than by anything she said, the shopkeeper explained to me how 'odd' they were, how different from the rest of the community. That attitude was new to me, surprising.

Before I'd even left the shop, I'd already decided to find out for myself in what way the shepherds were different. After all I had nothing in particular to do and the good mood the change in the weather had brought about in my inner world of mosses and ferns urged me on to action. Yes, I would attempt to discover the shepherds' secret. If I succeeded, it was quite likely that anything I learned would prove to be some universally applicable truth, not one restricted to the narrow world of Villamediana. Because in all times and in all places, indeed since time immemorial, there had been shepherds. And it was with such thoughts in my head that I turned my full attention to the goings-on in the happiest house in the village.

I soon came to realise that the peculiarity of its occupants was not restricted to their love of music or to the low esteem in which they held schooling. What was also noticeable – in a half-deserted village like Villamediana, how could you not notice? – was their sheer abundance, their quantity and the fact that their house was always crammed with people, not empty or half-empty like the majority of the houses in the village. Every time I passed the front door, I'd see five or six children playing there and there'd always be one I hadn't spotted before. Some were fair, some dark and there was even the occasional redhead and they were always well turned out. And it was rather the same with the adults, with them too it was difficult to keep track. One day I'd look up at the balcony and see two young women, the next day a third woman with an older man, rather short in stature, the day after that a dark, well-built man leaning on the balustrade smoking.

One evening, when I was with my neighbour, Onofre, I saw a white-haired old man going into the house.

'Does he live there too?' I asked, feigning amazement. The fact was the house seemed to be of limitless capacity.

'It's one of the shepherdess's husbands,' Onofre said. There was a malicious undertone to his words.

'One of her husbands? How many has she got?' This time my amazement was genuine.

'She's got two. The man we saw just now and another shorter man. But the short one's the boss, in fact, he's master of the whole house.'

I knew who he meant when he spoke of the master of the house, not only because I'd seen him standing on the balcony but also because I recognised him from the bar. He was always trying to get me to make up a pair for cards. And suddenly it struck me as odd that the shepherd should lack a partner to play cards with, especially in Villamediana, a village where there was no other entertainment. The word 'exclusion' floated into my mind.

My neighbour was smiling ever more maliciously.

'As I say, he's the boss. Everyone obeys him.'

'And how many people live in the house all together?' I asked.

'There's no way of knowing. It depends.'

'What do you mean, it depends?'

'I mean it depends how many are passing through.' Onofre was laughing quite openly now. Fancy a man like myself being unable to solve the enigma he set before me.

But it was not in the least difficult to understand what he was trying to tell me. Partly because his jokes tended to be full of sexual innuendo anyway, but also because of something he'd said earlier, which I remembered very clearly, something about the women of easy virtue who lived in Villamediana.

According to his fellow villagers, my neighbour was a 'stirrer', a 'mischief-maker' and a 'tittletattler' and nothing he said was to be taken seriously. However, as I subsequently found out, almost everyone in the village was in agreement with him as far as the family of shepherds was concerned. The mere mention of them provoked gales of laughter.

On the one hand, what they suggested to me fitted well with what I myself had observed. The music and the lights always lit, for example, or the studiedly 'petite cocotte' look adopted by the adolescent girls of the house, as well as the elusive behaviour of the women I'd seen on the balcony who – when it came to walking down to the bus stop on the main road – chose to take a long detour rather than go through the centre of the village. But, on the other hand, when I looked in at their front door, it was always the same people I saw. There were a lot of people, it was true, but they were always the same ones. There was certainly not the coming and going of men one might expect in a brothel. It was clear that this was a very special family. What was less clear was whether their specialness was of the kind so firmly endorsed by my neighbour and by others like him.

I asked Daniel, the village gamekeeper, about it. He was a serious man and not in the least narrowminded. Live and let live was his motto. I trusted his judgement and always accepted his invitations to join him for walks in the forest.

'Well, that's certainly the reputation they've been given and they're stuck with it. But this village is like that, always gossiping. If you listen carefully you can hear the constant buzz of people talking, usually talking ill of others. We're very backward here. It's not like in the city. In the city those girls would be no different from a lot of others. The fact that one got married when she was already pregnant and another after she'd had a baby, that's all it amounts to, nothing more. But, of course, because they're shepherds . . .'

That was the central issue, the fact that they were shepherds and, as I was soon to realise, in that fact lay the origin of the calumny. Not in their behaviour or their character, but in their condition as shepherds. What was said about them in Villamediana, was said about others in the region as a whole.

The clerk at the agency I rented the house from said to me once: 'Well, I must say I think you're wrong. You can't go leaving your front door open in this day and age, especially when there are shepherds about.' I'd happened to mention that I tended not to lock my door. 'They wait until there are gypsies around before they do any stealing. That's why gypsies have got such a bad name. Because they get blamed for all the burglaries the shepherds commit.' Then, to moderate what he'd said, he added that he was, of course, speaking in general terms, they weren't all thieves, it took all sorts, after all.

It certainly did, but – if one were to believe him or many of the others – the majority did have those bad tendencies, especially the ones who didn't own the sheep they tended and worked as hired hands. They were the unsociable ones who would have their knives out at the least provocation. Well, what could you expect when dealing, as one was, with alcoholics.

In the end I came to understand the role the inhabitants of the happy house played in Villamediana. They'd become marginalised, their role was that played in other parts of the world by the sick, by blacks or by people of a different sexual orientation. The fact is that every society, however small, always surrounds itself with a wall, an invisible one, but no less real for that and then tosses anything negative and foul-smelling into the area outside, like that wicked market gardener in the story who, when it came to getting rid of his weeds, always waited for cover of night and then made straight for his brother's farm.

The shepherds were beyond the pale, on the other side of the wall, in the circle of the guilty. And, it should be said, they've probably always been there, in all times and in all places. When

Calliope and her sisters spoke to Hesiod, they dismissed him with the words: 'you rustic shepherd, shame on you'. And when Christianity, which began as the religion of a humble and marginalised people, described the birth of the baby Jesus, it placed at his side the shepherds from Bethlehem for exactly the same reasons it later placed Mary Magdalene at the foot of the cross.

I shared my thoughts with Daniel and took advantage of one of our walks through the forest to ask him how the shepherds felt about their position; if it was true, as people said, that the majority were ashamed of their profession.

'The blacks aren't. The blacks tend to be very proud and if they can blacken their own name still further, they will,' he replied.

'Who are the blacks?' I asked, thinking perhaps it was the nickname given to one particular family.

'You mean you haven't noticed there are white shepherds and black shepherds?' And he began listing all the shepherds I knew in the village, explaining which belonged to which category.

'Why, you're right!' His classification seemed to me absolutely accurate.

Not content with simply listing the two groups, Daniel wanted to describe them too. He explained how the hair of some of the shepherds, usually the blue-eyed ones, would gradually become whiter and whiter and how their whole behaviour would undergo a similar transformation: they would become prudent, considerate, in fact as gentle as their looks. Others, though, became black as coal and could often be seen in the bar, drinking, carousing, ready to gamble away their money with anyone. In conclusion he said: 'In fact we're on our way to see two shepherds right now, one of whom, as you'll see for yourself, is black and the other white.' And leaving the village behind us, we set off in the direction of one of the plateaux.

The two shepherds hadn't been down to any village for a month. The black shepherd shouted a greeting to us when we were still some way off from the sheep pen and when we reached his side, he was there ready with a bottle of wine in his hand. He spoke in a sing-song voice and immediately started in on the tangled tale of some affair he'd had with a married woman, pausing only to let fly a curse or to throw a stone at the dog.

The white shepherd didn't even come over to us. Seated on a stone wall, he was busy cleaning a sheepskin. When I went over to offer him some of his companion's wine, he shook his head.

'Where are you from?' I asked.

'From around Segovia,' he replied in a very quiet voice. His eyes were pale blue, his eyebrows white as cotton wool.

'And what's your name?' I asked, in the same friendly fashion, having told him mine.

'Gabriel,' he whispered. Then, with only a muttered goodbye, he got down from the wall and walked away.

A little later I noticed that wings – white wings – had sprouted from his back and that, borne up on them, he'd taken flight and lifted off into the air. But that may just have been an illusion brought on by the wine given me by his companion, the black shepherd.

3. TO A village full of old people and with barely two hundred inhabitants, a stranger coming to stay is an instant novelty. They're not accustomed to receiving people, on the contrary, the scene they're most familiar with, the scene repeated year in, year out, is that of departure. Whole families have abandoned the village declaring that 'it's impossible to live in Villamediana'. And of course those who remain agree. They've stayed not because they wanted to, not because they value what they have, but because they've no other option. But then the normal course of events is reversed and a stranger, someone who obviously feels otherwise, arrives in their midst. He doesn't appear to be ill or to have come there in search of a dryer climate. Neither does he seem to be from some museum in Madrid as happens now and again when people

are sent to restore the statues in the church. No, this stranger has chosen the place because he likes it.

Such a conclusion is not only surprising, it's also flattering to those still living in the village. Everyone cheers up, they all want to talk about it. When they'd least expected it, life has given them a pleasant surprise and in bar and shop conversations are no longer limited to the usual subjects, to the family, to hunting and to work. Just by his presence, the stranger gives rise to the most diverse conjectures and suppositions. And later, whenever the opportunity arises, everyone will attempt to get into conversation with him, eager to find out just how much truth there is in their imaginings. Is it true that he likes Villamediana? Why? Because of the landscape? He wouldn't by any chance be trying to forget some unhappy love affair, would he?

Given this situation, the stranger has no option but to spread himself around. He'll be obliged to talk to everyone and to accept every invitation to go down to the bar for a glass of wine. And though spending all day walking from one part of the village to another will wear him out, he'll willingly carry out the task he's been set, because he too is astonished by the warmth of their reception, because he too is curious to find out what they are like, these countryfolk and shepherds who suddenly, from one day to the next, have become part of his life. He also knows that the situation will change after the first few days and that, once he ceases to be a novelty, he'll soon come to be seen as just another village resident. And the prospect of a life without complications cheers him: just two or three friends, the odd meal out, long walks and lots of reading, that's all he needs in order to live well.

However, starting up new relationships nearly always gives rise to some misunderstanding. You start chatting to someone with no other intention than that of passing the time pleasantly and exchanging a few anecdotes. But what if that person wants something more and tries to obtain or even demand that something more? Given that the newcomer speaks to everyone and opens the door of his house to all and sundry, extricating himself from this predicament may prove difficult.

The stranger soon comes to regret the attitude he adopted when he first arrived, because he genuinely dislikes the one person to interpret his behaviour as a sure sign of real friendship. A week goes by and he can find no way back, he doesn't know how to close the door he opened. And it seems to him he's made the same mistake he always makes, it seems that if the fault is in oneself, a change of address can resolve nothing; he fears that perhaps he's ruined the peace he'd hoped to find in Villamediana.

One person in the village did misinterpret my kindness: my neighbour, Onofre. When I arrived there he was getting on for sixty and, having been widowed very early on, he lived alone with his youngest son, a surly, grim-faced youth with an evil reputation amongst the other village youngsters. Since we lived right opposite each other and given the climate of affection that reigned at the beginning of my stay there, it was inevitable that I would have more to do with him than with anyone else. For example, it was from him that I gleaned my first facts about the village, concrete facts as well as tittle-tattle: how many acres the forest bordering the plateau covered; when the feast day of the place known as Valdesalce was held; how many soldiers there were in the signals barracks perched on the hill you could see from the main road.

Onofre was not the kind of man who, on becoming a widower, undergoes a radical change in ideas and adapts to doing all the housework for himself. He still considered preparing meals or sweeping out the rooms to be tasks unworthy of a man, a view, it should be said, that was fairly widespread in Villamediana society. I can still see the look of astonishment on the face of one little boy of five or six when he saw me bustling about in the kitchen surrounded by cooking pots: 'That's girl's work you're doing!' he said quite spontaneously, a comment that made me laugh but at the same time somewhat unnerved me. I immediately imagined myself being pursued around the village by children, amidst accusing cries of: Sissy! Sissy!

With no woman to look after him and with no desire or need to look after himself, my neighbour had plumbed the lower depths of squalor. He was perennially dirty and had got into the habit of eating constantly. Whenever he talked to me, I could actually see the food he was eating, chewed to a pulp, being churned around amongst his nicotine-stained teeth and my face and neck would get spattered by any random fragments that escaped from his mouth. I found it most disagreeable and had to make a real effort of will not to turn on my heel and simply remove myself from his presence. An even greater effort of will was required when he offered me the very bottle of wine from which his own greasy lips had just supped or when he bade me sit down amidst the eternal grime of his kitchen.

But the squalor was not restricted to the domains of his person and his home. His words were squalid too. One day he'd point to the shepherds' house and, as I described before, take enormous delight in vilifying the women living there, on another he'd pillory the owner of the local tavern, accusing him of having got rich on the proceeds of smuggling, or else he'd inveigh against the shopkeeper in the square, warning me never to buy anything from his shop because of the astronomical mark-up on all the goods. Like all gossips, he was also a coward, and he addressed these confidences to me in an undertone, in a whisper, lest the wind carry his words to the ears of whoever it was he'd just defamed.

Despite all this, what one noticed first about the man was not the filth but the beauty of his eyes. He had the blue, luminous eyes of a heretic, a visionary.

One day, just to pull his leg, I said to him: 'Can you remember being burned at the stake, Onofre?'

'When?'

'In the Middle Ages, when else?'

'Oh, drink your wine and shut up,' he replied, passing me the bottle. That was his favourite riposte, perfect for dealing with stupid questions.

However, the beauty of his eyes was not sufficient consolation and I did everything I could to reduce contact with him to a minimum. My front door remained firmly shut and I'd go out only when I knew he was taking his afternoon nap and, if he asked me to join him in a game of cards, I'd claim not to know how to play.

But it was all in vain. More than anything else and whatever the cost, Onofre wanted to be my friend and never missed a chance to proclaim the good news of our friendship to the village at large.

'We're the best of friends, we are,' he'd declare to anyone walking down our street on their way to one of the bars and then turn to me for immediate confirmation of what he'd said.

'Isn't that right? Wouldn't you say so? Bosom pals we are.'

I, of course, had no alternative but to concur.

More than that, he wanted me all to himself and used all the wiles of a jealous girlfriend to achieve this end. He'd follow me everywhere, interrupting my conversations with the shopkeeper, sulking whenever I asked a favour of someone else in the village.

He'd walk into my house, wearing a hurt expression and say: 'I hear you asked Daniel for firewood,' adding: 'My firewood's every bit as good as his, you know.'

Then, depositing a bundle of his own best firewood by the sitting room door, he'd depart in silence.

As time went on, he felt the need for a theory to explain the origin of our friendship and soon came up with the reason we two had ended up being such friends. The reason I'd come to live there was Luis, the bearded chap who'd rented the house before me. It was through him that I'd found out what a good sort Onofre was.

'Luis? Who's Luis?' I asked in confusion.

He gave me a knowing look and smiled, making it clear that he knew I was only joking. Who was Luis? Why, Luis was Luis, the old priest who'd come to live in Villamediana when he retired.

'You know who I mean,' he'd insist, clapping me on the back. 'You'd never have come here in the first place if he hadn't told you about me.'

That episode gave me much food for thought and, after a while, I came to understand Onofre's technique for dealing with reality. First, he'd invent a lie and then, having convinced himself it was true, he'd start spreading it around until, so to speak, it gained general acceptance.

This tactic sometimes had pathetic results. For example, one day he painted two blue windowframes on either side of the only aperture, a tiny kitchen window, on the otherwise blank façade of his miserable little house.

'When did you paint them? Last night?' I asked when we met. He pretended he hadn't heard me and made me feel rather as if I'd just told a child the truth about Father Christmas. From then on, as far as I was concerned, his house had three windows not one.

On another occasion he showed me a ring, telling me it had been a gift from his son and praising his son's generosity. I knew, however – indeed he himself had told me so only a month before – that he'd bought it from a travelling salesman.

Very slowly, as I came to understand him better, my opinion of him improved and our friendship ceased to be just another of his lies and became genuine affection. To be honest, his behaviour didn't strike me as so very unusual. All of us, at some time in our lives, feel the need to free ourselves from some painful truth and will resort to anything, especially lies, in order to do so. For the truth should never be given priority over suffering.

If Onofre was distinguished by anything it was his enthusiasm, the sheer energy he put into the carrying out of his stratagems. And, frankly, his personal situation cried out for such deceit. He lived in the most terrible solitude, I only realised just how terrible the day I asked him to lend me an alarm clock.

'I have to go to the city first thing tomorrow morning,' I explained.

'You mean you haven't got an alarm clock?' he said, giving me an incredulous look, as if unable to believe his ears.

No, I said, I didn't, I really didn't own an alarm clock.

He went back into his house, a pensive look on his face, and returned clasping a great silvery contraption. Placing it in my hands, he said, almost tearfully:

'For goodness sake get yourself an alarm clock! It really keeps a chap company!'

A shiver ran through me. I'd just heard an exact definition of solitude from the last person I would have expected it from. What else was solitude if not a situation in which even the ticking of a clock can be companionable?

I thought about the bars in the village and said to myself:

'The lives those places must have saved!'

4. THERE were only two bars in Villamediana. The best one, which had once been a social club, was on the main square and was furnished with special green baize card tables made from wrought iron and marble in the style prescribed by an earlier age. If one were to believe what the customers and the owners of the bar said, only those on the political left gathered there, those villagers who had sided with the Republicans during the Civil War and the young people in the village who refused to go to mass. On the other hand, and again this was only their opinion, the locals who frequented the other bar lived in servile submission to the village fascists and the priest and were supporters of the most rabidly right-wing politicians.

The other bar bore the unusual name of Nagasaki and was situated on the road leading out of the village. They played cards here too but the tables were made from aluminium and multi-coloured plastic. Unlike the regulars at the first bar, the customers who came here didn't classify the village bars according to ideological criteria, for them the factor tipping the balance in favour of one bar or another was purely economic. They considered the bar on the square to be the bar of the rich, of those who owned land and property. Their bar, on the other hand, was the bar of the poor, of the simple labourer, the farmhand.

The customers of each of these bars formed two distinct groups that rarely mixed. In the village as a whole, there couldn't have been more than ten people who frequented both bars indiscriminately. Some, amongst them the mayor, went to neither. They avoided taking sides and so could not allow themselves the luxury of seeming to favour one group over the other. After all, you never knew when another civil war might break out. Better safe than sorry.

In general terms, both sides were right. Although this may seem shocking to those unfamiliar with the evolution of fascism, the Nagasaki's clientele, the simple people of Villamediana, were in favour of a hard-line military government and embraced the kind of nihilism that can as easily fall prey to anarchy as to the ideas of a Mussolini or a Perón. Their vision of the world was imbued with a pessimism underpinned by endless proverbs and popular sayings. The clientele at the café on the square, on the other hand, were members of the highest stratum of village society, whose politics were half-enlightened, half-romantic. Like every militant socialist worth his salt, they claimed to believe in reason, although, as the wife of the bar's owner happily confided to me one day: the only good dictatorship is a left-wing dictatorship.

I spent more time at the poor man's bar. I was treated with excessive formality at the other place and their customers always made a tremendous effort to ensure that conversation there maintained a certain level. They were convinced, moreover, that I was a journalist and were constantly plying me with questions about current affairs. What did I think about the upcoming elections? What were my considered views on Spain joining the EEC? I found the role assigned me there distinctly uncomfortable and only went there for my after-lunch coffee. But at night, with the prospect of several hours ahead of me, I always made for the Nagasaki.

The Nagasaki clientele didn't bother me at all and only spoke to me when it was my round. They had no need of entertainment. All of them – from the owner down – were excellent conversationalists and weavers of interminable tales, mostly about hunting, that almost always ended in arguments. These arguments usually lasted until about three in the morning but, even so, rarely ended in any agreement. One of the regulars, an old shepherd called Agustín, used to take the same way home as me and always bade me goodnight with the same words:

'See you tomorrow, then. We can carry on where we left off because, you know, there was some real old rubbish being talked at the end there . . .'

I must confess that, at first, the main topic of conversation at the Nagasaki didn't attract me. Hunting has always seemed to me a cruel pastime and my habit of giving names to animals – something I've done since I was a child – prevents me ever doing harm to any creature, however repellent. Imagine, for example, that you have a cockroach living in your house and one day it occurs to you to christen that cockroach José María, and then it's José María this and José María that, and very soon the creature becomes a sort of small, black person, who may turn out to be timid or irritable or even a little conceited. And obviously in that situation you wouldn't dream of putting poison down around the house. Well, you might consider it as an option but no more often than you would for any other friend.

But the Nagasaki regulars were real hunters. They weren't the sort of hunters who, like Daudet's Tartarin, return from the forest and go on and on about their heroic deeds and exploits. Listening to them it was easy to comprehend what the old books say about hunting: that it draws down madness upon the hearts of men and that, basically, all hunters are like the unfortunate abbot who, on hearing his greyhounds barking whilst he was celebrating Sunday mass, simply dropped what he was doing and rushed off to give chase to the hare, pausing only to collect his rifle and his pack of dogs.

The subject of hunting took on an unusual grandeur on their lips. It seemed more an excuse to speak of man's solitude at night, lashed by icy winds . . . or to describe a man's sadness on returning home with his gamebag empty, after a whole day spent combing the forest, or simply as an excuse to recall their lost youth, for some of them, Agustín the shepherd for example, no longer had the strength to go after boars and wolves.

And beneath all the many variations on a theme, like a guiding thread, lay the idea of struggle. Not just of man against beast, but also amongst the beasts themselves. Snake against bird, weasel against rabbit, the bear against everyone else. It was the law – *dura lex, sed lex* – of nature, a law that not even man could escape.

'Do you know how a bear kills its prey?' the owner of the bar and one of the best hunters in the village once asked me.

I said that I didn't.

'It kills with one blow of its paw. Just one. And do you know what it aims for?'

Again, I didn't.

'It goes for the head. One blow and it'll rip your brains out. Just a single clean blow. It makes no odds whether it's attacking a calf or a man. It always goes for the head.'

Before continuing, he crossed his arms and leaned on the counter as he always did before launching into a story.

'I've only ever once seen a bear. Someone in the village killed it and it was left on display in the main square for a whole morning. When you see a bear close to like that, that's when you understand what a bear is. Every one of its claws is sharp as a dagger. The same goes for its teeth. It's a sight I'll never forget.'

'The man who killed it died three days later,' added Agustín.

'Really? Why was that? I was only a child then so I don't remember,' said the owner, surprised.

'I don't know whether it's true or not, but people say he died of shock. Apparently by the time he came back from the forest he'd gone a bit soft in the head. Just the fact that he'd managed to kill it, I suppose. Though it must be a tremendous shock suddenly coming face to face with a bear.'

'A shock? But, Agustín, how can you say that? I happen to know that he'd been after that bear for over a month,' intervened the group sceptic.

'You be quiet, you don't know anything about it!' said the bar owner, cutting him short. 'What's that got to do with anything? I spent five years hunting wolves . . . and what do you think happened when I finally caught up with them? My hair stood on end, that's what, because I never knew, at least not exactly, just when I might find them. That's where the surprise comes in, that's what shocks you.'

The sceptic cast doubt on the owner's argument, the latter produced another anecdote as an example, Agustín chipped in with something else he remembered, I asked a question . . . and so it went on into the early hours.

In the summer, we'd carry one of the tables outside and enjoy leisurely conversations beneath the stars, each of us with a beer in one hand. And towards August, when the scent of newly harvested wheat wafted to us on the breeze, everyone in the group became more than usually loquacious and cheerful. The hunting season was at hand.

5. YOU reached the highest point of the village by walking up the hill where I lived, at the top of which villagers had built their winestores or bodegas. From there, looking down to the right, an observer could see the village rooftops and the church's thick, cracked walls, whilst ahead and to the left, over a distance of some eight miles, stretched a plain bare of trees with the River Pisuerga in the background. Behind you lay the two high plateaux that formed a deep valley where they met and extended as far as the Astudillo forest.

Punctually each day, in straggling lines and small groups, the retired men of the village made their way up there to watch the peaceful evening hours pass by. As nearly all of them were – in the words of the old riddle – men who went on three legs, they'd get as far as my house and, greeting me with a lift of their stick, take the opportunity to rest from the climb by stopping to talk for a while, then, once they'd recovered, continue on up the hill.

That was how I became friends with Julián and Benito, two of Villamediana's elder statesmen.

The day we met, Julián said to me: 'Now, sir, I know you're cleverer than a rabbit, but I bet anything you like that you don't know the real reason behind this daily pilgrimage.' He was a stocky man with melancholy eyes and gnarled, sclerotic fingers.

'You're quite right, I don't,' I replied, sitting down on my doorstep to indicate that I had all the time in the world and could stay chatting to them for as long as they liked.

Julián sat down too, but on the stone seat opposite the front door. Benito, who was leaner and stronger, remained standing. He seemed to have a lot of problems with his eyes, because whenever he looked at us he would lean forwards, half-closing them and adjusting his glasses.

'But first you must clear up something else for me. What makes you say I'm cleverer than a rabbit?' I asked him.

'Of course. I'll clear up both points this instant,' said Julián calmly. Benito, who was always circumspect in the extreme, simply nodded. Yes, his friend would explain everything to me.

'The reason I'm convinced you're clever is because if you weren't, you wouldn't be sitting here at eleven o'clock in the morning on a working day. You'd be in the fields or in the factory, like all the other fools in this village. You may not know it, but all peasants are fools. And I'm the biggest fool of all.'

Benito, who until then had been nodding his head, now began to shake it. But Julián took no notice and, like a Moorish *cadi* dispensing justice, merely collected his thoughts and continued in the same sententious tone.

'That's the first point answered. Now let's move on to the second point. I spoke of a pilgrimage and I used that word because all us old men who trudge up this hill do so in a spirit of hope. We get up every day and ask ourselves: will I manage to get up the hill this morning? And that's what we're thinking about as we set off. We don't want to be left down below. Getting left behind is a bad sign. It means we're ready for admission to the biggest house in the village.'

'When he says "the biggest house" he means the cemetery, because it's never full,' Benito explained for my benefit.

'There was no need to explain, Benito,' Julián scolded him gently. 'Haven't I just said the gentleman's cleverer than a rabbit? And, anyway, I obviously wasn't referring to the town hall!' he concluded, turning to me with a wink.

I later discovered that it was often difficult to ascertain when he was joking and when he wasn't. You had to watch his eyes all the time.

'Mind you, the church is pretty big too,' said Benito, frowning.

'There you go, always thinking about the church. But no matter, Benito, no matter. If they were to take us to the church now, what do you imagine would be the reason? To baptise us?'

And then he added, addressing me again:

'Benito is very innocent, sir. Always has been. How he ever managed to get married I'll never know.'

'I may be innocent, but I'm sure to go to heaven,' Benito said, getting up and looking slightly grumpy.

It was a sunny spring morning and the first swallows were whistling through the clear air. After a moment spent contemplating their manoeuvres, Julián returned to the topic raised by his friend:

'You were quite right to say what you said, Benito. Because I must confess that there is something that bothers me and I'd like to take advantage of this opportunity to ask the gentleman here what he thinks. What do you think, sir, is there a heaven or isn't there?'

I too was watching the swallows, trying to buy time before giving my reply.

'They say there's no way of knowing,' I said at last, 'that each person must find the answer in his heart. But if you've always believed in its existence, ever since you were a child, I see no reason why you should stop believing in it now. It would be absurd to abandon a belief that's been with you all your life.'

Benito showed his wholehearted agreement by nodding his head vigorously.

'But what do *you* think?' asked Julián, fixing me with his eyes.

'Sometimes I think there is and sometimes I think there isn't.' I could find no other way out.

'Same here,' he sighed, getting up from the square stone bench. 'I'll tell you one thing, though, Benito. If there is a heaven, we'll both be going straight there,' he concluded, making his final preparations before continuing their ascent.

'Well, I certainly will,' replied Benito, adjusting his glasses. He was none too sure about his friend's spiritual future.

'Anyway,' they announced, picking up their walking sticks, 'on with the test.'

Whatever their declared reasons for doing so, they didn't climb up the hill merely to test out their strength, just as old fishermen don't go down to the harbour simply for a stroll. Installed up there on the highest point, the retired men of Villamediana could keep an eye on the work going on in the fields and on life on the plain; they could see who came and who went, how much time it would take for someone to finish their sowing and how much time another would take to plough a fallow field. And just as old fishermen can instantly recognise a ship on the horizon, those men could identify a tractor from miles away – there goes Purísimo, oh, and that's José Manuel getting started – where a stranger could barely make out even a shadow.

'Now you may be cleverer than a rabbit, but I'll bet anything you like that you can't see as many things from here as I can,' Julián said to me once. Julián, Benito and I were sitting on the stone bench outside one of the bodegas and the plain they kept such a close watch on lay stretched out beneath us.

'I'm sure you're right, but what makes you say so?' I asked.

'Because you only see what's there, whereas I see both what is there and what isn't there.'

'Such as?'

'Do you see that path?'

And with his stick he indicated a pathway that crossed the plain and disappeared into the plateau. Benito, as usual, leaned forwards and half-closed his eyes.

'What do you see there? Just a path and nothing more, right? I, on the other hand, see the path that leads to Encomienda. I mean that's what I think and when I think that, I see the place called Encomienda and in my mind's eye I see the big old house and the fountain. And it's the same with everything else. See those trees over there?'

'I can't,' said Benito. The trees were a fair way off, on the banks of the Pisuerga.

'Do you remember the plot of land where we had that party when we were young?'

'The place where we went swimming?'

'That's right, Benito. And that's what I mean. When I see those trees I see all the parties we held when we were young. I see the girls and the boys, I see Benito and myself. Not old and decrepit like we are now, but with our white shirts on and with all the grace of our twenty years. Isn't that marvellous?'

'It certainly is,' I said when he'd concluded these reflections. 'And I'd add something to what you've just said, and that's that new places always seem hostile to us. When I arrived in Villamediana, I spent the first week walking the streets of the village, from one end to the other, reconnoitring the territory, if you like. And I must admit it seemed the saddest, most desolate place in the world.'

'Call themselves Christians!' exclaimed Benito, suddenly angry.

Julián told him not to interrupt.

'Well, all I mean is that the village just seemed very hostile to me. Of course, then I could only see Villamediana with my eyes, I saw only houses, walls, windows . . . what you might call the outer shell. For example, I'd walk past your house and see only walls and windows. Now, though, when I walk by, I think: There's Julián's house. There lives the wisest man in Villamediana. That makes a big difference, I think.'

'See, Benito?' Julián said, laughing. 'You see how talking helps you understand people. It's very kind of you to call me "wise" but, as everyone knows, I'm nothing but a fool. The only wise man in the village is you, Benito, not me. Now you really do see things that no one else does! Do you remember that business with the statue?' Julián asked him, winking at me. Did I know what he was referring to? Indeed I did. It was something Benito had told me some months before when we were sitting on that same bench.

'Do you like this village?' Benito had asked me then.

'Yes, I do, very much. I really like it here.'

'Well, you would. It's not surprising really. There are a lot of things to see in Villamediana, loads of them. We even have a statue of Trajan . . .'

'A statue of Trajan?' I said incredulously because I'd never heard anyone mention such a thing all the time I'd been in the village. I glanced at Julián to see if he could enlighten me, but in vain. By some mysterious process of mimetism, he too had been transformed into a statue.

'Yes, Trajan! We have an equestrian statue of Trajan in the village!' Benito was talking with some vehemence, banging his stick on the ground for emphasis.

'What's it like?'

'It's made of gold. The whole thing is solid gold!'

'And where is this statue?'

I imagined a museum or some similar institution. However, Benito raised his stick above his head, traced a few circles in the air, and declared:

'Out there somewhere!'

'Don't you think that's remarkable! What I'd like to know is how he can describe in such detail something that hasn't even been discovered yet,' said Julián, guessing my thoughts.

'The council should find it any day now!' Benito said.

Two months had gone by since that conversation and the equestrian statue of Trajan had still not turned up. But by then – and this is what lay behind the wink – Julián had discovered the identity of Benito's informant.

'It seems an angel told him about the statue. What do you think of that?'

'I think he's very lucky,' I said, looking across at Benito's radiant face lit up by a beatific smile.

6. HOUSES that have never been lived in or, for example, holiday homes that have been built to be lived in only at certain times of the year do not tend to have ghosts. Although empty, they don't seem it, and any murmurings you hear coming from them are never overly querulous. Such houses know deep down that their solitude will not last for ever. Sooner or later someone will come. The doors will open, the lights will go on and they'll begin to live again.

On the other hand, houses that were lived in once but have since been abandoned seem even emptier than they really are and they begin to talk the moment they're left alone. It's said that the life they gave shelter to in days gone by never quite disappears and that they display odd bits of evidence to the passer-by, as if displaying old wounds. Thus a curious passer-by might find a kitchen utensil abandoned on the ground, the small mirror the house's former owner used when shaving, or a metal rod that was once part of a baby's cradle. And having listened to that revelation, the passer-by comes to realise that all abandoned houses are literally crying out for someone to walk through the front door and make themselves at home.

There were some three hundred houses in Villamediana and almost all had been abandoned fifteen or twenty years before I arrived. Beyond the church, for example, there was an area that seemed more like a cemetery for dead houses than part of the village. You would look in vain for signs of life in its deserted streets and squares. Nothing stirred, no light was lit. There were only shadows, ghosts, silence and, in the midst of that silence, the dull clamour of the abandoned houses calling: come in, come in, or whispering: over here, over here.

People in the village disliked any mention of the place and did their best to forget its existence; they were even ashamed of the dilapidated state of its half-ruined walls and roofs. The few times they spoke of it, they did so with repugnance. There's nothing but rats and snakes there now, they'd say, it's a danger to the health of the whole village. It's no use to anyone. It ought to be pulled down.

That very general way of talking, however, concealed an inaccuracy, or at least so it seemed to me one Sunday afternoon when, after climbing up to the belltower of the church, I was sitting there reading. For I had the distinct impression that somewhere there was a little boy walking around. Something, some noise probably, made me raise my eyes from my book and look down below me. And there I saw a small figure apparently strolling along a winding road, appearing and disappearing from view as he followed the path traced by the curves. He was walking along, his hands behind his back, with the serenity of one of those wealthy emigrants who returned from South America at the turn of the century. From time to time, he'd sit down on a stone bench and – like me – settle down to read.

Those last two details – especially the habit of walking with his hands behind his back – didn't particularly strike me and I gave no importance to what I'd seen. I did reflect on the behaviour of children, on the taste they often have for solitude and on how, as in that instance, they're not in the least bothered by having to walk through a place full of rats and snakes in order to be alone. I felt sure though that he must be a foreign child, for no village child would have dared to come there.

It didn't take me long to discover my mistake. My supposition was proved wrong when I was witness, again and again, to the same scene I saw that Sunday. On almost every afternoon that I went up to the church to read I'd see the boy strolling through the empty streets. I wondered if he didn't perhaps live there, if there wasn't a family still living in the area. I even thought they might be gypsies.

There was only one way to clarify the matter and that was to walk those same streets at night. Just as, when I first arrived in the village, I had gone out in search of the bright lights of the shepherds' house, so now I would seek out the lights of that family who seemed to have remained there in isolation. One window would tell me if that part of the village was truly dead or not. That same week, one night when I was on my way to the hunters' bar, I set off instead to find that window.

And there was life there; the quarter wasn't completely empty. But it wasn't the kind of life I expected to find. I'd imagined a kitchen, the clatter of plates at supper time, a snatch of conversation. Instead I found only a silent, solitary light in the low window of one of the big houses.

I approached, trying to avoid trampling the nettles that grew round about. I didn't want the people in the house, when they got up the next day, to realise that someone had been spying on them. But at the time what troubled me most, even more than the rats and the snakes, was the possibility of dogs. What would I do if two or three dogs suddenly appeared? 'Steal something as I fled,' I thought in answer to my own question. That at least would lend the episode coherence.

Luckily, nothing broke the silence and I gazed in through the window undisturbed. There was the little figure, bent over a table, intently studying a book by the light of a reading lamp. From the table the eyes of a cat glinted.

'There's a little boy I'd like to find out more about,' I remarked to Daniel. That was on a Sunday too, and we were out for a walk in the woods, he in the line of duty and I just to take a little exercise. I told him what I'd seen from the church and the explanation I'd come up with, though without mentioning my night visit. He burst out laughing.

'Yes, he certainly is an unusual little boy,' he said. I wanted to know what he found so funny. 'Once we've checked the woodlands, we'll go to his house. He does tend to hang around there, along with the rats and the snakes. But I didn't know he slept there too. I'll introduce you. Then you'll see just how unusual he is.' Again he burst out laughing.

As usual we had lunch in the woods and then headed off down towards the village. It was six o'clock in the evening by the time we reached the empty quarter. By day the house seemed smaller to me. It had been a beautiful house once with its portico and wide balcony, rather like the palaces that often end up being made into town halls; and although the upper floor was in ruins, it was the best preserved house in the whole neighbourhood. Tied to the grille covering the window I'd found lit on that other night was a bunch of thistles.

When we knocked, we heard the sound of something inside dropping to the floor, then a muffled cry. Finally, when it seemed to us that the silence had gone on much too long, we heard footsteps approaching, and Daniel elbowed me in the ribs to prepare me.

At last, the door was flung open, as if the person opening it were in a rage. I think I must have turned white at that moment, for before me stood a dwarf. From between his legs a Persian cat looked up at us, surprised, as if demanding to know our reason for coming there.

'Yes?' said the little man.

He didn't even reach my chest but he was no ordinary dwarf. Although small, he was well proportioned, straight-legged and had no hump. Unlike other dwarfs I'd seen before, he had a small head, small and pretty like a doll's.

His clothes were not in the least conventional either. Like the rich young masters of yesteryear, he wore gaiters, a waistcoat and a black jacket with tails that looked like a dress coat.

Daniel wasn't laughing now. He seemed embarrassed.

'I'd like to introduce a friend of mine,' he began and, no doubt because he was nervous, he made the introduction more than usually drawn out. He explained that I too was a stranger to the village and, like him, a keen reader, that perhaps we could become friends, that he lived too much alone in that gloomy neighbourhood . . .

The dwarf looked me up and down. His eyes were just like the Persian cat's, sometimes blue and sometimes grey. Just as I was about to speak, he turned his head and looked angrily at Daniel:

'I live in this gloomy neighbourhood because I want to! And what's more I'd like to be allowed to live here in peace!' I thought that at any moment he would slam the door in our faces. But I was not inclined to let such an occasion slip by me so easily. Here, I said to myself, was the most interesting person I had yet encountered in Villamediana and I had to get to know him. Disregarding the snub he'd just delivered, I held out my hand and told him my name.

I feared he might ignore me, even decline to acknowledge me. But no, he looked me up and down again, then proffered a limp hand, like the hand of a sleeping child.

'Enrique de Tassis,' he said.

'Tassis? Like the count?'

Suddenly I found my opening to the man: Juan de Tassis, Count of Villamediana, poet and friend of Góngora, who was slain for making fun of the king. No one thought of him as being from there, though they did his father. It was said in the village that the group of houses next to the baker's had been the palace of the first Count of Villamediana. Now, unexpectedly, I found myself before someone bearing the same name.

'No doubt you know him,' I said. That was a mistake. He turned towards me, a hurt look in his eyes. The cat's eyes followed exactly the same trajectory.

'Of course I do!'

In his desire to make his reply as emphatic as possible, his voice – already shrill – cracked. Then it was my turn to feel embarrassed and it fell to Daniel to break the silence that followed.

'You don't go walking in the woods any more, then?' he remarked, for lack of anything else to say. But such familiarities were unacceptable to Tassis.

'I do go as it happens, often, it's just that you haven't chanced to see me there,' he answered coldly and said, by way of an excuse: 'Now you must forgive me, but I was right in the middle of some studies.' And, without waiting for us to say our goodbyes, he shut the door and left us alone on the doorstep.

We both felt as if we'd made some kind of gaffe and once in the bar – perhaps regretting having been so polite – Daniel became angrier than I'd ever seen him before.

'Did you see the arrogance of the man?' he began, and from then on I found it hard to silence him. How if he ever had a child like that he'd rather let him die; how deformed people like that were born to suffer and to make others suffer; and anyway what was he doing living up there; the whole place should be pulled down and the machines that did it could get rid of the little count too while they were at it.

In order to calm Daniel down, I tried to justify the dwarf's behaviour, I tried to make him see that it was understandable, in a way, that having the misfortune to be as he was, he would naturally feel ill-disposed towards other people, that he would interpret any interest another person might show in him as merely morbid curiosity.

But the truth of the matter was that I was hurt too. The dwarf's scorn was a new experience for me. No doubt other people had regarded me as mere riffraff before but they'd never shown it so openly and had certainly never thrown it in my face as he had done.

I didn't go back to the empty quarter. I considered having any kind of relationship with Enrique de Tassis an impossibility. And anyway, when all was said and done, I myself saw no reason to go running after him; it made me wonder too if my behaviour was not, generally, a touch frivolous: observing, chatting, taking notes, the way a naturalist collects plants. Except that I wasn't dealing with plants, I was dealing with the people of a village called Villamediana. If the dwarf wanted to be on his own, why shouldn't he be, no one could stop him. He didn't exist just to answer other people's questions.

A month later I hadn't exactly forgotten Tassis but I had consigned him to memory. And so it would have remained, had fate not determined that I meet him again one summer afternoon when I was looking for Daniel in the forest. That's where our relationship really began, a relationship which, unfortunately, was to be limited to the seven walks we took together.

I saw him standing on the same path I was walking along, on the edge of the forest, looking at the stream bed that ran between the two plateaux that lay ahead. The wind kept snatching at the tails of his jacket.

I said a curt good afternoon and walked on.

'I rather hoped you might drop by my house again,' he said as I passed.

That was the last thing I had expected to hear him say.

He saw my surprise and made a grimace that was clearly intended as a smile.

'I know I was rather rude on that last occasion. But, to be honest, I don't much like these inane provincials and I count the man who was with you as one of them. Do you know what I mean? An eminent thinker, who once travelled in these parts, really hit the nail on the head when he said that the real scourge of this place wasn't insanity but inanity. I couldn't agree more,' and he laughed an unpleasant laugh, half-child, half-woman.

'I can't say it's a remark I've heard before,' I said drily.

'But you have heard of the Count of Villamediana, isn't that so? I got the impression last time that Juan de Tassis was not unknown to you.'

I nodded.

'A great poet, don't you think?'

I replied that I was no scholar and knew only two or three sonnets by him. But that, yes, he must have been a great poet for his death to have merited a poem by Góngora. And that I did know about the circumstances of his death; about how, when the palace was rife with rumours of his supposed affair with the queen, he walked past the royal couple wearing a cloak sewn with silver sovereigns and embroidered with the punning motto: My love is sovereign. And how it was a shame Felipe IV had taken it all so seriously, going so far as to have the joker killed.

He laughed all through my telling of the story in a way that a local might have termed 'peculiar'.

Then he set off towards the forest almost at a run and, as if addressing the trees themselves, he began to declaim Góngora's poem, which he knew by heart:

> Slandermongers all of Madrid,
> Why struggle to rewrite history?
> Who killed the count need be no mystery
> if you do as sense and reason bid.
> One does not have to be the Cid
> an upstart count to castigate.
> Such reasoning is inaccurate,
> vain lies concocted to invent
> some murd'rous villain on crime intent,
> – the impulse carried sovereign weight.

When he'd finished, he fell face down on the grass, his arms outstretched. I was scared.

'The Tassis family have always been odd,' he said to me once he'd calmed down a little and got to his feet. But he was happy. It was clear that the story filled him with energy. Perhaps too much energy. 'I do this walk every Friday at the same time. If it were just up to me I'd come more often but I don't like leaving Claudia alone,' he added in a more gentle tone.

I assumed Claudia was his Persian cat.

'If you come here on Fridays, I'd be delighted to talk to you. You're a cultured man. Not like those rude peasants from the village.'

I accepted his invitation and then we each went our separate ways.

The following Friday I made my way anxiously up to the woods. I wondered what we'd talk about and how I should behave towards a person like him; whether I should look at him – or rather, of necessity look down at him – or not; whether he'd like me to help him when he grew weary or whether, on the contrary, he'd consider that humiliating; and what would be the best course of action if he flew into one of his rages.

I was worried too that people would see us together. If they did, I felt sure I'd lose my good name in the village. Especially with Daniel. Because Daniel was still upset with the 'little count'.

The moment Tassis saw me, he guessed what was in my thoughts and we'd barely gone two steps before he'd resolved the matter in his own fashion.

'Do you know where the word "dwarf" comes from?'

The question caught me out, because, of all the words in the dictionary, that was the one word which, right from the start, I had forbidden myself to use.

'No,' I stammered. In the words of the poet, my reply fell to earth like a stone.

'Well, it comes from the Old High German *twerc*, but has its origin in the Sanskrit *dhváras*. I don't suppose you know what that means, do you?'

'No, I've no idea.' I was trying to act nonchalantly, as if we were talking about something like arithmetic.

'Well, it means a demon, something ugly and misshapen . . .'

'That's certainly not true in your case. You're not ugly,' I blurted out.

'How dare you!' he shouted and for a moment I thought that, in his anger, he was about to hit me. 'Please, no euphemisms where I'm concerned. Speak plainly.'

'I've said nothing that isn't true. You're neither misshapen nor ugly. You're very small but perfectly well-proportioned,' I said.

'I know all too well what I look like,' he said, tightlipped.

'What do you think you look like then?'

'I'm monstrous. That's the only word for me. All the rest is nonsense, a waste of breath.'

I've never quite known what to make of people who speak scornfully of themselves and their lives. But, in general, I feel such harshness is unjustified. I've often noticed that the harshest people only soften when it comes to judging the actions of the very life they claim to despise; and that then – feeling, of course, even more despicable – they tend to turn their weapons on the person nearest them rather than on themselves.

Even if Tassis believed what he said, his manner of speaking didn't impress me. All that occurred to me was what an excellent personnel officer he'd have made.

Nevertheless, the rules governing our relationship were established according to his wishes. My 'initial blunder' dictated that he would play the role of teacher and I of pupil. He would speak and I would listen. Somehow I had to be made to pay for that terrible act of compassion.

And, like good Jesuits, we both accepted the rules of the game.

'People like myself were a real headache to the wise men of past centuries,' Tassis continued, as we walked through the spot known as Valdesalce. 'According to them the world and everything in it were in God's mind from the very beginning, everything was preordained and indeed had already happened before creation. And the past, as well as the present and the future, were no more than a secretion from the mind of God. But what happened? Monsters like myself emerged. And then the wise men asked in amazement . . .'

He was getting himself worked up, as he had when he recited the poem by Góngora, and he paused to take a breath. His doll-like face, however, still bore that look of scorn. It occurred to me that his facial muscles perhaps lacked elasticity and that once they were set in a particular expression or grimace, it might be difficult for them to relax into a normal pose.

'They asked . . . but if absolutely everything was in God's mind right from the very beginning, what could he possibly want with monsters, invalids, paralytics? Is He not Good, infinitely Good?'

By this point Tassis was doubled up with laughter.

Even in my role as good pupil, I wasn't prepared to witness another scene like that of the first day and I suggested we continue our walk.

He agreed, but went on talking. He explained to me that in earlier ages it was thought that people like him had no soul, that they were not even considered to be human, that all manner of abuses were therefore permitted against them.

'It must have suited them to think that,' I said, interrupting. 'When the Spanish went to America and set about laying waste to everything in sight, the Court philosophers decided that the Indians weren't human either and reached that conclusion, mind you, basing themselves on the writings of Aristotle and others. They claimed the Indians were animals and that killing them was not therefore a sin. Have you ever seen the film *Blade Runner*?' I added.

'I don't care for the cinema,' he replied stiffly.

'I respect your right not to like it but I see no reason to be so proud of it. Only mediocrities take pride in their dislikes,' I said, momentarily stepping out of my role as pupil.

'*Touché!*' he said, laughing, and staggered about amongst the trees pretending to be wounded. Then he said: 'What about this film *Blade Runner* then?'

'Well, it deals with a similar problem, with the question of what is a man and who is endowed with human nature and who is not. I mean, the problem could arise again. In the year 2200 a schoolchild might ask: Is it all right to kill a robot? and the answer won't be that easy.'

'The teacher will just say: No, you can't kill a robot because they're too expensive,' commented Tassis and this time we both laughed long and loud.

That first outing became the model for all our subsequent ones and not only as regards the role each of us would take in the conversation or its unerringly intellectual, impersonal tone. Each outing was identical in form, length and route.

Each Friday we would walk for two hours, from seven in the evening until nine. We'd head off away from the plain – this part of the walk we did separately – and having climbed the plateau to our right would then meet up by the forest, beneath the first oaktree. There Tassis would explain the etymology of some word or other, just as he had that first day and, taking that subject as our starting point, we would walk along the little valleys – Valdesalce, Valderrobledo, Valdencina – that extended into the forest until, almost without realising it, we'd reach the plateau on the left-hand side, or rather the intersection of the two plateaux, at the top of the stream bed. We would sit there for a while and then follow the path home, in silence, each one thinking his own thoughts, but this time paying more attention to the landscape.

During that walk, which was repeated seven times, we touched on many topics, though I can't remember them all. Most, however, revealed to me a Tassis who seemed far more uncertain than he had on that first occasion, though no less talkative and arrogant. I would compare what he told me with what Daniel or Julián or Benito said and on the whole their thoughts seemed more valuable.

However, what he said to me on our seventh and last walk together was different. On that occasion what Tassis said really touched me and not just because it proved to be our final walk. That day I learned many things about him.

We were sitting at the intersection of the two plateaux, with the village below us and beyond that the plain.

'What do you think,' I asked, 'does Villamediana have a river or doesn't it?'

'No, it doesn't.'

'Well, the people in the village can't agree about it. Some say that, though it lacks water, there is a river with a valley, a stream bed and banks as well as bridges.'

'Bridges? Where?' He studied the stream bed with his blue-grey eyes and I realised that he'd never ventured any further than the local shop owned by a pale woman called Rosi, that he'd never been beyond the place where he did his shopping. Because the bridges (two bridges to be exact) were in the square itself.

'Between Rosi's shop and the shepherds' huts,' I lied, hoping to confirm my suspicions.

'Ah, yes. Now I remember,' he replied.

I realised he was afraid to risk other people's mockery. I realised too how terrible it must be to wake up, possibly from a happy dream, only to find that one's deformity is still there. I realised then that dawn must be the cruellest time for all those who suffer.

'The people in the village also say that, once, this river even flooded,' I said, in an attempt to dispel the thoughts going round and round in my head.

Shortly before, in an old programme for the village fiesta some years before, I'd read about a flood that apparently happened at the beginning of the century and it seemed peculiarly appropriate to mention to him the strange story recounted there. The author of the programme said that, during the flood, some local people had seen a white horse ridden by a man dressed in red and that the rider kept thrashing at the waters with his whip to drive them back. But he didn't know if that had really happened or if it was just the imaginings of a terrified populace. What most intrigued me about the story was its exactitude. It was such an archetype, it could have been an entry in a dictionary of symbols. As I remarked to Tassis, the part about the rider thrashing at the waters, for example, corresponded to the so-called Xerxes complex, because that was exactly what Xerxes had done. To say nothing of the rider all in red or the white horse. There was a mass of literature about what they represented.

But I saw that he wasn't listening and dropped the subject. Tassis wasn't interested in symbols, only etymologies.

'I'm boring you,' I said.

'No, no, it isn't that. It's just that today I'd rather talk about something else.'

'As you wish.'

'I'm going to tell you about something that can't be found in books,' he said, ironically, giving me to understand that he'd cottoned on to my latest habit. For since getting to know him, and as befits a good pupil, I too had taken to studying etymologies. 'It's to do with whether Villamediana has a river or not,' he added.

'You still think it hasn't.'

'Of course. Since it has no water, it has no movement and therefore lacks the vital ingredient. In all things, movement is the deciding factor. Movement means life. Stillness, on the other hand, means death.' He gave a triumphant laugh, as if he'd just been acclaimed the winner of some contest. But this time, unlike on other occasions, he gave me the impression that he was only pretending, that he didn't really want to laugh.

'All things, if they are good things, are related in some way to movement. Or to life, if you prefer. But whilst you cannot see life, you can see movement. I would say that movement is simply another name for life.'

'Go on.'

'If I say that a person is animated, I'm saying a lot of different things at once; I'm saying that the person has *anima* or spirit, for example, or simply that they're cheerful. But in fact all the word "animate" really expresses is life and movement. And the same goes, of course, for "animation" . . .'

He fell silent, as if something else had just occurred to him. But then he continued on in the same vein.

'And what, you might ask, about that excellent word "vivacious"? Where does that come from? Does that have anything to do with movement? 'Well, yes it does, a lot.'

'Where does it come from then?'

'From *vivax* meaning full of life, lively.'

It was the twilight hour when all the animals on earth fall silent. A gentle breeze was blowing and, in the west, the clouds were the colour of dark wine. Far off, the rooftops of Villamediana were growing dim.

'Have you ever read anything by the poet Carlos García?' he asked me. I said he wasn't a poet I was familiar with.

'Why do you ask?'

'Oh, no reason. It's just that a few poems he wrote about this time of day, the twilight, contain some rather similar thoughts.'

'The word "twilight" appears in any number of poems,' I protested.

'But the ones I'm telling you about are good!' he shouted. But, possibly influenced by the atmosphere about us, he soon reverted to a whisper.

'Carlos García speaks of the stillness of this hour. He says that this is the hour when all the birds go to rest, fall silent, when the roads empty of people and that, as the light fades, the landscape takes on the static quality of a stage set . . . and that the sky itself, with no sun travelling across it, with no shifting clouds, gives the impression of being just another backdrop.'

He was speaking very quietly, so quietly I could barely hear him. I didn't know this Tassis at all.

'Go on,' I said.

'That's all. All I wanted to say was that at this hour everything seems very still and that, because there are no reference points, time too seems to stop. In one way or another, it brings with it a remembrance of death.'

A little beyond where Tassis was standing there was a line of three tall plants. I noticed that only one of the plants was moving in the breeze.

'But there's always some movement, however slight. We hear the beating of our heart, we walk . . .'

'Yes, of course. And that's precisely what makes the twilight so special: it mingles life and death and that's why it has that capacity to make you feel simultaneously happy and sad.'

We spoke ever more quietly, he even more quietly than me. The silences between us grew longer and longer.

'The spectral hour,' I said at last, for it occurred to me that spectres never move.

'I'm getting cold,' said Tassis suddenly. I noticed an odd note in his voice and I looked into his face. His eyes were shining with tears.

We walked the rest of the way home in complete silence. I wanted to say something to him but didn't know what.

'Today's talk has made you sad,' I remarked when it came to saying goodbye.

'Oh no, not at all!' he exclaimed. But I knew he was lying.

'Would you like to go to the bar? We've never been there together.'

'No, thanks, I'd better rush. Claudia will be getting impatient when she sees I'm not home yet. Anyway, I have to do some shopping first.'

He hadn't even finished the sentence when he was already hurrying off to Rosi's shop.

The following Friday he didn't come to the forest, nor the Friday after that. When I think about it now, it seems to me I should have gone and searched him out and asked that we continue our walks together. But I did nothing and it was only much later that I went to see him. And I did so, moreover, for the very reason he'd forbidden: because I felt sorry for him. It was the worst thing I could have done.

During the installation of a bathroom in one of the houses in Villamediana some seventeenth-century frescoes were uncovered and because of that, some restorers came up from Madrid. I met one of them in the hunters' bar and he invited me over to see what they'd found. Viewing the paintings – the city of Jerusalem on one wall and some religious scenes on the other – didn't take us long, however, and we soon set to talking about things in general. Inevitably we passed from the name of the village to the figure of Count Juan de Tassis and from there – my fault, of course – to that of Enrique de Tassis.

'He's not a dwarf by any chance, is he?' exclaimed the restorer, opening his eyes wide, though I was even more surprised.

'Do you know him then?' I asked.

'He studied with me at university. And he's well-known in certain circles in Madrid.'

'Really?'

'His real name is Carlos García.'

I was so taken aback I couldn't speak. My companion was looking at me anxiously. He couldn't understand the reason for my sudden confusion.

Finally I asked him to give me a brief biography of Carlos García. He told me that he used to write and had published two volumes of poetry, neither of which, unfortunately, had been well received by the public.

'He gave classes in philology. Then he got it into his head that he was descended from the Count of Villamediana and he went a bit crazy. At least that's what they say. So he lives here now, does he?'

'Yes, but I think he'd probably rather not see you.'

'No, of course,' he agreed.

The following day, I went to the empty quarter with its abandoned houses and knocked at the door of the big house overgrown by nettles.

I had to wait a long time before the door opened, even longer than that first time I went with Daniel. And then he only opened it a crack.

'How's life treating you, Tassis?' I said by way of greeting.

'Much the same,' he replied. But he was considerably thinner and, unusually for him, his hair had become long and dishevelled.

He began to apologise for not going to the forest anymore. He said it was too cold now to go out walking and that he didn't like leaving Claudia on her own. I suggested we find another place where we could talk.

'It would be best to leave it till the spring. Anyway, talking doesn't solve anything.'

It seemed to me that he was anxious to close the door again so I bade him goodbye saying that, if he wanted to, we could resume our talks once the winter was over. But I myself knew that was impossible. I'd decided to leave Villamediana that Christmas.

'Do you know when the word "desolation" first came into use?' I heard him say as I walked across the portico.

'No,' I said, stopping.

'In 1612.'

'You shouldn't be bothering yourself with words like that,' I said.

He smiled, then closed the door.

The following spring, when I was already far from Villamediana, I received a letter from Daniel. It began with a joke, assuring me that the village girls had been most upset by my departure and all sent me their love. Towards the tenth line, however, the tone changed. 'I have something else to tell you, the dwarf's cat belongs to me now,' he wrote. And what I read from then on only confirmed what I'd suspected on that last visit.

7.   ALL THE young girls from Villamediana lived in other towns or villages, either studying or working as maids, and they only came back to their parents' house during the holidays. As Daniel said, 'It just wasn't fair', the young men of the village lacked opportunities for romance.

However, there were others who could take their place and of them, Rosi was the one who best filled the void left by the young girls. Although she was getting on for forty, she knocked ten years off nature by sheer will power, a miracle made possible by the fact that she still considered herself to be of marriageable age. In the village they called her Rita Hayworth – behind her back, of course – and she always wore gay, flowery dresses.

She was from quite a rich family, the owners of a market garden and was in charge of selling the produce and dealing with the customers, spending her days amongst the carrots and sacks of potatoes in a place that was half-warehouse, half-shop. She moved gracefully through this world, not allowing the rustic nature of her surroundings to influence the care she took over her appearance; she seemed more like an air hostess than a shopkeeper. I never saw her with a hair out of place, a button undone or a wrinkle in her coloured stockings.

'Now how may I be of assistance to you?' she would ask whenever I went to buy something there. She favoured such polite, roundabout phrases.

Sometimes I had the feeling that it hurt Rosi having to sell those rough products of the earth and that she envied the owners of the shop in the square, who, thanks to a refrigerator, sold a different kind of product, for example, butter and yoghurt, 'a better class of product' to use her own words.

Perhaps driven by such feelings, she was constantly sweeping and dusting the shop to expunge every last trace of soil that might be clinging to the beetroot, so that no one could ever say that in Rosi's shop they'd once stepped on a rotten apple, and so that her counter was as highly polished as a jeweller's.

Sometimes she'd sit down at the shop door, quite still, and gaze out at the main road. When would she get the chance to change her surroundings? Sad to say, never. She was irremediably tied to those vegetables. She couldn't just abandon her family. After all, someone had to look after her father, the old market gardener.

'Rosi asked me an odd question today,' Tassis said to me once, having first explained to me that the word 'shop' came from *scopf* meaning 'porch'. 'She asked me how long it would take the average family to get through a bottle of tomato concentrate.'

'And what did you say?'

'I said it would probably last a family about a week. Well, I had to say something.'

'It's not really such an odd question. I don't know, maybe she wants to start stocking some new products. She's always saying how fed up she is with selling potatoes.'

'I don't think I've made myself quite clear. An unforgiveable error,' admitted Tassis in his usual acid tones. 'To tell the truth, what was odd wasn't the question so much as what she did afterwards. She started making calculations about how many bottles there were to a crate and all that and then she turned to me and said that it would take six months.'

'Six months?'

'That's just what I said, six months for what? And then she explained that that was how long it would take to sell a whole crate of the stuff in Villamediana.'

'I still don't see what's so odd about it,' I said just to provoke him. But he let it pass.

'That wasn't necessarily so, I said, because if she started selling tomato concentrate to the signals unit on the hill, she'd need much more, at least a crate a week. And when she heard that, she could hardly contain herself for joy.'

'But they don't buy their supplies in Villamediana,' I said.

'That's why her behaviour seemed so odd to me. Why should that story about the barracks make her so happy? And then I had a hunch,' Tassis continued after a pause. 'It seemed to me that the only reason she was asking me that question was because I have no dealings with the other villagers. Not, as a mature person would, because she considers me to be intelligent. I don't know if you've noticed, but Rosi is not the most mature of people.'

For him maturity was a synonym for perfection and he considered its lack, where obvious, to be a grave defect.

Tassis' hunches were never wrong, still less when, as in this case, they were painful to him. I thought that probably all his assumptions were right. But even so, it was still no more than just another of the many anecdotes, one amongst hundreds, that came up during our walks and we both soon forgot about it.

However, the things one forgets are never completely lost. They go into hiding somewhere, in some crevice of the memory, and stay there, asleep but not dead. And they can, of course, wake up. Sometimes, a smell is enough to provoke it. At other times, a gesture. What helped me on this occasion was a hat.

I saw a man in a hat standing next to a van and I stood for a while watching him. I thought the hat suited him. He was a tall, good-looking man of about forty-five. 'He must be a lawyer,' I said to myself. But no, he most certainly wasn't; it seems that the van was his. He was just opening the back door.

He emerged bearing a crate embellished with a drawing of a tomato. That was when it all came flooding back to me: what Tassis had told me about Rosi's odd behaviour.

I didn't really need any confirmation but, nevertheless, I followed him into the shop.

'Ah, there's our crate!' exclaimed Rosi as soon as she saw the man. She was wearing a print dress in a reddish colour and her eyes and lips were discreetly made up. On the counter was a vase of flowers.

'Vitamins for the soldiers,' said the man.

'If you wouldn't mind waiting just one moment, I'll serve this other gentleman first,' Rosi said, excusing herself.

'That's OK, I'm in no hurry,' declared the man, taking out a cigarette.

The back room was in darkness but in its depths I could just make out a pile of something covered with a sheet of white plastic. There, no doubt, lay all the unsold crates of tomato concentrate Rosi had bought.

8.   IN SUNLESS December, all living things flee the land of Castile, and a man out for his daily constitutional will find no one to accompany him and no one to talk to. He will look ahead of him and to either side but to no avail. The plain is frozen hard, as is the sky, and between the two there is no one, not one arm raised in greeting. The peasant long ago finished preparing the ground for the next sowing, and now he doesn't even leave the village but passes the day at the bar or by his own fireside. As for the shepherds, there's no knowing where they've gone. There's not a sign of them anywhere; not in the bars, around the village, not even in the forest. They must be somewhere, of course, but they spend the whole day wrapped in blankets the same colour as the earth and it's as if they've become invisible.

The cold is intense but, despite that, the walker wants to walk, so off he goes, striding along some path that disappears off into the sky. Stopping at a crossroads, he pauses to clap his hands and jump up and down, stamping hard on the ground. But all in vain; this isn't the month of August and now nothing stirs in the fields; the flocks of birds that would normally fly up at the least noise have gone elsewhere. Even the snakes – like 'flashes of green green lightning' – that would slide from one field to another in the winking of an eye, are all in their nests, frozen, hibernating. No, there's nothing on the plain. Or, what's perhaps worse, there are only hungry crows, grown more listless than ever.

His walks grow ever shorter and finally even he gives up. He stays at home and spends half the day in bed because he has scarcely any wood left for the fire and – because the time to say goodbye is drawing near – he doesn't want to go begging for any more. He even forces himself to sleep. And he does sleep and he dreams.

He dreams he's inside Rosi and that a little blue light the colour of butane gas is guiding him on his journey. And he sees that the inside of Rosi is all made of glass, of a glass that grows thinner and thinner, so thin in the end that it breaks if you touch it. Still walking, still following the blue light, he reaches a small room, the most secret room, and he sees a cupboard and in the cupboard a row of bottles and on the bottles drawings not of tomatoes but of hats.

Then he wakes up and sees through the window that it's snowing. But a quarter of an hour goes by and he's sleeping again and dreaming again.

He dreams that he's walking across the snow to the bakery and that his friends from Villamediana, Julián, Benito, Daniel and even Tassis are there to greet him but they don't dare speak to him. They're all wrapped in blankets and stamping their feet on the pavement.

Numb with cold, he reaches the square and, since it's the Christmas holidays, he finds it odd not to see any children there. But this isn't the moment to stop and think and he starts running towards the bakery.

'Ah, paradise!' he exclaims as soon as he goes in. But it isn't just the pleasant smell coming from the wood-burning stove, nor is it a reference to the weather. At least it isn't only that.

He cries out to protect himself, to mask the other more

compromising cry rising in his throat. For, amongst the baskets of bread and wrapped in the smell of freshly baked flour, is a girl of about twenty reading magazines and the girl is wearing only the briefest of silk nightdresses with a low-cut neck that reveals a breast the size of an apple.

9. IN ACCORD with the belief that one has to say goodbye to places as well as people, I asked Daniel to go with me and take one last long walk before I left Villamediana for ever. I wanted those places to remain in my memory so that later I could more easily remember all the times I'd spent there.

That day – though it was only three days before Christmas – the clear blue sky seemed utterly spring-like and, unusual at that time of year, the windows and doors of all the houses stood open. The snow was melting fast and by the afternoon all that remained were a few white patches in the hollows of the rocks on the plateau. As Daniel said when we set out, this wasn't Castile, it was the Mediterranean.

The weather – so different from the winter in which I'd arrived – did wonders for the ferns and mosses of my inner self and lessened that sense of sadness that crops up in all the popular songs about goodbyes.

Slowly we walked through all the places I'd visited that year: Valdesalce, Valderrobledo, Valdencina, Encomienda, Fontecha, Ramiel . . . and sometimes, in Valdesalce for example, I'd tell Daniel things that I'd kept from him until then. I wanted to leave things between us absolutely clear.

'I never said anything to you before, but I did actually make friends with the little count. He's a most unusual person as you know,' I began, and then told him all about our Friday meetings.

'I know you think I hate him and that's why you never told me. But I really don't. I feel sorry for him. Maybe it's worse to feel sorry for someone than to hate them, but that's how it is. Right now, I'm almost sure he's run out of firewood. At any rate I haven't seen any smoke coming from his chimney.'

'And you'd like to take him some.'

'I've got a bundle at home ready. It's just a question of delivering it to him.'

Daniel was, in the best sense, a good man.

But that wasn't the dominant mood of the conversation during our last walk. We left unpleasant topics completely to one side. We just walked and, as we walked, we remembered the time we watched the night games of the hares, the lunch we'd had with the shepherds and the jokes that were told afterwards, the argument we'd had with a group of hunters.

Warmed by the south wind, we talked about the funny things that had happened to us during that time.

'Stop here, Daniel. Now this is a sacred place for me,' I said as we rounded a corner and came across a beehive.

'Something to do with a woman I bet.'

'Well, yes, but not in the way you mean. Do you remember how during those first few months I used to go around all the time in a tracksuit?'

'Yes, I do.'

'Well, one day I was having a quiet walk around here when I suddenly remembered my kitchen. I mean I suddenly remembered that I'd left a pot boiling on the stove. I could already imagine the house in flames and I was off like a shot. I came tearing round this bend at full pelt and right here, right where we're standing, I ran slap into the whole female population of Villamediana out for a stroll. Some thirty of them, at least, married women, newlyweds, widows and grandmothers . . . and, of course, I couldn't stop to talk, I had to get home as fast as I could. And when I passed them, you should have heard the applause, Daniel! . . . when I tell you that even one of the grandmothers cheered me on, need I say more? I felt really touched. It was the first time in my life that I'd been cheered on as a runner. At last I understood how Zátopek must have felt.'

'Well, you know what women are like,' remarked Daniel. It was clear that some subjects were dearer to his heart than others.

Finally, crossing the plateau, we dropped down to the hill where the bodegas stood. There we saw Julián and Benito immersed in their task of surveying the plain, but I indicated to Daniel that I'd rather continue on, that I'd prefer not to stop there just then. I felt quite incapable of saying goodbye to those two old men.

At nightfall – still following the recommendations of those popular songs for when 'the time has come to say goodbye' – we went drinking. In Villamediana itself to start with, then in the next village along and later still in the bars on the main road. The next thing we knew we'd missed supper and we were, as another line from the song would have it, free from all sorrow.

'It's time we did something serious!' said Daniel opening his car door.

Then, having committed our first traffic offence of the night, he drove us to a club.

The plain to the north and the south; a row of warehouses towards the west; two lorries to the east; those were the cardinal points of *Las Vegas*. The sign was lit up in red neon.

There were two girls behind the bar and two more in front. The two behind the bar served us.

As far as I can remember, I spent the two hours we were there discussing the social and political problems of the Dominican Republic. I believe I received detailed and fairly well-documented facts which I subsequently forgot completely.

Daniel, for his part, tried to learn a few words of Portuguese, every now and then bursting out in loud laughter. I don't know what the words were that he found so funny. I only remember that he paid for them in beer.

'If you want whisky, you'll have to teach me nicer words,' he said to the girl.

When we left *Las Vegas*, he was smiling and happy.

'Did you notice the way that little Portuguese girl looked at me?' he asked as we committed our second traffic offence of the night.

'What do you mean?'

'You know, as if she was in love with me.'

'Really?'

If he hadn't been driving, I might have said more but I didn't want to distract him.

'I mean, she didn't look at me the way professionals do. She didn't look at me with a cold professional eye. I'm serious. Don't you believe me?'

'Of course I do.'

'How did you get on?'

'I didn't notice anything special about the way mine looked at me. She seemed rather like a schoolteacher. I mean, she looked at me the way a schoolteacher would.'

The night was full of stars, there wasn't another soul on the road, and I too felt happy.

We agreed to have one last drink at my house and made a stop on the hill first. From there you could see even more stars. Suddenly Daniel said: 'The Three Wise Men are on their way.'

IN SEARCH OF
THE LAST WORD

YOUNG AND GREEN

ALONG time ago, when we were still young and green, a man with a moustache and a checked cap arrived at the primary school we went to and announced in a grave voice that he'd come to take a group photo of us, the first we'd ever had taken. We listened to him and giggled, because he looked so funny, especially in that cap, and also because up until that moment we'd never even heard the term 'group photo'. Then, jumping in all the puddles and throwing our satchels in the air, we followed our schoolmistress to the colonnade by the church.

The minute we arrived, our exuberance flagged a little – happiness is never entirely unqualified – for sitting primly on the benches arranged there were the secondary school girls, our sworn enemies of the time: a lot of stuck-up ninnies who wouldn't even deign to greet us in the street. 'Let he who has never cast a stone raise his hand,' the parish priest would say each time one of the girls went running to him with some tale. And every hand stayed firmly in its pocket, every eye remained fixed on the floor. Now, alas, they were there before us, waiting, equipped with combs and scissors, a malign smile on their lips.

'Well, what are you waiting for? Off you go now, your friends from the girls' school are here to spruce you all up!' the schoolmistress said encouragingly, addressing the boys in particular, and she seemed mystified by the look of disgust on our faces at the prospect of that 'make-up' session. She didn't live in the village and so knew nothing of the generational war being waged in Obaba.

Their attempts to smarten us up involved much pinching, hairpulling and other such incidents but, at last, after lining us up on some stone steps, all the village girls and boys, we were about nine years old at the time, duly had our picture taken, united for ever even though soon, like travellers with different destinations, we were all to wade into the river of life and be parted for ever.

A week later a sheaf of photographs arrived back at the school and everyone wanted to see how we'd come out. There we were, serious little girls and even more serious though not so little boys, displaying a gravity worthy of Roman statues. But it wasn't in fact a question of gravity, or even of dignity or of any other word ending in '-ity'. It had to do purely and simply with the solemn vow of vengeance sworn (most solemnly of all by those of us with curly hair) only moments before.

'There will be more stones,' said our faces. 'And soon,' added our tight lips.

The schoolmistress distributed copies of the photo and told us to take good care of them, for later on, when we got to be her age, for example, we'd be really pleased to have a photo like that to look back on. And, like the good students we were, we carefully put the photo away and, no sooner had we done so, than we forgot all about it. For, as I said, we were young and green then and not in the least preoccupied with the past.

The fact is that the world was more than enough for us. It spread itself before our eyes like a peacock's tail and each day brought us a thousand different things with the promise of a thousand, ten thousand or a hundred thousand more new things to come. And what was the world? It was impossible to say really, but it seemed immense to us, unbounded by time or space. At least that's how we imagined it to be and that's why the addresses on the letters we wrote were so long. Because it was not enough for us to indicate to the postman, for example, the name of our cousin and the city in which he lived; to make things absolutely clear we had to specify in which province the city lay, in which country the province was, and in which continent the country. Then, at the end of this whole long list, we would write in large letters: Planet Earth. Just in case the postman got the wrong galaxy.

Winters and summers passed and, like people playing the

Game of the Goose, we moved on from the square we started on. Sometimes we advanced easily, jumping from goose to goose; at other times we swerved away from the luminous landscapes and fell into prisons, into infernos. Then came the day on which we got out of bed, looked in the mirror and saw that we were no longer nine years old, but twenty or even twenty-five and that, although still young, we were no longer green.

Amazed, we went feverishly over our whole existence. How had we got here? How had we come so far? Was it true that we felt more tired now than we used to at primary school; was it true that the geographical specifications on our letters were now so brief; and what other things, apart from them, had changed? The question seemed a complex one and, after giving the matter much thought, we thought – like characters in a puppet show – that the best thing would be to think it all through again.

In the midst of this confusion, and exactly as our school-mistress had predicted, we remembered that first group photo. We got it out now and again from amongst our old exercise books and begged it to reveal to us the meaning of existence. And the portrait would speak, for example, of sorrow and bring to our notice the two sisters, Ana and María, stopped for ever on square number twelve of the Great Board; or else, it would ask us to ponder the fate of José Arregui, our classmate who, from being a smiling boy standing half-way up the stone steps, had grown to be a man, a man tortured and then found dead in a police cell.

But not all the answers the photo gave were sad ones. On the whole, it simply underlined the old saying that to live is to change and made us smile at the paradoxes those changes throw up. Manuel, our finest warrior in the battle against the secondary school girls, had ended up marrying one of them and now had the reputation of being a rather henpecked husband. Martín and Pedro María, two brothers who never went to catechism classes, had both become missionaries and now lived in Africa.

However, my interest in the photo soon evaporated. Its

answers became rather stupid and repetitive and never really surprised me. I still needed to go on asking the questions but in another way, in another place.

The photo remained on my bedside table for a whole year – and might well have stayed there for ever – until a colleague at work came to my house and asked if he could borrow it. He said he'd just set up a dark room and that, since he was still in the process of trying it out, he could blow the photo up for me to five or six times the original size.

'Then you can hang it on the wall,' he suggested.

It was then, when my colleague had finished his work, that the old photo spoke clearly and revealed its secret. For once it was enlarged, I discovered in it a detail that had gone unnoticed before, and that detail set me off on the trail of some surprising facts.

But before I say what happened I should confess that it is not usual for a writer to be both participant in and witness to any stories worthy of the telling, indeed that may be why we're usually obliged to invent them instead. Nevertheless, just this once the rule will be broken. On this one occasion the author will extract his narrative material from his own reality. His work will be that of narrator rather than creator and although those two words may sound similar, they are not at all the same thing.

And now the prologue is done, let's get down to the story and continue, word by word, until we reach the last one.

The enlargement made by my colleague was, as I've said, some five times the size of the original photo, and because of that I could pick out details that before had been only blurs: the weeds growing in the cracks and joins of the stone steps, the buttons on the coat of one of the children being photographed.

Whilst looking at this sort of detail I happened to notice the right arm of a classmate called Ismael, the bad boy of the class. He had slipped his arm underneath the flap of the satchel clasped to his chest, so that the fingers of his hand were poking out the other end. The hand was not empty. There was something sticking out of it.

'A knife?' I thought, recalling that he was in the habit of carrying one around with him. But it couldn't be, it definitely wasn't anything sharp. It was then that I decided to resort to a magnifying glass to find out what it was. There was no doubt about it, what Ismael had in his hand was a lizard.

'He probably wanted to frighten the child in front of him,' I thought, remembering how scared the children in Obaba were of lizards.

'Never go to sleep on the grass,' our parents would tell us. 'If you do, a lizard will come along and crawl inside your head.'

'But how will it get in?' we'd ask.

'Through your ear.'

'But what for?' we'd ask again.

'To gobble up your brains. There's nothing a lizard likes more than human brains to eat.'

'And then what happens?' we'd insist.

'You'll go crazy, just like Gregorio,' our parents would say straightfaced (Gregorio was the name of one of Obaba's 'characters'), adding: 'That's if you're lucky of course. Because the fact is the lizard didn't actually eat much of his brains.'

Then, so as not to alarm us too much, they'd tell us that there were two ways of protecting oneself against lizards. The first was not to go to sleep on the grass. The second – assuming that the lizard had already managed to crawl inside your head – was to run as fast as you could round seven villages and ask the parish priest in each of them to ring the church bells, because then, unable to bear all that bellringing, the terrified lizard would leave your head and run away.

Such were the ideas haunting me as I studied the photo and it occurred to me that the scene I'd just discovered could be interpreted as an attempted prank. That little devil Ismael probably held the lizard to the ear of the classmate immediately in front of him – Albino María by name – so that, out of disgust and fear, the latter would move and ruin the whole group pose. For some reason

Albino María had withstood this act of aggression and there had been no need to retake the photo.

But something wouldn't let me accept that interpretation so easily. That something was the memory of what had subsequently happened to Albino María, who in only a short time had gone from being one of the school's brightest students to being one of its most stupid, growing progressively worse, becoming more and more confused until finally he was incapable of even reading or writing; a sad process that only came to a halt some years later, by which time Albino María had joined the ranks of the village idiots.

I pondered life's ironies as I looked at the photo and it seemed to me that the lizard held so close to Albino María's ear was, in some obscure way, an augury of all that happened to him later on. Symbolically speaking, Ismael's gesture united past with future.

But was that union in fact purely symbolic?

At certain times – at dusk, for example, walking down the street along with a lot of other people – we are assailed by the most unexpected questions . . . and every time I went out for a stroll that was the question that kept returning again and again. What if that relationship were *more physical* than it at first sight appeared? What if the lizard really had crept inside Albino María's ear? No, it simply wasn't possible.

However, contrary to my expectations, the hypothesis grew in strength. One day I was looking at the photo again and I discovered that what Ismael had in his hand wasn't a full-grown lizard, but a baby lizard, something that really was small enough to slip into someone's ear. Then I consulted encyclopaedias and nature guides and learned that the variety *Lacerta viridis* could in fact prove dangerous to man although – at least in those particular books – the nature of the danger was never specified.

Then it suddenly occurred to me to wonder about the eardrum. If the lizard had managed to get into the ear, the boy must have had a pierced eardrum. There was no other explanation.

My natural impatience meant that I had to find out the truth or falsity of my reasoning as soon as possible. I picked up the phone and called my uncle, an emigrant who had made his fortune in South America and then returned to live in Obaba.

'You know I don't go out much any more. You'll have to ask someone else, I'm afraid,' he replied, without showing the least curiosity about the subject. In fact the only thing he was interested in were the literary gatherings held at his house on the first Sunday of every month. 'Now you haven't forgotten our arrangement, have you? We've got a meeting next Sunday,' he said.

'Don't worry, I'll be there, and with no fewer than four stories.'

'The uncle from Montevideo will be pleased.'

That's what he liked to call himself: 'the uncle from Montevideo'. He'd lived for a long time in that city and still had some business interests there, a couple of bookshops and a bakery.

'Are you sure? You never usually like anything I write! According to you all my stories are plagiarised!'

'Well, it's true, isn't it? All you writers today ever do is plagiarise. But hope springs eternal . . .'

'All right. You can tell me all about it on Sunday.'

'And see if you can bring another writer with you. The more the merrier.'

'I'll try, uncle, but I can't promise anything. People are afraid of you. Is there anything in the world he does like? they ask themselves. Apart from nineteenth-century novels, that is.'

At the other end of the phone, my uncle chortled.

'So who could I ask about Albino María?' I said.

'Why don't you phone the bar? All you have to do is say you're conducting a survey about the physically handicapped. The word "survey" works wonders these days.'

I followed my uncle's advice and got the result he'd predicted. The woman who owned the bar seemed very interested.

'Yes, you're right, I think he is deaf. Hang on just a minute, I'll go and ask some of the others at the bar,' she said.

While I waited, I came to the conclusion that the general tendency of stories is to grow ever more complicated.

Then I heard her say: 'Yes, that's right, he's completely deaf in his right ear.'

It seemed to me that the moment had come to consult a doctor, because, as the photograph clearly demonstrated, the lizard – always supposing that it *had* managed to creep inside his ear – could only have done so from that side.

I need few words to summarise what happened next. At first the doctor I consulted – a friend of mine, who was also very keen on literature – said that what I told him was an impossibility. But, being of an experimental turn of mind, he accepted the idea as a working hypothesis.

'I'll go to the hospital library and consult the data base. We're certain to have something on tropical diseases. Call me back in a few days.'

But I didn't need to call him back, he called me, the following morning.

'Well, it seems it is possible,' he said, without even a hello.

'Are you serious?'

It was a hot summer's day, but the sweat dampening my palms at that moment had nothing to do with the temperature.

'Massieu, Pereire, Spurzheim, Bishop . . .'

I realised he was reading off the computer screen.

'Who are they? People who've written books on the subject?'

'Well, on tropical diseases in general. But the computer gives the chapter titles of the books and every one of them has something on the dangers posed by lizards. *On lizards and mental pathology* . . .'

He was reading from the screen again.

'I've spoken to my colleagues,' he went on, 'and we're all agreed. If what you believe were true, though it probably isn't . . .'

'Of course not. That's what I think. That it's just a possibility, I mean,' I said.

'Right. But what I was going to say was, that if it were true, it would be the first case known in Europe. Interesting, eh?'

'Do you want to come to Obaba next Sunday?' I broke in. 'It's one of my uncle's literary dos. You remember my uncle, don't you, the one from Montevideo?'

'How could I forget? He demolished my story in about five seconds flat. Never mind that it was the first one I'd ever written,' he said laughing.

'Look, I'll tell you what we'll do. On Saturday we'll leave here in the evening and go to a village on the coast. No, I won't tell you which village exactly. Just that we're going to visit someone. Oh, all right, it's Ismael. I see there's no point trying to keep any secrets from you. Yes, he lives there now, he owns a bar next to the beach. And then afterwards, we can drive back to Obaba. We could even have a swim.'

He remained silent a moment.

'Will your uncle put up with a plagiarist like me?'

'According to him everything that's been written since the nineteenth century is just one long act of plagiarism. So if that's all you're worrying about, don't be.'

'OK, I'll come. I'd like to meet Albino María.'

He sounded uneasy. But his unease was that of the literary man, not of the doctor.

'Fine. Right. I'll pick you up on Saturday at seven. If there's any problem, call me.'

But there was no problem. At just after seven the following Saturday, our car joined the motorway. The journey to Obaba had begun.

The village on the coast was less than an hour from our town and we took advantage of the remaining daylight to walk along the seafront and have supper out in the open air. Then, when it was eleven o'clock, we drove down to the beach and went to the bar run by my old classmate.

'Have you seen what the place is called?' my friend said pointing up at the neon sign.

'The Lizard,' I read.

'It looks like Ismael hasn't lost his old interests.'

'So it would seem.'

The bar was packed with adolescents and we had a hard time finding a suitable place from which to spy on him. Finally, thanks to the generosity of some motorcyclists, we occupied the bit of the bar they'd been using to put their helmets and gloves on. Then we sat down on the stools, our eyes fixed on Ismael.

He was as thin as ever, but he no longer looked like the wild boy of Obaba. He'd changed a lot. He was wearing an orange T-shirt emblazoned with some slogan in English and had blonde highlights in his dark hair. When he saw us, he walked the length of the bar to greet us.

'What a surprise! What are you two doing here?'

It wasn't only his appearance that had changed. He seemed relaxed and his smile was friendly. What would the photograph say to me next time I looked at it? Probably nothing. It had told me often enough already that 'to live' and 'to change' were synonymous.

'As you see, even we manage to get out occasionally,' we replied but were unable to continue the conversation because Ismael had to attend to a group of youngsters who were shouting for him.

Before he left, he offered us both a cigarette and – pointing to a seascape, one of the many he had hanging on the walls – made some comment about how polluted the sea had become.

'I never thought Ismael would turn out to be an ecologist,' I said.

'I bet he goes surfing too,' my friend whispered.

Half an hour later, with the bar still filling up with people, we broached the matter that had brought us there. We told him we were curious about the details of something that had happened when we were both at primary school, that there was no reason for him to be worried, our interest was, so to speak, purely scientific.

A mixture of fear and distrust surfaced in Ismael's eyes. It was the look of the nine-year-old with a knife in his pocket. At least that hadn't changed.

'Go on,' he said.

'You're very keen on lizards, aren't you?' I began. But not in any accusatory tone, I said it brightly, playfully.

'What makes you say that? Because of the name I gave the bar?' His tone was unpleasant, almost threatening. But I knew he was a coward, I'd known it ever since primary school. He was a little devil then, but not up to fighting anyone face to face.

'No, I don't mean that. I mean the lizard in the photograph, the one you were holding to Albino María's ear. What I want to know is did the lizard crawl inside his head or not?'

'What are you talking about? You must be mad!' he shouted, then stalked off and set to washing up some glasses.

'You've offended him,' my friend said.

But Ismael was back with us again.

'I'd have expected better from you. Do intellectuals like you still believe rubbish like that? Frankly, I'm disappointed.'

Ismael was still talking very loudly. His every gesture spoke his scorn. The motorcyclists along the bar from us were looking in our direction. It was beginning to look as if a fight was on the cards.

'Don't get so upset, Ismael,' I replied, imitating the Obaba accent. I felt euphoric. The two gins inside me were beginning to take effect.

'I'm in my own place and I can do what I like! And I won't have anyone coming in here making stupid accusations!'

I decided then to adopt Obaba behaviour patterns. I took his hand in mine, a gesture that meant I was on his side and loved him like a brother. After all we were from the same place, weren't we? We'd appeared in the same photo. Surely that was enough. How could he not trust me?

'You know perfectly well I've got nothing against you personally!' I said.

'We're just interested in this one small thing. I'm treating Albino María's deafness and I just wanted to know exactly what happened that day, that's all.'

I was amazed at my friend's deftness. That was without doubt the best way of approaching the subject.

The reaction was quick in coming. The anger in Ismael's eyes subsided.

'Why do you want to know?' he asked.

'Well, according to Albino María's mother, that was the day he started to go deaf.'

I was astonished at how good my friend was at lying.

'OK, I'll tell you the truth. Not that I think it will be much use to you,' said Ismael, drying his hands on a cloth. 'I don't actually know what happened to that lizard. It's true I had it in my hand . . . to play some practical joke, I suppose, so that the photograph would turn out funny, with everyone in front moving about and shouting . . . I imagine that's what I wanted. But I don't know what happened afterwards. I do remember that it slipped out from between my fingers. But I don't think it got into Albino María's head. To be frank, that simply doesn't seem possible.'

'No, of course not. We don't think it is either. But we were just passing and it occurred to us to pop in and ask, that's all.'

My friend's tone was conciliatory now.

'I *was* very naughty when I was little. Really naughty!' said Ismael, smiling.

'We all were in our own way. You'd never think it to look at me, but I actually burned down my grandfather's house. Not on purpose, of course,' my friend confessed.

'Good grief!'

It was clear that such remarks were very much to Ismael's taste. Perhaps they helped ease his bad conscience. After a brief farewell, we left the pub and walked back to the harbour car park. Back in the car, my friend and I – both a little disappointed – recalled what Balzac said: that life does not provide us with nice, rounded stories, that it was only in books that you found good, strong endings.

'We'll never know what happened with that lizard,' I said.

'That remains to be seen. Before we finally close the file on the subject, we have to talk to Albino María,' my friend replied.

'We could probably visit him tomorrow. He hardly ever leaves Obaba.'

'Let's hope so.'

'Speaking of Balzac and good endings, what's the best story you know? I mean, in your opinion, which story has the most satisfying ending,' I asked suddenly. There were scarcely any cars on the road at that hour and the solitude of the motorway created a favourable climate for confidences.

'I'm not sure I could say just off the top of my head,' my friend answered.

'Well, if you like, I'll tell you what Boris Karloff's reply would have been. I bet you can't guess what Boris Karloff thought was the best story in the world,' I said.

'No, I can't, but I bet it was some horror story.'

'It was the story about the servant from Baghdad.'

'Which story is that?'

'I'll tell it to you if you like. With a cup of coffee in front of me, of course.'

'OK. It'll be good training for tomorrow's session. With your uncle sitting in judgement, we need all the practice we can get.' We stopped at a motorway café. Then, seated at a corner table, I recounted the old Sufi tale to my friend. And I did so in exactly the same words I'm going to use now to transcribe it. The story about the lizard and the last word of that story can wait.

THE RICH MERCHANT'S SERVANT

ONCE upon a time, in the city of Baghdad, there lived a servant who worked for a rich merchant. One day, very early in the morning, the servant went to the market to do the shopping. But that morning was different from other mornings, for he saw Death there in the marketplace and Death looked at him oddly.

Terrified, the servant returned to the merchant's house.

'Master,' he said, 'lend me your fastest horse. Tonight I want to be far from Baghdad. Tonight I want to be in the far city of Isfahan.'

'But why do you wish to flee?'

'Because I saw Death in the marketplace and he gave me a threatening look.'

The merchant took pity on him and lent him the horse, and the servant left in the hope that he would be in Isfahan that night.

That afternoon, the merchant himself went to the marketplace and, as had happened before with the servant, he too saw Death.

'Death,' he said, going over to him, 'what did you mean by giving my servant a threatening look?'

'What threatening look?' replied Death. 'It was a look of pure amazement. I was simply surprised to see him here, so far from Isfahan, for it is tonight in Isfahan that I am to carry your servant off.'

Regarding stories

AFTER listening to the story about the servant, my friend grew thoughtful. He stared into his coffee cup like someone trying to extract some meaning from the dregs. At last he said: 'I agree with Boris Karloff. It really is an excellent story.' And, as happens in all late-night conversations worthy of the name, that remark brought with it a rather metaphysical question, not at all easy to answer:

'But why is it good? What makes a story good?'

'I know a much better story than that,' exclaimed someone sitting near us, a man with a foreign accent.

Surprised at the presence of that unexpected witness, my friend and I turned round.

'It's me,' the man said.

But we'd never seen him before in our lives. He was an elderly man with white hair and beard. Although he was bending towards us, almost crouching, he seemed extremely tall to me. He must have been over six foot five.

'I know a much better story than that,' he said again. His breath smelled of whisky.

'Tell it to us then,' we said at last. I wondered what country he came from. His clothes betrayed his foreignness.

He solemnly raised one hand and asked us to wait a moment. Walking over to the bar, he stood head and shoulders above the other customers. He really was very tall.

'We'd better go somewhere else,' I said to my friend and added, to reinforce my decision, that otherwise we wouldn't be able to talk about things in peace.

The white-haired old man seemed an interesting character, but he was also extremely drunk. Besides, we had to drive on to Obaba.

'Have you spoken to the uncle from Montevideo? Does he know I'm coming too?'

'Yes, I've warned him. He was thrilled when I told him that you'll be reading something too. You know what he's like. The more victims he has, the happier he is.'

'We'd best get to bed early then. We've got a hard day ahead of us tomorrow.'

'OK, let's go,' I agreed, smiling.

But the tall man was back already. This time he was wearing a hat and carrying a whisky in one hand.

'My story really is very interesting,' he insisted. When he went to sit down, he tripped and fell on top of us.

'I'm so sorry.'

'We're all ears,' said my friend. The old man took out a small tape recorder from his jacket pocket and placed it on the table.

'The story is entitled "The Monkey from Montevideo",' he said, pressing the record button.

But he got no further. His tongue was thick with drink and he stumbled over his words, some of which were in English. With a sigh he switched off the tape recorder.

'It can't be done,' he said apologetically, repeatedly covering and uncovering his ears with his hands.

'No, you're right. It's much too noisy in here,' said my friend, getting up, 'and anyway we really must be going. Another time perhaps.'

'It's a real pity,' he said, once all three of us were on our feet.

'It certainly is. But what can we do? Maybe we'll meet again. We'd love to hear your story.'

I was on the point of inviting him to the gathering to be held a few hours later in Obaba but, although such surprise moves usually pleased my uncle, in the end I didn't dare. The old man's liking for the bottle frightened me a little. When we went to the bar, the waiter told us our drinks had been paid for.

We waved to the white-haired old man to thank him and he

responded by raising his hand to the brim of his hat. Then we left the café and walked back to the car.

'We were talking about what makes a good story,' said my friend when we were barely half a mile down the motorway. The subject obviously interested him.

I pulled his leg a bit, teasing him about his love of serious conversation. In fact, I really admired the adolescent, still full of uncertainty and utterly immune to frivolity, who lived on inside the doctor. He was not at all a typical example of late twentieth-century man.

'We could begin by recalling some stories we've enjoyed and see if we both agree about their quality,' I suggested, dipping my lights so as not to dazzle the driver of the red Lancia that had just passed us.

'I think that was Ismael,' said my friend.

'What?'

'I think it was Ismael driving that Lancia. At least it looked like him.'

'He'll be going to Obaba to spend Sunday, like us,' I said.

'I told you the lizard story still had plenty of mileage in it,' laughed my friend.

'Just like the one the old man wanted to tell us, the one about the monkey from Montevideo. I'm sure we'll hear the whole thing one day.'

'So we're back to where we started. We need to clarify our ideas before that occasion arises. Otherwise we won't be able to tell him if his story is good or bad, and the old man will be disappointed,' said my friend. I noticed that he was becoming more and more animated.

'You begin. Tell me a story you think is good.'

'I'd choose one by Chekhov.'

My friend then gave me a summary of one called 'Sleep': Varka, a very young maid working in a rich house, could never get to sleep. What stopped her was the baby she was in charge of, an insomniac baby that cried all night. She cradled it in her arms and sang it sweet songs, but all in vain. The more she longed for sleep and the more exhausted she became for lack of it, the more the child howled. And so it went on day after day, until one morning, the parents of the child leaned over the cradle to say good morning and realised with horror that . . .

When my friend had finished, I began to tell him a story by Evelyn Waugh entitled 'Mr Loveday's Little Outing': A high society lady takes pity on a kindly, mild-mannered old man who has spent the last twenty-five years locked up in an insane asylum. 'Why is he kept locked up? He seems such a kind person, so normal . . .' the lady asks the doctor. 'He's here of his own free will. He's the one who doesn't want to leave. He must have been very different before because, according to what we were told, he killed a young girl, apparently for no reason whatsoever, when she was out for a quiet cycle ride. But things are different now. After all this time, he ought to be out in the world.' Then the lady tries to convince the old man that he would be much better off outside, that freedom is a marvellous thing, even offering to help him make the necessary arrangements. 'I don't much want to leave here,' says the old man, 'but you've convinced me by what you've said. Yes, I think a change of air would do me good. And besides, there is one thing I'd like to do.' And so the kindly, mild-mannered old man regains his freedom. But only a few hours after leaving, he's back at the asylum. Meanwhile, not far away, a lorrydriver finds a bicycle lying by the roadside, and . . .

'Excellent. We agree then. That's my idea of a successful story too. There's another one I like, about a necklace. It's by Maupassant. Do you know the one I mean?'

'I do but it's ages since I read it,' I said as we overtook a caravan.

'The protagonist was called Mathilde Loisel, wasn't she? Yes, I think that was her name,' my friend began.

But he was forced to fall silent again for a moment before continuing because the driver of the caravan – either annoyed at us for overtaking him or because he was in playful mood – accelerated until he was almost alongside us, on our left, making a hell of a noise.

I braked and let him get ahead of us. My friend and I needed silence.

'Have a good time in France,' we both said when we saw the French number plate.

'Mathilde Loisel lived in France too. She lived in Paris,' my friend went on, 'in the elegant Paris of the eighteenth century. She was married to a boring civil servant and her life with him was far from stimulating. And then one day she received an invitation to go to a ball held by the Minister, M. Ramponneau. This good news, however, only made Mathilde sadder still. She wanted with all her heart to go to the ball but how could she? What dress could she put on? What jewels could she wear? Then she suddenly remembered a childhood friend of hers who had married a very rich man. Why not ask her if she could borrow some jewels? She decided she would and she got the jewels, amongst them a beautiful pearl necklace . . .'

'Ah, now I remember. Having danced until she dropped, Mathilde Loisel suddenly realised that the pearl necklace her friend had lent her was no longer around her neck. She'd lost it . . . isn't that what happens?'

'Exactly. Mathilde had lost the necklace. But, of course, she couldn't tell her friend what had happened. She had to give it back to her. And so she mortgaged everything she had, even her life, in order to be able to buy another necklace.'

'Yes, the whole affair proved disastrous for her. She had to work day and night to earn enough to buy another necklace. And then, just imagine, some years later, walking along the street, she meets her childhood friend. And what does she discover? That the pearls on the necklace she had lent her were fake, it was costume jewellery!'

'You won't believe this, Mathilde,' said her friend, 'but this necklace hasn't been the same since you wore it to that ball, the pearls have a different quality about them altogether, almost as if they were real.'

That story was followed by another by Schwob, the story by Schwob by one by Chesterton and then, telling tales as we went, we left the motorway and took the road that winds through the mountains to Obaba. We opened the car windows.

'When we were little, we used to call this road "the road of moths",' I said to my friend.

'I'm not surprised,' he replied. In the beam of the car lights, an infinite number of white moths could be seen fluttering about us.

'It looks like it's snowing,' added my friend.

'We often came this way when we were small. By bike, of course, like the girls in Evelyn Waugh's story. We'd spend the whole summer riding around on our bikes.'

'But why are there so many moths?' asked my friend.

'I think this particular variety of white moth feeds on mint. And the woods we're passing through now are full of the stuff. I imagine that must be the reason.'

Inspired by what I'd just said, I stuck my head out of the window and took a deep breath of the warm summer air. Yes, the woods still smelled of mint.

We drove the next mile or two in silence, each of us immersed in his own thoughts, observing the moths, watching for stirrings in the woods. From time to time, where there was a stretch of road with clear views to the side, we could make out the bright lights of houses on the slopes of the mountains, distant and solitary.

When we were only half an hour from Obaba, we saw a small white cloud form in the sky amongst the stars. The small cloud was followed by the noise of a rocket exploding.

'There must be a fiesta in one of the villages near here,' said my friend.

'That one down there,' I said, pointing to a belltower whose silhouette stood out above the trees.

'It seems moths aren't too keen on fiestas. Look, they've disappeared.'

My friend was right. At that moment, the car headlights showed only the coloured flags adorning the roadside.

We parked the car right at the entrance to the village, on a hill. From there, as if from a high balcony, we looked out over the whole square and could watch the dancing. The music from the small band came to us in gusts, depending on which way the wind was blowing.

'So what conclusions have we reached about stories then?' my friend asked.

He didn't want to go down and mingle with the crowds without first clarifying the question, at least to some extent. And to tell the truth I felt exactly the same. It was nice up on that hill, ideal for daydreaming and smoking.

We didn't stay there long but, even so, we managed to make a fairly reasoned analysis of what it was that writers as fine as Chekhov, Waugh and Maupassant set out to achieve when it came to writing their stories; and, in conclusion, we managed to establish the characteristics of the genre and were left with a sense of having had a highly profitable conversation.

In the first place, there seemed to us to be an evident parallel between stories and poems. As my friend said when summarising what we'd talked about, both come from the oral tradition and both tend to be short. Moreover, and because of those two characteristics, both have to be intensely meaningful. The proof is that bad stories and bad poems end up being, as someone else said, 'futile, empty and trite'.

'Looked at like that, the key doesn't lie in making up a story,' my friend concluded. 'The truth is that there are more than enough stories. The key lies in the author's eye, in his way of seeing things. If he's really good, he'll take his own experience as his material and extract its essence, something that has universal value. If he's a bad writer, he'll never get beyond the merely anecdotal. That's why the stories we talked about tonight are good. Because they express essential things and aren't just anecdotes.'

The band hired to make the fiesta go with a swing was playing a very slow, sentimental number. The couples who only a moment before had been bouncing about to the music were now clasped to one another, barely moving.

'That's why so many stories have been written on the great themes,' I said, taking up the thread of the conversation again. 'I mean stories that turn on themes like death and love and the like. In fact exactly the same thing happens with songs.'

'Didn't Valentín send you something about that?' he said.

'Which Valentín? The one who lives in Alaro?'

'That's the one.'

My friend was referring to a writer we often saw.

'That's right, he did. He sent me a manual by Foster Harris. If I'm not mistaken,' I went on, 'Harris has some very odd theory about the short story. According to him, a story amounts to nothing more than a simple arithmetical operation. Not an operation involving numbers, of course, but one based on the addition and subtraction of elements such as love, hate, hope, desire, honour and other such things. The story of Abraham and Isaac, for example, would be the sum of pity plus filial love. The story of Eve, on the other hand, would be a simple subtraction, love of God minus love of the world. Moreover, according to Harris, additions tend to produce stories with happy endings and subtractions ones with tragic endings.'

'So he ends up saying more or less the same as us, then.'

'Yes, although his theory is even more restrictive. Anyway, who knows? Maybe that's all we are, a few unfortunates ruled by the most elementary arithmetic.'

'Even so, what we've said doesn't seem to be enough somehow. And having a way of looking at the world which is capable of capturing the essence of something isn't enough either. A good story has to have a strong ending too. At least I think it does,' my friend asserted.

'Oh, I agree, I think a good ending's indispensable. An ending that's both a consequence of everything that's come before and something else besides. And the need for such an ending would explain, I think, the abundance of stories that end with a death. Because death is the ultimate definitive event.'

'Absolutely. Just look at the Chekhov story, or the one by Waugh, or at the story about the servant from Baghdad you told me in the café. They're all packed with meaning and they all have very powerful endings. The story about Baghdad reminds me of what happened to García Lorca. He flees from Madrid thinking he's going to be killed there, and then . . . it's almost a prophetic story, really excellent. The best of the night in my view.'

I smiled at my friend's words. At last he'd returned to the story I'd told him in the café. The moment had arrived to produce the card I had hidden up my sleeve.

'Oh, there's no doubt it's good. But if it was my story I'd change the ending. I hate all that fatalism,' I said.

My friend looked at me in astonishment.

'I'm serious, I really dislike the fatalism in that story. It seems so implacable, the kind of thing reflected in the saying that life is just like a throw of the dice. What the story is telling us is that we're born with a fixed destiny and that our will counts for nothing. We have to accept our destiny, whether we like it or not. If death comes for us, we have no alternative but to die.'

Shrugging his shoulders, my friend gave me to understand that he saw no other option.

'If you say so. But to me it seems the only possible ending for the story,' he explained.

'Well, I've given it another one.'

'You mean you've written a variation on the story?' he said, raising his eyebrows.

'I certainly have. And here it is.'

And from a file I'd left on the back seat of the car I took out two pages covered with writing.

My friend burst out laughing.

'Aha! Now I understand. I thought there was something fishy going on when you started talking about the literary tastes of Boris Karloff and all that. One minute we were talking about lizards and what Ismael had got up to and suddenly, with no explanation, you'd gone and changed the subject. Of course! You just couldn't wait to show me what you'd written. It's true, isn't it? You'll never change!'

His last words were a reference to the reputation I had amongst my friends, who all agreed that I would do absolutely anything just to get a chance to read them my stories.

'Lord, pardon this your incorrigible servant!' I said raising my eyes to heaven.

'Oh, all right, but let's go down to the square first. I'm only prepared to listen to your variation on the story with a beer in my hand,' said my friend.

'And I'll have to pay for the beer, I suppose.'

'Of course.'

'A writer's lot is a hard one. You even have to bribe people just to be able to work,' I exclaimed before getting out of the car.

In the square we saw that the musicians in the band had taken a break and that an accordionist had replaced them on the stage. The two or three bars available and the area around them were crammed with people all shouting to each other and laughing.

It was almost harder getting the drinks than it had been determining what made a good story. At last we got them and – spotting some benches along the path near the cemetery – we fled the noisy bars.

We both felt happy. Our night was becoming more and more like the meetings held once a year in England by members of the Other Society. The only difference was that our meeting was not being held in a hotel in Piccadilly and our stories were not, at least in one sense, gothic.

And having reached this stop on the road, I will again pause to transcribe my variation on the story as I told it to my friend. The journey towards the last word will continue later.

DAYOUB, THE RICH MERCHANT'S SERVANT

ONCE upon a time, in the city of Baghdad, there lived a servant who worked for a rich merchant. One day, very early in the morning, the servant went to the market to do the shopping. But that morning was different from other mornings, for he saw Death in the marketplace and Death looked at him oddly.

Terrified, the servant returned to the merchant's house.

'Master,' he said, 'lend me your fastest horse. Tonight I want to be far from Baghdad. Tonight I want to be in the far city of Isfahan.'

'But why do you wish to flee?' asked the merchant.

'Because I saw Death in the marketplace and he gave me a threatening look.'

The merchant took pity on him and lent him the horse, and the servant left in the hope that he would be in Isfahan that night.

The horse was strong and swift and, as he had hoped, the servant reached Isfahan just as the first stars were coming out. Once there, he went from house to house, begging for shelter.

To any who would listen he said: 'I'm running away from Death and I need somewhere to hide.'

But the people were frightened at the mention of Death and they all shut their doors to him.

For three, four, five hours, the servant walked the streets of Isfahan in vain, knocking at every door and growing wearier by the minute. Shortly before dawn he reached the house of a man called Kalbum Dahabin.

'In the marketplace in Baghdad this morning Death gave me a threatening look and so I have fled the city to seek refuge here. Please, I beg you, give me shelter.'

'You can be sure of one thing, if Death gave you a threatening look in Baghdad,' said Kalbum Dahabin, 'he won't have stayed there. He'll have followed you to Isfahan. He must be within our walls already for the night is nearly over.'

'Then I am lost!' cried the servant.

'Don't despair yet,' replied Kalbum. 'If you can stay alive until sunrise, you'll be saved. If Death has decided to take you tonight and he fails, then he'll never be able to carry you off. That is the law.'

'But what should I do?' asked the servant.

'We'll go straight to my shop in the square,' ordered Kalbum, shutting the door of his house behind him.

Meanwhile Death was approaching the gates of the city of Isfahan. The sky was beginning to grow light.

'Dawn will be here at any moment,' he thought. 'If I don't hurry I'll lose the servant.'

At last he entered Isfahan and sniffed the thousand smells of the city, searching out the servant who had fled Baghdad. He instantly discovered his hiding place: Kalbum Dahabin's shop. He was off like a shot, running in that direction.

A light mist hung over the horizon. The sun was beginning to regain possession of the world.

Death reached Kalbum's shop. He flung the door open and . . . he couldn't believe his eyes. For in that shop he saw not just one servant, but five, seven, ten, all identical to the one he was looking for.

He gave a sideways glance at the window. The first rays of sun were already filtering through the white curtain. What was going on here? Why were there so many servants in the shop?

He had no time to find out. He grabbed one of the servants in the room and rushed out into the street. Light was flooding the whole sky now. That day the neighbour who lived opposite the shop in the square was cursing and furious.

'When I got out of bed this morning and looked out of the window,' he said, 'I saw a thief running off with a mirror under his arm. A thousand curses on the blackguard. A good man like Kalbum Dahabin, the maker of mirrors, deserves to be left in peace!'

Mr Smith

SOMEONE was waving to us as he approached the bench where we were sitting. The cemetery path was half in darkness and we could not at first make out his face and – bearing in mind that we knew no one in that village – we simply assumed he was one of those enthusiastic types you get at all fiestas, the sort who feels happy and wants to be everybody's friend. But, gradually, his silhouette grew clearer. We saw something white on his head.

'He's very tall. He must be over six foot five,' I said to my friend.

'And he's wearing a hat,' my friend said to me.

'And he's got white hair and a beard.'

'Therefore . . .'

'It must be the old man from the motorway café,' we concluded, both exploding in laughter at the same time. When he reached us, the old man leaned his back against the lamppost next to the bench.

'I know a much better story than that!' he exclaimed by way of greeting.

'He seems to be following us around almost the way Death followed the servant from Baghdad,' I whispered to my friend.

'No, it's not that,' my friend replied. 'It's just that, like you, he'll do anything in order to get to tell his story. There's no doubt about it, he's your natural soulmate.' Then to the old man he said, 'Do come and join us.'

The old man came over to us, but indicated with a gesture that he preferred to remain standing.

'Would you like some beer?' my friend asked.

He shook his head.

'I prefer whisky,' he said.

'You say you know a better story. But better than what?' I asked him. I wanted to find out just how aware he was of what he was saying.

'Baghdad, Isfahan, bah!' he replied.

My friend and I looked at each other. He wasn't as crazy as he looked.

'What's your name?' we asked him.

'Smith. My name's Smith.'

This time it was his turn to laugh.

'At least tell us where you're from. You're not really a stranger to these parts, are you? Were you born around here?'

'Be quiet! My name is Smith!' he said, adopting a fierce expression and placing a finger to his lips.

'Sit down with us then, Mr Smith,' my friend suggested. 'Sit down and tell us that wonderful story of yours. You'll find no better audience than us. And we promise never to ask you your real name.'

This time he did sit down in the space made for him by my friend, not on the lower part of the bench, but on the back, like a teenager.

'I'm afraid I can't tell you the nice story now, the one about the monkey from Montevideo. Sorry, my friends.'

'That's fine, but you must tell us another story,' we insisted.

'Something from your own life, for example. It's not fair to promise us great things and then tell us nothing.'

'All right, my friends, a story. It's not the nicest one, but the truest. Something that happened to me a long time ago.'

'Go on.'

He stood up again and brushed the dust from his jacket and his trousers as if wanting to spruce himself up a little first. Then he took out the small tape recorder from his pocket and, after a couple of failed attempts, pressed the record button.

The red light was on, he had to begin. Mr Smith gave a little sigh and began to tell us his story, which he intoned rather than spoke.

178

The road to the last word is a long one. I'll pause again here and write down the story that Mr Smith told us on that cemetery path. I'd be neglecting my duty if I didn't. As someone once said: 'Let nothing that has been lived be lost.'

I've transcribed the story almost exactly as it was on the tape, merely correcting, or rather, translating a few words and expressions originally in English. I felt they spoiled the flow of the narrative.

Just one more point. The story was untitled and it was my friend and I who gave it the title it now bears: 'Maiden name, Laura Sligo'.

Here it is then. Over to Mr Smith.

Maiden name,
Laura Sligo

LAURA SHELDON (maiden name, Laura Sligo), was looking out from the village of La Atalaya at the vast expanse of jungle and listening to the songs of all the inhabitants of the Upper Amazon, to the song of the *arambasa*, of the *papasí*, of the *carachupausa*, of the duck known as the *mariquiña*, of the shy *panguana* that dies after laying only five eggs and of the blue parrot known as the *marakana*. And to the song of the *huapapa* and of the *wankawi* and of the great *yungururu*. And also to the song of the sad *ayaymaman* whose cry is like that of a lost child.

She was listening to the songs of all these birds and of a hundred more and of another hundred still.

But she was not only listening to the birds; she was also listening to the fish of the Unine, of the Mapuya and of the other rivers in the region, as she sat there, at the door of a shack in La Atalaya, so far from Iquitos, gazing out at the jungle, especially at the green Tierra Alta where the Unine rises, for that was where all the tracks left by her missing husband, Thomas Sheldon, pointed. It was late evening and Laura Sheldon (maiden name, Laura Sligo) was wondering what could have happened in that jungle, as she sat listening to the birds and to the fish, as she sat listening to the song of the brilliant *akarawasu*, of the *gamitana*, of the *shiripirare* and of the *paichea*, which grows to a length of nearly ten feet and has a tongue made of bone, and of the *añashua*, the electric eel that kills with one flick of its tail, and of the *shuyua*, which can walk on land, and of the *paña* or *piraña* and of the *maparate* and of the *palometa*, which is good to eat.

She was listening to the songs of all these fish and of a hundred more and of another hundred still.

But she was not only listening to the fish and the birds, she was also listening to the snakes that slither up and down the trees, as she sat there at the door of the shack, looking out at the jungle and thinking about the letter she had received a year before in Dublin: If lost, return to sender: Doctor Thomas Sheldon, Napo Street, Iquitos, Peru, said the return address on the letter, in which her husband declared his intention of journeying deep into the jungle. He wanted to forget the faces of the soldiers he had seen die in Verdun and in Arras, he wanted to forget the terrible bayonet wounds which – God knows – he had been unable to treat; he felt terribly disillusioned with himself and with the world and his primary aim was to cast into the Amazon river the medal awarded to him for his work as Medical Captain. It was a year since she'd received the letter in Dublin and after that there had been nothing, only silence. And Laura Sheldon (maiden name, Laura Sligo) feared that Thomas might already be dead and lying at rest near the source of the Unine, in that same Tierra Alta she was contemplating then as she listened to the fish, the birds and the snakes of the jungle, to the *afaninga*, that whistles like a young boy, and to the *mantona* with its ten colours and to the *naka*, which is small but very poisonous, and to the black *chusupe*, that grows to a length of sixteen feet and bites like a dog, and to the giant *yanaboa*, with a body the thickness of a well-built man, and to the *sachamana* and the *yakumana*.

Laura Sheldon (maiden name, Laura Sligo) was listening to the way the songs of all the snakes – and the songs of a hundred more and another hundred still – blended with the songs of the fish and the birds, as she sat there at the door of a shack in La Atalaya, thinking about her husband and unconvinced by what César Calvo and I kept telling her:

'I think the doctor went up the Ucayali and then bore left towards the Unine,' César Calvo, the wise man of Iquitos, was saying. 'And if that is the case, then you've no need to worry. The doctor will now be amongst the Ashaninka, who are a good people. The Ashaninka don't attack *viracochas* like your husband. I mean, white people who come in peace.'

As well as being a wise man and an expert on everything to do with the jungle, César Calvo was also a good and prudent man. He spoke of the Ashaninka, but not of the Amawaka, the tribe living to the right of the Ucayali, by the shores of the Urubamba, an option that would prove fatal to a *viracocha*, whether he came in peace or not.

'Now you have less reason to despair than ever, Laura. For the first time in three months, we have a firm trail to follow. Tomorrow or the day after tomorrow we will find your husband, I'm sure of it,' said I, the man she had hired as a guide in Cuzco, when she was still a beautiful girl just arrived from Dublin, and not a woman worn out and wasted by the jungle. I was fond of her, I felt myself to be her friend and I would have given anything to be of consolation to her.

But she wasn't listening to us, only to the inhabitants of the jungle: to the *carachupausa*, the *papasí*, the *huapapa*, to the *yungururu*, the *ayaymaman* and to the *yanaboa* and the *naka*; and also to the *makisapa* monkey and to the *wapo* toad and to the *cupisu* turtle.

And then, suddenly, the whole jungle fell silent. The birds fell silent, the fish and the snakes fell silent, all the other animals fell silent, and, alone in that silence, only the lament of the *ayaymaman* could be heard, calling out like a lost child again and again. Night had fallen on the Amazon.

Laura Sheldon (maiden name, Laura Sligo) turned her head in the apparent direction of that solitary song and then, huddled in her chair, she burst into tears. And for a long time there were only two songs in all that vastness: Laura's sobs and the cry of the *ayaymaman*.

It had grown completely dark when César Calvo, the good man of Iquitos, went over to her and spoke to her like a brother.

'We will find him. But now you must sleep. We have a long

182

day ahead of us tomorrow, seven hours to the Unine and then about the same again to the land of the Ashaninka. You must sleep. I'm going to see if the canoes are ready and to reach an agreement with the Indians. I hope they're in the mood for rowing,' he added before going off towards another of the shacks in La Atalaya.

Then it was my turn to go over to Laura, not like a brother, but like a man who could not recall ever having met a woman quite like her: so intelligent, so brave, so very nice.

'Cheer up, Laura. Tomorrow we'll find your husband, you'll see. And when you throw your arms around his neck I want to see you laugh out loud because I've never seen you laugh. And it's about time I did, I think.'

She forced a smile, put a hand on my arm and told me not to worry, she was feeling better already.

Shortly afterwards César returned, saying that everything was in order and that each of us would go in our own canoe with two rowers, at least as far as the Unine.

'Only as far as the Unine?' I asked.

'That's right. Once we reach the Unine we'll have to shift for ourselves. The Indians from La Atalaya will have nothing to do with the Ashaninka.'

We remained a little longer beneath the starless night sky, looking over in the direction of the green Tierra Alta we hoped to traverse. Then we went into the hut and lay down to sleep, wrapping ourselves up in great sheets of canvas, a protection against the tiny *piri* bats, the most efficient bloodsuckers in the jungle.

However, it wasn't the *piri* that kept me from sleep a good part of the night, it was concern about the Amazonian rains which would soon be upon us. César Calvo, the wise man of Iquitos, never spoke of them but I knew he was worried too. If we didn't hurry, the rains would cut off our path back, forcing us to remain amongst the Ashaninka, isolated from civilisation, until the waters of the river became navigable once more.

The Ashaninka were good people, of course, excellent people, but, nonetheless, nothing had been quite the same in the jungle since the advent of the rubber tappers and their Winchester rifles. It was best not to take risks and to make the return journey as quickly as possible.

The following morning, once we had each taken our place in the three canoes César Calvo had hired, we began our journey up the Ucayali, the canoes forming a line with Laura and her two rowers in the middle. Seven hours later, having met with no mishaps, we could see the waters of the Unine, almost yellow in colour, mingling with those of the Ucayali, and we knew the moment of truth had arrived. We would soon be among the Ashaninka. Laura would at last know her husband's fate.

Almost immediately, the Indians raised their oars and pointed to the red trees rising before us on one of the small islands in the river. As César explained later, they were *palosangres*, a species typically found at the mouth of the Unine.

With extreme caution, the Indians replaced their oars in the water and rowed us to the shore. As far as they were concerned, the journey was at an end.

'Are you sure you won't go on?' César asked them once he had handed them the money promised them in La Atalaya. 'I'll pay you double if you'll take us up the Unine,' he added.

But it was useless, they were much too frightened. After a curt farewell, they climbed into two of the canoes and rowed off towards their village. About us screamed hundreds of monkeys, the half-crazy *makisapa* of the Upper Amazon.

Then César Calvo, the wise man of Iquitos, looked up at the sky and said:

'There's still plenty of daylight; our best bet would be to continue our journey on foot along the banks of the Unine, that way we'll avoid the whirlpools at the mouth of the river.'

'Fine,' I said and, taking out my machete, I plunged in amongst the *palosangres* and began to clear a path ahead. He and Laura followed me carrying the one canoe the Indians had left us.

We walked for about four hours, never leaving the shores of the Unine and guided by the sound of its rushing waters. Then we looked for a beach and settled down to spend the night, our first night in Ashaninka territory.

'Who'll take the first watch?' asked Laura Sheldon (maiden name, Laura Sligo) once the tent had been put up and fires lit around it.

'I'll take two watches, yours and mine,' I answered.

She shook her head and frowned, as she always did when she was about to get angry.

'And no arguments,' I said to her, sitting down on a treestump on the beach and making it clear that my watch had already begun.

'He's a strong young man. He'll survive,' smiled César Calvo, the good man of Iquitos, and any dispute was thus resolved. Shortly afterwards, the two of them were sound asleep in the tent.

The only sound in the whole jungle was the murmur of the Unine flowing close by and the crackling flames of the fires protecting the tent. Where were the birds and snakes whose songs had accompanied us all day? Where were the boisterous *makisapa*? Perhaps they were hidden amongst the branches of the *palosangres* that fringed the beach, watching us, waiting for a moment's inattention on our part to leave their lairs and attack us. But I was in no mood to give them that chance. I kept my eyes fixed on the jungle, alert to the slightest whisper, the slightest crack of broken twigs and only looked away when, getting up from my seat to stretch my legs, I glanced across at the tent and comforted myself with the thought of Laura. I was the guardian of her sleep and that made me happy.

I was still thinking about her when I was startled by the triumphant call of a *makisapa*. 'It must be dawn already,' I thought to calm myself. And just then a *naka* viper entered the circle of burning logs that protected me and buried his two small fangs in the ankle of my right leg.

'What's wrong?' exclaimed César Calvo, rushing out of the tent. My howls of pain had woken him.

I showed him the snake lying about a yard away from me. I had sliced it in two with my machete.

'A *naka*!' cried César, opening his eyes wide. Then he picked up the machete and made a long cut in the place where I had been bitten.

'What's wrong?' asked Laura, who had followed him out of the tent. But her question remained hanging in the air, unanswered, for César was bending over me, sucking the blood from the wound.

'Oh, my God!' said Laura when she realised what had happened. And she said it with such sadness that, for an instant, I forgot the pain. It was proof that she was fond of me too.

After half an hour César said: 'I think I've got nearly all the poison out.' It was daylight by then and the songs of the inhabitants of the jungle again enveloped us. By the side of the tent a great dark stain sullied the dry earth of the shore. The blood from my wound.

'Does it hurt?' asked Laura.

'It's not too bad,' I lied.

I was determined not to slow our progress and I began taking down the tent and gathering up the things we needed to put in the canoe, more energetically than ever, in fact, as if the bite had given me renewed strength.

'Shall we go on?' I asked. They both looked at me apprehensively, afraid that at any moment I might collapse. But, as César had said, I was a strong young man. I could withstand the poison that was still inside me.

We dragged the canoe down to the water and, with all three of us rowing, we set off up the Unine, towards the green Tierra Alta where we hoped to find Doctor Sheldon. We had been on the river for about two hours when a new song joined the habitual song of the jungle inhabitants. It was monotonous, repetitive.

The wise man of Iquitos raised his head to listen harder.

'The *manguare* have begun to sound,' he said, explaining that this was the name the Ashaninka gave to their wooden drums.

'We're getting near, then,' I sighed. I couldn't wait to get there. I was feeling weaker and weaker and my ankle was terribly swollen. I wasn't so sure now that I could withstand the *naka*'s poison.

The good man of Iquitos nodded. Yes, any moment now the Ashaninka would appear. Then he added something he had kept secret until then:

'The Ashaninka are good, honest warriors. They'd never kill anyone in an ambush,' he began. Laura and I remained silent. 'They don't use curare,' he went on, 'it's not the virulent, painful poison that the Amawaka, for example, extract from snakes. They use a poison taken from the *tohé* plant, which kills instantly and painlessly.'

I think it was then that Laura and I realised the great danger we were in. César Calvo certainly chose his moments for telling us such things.

'But I don't think they'll harm us. As I've told you before, they don't attack *viracochas* who come in peace.'

Meanwhile, the *manguare* were beating in the jungle, growing louder and louder. The Unine river began to narrow.

I soon became incapable of rowing. I lost all strength in my arms and it hurt me just to move my leg. And yet I did not feel unhappy, it was as if the pain were unimportant. After all, I was next to Laura, the beautiful girl I had met in Cuzco, the woman I cared most about in the world and what mattered was that she find Doctor Sheldon and return with him before the rainy season set in, so that she would not have to stay here amongst the Ashaninka. For the Ashaninka were a very noisy people, constantly beating those drums of theirs, their *manguare*, and that wasn't what I wanted for Laura, I hated to hear her crying the way the *ayaymaman* cried.

'I'm not crying,' Laura said.

I sat up a little and opened my eyes. I was no longer in the canoe, but lying down on a beach by the Unine river. And indeed Laura wasn't crying, she was smiling as she mopped the sweat from my brow with a white handkerchief.

'We've given you some quinine and the fever's gone down considerably,' Laura said. She was still smiling.

I felt ashamed. I had no idea what I might have said in my delirium. I feared I might have declared my true feelings for her.

'Can you hear the drums?' asked César Calvo, kneeling down beside me.

It was impossible not to. The clamour of the *manguare* filled the jungle.

'I hope the Ashaninka come soon. Only a *shirimpiare* can save your life now,' he added.

'A *shirimpiare*?' I asked.

'That's what they call their medicine men.'

I tried to get up, but in vain. All my strength had ebbed away. I believed the time to say goodbye had come.

'Laura, César, listen to me a moment,' I said. 'It's best if you leave me here. You go on alone and find Doctor Sheldon before the rains come. I'd just like to say how glad I am to have known you both.'

'You silly boy!' exclaimed Laura, laughing, and the good man of Iquitos laughed too. They hadn't the slightest intention of abandoning me.

I went back to sleep, but this time I slept calmly and dreamed we were roasting monkey meat and that the three of us, Laura, César and I, were having a party. But there was too much noise at the party, as if we were not the only people there, as if there were many other people, all of whom were eating, singing and shouting.

Worried by what I heard, I opened my eyes again to find that the visitors we had so long expected had arrived. Before me stood three Ashaninka and behind them another ten, another hundred, another thousand. They filled the whole beach, waving their bows and arrows. They were completely naked, their faces and bodies daubed with red and black paint.

César Calvo and Laura were trying to talk to the man who was apparently the leader of the group. They pointed at me again and again and I thought I could make out the two most important words to me at the time: *naka* and *shirimpiare*. Then I lost consciousness.

I did not come to until many days later and I was not a witness to what happened after the Ashaninka had agreed to take us to the place where they were living. However, according to what César Calvo told me later, we entered the village surrounded by children and in the midst of general merriment. It seems the Ashaninka were much taken with Laura's blonde hair and whenever one of the Indians touched it, the others would explode into loud laughter.

Then the majestic figure of Pullcapa Ayumpari, the *shirimpiare*, had appeared, the only Ashaninka with the right to paint his body and face in three colours, with white as well as the red and black that the others used.

'I realised at once that he would do us no harm. He looked at your ankle and frowned as if he were concerned about the swelling,' César said.

'The Ashaninka build two huts for each individual,' he went on. 'One, which they call *tantootzi*, for the family and the other, which they call *kaapa*, for their guests. Pullcapa Ayumpari ordered you to be taken to his own *kaapa*. Laura and I were given a good hut on the other side of the village. Can you really remember nothing of what happened?'

'Very little,' I replied. 'I remember that the Ashaninka looked after me and that I slowly began to feel better. Apart from that, all I remember is the rain. The noise it made on the roof of the *kaapa* used to wake me up.'

'Of course. You were hovering between life and death for twenty days. More than enough time for the rains to begin.'

César Calvo was absolutely right. I had spent twenty days in the house of the *shirimpiare*, Pullcapa Ayumpari, and when I left, I was completely cured. An old woman signalled to me to follow her and led me to the hut occupied by my companions. As soon as I entered I saw Laura and my heart leapt: she was a lovely woman again, the same beautiful girl I had met in Cuzco. It seemed the

Ashaninka had also been ministering to her and had restored her to health as well.

Laura let out a yell and threw her arms around me. She was laughing and crying at the same time and kept saying how glad she was to see me again. She had feared the worst.

Yet she was downcast. She had discovered nothing about her husband. There was no trace in the village of Doctor Thomas Sheldon.

'The Indians don't want to tell us anything,' said César Calvo. 'Either that or they can't. Every time I ask them something they just burst out laughing. It's the same with the old woman the *shirimpiare* has placed at our service. I try to worm things out of her but it's useless. She just laughs and goes on with her work.'

'I'm sure they know something,' sighed Laura. But she was not convinced by what she said.

This was not the journey's end we had expected. Danger and even death, yes, but we had also expected some news of Laura's husband. In fact just the opposite happened. They treated us like honoured guests but told us absolutely nothing.

And meanwhile, it rained, endlessly. It rained on the huts, on the trees and on the fields. The only song to be heard in the jungle was that of the rain.

'That's why we're still here,' said the wise man of Iquitos, 'because the waters of the Unine are running so high it would be impossible to row down it. As soon as the rain stops, they'll take us back to La Atalaya.'

Little by little, an idea began to take hold of me, that of searching Pullcapa Ayumpari's *tantootzi*. If Doctor Sheldon had come up the Unine – and we knew that such a possibility existed – there must be some evidence of him in the village. To find out what had happened to him, all we had to do was get into that *tantootzi*, the most likely place to find such evidence.

I mentioned my idea to César Calvo.

'We can't let Laura go back emptyhanded. There's nothing

worse than uncertainty. She has to know if her husband is alive or dead,' I said.

'It's very risky. An Ashaninka cannot forgive someone who goes into his house to steal. The punishment is death. Always, without exception.'

I remained silent for a long while, watching the rain.

'The rainy season will be over soon and on that day the Ashaninka will hold a celebration. But not here in the village. They'll go to the shores of the Unine,' whispered the wise man of Iquitos, adding: 'That's our only chance.'

'I'm going to give it a try,' I said.

César Calvo nodded, smiling. He was not unaware of the motives that lay behind my decision.

'I'm afraid otherwise Laura may go mad,' I said in justification of my action. 'She seems more and more turned in on herself. She spends hours staring out at the jungle, without saying a word.'

'Yes, we must do something,' said César encouragingly.

Hardly a week had passed before the blue sky returned to the Amazon. The Ashaninka greeted it with laughter and shouts, with an enthusiasm which to us, the inhabitants of another world, seemed childish. Nonetheless, their high spirits were enviable. They were happy, we were not.

The preparations for the celebration began very early. Warriors, old men and children allowed themselves to be adorned by the women. Seated at the doorway of his *tantootzi*, Pullcapa Ayumpari was arrayed like a peacock. He would without doubt be the most distinguished figure at the celebrations.

By midday, the village was practically empty. Only three warriors remained on guard at the entrance, but they were too drunk on *chuchuwasi* to carry out their duties. The moment to take action had arrived.

'I'm going to have a look round the *shirimpiare*'s hut. I may find something,' I said to Laura before leaving. She was lying down on her bed with her eyes closed, even more downcast than usual.

'You are a brave boy,' she said, opening her eyes and making an attempt at a smile. I took that smile, locked it in my heart then left, absolutely determined to discover something.

Pullcapa Ayumpari's *tantootzi* was much darker inside than one would have expected on such a bright day and it took some time before my eyes could make out what any of the objects scattered around the room were. Finally I managed to identify the clay containers in which the *shirimpiare* kept his ointments, as well as some masks that I had never seen him wear but which were presumably for use in religious ceremonies. I made my way over to the bed, which was no larger or more luxurious than those we had in our hut, and then I stopped. Something was not quite right here. But what? I realised that my eyes had glimpsed something, but I couldn't put my finger on what it was. I searched every corner but could find nothing unusual.

'I can't see it now, but I did see something,' I thought and then returned to the part of the *tantootzi* I would have seen on first entering the hut.

Then I spotted it. It was rectangular in shape and lay amongst the clay containers. It looked like a book. My fingers confirmed that impression. The cover read: *Discours sur les sciences et les arts* Jean Jacques Rousseau. And on the third page, in tiny writing, were the words I had so longed to see: If lost, return to Thomas Sheldon, Medical Captain, Fleury, Normandy.

A shaft of light entered the hut, as if a ray of sun had managed to pierce the roof of the *tantootzi*. But – as I realised when I looked up – that was not the source of light. The light was coming from the door, which was slightly ajar. A red hand was slowly pushing it open. Before I had time to react, an Ashaninka was standing before me. His face and body were painted in many colours.

'Pullcapa!' I cried, not out of terror or fear of the punishment that awaited me, but out of the shame I felt the moment I recognised him. It was not right to betray the man who had saved my life. 'I did it for Laura,' I said, showing him the book.

Pullcapa Ayumpari simply stretched out his hand, the way a father would to a small child, calmly, without a trace of displeasure or anger. I obeyed and took his hand. It was like being five years old again.

'Now I understand what it means to be a *shirimpiare*,' I thought as we both followed the path that led into the jungle. He was a father to everyone, a great tree, a good river; a man who had suffered only in order to struggle with the Great Enemies who destroyed his brothers, weaker than himself. I remembered what César Calvo had told me, but I did not fear for my life.

Still silent, Pullcapa Ayumpari led me to a clearing in the jungle full of small mounds made out of pebbles from the river. Each mound, surrounded by bows and arrows, was adorned with white flowers. I understood that this was where the Ashaninka warriors were buried.

Pullcapa let go of my hand and indicated that I continue along the path. Again I obeyed.

Twenty paces on was one solitary mound. There were no flowers this time, only a gold object with three ribbons.

'So he didn't throw it in the river,' I thought sadly. For that golden object was none other than the medal the army had bestowed on Thomas Sheldon, Medical Captain. One of the ribbons, the larger one, bore the cross and colours of the Union Jack. The other two represented the Red Cross and the Republic of France.

'You suffered greatly. Now rest in peace,' I prayed as I knelt.

When I returned to where I had left Pullcapa, I found myself alone. The *shirimpiare*, the good father of all the Ashaninka, had returned to the celebrations by the Unine.

'I want you to be the one to tell her. I don't feel able to,' I said to César Calvo. He was much surprised by what I had told him. He just could not understand Pullcapa's behaviour.

'Oh well, it's better this way. Don't worry. I'll go and tell Laura now,' he said.

I spent that afternoon wandering through the jungle that surrounded the village. I envied the Ashaninka, whose voices and laughter I heard each time I approached the river, and I felt sad not to be able to share their happiness and innocence. I wondered how Laura had reacted to the news that her husband was dead. But that was not the only question I asked myself. There were many others, all of them difficult, perplexing ones. What was I going to do? Should I speak to Laura before the journey was over and she returned to Dublin? What if she felt nothing for me? But the only answer to any of these questions was to keep walking, to keep thinking, to keep searching.

When I returned to the village at nightfall, a group of warriors offered me some *chuchuwasi*. They were happy, very happy, and wanted me to be happy too. I accepted their offer and took a drink.

'Not bad,' I said.

The *chuchuwasi* was not dissimilar in taste to cherry liqueur – I liked it. I drank a second draught then a third and a fourth. Two hours later I was completely drunk and as happy as they were.

I don't remember how I made it back to my bed nor what I got up to during the hours spent with the warrior drinkers of *chuchuwasi*. To judge by the mocking looks I received when I woke up, however, I assume my behaviour must have been rather comical.

'Ah, so you've opened your eyes at last,' said César.

'I had no idea my head was made of ground glass,' I moaned. The slightest movement made my temples pound. I had no alternative but to remain lying on my bed.

'It's odd your head should hurt so much. I can't imagine why it should,' said Laura ironically. I saw that she was smiling and had emerged from her dejection of the previous days.

'The worst thing must have been the uncertainty,' I thought. 'Now that she knows what really happened, she feels better.'

'I think I'll just go back to sleep for a bit,' I said.

'Oh no you won't,' said César. 'We're leaving. The Ashaninka are taking us back to La Atalaya.'

'When?' I exclaimed, sitting up. I had suddenly forgotten about my headache.

'Right now. The canoes are ready,' said Laura pointing to the window. I stood up and looked outside. The group charged with our return were waiting in front of the *tantootzi*. I counted six canoes and fifteen oarsmen.

'It looks like we'll have quite an entourage,' I said.

'Like royalty,' smiled César Calvo.

Laura went over to the old woman who had helped us with the domestic chores and presented her with a lock of her fair hair; she should keep it as a souvenir, for she had been very kind to us all. Then we rejoined the Ashaninka who were to accompany us down the Unine.

Before we set off into the jungle, we looked back towards Pullcapa Ayumpari's *tantootzi*. He was standing at the entrance, watching us.

'Wait just a moment. I'd like to thank him,' said the wise man of Iquitos. Asking one of the oarsmen to accompany him, he went off to perform that final act of courtesy.

'What did he say?' we asked when he came back.

'He simply wished us a good journey,' sighed César Calvo. It seemed to me that it pained him deeply to leave that good father of the Ashaninka.

We looked back at the village one last time, waving to the men and women who had gathered outside the huts. Then we went down to the river.

The jungle, so silent during the rainy season, was once more full of life and, as we were carried swiftly down the Unine, we listened to the songs of all the inhabitants of the Upper Amazon, the song of the *arambasa*, of the *papasí*, of the *carachupausa*, of the duck known as the *mariquiña*, of the shy *panguana* that dies after laying only five eggs and of the blue parrot known as the *marakana*. And of the *huapapa*, and of the *wankawi*, and of the great *yungururu*.

We were carried swiftly down the Unine to the sound of the songs of all these birds and of a hundred more and of another hundred still.

But we heard not only the songs of the birds, we also heard the fish in the river which, from time to time, approached our canoes and followed us with the same tenacity as I, at that moment, followed my memories; and my memories were of a *tantootzi* and a *shirimpiare* and the hands that had healed my ankle and a book by Rousseau and a medal from the army placed on a mound of pebbles.

And suddenly the scream of a *makisapa* rose above the other songs of the jungle, startling me.

'The medal, of course!' I cried and the two Ashaninka in my canoe both laughed out loud.

At last I'd found the missing piece to the jigsaw puzzle of my memories. How could that medal possibly still be so golden. And the ribbons? How could they have preserved their colour in a climate like that of the Amazon? Hadn't it been over a year since Doctor Sheldon had disappeared into the jungle?

All the answers pointed in one direction.

The Ashaninka said goodbye to us as soon as we reached the Ucayali, leaving us their finest canoe and showing us how best to row in order to make our way downriver. Then they rowed back against the current, glad to be able to return to their village.

'They seem so happy!' exclaimed Laura.

'Well, we're headed in quite a different direction,' smiled César Calvo, getting into the canoe.

'To La Atalaya!' I said in a tone of voice intended to be carefree. But the answer I had stumbled upon while we rowed down the Unine continued to rankle; my voice failed me and I merely succeeded in sounding lugubrious.

To avoid the risk of colliding with the many uprooted trees left behind by the previous months of flooding, we proceeded very slowly down the Ucayali. By the time we reached La Atalaya, it was nearly night.

A little later, I was sitting in the same place Laura had sat before we left for the Unine, the same place from which she had looked out at the jungle and, hearing the song of the *ayaymaman*, had wept. I could find no peace there either.

The wise man of Iquitos came out of the shack and sat down beside me.

'Yes, I'm thinking about him too,' he said.

'About Pullcapa Ayumpari you mean?'

'Yes.'

'Thomas Sheldon,' I said sadly.

César Calvo nodded.

'I first became suspicious the day he spared your life. A true Ashaninka could never have done that. That's why I went to thank him this morning, because I wanted to see his face. The coloured clay can hide a pale skin, but not the eyes. And, of course, his eyes were blue, the typical blue eyes of an Englishman.'

'But how did he come to be *shirimpiare*?'

'Well, he is a doctor. He probably arrived at the village, taught the previous *shirimpiare* a few things and then the latter no doubt adopted him as his son and named him his successor. I'm sure that's what must have happened.'

'There's just one thing I'm not sure about, César. I don't know if I should tell Laura. And I'm sure you know why.'

Then we heard a cough. Someone wanted to warn us of their presence.

'César's right. Thomas cured the old *shirimpiare* who then gave up his post to him. He tells me so in this letter I've just found amongst my clothes.'

Laura was standing behind us, holding a piece of paper in her hand.

'I thought you were asleep!' I exclaimed.

'I heard everything,' said Laura looking me in the eyes.

For a moment the three of us were silent.

'What should we call you from now on?' I asked at last.

'By my maiden name. Laura Sligo.'

Then she spoke much more directly than I had dared to.

'Thomas tells me you're in love with me. Is that true? Don't forget we have César Calvo here as our witness.'

A month later the two of us were in Dublin.

FINIS CORONAT OPUS

FINIS coronat opus, said Mr Smith, switching off his little tape recorder. Then, before my friend and I had time to say a word, he had thanked us for listening to the story and was hurrying off towards the village square.

'Where are you off to?' we called after him. But he continued on, walking ever faster. Striding along in his white suit, he looked like a master of ceremonies urgently needed back at the festivities.

'Who do you think he is?' I said.

'I don't know. But one thing's for sure, he's a writer,' said my friend.

He too was a little disconcerted by what had happened.

From our vantage point, the world seemed a peaceful, silent place. A south wind was blowing – the wind of madmen and of all those unsatisfied beings ceaselessly searching for something, the wind of the poor in spirit, of those who sleep alone, of humble daydreamers – and it awoke in us the illusion that everyone and everything were in their right place, exactly where they should be: the stars high up in the sky; the mountains and the forests sleeping placidly around us; the animals all sleeping too and hidden away somewhere – some amongst the grasses, others in pools in the rivers, the moles and mice in burrows beneath the earth.

We would like to have stayed there because – at least compared with the dank Amazon that Laura Sligo and her friends had wandered – it reminded us of the ineffable gardens described in old novels. But we had to get up and continue our journey. We couldn't arrive at the reading the following morning jaded from lack of sleep. One more beer and we'd call it a night.

We walked the path from the cemetery to the square in silence, convinced that, if we spoke, we would disturb the beneficent spirits at that moment stirring within us, who would then escape through our open mouths to their home, the upper spheres. We had plenty of time, the summer was only just beginning. The time would come for us to comment on the story Mr Smith had just told us.

Once back in the whirlpool of the fiesta, our eyes scoured every corner of the square. But there was no white suit to be seen, no hat stood out above the crowd.

'Our honest old man appears and disappears as if by magic,' said my friend.

'Let's drink our last beer to his health,' I replied.

'Good idea. I'll go and get us a couple of bottles.'

He managed this more easily than the first time and we went and sat down on the church steps. According to the church clock it was two in the morning.

'You see, everyone plays their own game,' I said to my friend, after taking my first sip of beer and pointing to the two groups that had formed at the fiesta. Because by then not everyone at the fiesta was dedicating themselves solely to drinking and holding loud conversations in the bars. A fair number of couples had broken away and wandered off into the dark to dance and kiss.

'Those who are inside want to get out and those who are outside want to get in,' my friend remarked.

'What?'

'Oh, nothing, just a bit of nonsense,' he said by way of excuse. 'It's something my grandfather was always saying. He said that married people tend to envy single people and vice versa. In other words, those who are inside would give anything to get out and those who are outside would give anything to get in.'

'And what made you think of that now?' I asked.

'From what I see in the square. It just occurred to me that many of those who are dancing would rather be in the bar, whilst many of those in the bar would rather be dancing. Such is life!' he said with a theatrical sigh.

'My father had a similar saying. He said that in heaven there's a huge cake reserved solely for married people who've never once regretted getting married. The cake's never been touched.'

We both laughed at the scepticism of our elders. Their view of love was very different from that of the Mr Smith whose health we were drinking.

But our state of mind predisposed us more to melancholy than to joking and we soon dropped the funny remarks. It was fine that there was a fiesta going on, but we didn't want its atmosphere to infect us, not that night. My friend and I formed a third group at the fiesta. And we fell silent again, letting ourselves slip back into our earlier mood, thinking and now and then listening to the slow, gentle tunes the band was playing. And when the clock chimed half past two, we finished our beers and walked back to the car.

'What time does tomorrow's session start?' my friend asked.

'My uncle didn't say but I imagine it'll be around ten.'

'As early as that?'

'Well, at ten we'll have breakfast. We'll start the stories around eleven.'

'How many are you going to read?'

'About four. And you?'

'I'm not sure yet. Only one I think. I'm there to listen rather than to read. And your uncle? Will he read something?'

'He didn't tell me that either. But I'm sure he will. I imagine he'll read some short essay. "On why the nineteenth century was the second and last Golden Age", or something like that.'

'We're in for a good time then.'

'I hope so. Besides, you know how well we always eat on these occasions!'

'Like princes!' exclaimed my friend emphatically.

We were back at the car. The noise and music from the fiesta was far from us again and my friend and I – at peace at last, breathing easily and enjoying the quiet – smoked a farewell cigarette. Our final reflection was dedicated, of course, to Mr Smith.

'It's a shame he didn't come with us. He wouldn't have made a bad companion at tomorrow's session,' my friend said.

'It's my fault. I did think of inviting him, but then I lost my nerve,' I replied.

'There have been a lot of unknowns tonight, haven't there? Ismael's lizards, Mr Smith's stories . . .'

'I should say! I haven't had such a strange night for ages!'

'Nor have I. But it's been really good. It's nights like this that make life bearable.'

'Anyway, let's go,' I said, starting the engine.

There were one hundred and twenty-seven bends in the road between that village and Obaba: eighty uphill, rising gently to the top of a long slope and from there, over the other side of the mountain, another forty-seven downhill. It took a little over half an hour to drive, through forests all the way, leaving the sea behind us.

Despite all the bends our journey along the road of moths that night turned out to be a safe, quiet drive through the trees; the lights of the few cars coming in the opposite direction were visible long before they reached us.

'How do you know there are one hundred and twenty-seven bends?' my friend asked me when we'd already driven round twenty of them.

'I told you earlier that I spent my whole childhood cycling round here. The number of times I've ridden up here, pedalling furiously and shouting: forty! forty-one! forty-two! I know these bends by heart,' I went on, 'See that one up ahead? Well if you count the bends coming from Obaba it's number one hundred. But if you count from the village we've just left, it's number twenty-seven.'

'It must be a very special place for you,' my friend said, smiling.

'Not just because it's the hundredth one, but because of the fountain there used to be up here. Well, that still is up here. You saw the ditch that crossed it,' I replied . . . speaking in the past tense, of course, because no sooner had he asked the question than bend number one hundred was behind us.

My friend remained silent and I let myself be carried along by memories.

'This road meant a lot to us. As did the bicycle, of course. For the children in Obaba, from about the age of seven onwards, learning to ride a bike was the number one priority. The arithmetic and grammar they taught at school didn't matter, neither did the Bible history they talked about in the church sacristy; the only thing that mattered was attending the cycling classes held by the older boys in the square in Obaba, and securing a place amongst the elect group who could go anywhere on two wheels. And if you couldn't do that by the time you were nine or ten, then you became marginalised, a second-class kid . . .'

I cut short the thread of my memories at that point and indicated something to our left. We had just entered the straight stretch of road which, counting from Obaba, followed bend number eighty-eight. It formed a natural belvedere from which, by day, you could see first the broad valley and, beyond that, the beaches and the sea.

'The view's pretty good at night too,' said my friend.

'See those lights in the distance?' I asked.

'What are they? Houses or ships?'

'Ships.'

We slowed down and drove that stretch of road staring out at the lights, slightly astonished at how near the coast seemed to be, simply because the air was so clear.

'How much farther to the top?' my friend asked once the view had disappeared. We were going uphill again now.

'About another forty bends. But don't worry, once we get there we can look down on the whole valley of Obaba. Just a few more and we're home! It's hard going though, isn't it?' I added.

'It certainly is. And you say you used to come up here on your bikes . . .'

'A couple of times a week, what's more.'

'You were real cyclists then!'

'Not as good as Hilario, though . . .'

'Hilario?'

'Yes, Hilario: the best racing cyclist in the world. And born in Obaba into the bargain.'

Naturally my friend didn't know who I meant and so I settled down to the eleventh memory of the night – too many perhaps for one journey, too many, even, for one book. But that night my memory was like dry tinder which the heat generated by the landscape set burning.

'He had a pale blue racing bike, one of those that are light enough to lift on one finger,' I began, once I'd apologised for my fondness for memories, 'and every evening he'd put on his shorts and his bright-coloured jersey and cycle off to train along the roads round the village. Whenever he passed us we'd shout: "There goes Hilario!" And when he cycled up behind us and overtook us on this very road, we'd always be full of appreciative comments: "Did you see the way he passed us? Like a bat out of hell! He's an amazing cyclist!" In short, we admired him. We ourselves sped downhill crouched right over the handlebars, and we were pretty good, miles better than the fainthearted cyclists who rode sedately round and round the square, but compared to Hilario we were nothing. He was in a class of his own. And if, for example, one of the older boys suggested to us that Hilario wasn't really that good, we'd immediately say: "What do you mean he isn't that good? How come they let him wear that cycling jersey then?" And if the boy made some remark along the lines of "Anyone can get a jersey", we'd burst out laughing: "Oh, they can, can they? Why don't you go and ask for one then? Go on, and let's see what you come back with!" Well, when you're a child, all arguments tend to be *ad hominem* since it's generally assumed that the motivating force behind most human actions is envy. Not such a false assumption, it must be said.

Besides, we had proof. There were, for example, the three photographs hanging on the walls of Obaba's smartest bar: Hilario smiling, Hilario with his arms raised in triumph, Hilario crossing the finishing line first. It was no use some envious villager trying to convince us otherwise. Our faith in him was unshakable.

And one day, before we'd had time to grow up a bit, a cycle race was announced. The race would pass right through Obaba, along the very road we're driving now. "And Hilario's competing too," someone must have said. And the news became a chant that we never tired of repeating amongst ourselves.

The day of the race arrived, a Sunday, and we all went up to the top of the pass, where we're going now in fact . . . and what's more we walked up; our parents wouldn't let us go on our bikes because of all the cars and as soon as we got to the top, we went and sat down on that mound over there, do you see it?'

'Yes, yes, I see it,' said my friend.

'We came up here to get a better perspective on the race and because this was the final uphill stretch on the route.'

'And. . . ?'

'Well, we were sitting on the mound when, suddenly, a murmur ran through the crowd, horns sounded, a rocket exploded, and the cyclists were upon us. "There are three breakaways! Three breakaways!" someone shouted and we all craned our necks, preparing ourselves to see Hilario. Because, of course, we just took it for granted that he would be amongst the three in the lead; we hadn't the slightest doubt. We waited a little longer and then the three cyclists appeared around the bend, about to make the sprint to the top and win the mountain prize. "Come on, Hilario!" one of us shouted. But why that cry of "Come on, Hilario!"? Was he amongst the three? No, he wasn't. It was odd, but not one of the three leaders was Hilario.

"Did you see the state they were in? They could barely control their legs!" one of us said, breaking the silence that had fallen over the group. "You're right, they were absolutely shattered. The main group will soon catch them up," said another in support of this. "Hilario's probably saving himself for the final attack. It's almost better that way. You know what a great finishing sprint he's got. . . !" said another.

'And the main group passed and no sign of Hilario,' my friend guessed, silently pointing to the lights in the valley below us. The lights of Obaba.

'Well, we didn't see him at any rate. We saw a caravan of publicity cars, we saw motorcyclists in black leather, we saw cyclists of all sizes and colours, but as for Hilario, not a sign. And when the main group whistled past and headed off downhill, we were all confused, we didn't know what to think. "What's going on?" one of us exclaimed angrily. Because it seemed more like a cruel blow from fate rather than any failure on the part of Hilario.

And so, slightly crestfallen, we started walking down the hill, home. "The one time the race comes through Obaba and he has to go and fall off," said the one rather angry member of our group. "Fallen off?" the rest of us exclaimed. "Of course he must have fallen off! Why else would he drop out?" he argued. "Knowing how tough Hilario is, it must have been a really bad fall. You don't think he could have hurt himself, do you?" asked the youngest amongst us.

Soon we were all sorrowing over the misfortune that must have overtaken that flower of Obaba, our knight, Hilario. And then, when we'd reached that wide curve we passed just a short time ago, we heard the sound of car horns. We looked back and . . . I bet you can't imagine what we saw. Well, we saw a clapped-out old lorry with a big broom attached and in front of the lorry . . .'

'Hilario!' said my friend.

'That's right! Hilario in his black shorts! Hilario in his bright-coloured jersey!

A hole opened up in our stomachs. "He's coming in last!" we shouted, almost on the verge of tears. And at that precise moment, possibly out of respect for us and for our disillusion, the sun slid behind a cloud.

I don't know how long we stood there, openmouthed and with that hole inside us. As far as I was concerned, the moment seemed an eternity. And, at last, when both lorry and cyclist reached us, a querulous cry left our throats: "Come on, Hilario!" . . .

And with that shout both the cycling race and our childhood ended.'

My friend thought highly of the story and advised me to try and get it published. In his opinion it certainly didn't belong in the category of the 'futile, empty and trite' and therefore fulfilled one of the conditions of good literature. Any reader could see him or herself reflected in that mirror full of children and bicycles.

Although grateful for my friend's kind words, I had no intention of following his advice. Publishing my memories of a cycling idol seemed an irrelevance, especially since for me the search for the Last Word – of the other story, the one about the lizards – was becoming ever more pressing. But, immediately following our conversation, on the next bend, something unusual happened, an event I did feel obliged to record. 'It is not for the writer to scatter stories that chance has brought together,' I thought, and I acted accordingly.

So on with the story of what happened along the road. But before I do anything else, I would first like to refer to a letter the writer Théophile Gautier wrote shortly after passing through a village very similar to Obaba, for what he said in that letter very much expresses what my friend and I felt at that point on our journey.

Gautier recounts the following story to his esteemed friend Madame Devilier:

When I got there the village was holding a celebration and everyone was gathered in the square. I joined those men and women of the countryside and do you know what I saw? A fine crystal glass had been placed on the ground and a dancer with powerful, agile legs was spinning and turning around it. He would dance away from the vase, approach it and again move away; sometimes, when he leaped into the air, for example, it seemed he would fall on top of the fragile glass, that he would trample and break it. But at the very last moment, his legs would part and he would dance on, smiling and happy, as if it cost him not the least effort. Then he would move away, draw near and move away again. However, as the turns he gave around the glass grew ever tighter, one felt he must inevitably crush it, so much so that, in expectation of that outcome, we who were gathered there, found ourselves breathing to the rhythm of the bells the dancer wore on his ankles, our anxiety waxing and waning in time to them.

Suddenly, the whole square fell silent, the bells too. The dancer sidestepped the glass just barely brushing it. Realising that this jump would be the last, I closed my eyes, just as I would to avoid seeing the fatal axe blow dealt by the executioner. Then I heard an explosion of applause. I opened my eyes again and . . . there stood the glass, intact. The dancer gaily scooped it up from the ground and drank the white wine it contained.

That dance had a profound effect on me. It seemed to me that women and men like you and me are just like that crystal glass and that very often we feel as if there were some invisible dancer turning and spinning around us, the dancer who bestows, directs and snatches away life, the dancer who, clumsier than that dancer in the square, will one day fall upon us and shatter us.

Gautier was not lying. The dance really did have a profound effect on him and he never forgot it. The proof is another passage that appears in chapter nine of his memoirs:

Once, when I was staying in Madame Cassis' house, I suddenly remembered an old friend of mine. And no sooner had I mentioned his name than that same friend, whom I believed to be in Greece, appeared as if by magic in the room. A shiver ran through me, because that same week I had experienced two other *coups d'hasard*. I had a feeling that hidden forces were walking behind me and were determined to sport with me, the way a dancer spins and plays around a glass tumbler.

But that's enough of Théophile Gautier and of the two long quotes I chose as illustrations of a most unusual feeling. It's time to move on again to the 'next bend' in the road, to what happened when my friend and I had almost reached Obaba and were within sight of the palm tree hung with lights that the uncle from Montevideo had left switched on, as he always did when he was expecting visitors.

We were driving down the middle of the road, chatting about that habit of my uncle's, when, suddenly, after bend number twelve, we saw a car parked at the side of the road. A red Lancia.

'Isn't that. . . ?' I began. But before I could finish my question, the person I was thinking of emerged from behind a thicket.

'Ismael!' exclaimed my friend.

By then our headlights were full on him and you could see with absolute clarity the small flattened head and the round eye peeping out from the hollow formed by Ismael's cupped hands.

'Did you see what he's got in his hands?' I said.

'There's no doubt about it,' whispered my friend, 'it's a lizard.'

It was then that we felt the proximity of that dancer who bestows, directs and snatches away life. I don't know how much it was just a consequence of our tiredness and the idle talk we'd enjoyed that night. Perhaps we'd talked and drunk too much, but whatever the reason, the fact is we were frightened. It seemed to us that, like Gautier, we too were at the mercy of dark forces, the same forces that had planned and organised many of the things that had happened to us prior to that night: they had furnished us with the opportunity to enlarge the school photograph; they had called our attention to the lizard held next to Albino María's ear; they had arranged for us to discover the article on lizards and mental pathology.

'What is the man up to?' said my friend as we passed.

'I don't know and I don't care. We've had quite enough adventures for one night,' I answered, putting my foot down on the accelerator. My one desire was to get away from that old primary school classmate of mine as fast as possible. I didn't even feel like waving to him from the car.

'We'll think about it all tomorrow,' I said.

'That's fine by me. First things first.'

My friend was as anxious as I was to forget what we'd seen.

'Yes, we need to be in good shape for tomorrow's session. As you see, the palm tree's all lit up ready. We can't disappoint the uncle from Montevideo.'

'Of course not. Games should be taken very seriously.'

And that was how the Ismael affair came to be postponed but not concluded. *Ad maiorem literaturae gloriam*, I hope.

We parked the car by the illuminated palm tree, at one corner of my uncle's garden.

'Let's see what's in the post for us,' I said to my friend, plunging my hand into the wooden letter box. I drew out a piece of paper.

'The programme, I assume,' my friend guessed correctly.

'Yes, you know what he's like, the same old ritual.'

And going over to stand in the light from the palm tree, we read the note my uncle had written.

'Breakfast at ten with orange juice, fresh croissants, pancakes and butter, coffee and tea, but no jam because I haven't managed to find any that I like. From eleven to one, the reading of stories on the porch at the rear of the house, because it's the coolest place at that hour. At one o'clock, martinis in the garden served with an olive and a slice of lemon. Any discussion of the stories read earlier is strictly forbidden, since an argument might ensue which could provoke serious digestive upsets. Instead, we will speak only of trivial things. At two, lunch, which is top secret, but if I say it's in the hands of Antonia from the Garmendia house, I need say no more. At four, coffee and the first cognac. At five, the second cognac and an analysis of what was read in the morning. A word of warning: I have changed my mind. I am no longer against plagiarism. See you tomorrow.'

'He's got something up his sleeve,' I said, reading those last lines. Then, in utter silence, we mounted the stairs to the bedrooms on the top floor of the house. It was three fifteen. Five minutes later we were both asleep.

IN THE MORNING

A BACK stairway connected the two floors of my uncle's house and at a quarter to ten, well showered and even better shaved, my friend and I came down it. My uncle had not yet returned from buying the fresh croissants that formed part of the programme and the air was full of that sloth peculiar to Sunday mornings. 'It will be extremely hot today, especially along the coast, with temperatures reaching eighty-five to ninety-five degrees Fahrenheit,' said the radio in the kitchen, its murmurings a further invitation to remain in that state of semi-consciousness.

After a brief visit to the library, we went and sat down on the porch at the rear of the house.

'It's a 1928 edition of *Nana*,' my friend said, opening the book he'd just taken from my uncle's 'Zola shelf'. But I paid no attention to his remark. 'What are you looking at?' he added when I failed to respond.

'Sorry,' I said. 'Have you seen what's over here?'

'Something your uncle's written?'

'I think they're translations he's made, and you can bet he's up to no good with them. If I'm not mistaken, he's discovered yet another example of plagiarism, carried out, needless to say, in this ridiculous twentieth century of ours!'

I passed my friend the two sheets of paper I'd picked up.

'Shall I read what it says or would that be flouting the rules of the programme?'

'Of course it would. But, since he's not back yet, it's a luxury we can allow ourselves. But be careful, if you hear him come in, stop reading at once and look studiously out of the window.'

'I'll do better than that. I'll point to that apple tree over there and say: "An apple a day keeps the doctor away." It'll seem perfectly natural to your uncle. He won't suspect a thing.'

'Perfect. You can begin.'

'Well, the title on the first page is "Odin, or a brief story by a writer currently much in vogue, in a translation by the uncle from Montevideo." '

And this is what follows:

'King Olaf Tryggvason had embraced the new religion.

One night an old man arrived at his court, wrapped in a dark cloak and wearing a wide-brimmed hat that hid his eyes. The king asked what the stranger could do. The stranger replied that he knew how to tell tales and to play the violin. He played old tunes on the violin and told the story of Gudrun and Gunnar; finally, he touched on the birth of the old god Odin. He told of the arrival of three sorceresses and how the first two had wished him happiness . . . whilst the third, full of wrath, announced: "The boy will live no longer than the time it takes for the candle at his side to burn down." And his parents blew out the candle so that Odin would not die. Olaf Tryggvason did not want to believe the story. The stranger again assured him that it was true and, taking out a candle, he lit it. Whilst everyone watched the candle flame burning, the old man announced that it was getting late and he must be going. When the candle had burned down, they went out to look for him. Not far from the king's palace, Odin lay dead.'

My friend lay the first sheet down on the table and was about to read the second. I suggested he do so quickly. According to the radio in the kitchen it was already ten o'clock.

'He'll be here soon,' I said, remembering my uncle's punctuality.

'Right, the title on the second sheet is: "Passages taken from certain dictionaries learned by heart by that same fashionable author." '

'He's obviously keen on long titles.'

'The three paragraphs are about the hunter Meleager . . . "There was a rumour," says the first one, "that Meleager was not the son of King Aeneas but of the god Ares. Seven days after the birth of the boy, the Moerae appeared to his mother Althaea and told her that the fate of her son was closely linked with that of the brand burning in the hearth. They said that once the brand was burned up and had become ashes, Meleager would die. Althaea removed the brand from the hearth and, having extinguished it, put it away in a box" . . .'

'Now read the second paragraph,' I told my friend.

'The second one says . . . "And the Moerae, who are the godmothers of fate, went in search of her and predicted that if the brand from the hearth was ever consumed completely and became ashes, her son would also be consumed and die. Then Althaea removed the brand and, having extinguished it, put it away in a box. But it happened that Meleager, who was out hunting in Calydon, killed his uncles, Althaea's brothers. Learning this, Althaea grew angry and threw the brand that had been linked with her own son's life into the fire. Meleager died instantly" . . .'

'I think he's coming,' I said.

'The third paragraph is very short,' my friend replied.

'Well get on with it then. Come on.'

' "Amongst Celtic people, the figure of Odin goes by the name of Arthus or Arthur, as can be seen in the Norman *chasses du roi*. According to Dontenville, the myth underlying all of them is that of Meleager." '

Then we heard a voice say: 'The reading session begins at ten.'

One of the nineteenth-century novelists he so admired might have described my uncle as follows: a plump, heavily built man of about sixty, with dark skin and a fine bald head, who usually dressed in blue and yellow. The caricature of him that hung in his library depicted him as half *bon vivant* and half Roman senator, but omitted his most marked characteristic: the vivacity of his small, dark eyes. For my uncle never had the resigned, sceptical look of a man who has lived a lot and has no further interest in seeing more of life, but of a man in whose eyes there still shines the enthusiastic, mischievous, joyful spirit of someone off to their first party. That — the spirit so evident in his eyes — was at the root of his literary gatherings, his ceremonies, his illuminated palm tree, at the root of his struggle against the banal way of life the world otherwise offered him.

'What do you think programmes are for?' asked my uncle coming over to us, smiling.

But the question was purely rhetorical and we embraced and greeted each other, laughing.

'And I'll tell you something else,' he went on. 'What you've just read is water under the bridge. I certainly wouldn't make fun now of anyone capable of plagiarising that well.'

'Yes, we've noticed your new attitude towards plagiarism. And to be honest we find it very odd,' I said.

'But how did you find out?'

'From the note you left us in the letter box, uncle.'

'Oh, of course! I'm so pleased with my change of mind that I can't keep it to myself and I take every opportunity to let others know about it. But we'll talk about that later. Now I'm going to give you breakfast.' And, saying that, my uncle laughed to himself.

'He's up to something,' I said when he'd slipped away to the kitchen.

'Plagiarism is the goose that laid the golden egg! You bet it is!' we heard him say.

During breakfast we spoke only of everyday things. And when there wasn't a single croissant, pancake or bun left on the tray, we each picked up our second or third cup of coffee and began the reading session.

I read the first four stories: 'Hans Menscher', 'How to write a short story in five minutes', 'Klaus Hanhn' and 'Margarete and Heinrich, twins'. Then it was my friend's turn. He read 'I, Jean Baptiste Hargous'. And finally my uncle set forth his new theory with a text entitled 'How to plagiarise'.

Once again, the last word will have to wait. It would be inappropriate to continue the search without first setting down the above-mentioned stories.

HANS MENSCHER

IN HAMBURG, not far from the Binnenalster lake, there is a house whose neglected state stands in contrast with every other house in that part of the city and which would appear to be utterly dead were it not for the roses that still bloom in the garden even today, doing their best to overflow the railings that separate them from Vertriebstrasse, the street linking the lake and Eichendorf Square.

Any passer-by chancing to pause outside the house will notice the peeling plaster of its walls, the faded paint on both front door and window frames, and recognise the air of desolation that clings to all abandoned houses, a desolation that speaks to his own heart, perhaps itself an abandoned place. But he sees no statue there, no plaque, no sign to excite his curiosity, so the passer-by lingers a little longer, thinking how lovely the rose gardens must have been and then continues along the road. He reaches the shore of the lake, sits down on the jetty and looks out at the fragile sailing boats, watching them slip along, bobbing up and down each time a motorboat passes, making rings in the water; and barely has he begun his contemplation than he has forgotten all about the abandoned house he stopped to look at in Vertriebstrasse. He has thus missed the opportunity of knowing that the painter Hans Menscher lived there, and was found dead in that very garden on 27th July 1923.

Had the passer-by shown more curiosity and, prompted by the need to know why the house had been abandoned, asked for more details, perhaps – as happened with me – someone would have delved into their memory to recall that July morning and then, with the expression of one trying but failing to remember something, directed him instead to the city's central library.

'If you want to know what happened to Menscher, look in the

newspapers of the time. They're bound to have something about him.'

The passer-by will then endeavour to follow his informant's advice for, like all passers-by, he too has gone out into the street in search of something to relieve the monotony of his life, without knowing quite what that something might be, and following the trail of the painter Menscher seems as good a way as any of spending the afternoon. Continuing with our hypothesis, it would not be long before the passer-by was sitting down in front of one of the many newspapers which, the day after Menscher's death, described what happened in the house on Vertriebstrasse.

Were he to choose the same newspaper I chose, the *Bild Zeitung*, the passer-by would read: 'Hans Menscher, the painter and close friend of Munch, never really fulfilled the promise of his early work. It would not, we believe, be an exaggeration to say that Menscher was lost to painting the day he went mad, rapidly becoming the laughing stock of all who observed him painting in the garden of his house.'

The first reaction of the passer-by, who is now the reader, would be one of surprise. He would probably remember the names of painters whose genius verged on madness without having any ill effects on their work – quite the contrary – and he would want to know the details of the madness from which, according to the journalist, Menscher suffered; a madness which brought about not only his failure as a painter, but also made of him a public laughing-stock, a figure of fun.

Needless to say, there will be no shortage of such details in the article. Indeed, the passer-by, who is well aware of the vileness of life but does not care to dwell too much upon it, will find himself obliged to skip most of the anecdotes that the journalist – with the malice ordinary people reserve for those different from them – poured into his work. And when, at last, the passer-by comes across the concrete fact on which the idea of Menscher's madness was based, the fact will strike him as banal, because it will turn out that Menscher's madness consisted in a view of pictorial art that is taken absolutely for granted today: the idea of painting according to the dictates of the imagination.

'As many Hamburg citizens who walked down his street will know,' the journalist writes, 'the painter seemed incapable of seeing what was right in front of his eyes. After looking hard at his rosebushes, he would take up his brush and with just a few strokes produce, for example, a Mediterranean landscape, a field of almond trees. And if he turned his gaze on Vertriebstrasse, a Greek square or some other exotic landscape would appear. But that was not the worst of it . . .'

Indeed, it wasn't, the worst thing was that people – the bored citizens of Hamburg – would stand on the pavement and keep plying him with questions and the unfortunate Hans – 'unfortunate' being the correct epithet for someone blind to the evil intentions of others – would reply as if *'he really was, body and soul, in the midst of a Mediterranean landscape or in a Greek city, even speaking in some sort of Italian or Greek . . .'*. The italics are, of course, the journalist's.

That was the worst thing, the fact that Menscher slowly became what the English call a 'village idiot' and because of that – again I yield the floor to the journalist – 'no one considered what the consequences of that alienation from reality might be'. The consequences were his tragic death one July morning.

The *Bild Zeitung* journalist relates the circumstances surrounding the incident with a certain glee:

'As many of us who stopped in Vertriebstrasse had the opportunity to observe, for the whole of this past year Menscher painted only one subject. A Moorish city, always the same Moorish city . . . White streets, mosques, medersas, men wearing long robes, women with their faces veiled . . . That was what appeared in the paintings. And along with that mania, there arose in him a rare joy, a joy many considered pathological. When questioned about it, the painter explained the reason for his state of mind as if it were the most natural thing in the world. He said that he was having a love affair with Nabilah, a woman he had met in the city of Jaddig that appeared in his paintings. For those of you unfamiliar with the name, Jaddig is a city situated on the coast of Arabia.'

I imagine Menscher speaking from behind the railings round his garden and I imagine the faces of those who listened to him. I cannot bear that image, it wounds me. On reflection, though, perhaps Menscher really was mad, because only madmen can bear the mocking smiles of the people who address them.

'It seems,' writes the journalist, and it is not hard to imagine a mocking smile on his lips too, 'that the relationship between Menscher and Nabilah was a most passionate one. An old friend of the painter, whose name must remain secret, explained to me that Menscher had spoken to him of that passion in lurid and intimate detail, the kind of detail which, for obvious reasons, we cannot go into here.'

The journalist then emphasises what he said before: 'According to what his childhood friend tells me, the painter spoke of Nabilah as if he had really and truly lain with her in some lowly bed in the city of Jaddig. It is possible that Menscher died believing this to be so . . . That he died or was killed, because it is still unclear as to what exactly happened.'

The journalist is, at last, back on familiar ground. He knows that readers of the article will appreciate the sincerity required in recounting such tragic events and he does his best to achieve this.

'Some months ago,' he writes, 'the painter began to paint a very different image to the one described earlier. There was no longer joy in his heart. On the contrary, he seemed distressed, frightened. When anyone asked him the reason for that change, Menscher replied saying that he had seriously violated the ancient customs of Arabia, which not only forbid carnal relations before marriage but also any relationship between an Arab woman and a foreigner; he and Nabilah had been found out, and now her family were looking for him with the intention of killing him.

Naturally, no one believed his story, although many people felt sorry for Menscher and pitied his sufferings. They thought too that he would get over his bad spell and go back to being happy again.

Unfortunately the exact opposite happened. Menscher's fear became terror and that terror caused him to cry out and run madly from one side of the garden to the other. Menscher asked for help from those who, with a feeling of impotence one can easily imagine, watched from the pavement, uncertain whether to laugh or cry. Now, however, we all know that the situation merited the second reaction, for Hans Menscher is now dead. He was found stabbed to death in his garden yesterday morning, the twenty-seventh of July. The dagger that put an end to his life was authentically Arabian, with a long blade and a damascene hilt – a detail that has been remarked upon in every café conversation.'

The passer-by who made that walk to the library does not feel disappointed. His curiosity has provided him with an entertaining afternoon and he now has a story to tell at supper time. Contented, he goes down the steps of the building and is lost amongst the crowd. However, that passer-by will not have had the luck which, purely by chance, I had; a stroke of luck, as I will now explain, that allowed me to discover how the Menscher story ended.

It happened that I was invited to the house of a retired judge and when he told me that he was writing a book on unsolved court cases, it occurred to me to ask him about the mad painter and the matter of the Arabian dagger that had killed him.

'That case,' he said, 'was indeed never solved.'

Seeing that I was clearly hoping for a more detailed reply, the judge asked me to follow him. When we reached his study, he took down a file from the bookcase and placed in my hands an envelope bearing a seal. My hands trembled: the seal bore Arabic characters.

'Read what the letter says.'

The letter was written in English, a language I do not know well, but well enough to see that it was a request from the police in

Jaddig for information on a German subject, Hans Menscher, giving as a justification for that request a complaint made in their offices by a woman called Nabilah Abauati. In her statement Nabilah Abauati declared that on the night of the twenty-sixth to twenty-seventh of July 1923 three members of her family had murdered the above-mentioned German citizen.

'So,' I asked, 'what really happened?'

'You're forgetting that I deal only in unsolved cases,' smiled the judge and indicated that it was time for us to rejoin the other guests gathered in the drawing room.

How to write a story
in five minutes

TO WRITE a story in just five minutes you need – as well as the customary pen and blank paper, of course – a small hourglass, which will provide accurate information both on the passing of time and on the vanity and worthlessness of the things of this life and, therefore, of the actual effort you are at this moment engaged in. Do not for an instant consider sitting yourself down in front of one of those monotonous and monotone modern walls; let your gaze lose itself in the open landscape that spreads itself before you outside your window and in the sky where seagulls and other such medium-weight birds trace the geometry of their fleeting pleasure. It is also necessary, though less essential, that you listen to music, to some song whose words are incomprehensible to you, a song in Russian, for example. Having done this, turn inwards, bite your own tail, peer through your own personal telescope at the place where your entrails are silently working away, ask your body if it is cold, if it is thirsty, if it is both cold and thirsty or suffering from any other kind of discomfort. If the answer is in the affirmative, if, for example, you feel a general tickling sensation, do not fall prey to anxiety, for it would be strange indeed if you managed to settle down to your work at the first attempt. Look at the hourglass, whose lower portion is still almost empty, and you will see that, as yet, not even half a minute has gone by. Don't get nervous, go calmly to the kitchen, taking small steps or dragging your feet as you prefer. Drink a little water – if it's iced water, take the opportunity to splash some on your neck – and before returning to sit down at the table take a nice, quiet leak (in the toilet, that is, because peeing in the corridor is not, in principle, an essential attribute of the literary man).

The seagulls are still there, so are the sparrows, and there too – on the shelf to your left – is a large dictionary. Pick it up with the greatest of care, as if it were charged with electricity, as if it were a platinum blonde. Then – taking care to notice the sound the pen makes as it scratches the surface of the paper – write down this sentence: 'To write a story in just five minutes you need.'

There you have your beginning, which is no small thing, and barely two minutes have passed since you sat down to work. You not only have the first sentence, in the large dictionary you are holding in your left hand you also have everything else you require. That book contains everything, absolutely everything; believe me, the power of those words is infinite.

Let yourself be carried along by instinct and imagine that you, yes, you, are the Golem, a man or woman made up of letters, or rather, constructed entirely of symbols. And allow the letters of which you are composed to go forth – the way one stick of dynamite sets off all the others – in search of their sisters, those drowsy sisters asleep in the dictionary.

Some time has passed but a glance at the hourglass shows that not even half the time at your disposal has gone.

And suddenly, like a shooting star, the first sister awakens and comes to you, enters your head and lies down, humbly, inside your brain. You must write that word down at once and write it in capital letters for it has grown on the journey. It is a short word, agile and swift; it is the word NET.

And it is that word which puts all the others on their guard and a noise, like the one you might hear on opening the doors of a drawing class, fills the whole room. After a short while, another word appears in your right hand. Ah, my friend, all unwitting you have become a magician. The second word grabs the penshaft, slides down it, leaps on to the nib and scrawls something in ink. The scrawl says: HANDS.

Just as if you were opening a surprise packet, pull the end of that thread (forgive me if I seem over-familiar, we are fellow travellers after all), as I was saying, pull the end of that thread as if you were opening a surprise packet. Then greet the new landscape, the new sentence that comes wrapped in a parenthesis: *(Yes, I covered my face with this dense net the day my hands got burned.)*

Three minutes have just passed. But behold you have barely written down the previous sentence when many more sentences, many, many more, come to you like moths drawn to the flame of a gaslamp. You have to choose, it's painful, but you have to choose. So, think hard and open the new parenthesis: *(People felt sorry for me. They felt sorry, above all, because they thought my face must have been burned too; and I was convinced that the secret made me superior to them all and mocked their morbid curiosity.)*

You still have two minutes. You don't need the dictionary now, don't waste any more time looking up words. Pay attention to your own inner fission, to the contagious verbal sickness that grows and grows in you and will not stop. Quickly, please, write down the third sentence: *(They know that I was beautiful once and that every day twelve men would send me flowers.)*

Now write down the fourth sentence as well, which comes treading hard on the heels of the previous one and says: *(One of those men deliberately burned his face, thinking that this would put us on a level, place us in the same, painful situation. He wrote me a letter saying: Now we are equal, take my action as a proof of my love.)*

And the last minute is just beginning to empty itself out when you are already in the middle of the penultimate sentence: *(I wept bitterly for many nights. I wept for my own pride and for my lover's humility; I thought that, to be absolutely fair, I should do the same, I should burn my face too.)*

You have to write the last part in less than forty seconds, time is running out: *(If I did not do so it was not because I feared the physical suffering involved nor out of any other fear, but because I understood that a loving relationship that began with such a display of strength would, necessarily, have a far more prosaic ending. On the other hand, I could not let him know my secret, it would have been too cruel. That's why I went to his house tonight. He too had covered his face with a veil. I offered him my breasts and we made love in silence; he was happy when I plunged this knife into his heart. And now all that remains for me is to weep for my own ill fortune.)*

And close the parenthesis – thus ending the story – just as the last grain of sand drops into the bottom of the hourglass.

KLAUS HANHN

I T WAS the second day to dawn in the month of September, a
Monday, and Klaus Hanhn opened his eyes surprised to find
that the three alarm clocks lined up on the carpet in his bedroom
had just gone off, one after another, each one ringing out and
demanding, as they always did, that he get up, get up and go to
work, as soon as possible.

The clocks told him that it was five fifteen in the morning. The
message was strident and unpleasant.

As soon as he was fully conscious of his situation, Klaus Hanhn
gave an angry sigh and closed his eyes again. There was no reason
for the clocks to have woken him, not on that Monday, not on that
second day of September. For that was the day he had chosen as the
day on which he would Change His Life; it was both the day of his
forty-seventh birthday and the day on which his Great New Era
was to begin. No, the three clocks that he usually needed to rouse
him from his leaden slumbers had not gone off because he wanted
them to. They had done so only because of some aberration on his
part the night before.

He drew his hands out from under the sheets and, without
bothering to switch on the light, groped for the clocks on the
carpet. But no sooner had he turned the first one off than he gave up
and lay back in bed again. In fact, it rather suited him to listen to the
clamour. It highlighted this moment he was living through, it
made him more intensely aware of the nature – the good nature of
course – of the New Era he had just entered upon. Let them ring
and clatter out the warning that it was five fifteen in the morning,
that, however sleepy he felt, he had no alternative but to go to
work. What did he care? He was no longer in their sway. Let them
ring. He was not going to obey, not now or ever again.

'Who's going to stop you staying in bed, Klaus?' asked his little brother Alexander from inside. Alexander was dead, or at least that was what they'd told him: that he'd been dead for many years, that he'd drowned amongst the reeds of the River Elbe when they'd gone on a trip there with their schoolfellows. But he didn't believe them. He knew that Alexander had simply changed places. Ever since that day he had been not outside, but inside, and from time to time he spoke to him, especially at moments of importance. It filled him with joy to hear his brother's childish voice and he almost always followed his advice. Because he loved him very much, very, very much.

'No one, Alexander. No one can,' he replied, smiling. Then he turned over and went back to sleep.

Some hours later, when the sun shone directly into his eyes and woke him from that second sleep, he felt full of contradictory feelings, sudden as the onset of palpitations. He felt excited and happy, because the manner of his waking confirmed the reality of his changed life; but, unfortunately, there was fear there too. A vague, dull fear that might well go on growing throughout the day, little by little, the way a headache grows until it becomes intolerable. What would the future bring? Would it give him everything he needed? He had no way of knowing and his brother Alexander didn't have the answer either. But, despite that, he tended to the belief that all the work of the previous months would bear fruit. The important thing was not to allow himself to succumb to fear. It was the morning of the second of September. Another twenty-four hours and he would be out of danger.

Klaus Hanhn raised the blind and saw that the sky on this his Decisive Day was cloudless. It was a good sign. After white, his favourite colour was blue.

'Klaus Hanhn?' he asked, leaving his bedroom and walking into the middle of the living room.

The large mirror there framed him completely, from head to foot. It was oval in shape and could be inclined forwards or backwards by means of a wooden hinge. That morning it was inclined forwards making Klaus look rather smaller than he really was.

The image nodded, smiling.

'Well, in that case, many congratulations,' he said, bowing.

The figure in the mirror hurriedly returned his bow and then stood there looking at him, direct, serious, searching. Yes, there was no doubt about it, he was forty-seven years old. The wrinkles told him he was, the deep lines on his forehead told him, his very expression told him. And, on reflection, it seemed absurd, it was very difficult to fit all those years into the anagram of his life. For where were the events to fill up all that time? He couldn't find them and even Alexander was not much help in that particular enterprise, since his brother – a mere child after all – knew nothing of the passing of time. But, despite that, there was no denying the facts. He was forty-seven years old. Perhaps it was too late to change his life.

'Is it too late, Klaus?' he asked the mirror.

But before anyone could answer the question, the mirror emptied and their conversation was interrupted. The noise of hundreds of car horns drifted up from the street.

'A traffic jam, Klaus. A beautiful sight, eh?' Alexander remarked when Klaus opened the window and leaned out.

'It certainly is, Alexander,' he agreed.

Surrounded by cars, the traffic lights on Bulachweg changed vainly from green to red and from red to green. Opposite his front door, a man delivering bread was cursing the traffic jam that had boxed in his van between two buses.

With his gaze fixed on the van, it occurred to Klaus Hanhn that for the third time that morning – the blue sky and the alarm clocks had been the other instances – destiny was taking the trouble to send him signals to help him understand the advantages of his new way of life. For he too, in that past he had only just left behind, had been a humble baker's deliveryman; from six in the morning until five in the afternoon, every day, even on Saturdays. His life had consisted of just that, of delivering bread, ordinary bread to the shops, speciality and specially ordered bread to the houses of the wealthy in the prosperous parts of the city. He was all too familiar with the traffic jams that held up deliveries and lengthened the working day. That very Monday he could have been in the same situation as the deliveryman sitting there shouting and fuming in his van. But the fact was that his clocks said it was ten past ten and he wasn't out there. No, he wasn't out in the street, but at home. And what's more, he'd unplugged the phone. No one could call him, no one could ask him why he hadn't gone to work.

Destiny smiled on the brave, for he had been brave. He would never go back to the van.

This second of September had to be different in every way from other days, even in its most insignificant details, and so instead of his usual shower Klaus Hanhn took an invigorating bath with the water at 70°F. Then he returned to the living room and breakfasted on tea, toast and butter, sitting on the sofa, naked, with the sun shining full on him. He wanted to dry in the sun, slowly. From that day forth, he would always live that way, sweetly and slowly, like a sleeping fish letting itself be borne along by the current.

When he'd breakfasted, he plugged in his phone again and called a taxi. He put his clothes on over his still damp skin and went down to the front door.

Half an hour later he was going into one of the plushest department stores on Avenue Kieler. He asked to be shown their most expensive clothes and the shop assistant, dropping the bored tone she had adopted when greeting him, asked him what sort of clothes he meant.

Klaus explained that he wanted a complete head-to-toe change of outfit. He needed underwear, socks, a shirt and a pair of shoes all in blue and then, and this was the most important part, a light summer suit, in white. And he wanted to wear it now. If they wouldn't mind – he knew they wouldn't – he would leave the clothes he was wearing with them.

'Are you sure you want a summer suit? Summer won't last for ever,' argued the shop assistant with a look of unexpected complicity. She pointed to the small calendar next to the cash register. Autumn was nearly upon them and it could be very chilly.

'It's always summer on the island of turtles,' said Klaus with the same complicit smile worn by the shop assistant.

'Whatever made you say that, Klaus?' he heard a voice say. Alexander's tone was sharp, reproachful.

Klaus' smile vanished from his face. That remark about the turtles – a travel agent's slogan – could be seen written in huge letters across a background of palmtrees on nearly every advertising hoarding in the city. His witty riposte meant that the shop assistant was now in possession of information that could put his whole New Era at risk.

'You've acted unwisely, Klaus. This woman will remember the answer you gave. Let's just hope the information never reaches certain other people's ears,' whispered Alexander.

His little brother was right. He wanted to live peacefully, like a sleeping fish, letting himself be borne along by the current; but, even when asleep, fishes ensured a happy ending to their dreams by always keeping one part of their brain alert. He should follow their example. He should not forget the existence of other fish, unsleeping, vigilant, more powerful than he; fish that could smell blood and track it down to its source. He must beware of them. Another twenty-four hours and he would be safe. Until then he must act prudently.

'Where are you going?' exclaimed Klaus when he saw the shop assistant making for the telephone installed at the other end of the counter. His expression was one of anguish.

'She's going to call the police. Kill her, Klaus! Kill her now!' Alexander shouted. Being a child, he could not distinguish between good and bad and sometimes behaved foolishly. Especially when he was frightened.

'Don't talk nonsense, Alexander!' he shouted back. Then, his hands drenched in sweat, he followed the shop assistant over to the phone. But she was still smiling at him. She seemed to suspect nothing.

'We don't keep all our stock here in the shop. We have to get some things from the warehouse in the basement,' she said. Then, lowering her eyes and putting her lips to the phone, she asked: 'Have we got any blue shoes?'

The shop assistant hung up and at the same time nodded to him. Yes, they did have blue shoes. He would leave the shop dressed just the way he wanted. In a couple of minutes she would return with all the clothes he'd asked for.

Klaus took advantage of the shop assistant's absence to speak with his younger brother. They must not lose their heads and succumb to fear, because fear was the worst counsellor: it concealed the roads leading to salvation and lit instead those that led straight into the abyss. Moreover, he almost never acted the way he had when he'd made that remark about the island of turtles.

'You're right, Alexander. I'm usually very prudent. If I weren't, I wouldn't have reserved tonight's air ticket six months in advance.'

But the shop assistant was calling him over. Klaus broke off his inner dialogue and went to try on the white suit.

By the time he left the shop it was gone midday and the sun's rays were falling vertically on Avenue Kieler. The pavements were filled with lunchtime office workers making for the park around the Binnenalster lake.

Choosing the opposite direction, Klaus began walking towards the St Pauli district, in one of whose streets – Brauerstrasse – was the city's most famous beauty salon for men, Sebastian.

It was not the first time he'd made that walk but nevertheless he had the impression that, from the moment he set out, everything was completely new and different: what he saw, what he heard, what he felt. Luckily for him, the novelty lay not outside but inside himself. For the Klaus Hanhn of that second day of

September had nothing whatsoever to do with the former baker's deliveryman who, late on Saturday afternoons, would go to the salon and make do with only the cheapest services offered. And that impression grew stronger with every sideways glance at the shopwindows he passed, because all the reflections, in all their multiplicity, spoke of the same thing: of a rich man dressed all in white, enjoying a summer stroll.

'Klaus Hanhn?' he asked, stopping on the pavement.

Alexander warned him that talking to a florist's shopwindow was a little eccentric and that passers-by might begin to ask questions. But he didn't care about passers-by. All that mattered was that new man clasping a bunch of tulips to his chest.

'So you're Klaus Hanhn!' he exclaimed, putting on a surprised face.

The figure in the reflection nodded and began to laugh. But his laugh was not a guffaw, it was a soft tremor that emerged from some place far from his heart and gradually expanded outwards to his skin. That laugh had lain submerged since he was six or seven years old, and now at last it lived again.

'Aren't you laughing, Alexander?' he asked as he walked on.

'Can't you see that I am?' replied his brother.

He reached the door of Sebastian's almost without realising it. Happiness made distances seem much shorter, there was no room for weariness in a happy heart.

Manicures, French lotions, facial massages using a method imported from the Orient – that's what the poster said, 'imported' – exclusively for you. Klaus read the list with amusement and then firmly pushed open the door. He was prepared to try each and every one of the house's specialities.

A young woman led him to a room rather like a dressing room.

'Do you think you could make me taller? I'd like to be as tall as you,' he joked. The woman was in fact very tall.

'There are some things I can't do, at least not yet. But I will leave you looking more handsome,' she replied, rubbing a reddish liquid into his face. Her accent recalled the proximity of the St Pauli nightclubs.

'That'll do fine,' Klaus said. In fact, he didn't need to be any taller. According to the travel brochure, the inhabitants of the island of turtles were all fairly short in stature.

'First I'll give you a full body massage. Put your nice clothes on those hangers over there and lie down,' ordered the masseuse in decidedly professional tones. She pointed theatrically to the place – to 'those hangers' – rather like an airhostess indicating the emergency exits.

Klaus Hanhn recognised the gestures and his thoughts drifted off to the journey he would make that night. He thought about the airport, the suitcases he had checked in the day before, the twenty gift-wrapped belts he'd placed in those suitcases and the ten thousand marks – folded and refolded – contained in each of those belts. Twenty belts, two hundred thousand marks. The treasure that was to provide the foundation of this New Era of his Life.

Then he thought of the savings which would allow him to do without that treasure for a sensible period of time. Far off on the island of turtles. Eight hours from now night would fall and the red, winking light of the plane would make its way through the darkness of the sky.

The hands of the masseuse pressed into his flesh, producing tiny spasms of pain which as suddenly became pleasure. He closed his eyes in order, mentally, to follow the flight path of the plane until it landed on the island. But there was so much joy in his heart that he couldn't think. It blinded him, the way the sun blinds those who look directly at it.

The objectives he'd set himself for the morning of his birthday ended there, with the visit to Sebastian's beauty salon. Out on the pavement of Brauerstrasse again, Klaus hesitated over which direction to take. He looked at his watch. It was two o'clock.

'Which is the best restaurant in this sad city, Alexander?' he asked as he looked up and down the street, completely empty at that hour. But his little brother knew nothing about the banal facts of the world and remained silent. 'I'll go to the Paris restaurant,' Klaus decided after a moment's thought.

It was a restaurant frequented by all the wealthy inhabitants of the prosperous parts of the city, the ones who ordered speciality breads for their family suppers. It was bound to be excellent. Moreover, it was in the Stadtpark, not far from Brauerstrasse.

Klaus raised an arm and hailed a taxi.

'The Paris restaurant, please,' he said to the driver with feigned tedium. He tried to disguise his normal accent.

'There's no need to talk like that, Klaus. You're wearing so much cologne, no one would dare question your high social status,' said Alexander with a little smile he intended to be ironical.

The dining room of the restaurant was broken up by golden columns and the tables – about twenty at most – were scattered around a huge glass aquarium. Through the restaurant windows you could see the trees in the Stadtpark, their leaves already stained with red. The napkins were blue and the tablecloths white.

Klaus Hanhn sat down at a table near the aquarium, with his back to the other customers. He wanted to dine facing the tropical fish that swam in the aquarium.

'It would be a good idea to get accustomed to what we'll be seeing on the island of turtles, Alexander,' he remarked.

'What's your name?' he said in a firm voice. The question was directed at the waiter who'd just approached him bearing the menu.

'Marcel, *monsieur*,' replied the waiter, rather ruffled.

'*Très bien*, Marcel. I want your best advice. Today is my birthday.'

Klaus was looking apprehensively at the menu he held in his hands. Despite the fact that the ingredients of each dish were given in brackets below, in small writing, in a manner he could understand, most of the names written there were utterly incomprehensible to him.

'Our *savarin* is excellent, *monsieur*,' the waiter advised him, having murmured a few words of congratulation.

'*Savarin* it is then.'

Klaus tried to find that particular dish and ascertain its ingredients. But he couldn't. He got lost in that strange menu.

'Isn't that rather a strange name for a meat?' he hazarded.

'Forgive me, *monsieur*, but it is in fact a fish. But you're quite right. It is rather a strange name,' agreed the waiter giving him a friendly smile.

'Of course, of course,' he said hurriedly.

'You've made a fool of yourself,' he heard a voice say. His brother's voice was sharp, as it always was when he wanted to hurt him.

They were brothers and they loved each other, but there were times when Alexander didn't seem to understand him.

'You know what Marcel will say as soon as he gets to the kitchen, don't you?' he went on in that same sharp tone. 'He'll say that the customer sitting at the table next to the aquarium is a fraud, a vulgar man putting on the airs of a rich one. You really made a fool of yourself there, Klaus.'

A cold sweat broke out on Klaus' forehead and hands. He was still looking for that *savarin*.

'There it is, *monsieur*,' said the waiter helpfully, bending over the menu.

'I can see it! I can see it!' said Klaus brusquely. The dish (*Savarin scandinave avec brocoli d'aneth*) appeared in a separate section of the menu, amongst the ten dishes recommended by the chef that day.

The price of the dish made him open his eyes wide. It was ten times the price of any meal he'd eaten in his long and still very recent past.

'Fine. Bring me that,' he ordered the waiter. But he was stunned by the price and had to make a tremendous effort not to show it.

'You think like a poor man, Klaus. You're rich and you still

233

think like a poor man. You'll never change,' the sharp voice said reproachfully.

'Be quiet, Alexander!' All those years together and he still didn't understand what made his little brother tick. Sometimes he turned against him, for no reason. It was as if he enjoyed making him suffer.

'And as an *hors d'oeuvre, monsieur?*'

'*Crêpes de roquefort,*' replied Klaus, without knowing what it was he was ordering.

'And a white wine of the region? A Rhine wine perhaps?' The waiter was still smiling but not as warmly as before. For a moment Klaus thought he caught an air of mockery in his look.

'Perfect! Just what I need! A Rhine wine!' agreed Klaus enthusiastically. But his enthusiasm rang false.

When the waiter disappeared off amongst the columns, Klaus tried to fix his attention on the trees, still full of sun, in the Stadtpark, or on the tropical fish in the aquarium. But it was in vain that he tried to redirect his thoughts. Again and again they returned to the *savarin scandinave* that had made a fool out of him. All morning he'd been the sleeping fish he wanted to be, thinking he was being borne along on a gentle current. A dream, nothing but a dream. A slight disturbance of the waters was all it had taken for him to wake and realise that the current didn't exist. He wasn't in the sea, he wasn't in a river; he was in a fish tank, just like those tropical fish in the restaurant. Except the fish tank he lived in was smaller. It suffocated him, made him sweat.

'It's all your fault, Klaus,' said the sharp voice.

Alexander's reproaches increased the anxiety he was feeling at that moment and he was pleased to hear the waiter's voice at his side. He had brought him the bottle of Rhine wine.

'Would you like to taste it, *monsieur?*'

The wine was the colour of amber. Klaus nodded.

'Do you have any paper?' he asked, after approving the quality of the wine.

'Paper, *monsieur?*' The waiter wore a look of incomprehension.
'To write a few short notes. Can't waste any time, you know.
I'd like to, but I can't.'

'Now you've got it, Klaus. Now you're talking,' he heard
inside him and Klaus smiled with satisfaction. Alexander's voice
was no longer sharp.

'Would a few postcards do?' said the waiter going over to the
sideboard beneath the aquarium. 'There's a picture of the
restaurant on the front,' he went on, returning to the table and
placing a few cards on the cloth.

'Fine, Marcel. Many thanks. They'll do nicely,' said Klaus
picking up the wine bottle and refilling his glass.

He addressed the first note to his company's personnel
director. He justified his absence from work – as well as his
presence in an expensive restaurant – with an allusion to a sudden
decision to get married. He hoped he would understand and
assured him that he would be back on the van as soon as possible.

However, the tone of the note changed in the last two lines.
The postscript read:

'I shouldn't be away for much more than thirty years. And I
would be most grateful if by that time you could be dead.'

Klaus heard Alexander giggling inside him and he too laughed.
He knew the head of personnel very well and could imagine his
hysterical cries when he finished reading the card. That's why he
wrote to him, just to sour his life a little.

'You should have killed him,' whispered Alexander.

'Be quiet, silly,' Klaus said, but affectionately, the way one
says such things to children. That amber-coloured wine was
putting him in a good mood.

He took more trouble over the second note and was still
finishing it when the *crêpes de roquefort* arrived on the table.

'Your little fish bids you farewell, for ever. By the time you
receive this postcard, I'll be far away. I know you won't understand
but it doesn't matter. You never understood about Alexander and

that doesn't matter either. I doubt that you'll miss me. It's better this way. I'd write more but I don't know what to say. Have fun.'

He signed both cards, wrote the addresses and handed them to the waiter.

'Could you make sure these get posted, Marcel?'

'Of course, *monsieur*. We'll post them tomorrow.'

'Thank you, Marcel.'

'I think you may need more wine, *monsieur*,' remarked the waiter, pointing to the almost empty bottle on the table.

'Yes, bring me another bottle, please. I always need to be in a good mood before I can write,' smiled Klaus. The waiter returned his smile and served him what remained of the first bottle.

Neither the wine nor the meal agreed with him. He grew hotter and hotter and when – as he was trying to do justice to the *savarin* – he took off his jacket, he saw with disgust that the sweat from his armpits had darkened the blue of his shirt. The stains were even visible in the distorted image one of the golden columns gave back.

'The bill, please!' he shouted suddenly and all the remaining customers in the restaurant turned round to look at him. He had decided to abandon that disgusting *savarin* and leave as soon as possible. He needed air, he was suffocating. 'Marcel, the bill!' he cried again.

The waiter ran over to him, taking short steps to disguise his haste.

'You're leaving, *monsieur*? You don't want anything else?' His face bore an expression of alarm.

'Yes, I want to leave!' Klaus' right hand grasped one of the corners of the tablecloth.

'Please, be patient. I'll bring you your bill right away. I'm so sorry, *monsieur*.'

'No, no, I'm sorry, it's just that I have to go home,' said Klaus, excusing himself and lowering his voice. After all the shouting he felt empty and drained. His head felt heavy.

'I'll be back in a minute, *monsieur*.'

His head not only felt heavy now, it was spinning too and he had difficulty getting up from the table. Afterwards, when he had already bumped into the aquarium twice, he decided to lean against one of the columns and wait there for them to bring him the bill.

'Lovely fish, Marcel, really lovely,' he remarked when the waiter returned. He paid for the meal with two one hundred mark notes. 'Keep the change,' he added. The change was forty marks.

'How generous you've become, Klaus! You can tell you're drunk.'

Alexander's voice contained an obvious note of mockery.

'Thank you very much, *monsieur*,' the waiter said, almost bowing.

'Don't forget the postcards, please. They're most important to me. I'm serious, Marcel. Affairs of the heart. You know what I mean.'

He found it difficult to enunciate, his tongue got entangled with the words.

'Don't worry, *monsieur*. I won't forget.' The waiter was gradually, gently, hustling him towards the door.

'Anyway,' Klaus began, stopping and turning round, 'the fish on the island of turtles are much prettier. I mean it. Much much prettier. You get some really incredible fish there.'

'Of course, *monsieur*. Would you like me to call you a taxi? I'll call you a taxi if you want me to. It's no bother.'

'I may not have appreciated that *savarin* as I should have, Marcel. I'm sorry. If you only knew. . . ,' said Klaus, with a look of genuine desolation. The fact that he had been unable to finish that dish began to take on great significance for him. It symbolised all the other failures in his life.

'Another day, *monsieur*. Come back another day. You'll really enjoy it then, you'll see. We all have our off days,' the waiter said consolingly, sighing.

'I don't think I'll be able to come back, Marcel. Seriously. Really. In a few hours . . .'

'Shut up, Klaus. You're a fool. You always have been,' he heard a voice say inside him.

Klaus was almost on the point of revealing his travel plans to the waiter, despite Alexander. But one glance at the aquarium stopped him. The tropical fish were all gathered in one corner of the tank, observing him gravely. They didn't think much of his attitude either. Why was he talking so much? Didn't he know when to shut up? His brain was unworthy of a fish. He couldn't see the warning signs.

Klaus put a finger to his lips.

'Shut up!' he said to himself.

'Would you like me to call you a taxi, *monsieur*?' repeated the waiter.

'*Merci beaucoup*, Marcel. You're very kind. I am actually feeling a little unwell.' The waiter rushed off to the telephone.

'So you're unwell, are you? Don't make me laugh, Klaus,' said the harsh voice.

'You're very cruel sometimes, Alexander. I know I've drunk a bit too much. After all, it is my birthday,' replied Klaus, a complaining note creeping into his voice.

The tropical fish were swimming back and forth in the tank again. Klaus gave them a knowing wink.

'I'm a thinker too, my friends!', he told them.

'The taxi won't be long, *monsieur*. It will wait for you at the gate to the park,' the waiter announced.

'Many thanks, Marcel. I mean that,' said Klaus, slapping him on the back. Then he stumbled out of the restaurant and walked over to the taxi.

An hour later he was opening the door to his flat. He had made the journey with the taxi windows down and he no longer felt quite so dazed. But he was still glad that he had everything prepared. The most important part of his luggage was already at the airport. The rest – an overnight bag – waited in a corner of the living room. All that remained was for him to rest a little and then say goodbye to that cheap flat. He didn't like it but, nonetheless, he had lived there for forty-seven years.

Before sitting down on the sofa, he brought the three alarm clocks into the room and took out the old hunting rifle from the cupboard where he had put it the night before. Klaus kissed the rifle and laughed.

'You're drunk, Klaus,' said the harsh voice.

'Thanks very much,' he said to the rifle. He had bought it from a workmate two years earlier and had only used it once.

'Yesterday morning,' thought Klaus, surprised. It seemed much longer than that since he had used it to hold the bank manager's family hostage. But the impression was entirely false, only twenty-four hours had passed since then. 'I'm calling from your home. I have your wife and two daughters with me. I presume that you do at least love your daughters. I need two hundred thousand marks. It's up to you if you bring them to me or not, but it would be best if you did so without a word to anyone else, since I forgot to mention that I have a rifle in my hand with six bullets in it. Bring the money and no one will get hurt.'

However, later – Klaus recalled with sadness – he had had to kill them all, not because he wanted to, but because of Alexander, because Alexander, being only a child, didn't understand how horrible death was. Generally, he took no notice of him and refused to follow his orders to kill. He only obeyed when he was upset.

'And, unfortunately, yesterday I was very upset,' thought Klaus, yawning.

'You've drunk too much wine, Klaus. You're talking nonsense,' said the harsh voice.

'I'm sleepy, Alexander,' he replied. His eyes were closing.

'Get up at once, Klaus. You can sleep all you want to on the island of turtles!' shouted Alexander. 'You're here now and you haven't even looked at yourself in the mirror. You should take a bit more care over your new appearance,' he added afterwards in a gentler voice.

'All right, Alexander, all right,' said Klaus obediently. Sometimes his little brother bored him. Why make him get up at a moment when even his white suit weighed heavy on him. He didn't understand how he could be so capricious.

'Klaus Hanhn?' he asked, having planted himself in the middle of the room.

The figure in the mirror nodded, just as it had that morning, but not as enthusiastically as he had hoped. The white suit looked good, as did the rifle inclined against his chest, but everything else was wrong. Especially his face. The sweat had ruined the work of all those skincreams. The red blotches had appeared again.

'The greasy skin and the blotches,' the doctor had said, 'are congenital in nature.'

He remembered that he still had one bullet in the rifle chamber and he levelled the weapon at his own image, at the red blotches on his face. He took his aim of the target – sure, unmoving – opening and closing one eye. From the other side, in ironic symmetry, the other marksman reflected back.

'I'd be sure to win,' shouted Klaus, laughing out loud and throwing the rifle to the floor. The figure in the mirror laughed just like him and he too withdrew from the duel. Both of them were decidedly drunk.

He was just about to pick up the rifle again when the telephone rang. Startled by the ringing, Klaus wheeled around and fell onto the sofa.

'I don't want to talk to you!' he shouted. 'I've explained it all on the postcard!' The telephone kept ringing. Its sheer persistence irritated him. 'I've celebrated my birthday already! I dined on *savarin!*'

Remembering that dish brought on another fit of laughter.

The laughter and the ringing ended at the same time and Klaus took advantage of the quiet to see what time it was by the three alarm clocks. It was just a few minutes before five o'clock.

'Four hours before I get the plane,' he thought with a grimace of boredom. They would seem like an eternity. Even longer with the headache he could feel coming on.

'So much time!' he sighed, rubbing his eyes. He could go to the airport now, but it wouldn't be wise. Anyway, he didn't feel like moving.

'Get up this minute, Klaus!' ordered Alexander seeing him leaning back against one of the arms of the sofa. 'Don't go to sleep without setting the alarm clocks!' he warned.

Alexander's proposal seemed reasonable. Whether he wanted to or not, he would end up going to sleep and it was best to take precautions. Yes, he would go to sleep for a couple of hours and then go to the airport. Given the circumstances, that seemed the most intelligent thing to do. These final steps had to be taken calmly.

Without getting up from the sofa, he reached out and began to set the alarm clocks. He set the first for two minutes to seven, the second for one minute to seven and the third for seven o'clock exactly. One of the three was bound to wake him.

He stretched out on the sofa and, knowing that sleep would not be long in coming, he forced himself to think about that dreamed-of island of turtles. The island was small and in the shape of a snail. However – if the information given him by the travel agency was correct – it lacked for nothing and was suitably equipped to welcome all first-class visitors. It had two hotels, about two hundred bungalows and one hundred country cottages. And there was more: garages, cafés and restaurants, three large cinemas and a small port bobbing with white yachts. The whole island was full of life and colour, and such was the *joie de vivre* of the islanders that they spent the whole day singing. The palmtrees were not to be sniffed at either. They were the tallest palmtrees in the world; they fringed the beaches. And the beaches – that was the most marvellous part – were tremendously wide and long and encircled the island like a ring of sand. The sea was blue in the morning and emerald in the evening and the vast majority of the fish were red.

OBABAKOAK

Klaus looked hard at those red fish. They let themselves be carried on the emerald waves, advancing and retreating. It was as if the sea were rocking them to sleep.

'You were right, *monsieur*. They are lovely fish. Far lovelier than the fish in the restaurant,' said someone at his side. Klaus opened his eyes and saw that it was Marcel, the waiter from the Paris restaurant. Along with his bow tie, he was now wearing a pair of swimming trunks, white with black dots.

'We don't eat *savarin* on this island, Marcel,' he said. But the waiter had vanished from the beach.

'He must have gone for a swim,' he thought, looking out at the emerald sea. But only red fish were swimming there.

'He must have drowned,' he decided, lying down again on the sand. He felt the heat of the sun on his face, especially on his eyelids.

'Klaus, get up this instant!' he heard a voice say shortly afterwards.

On the very spot where the waiter had stood there was now a child. He was wearing yellow trunks and was smiling scornfully at him.

'What are you doing out there, Alexander?' Klaus asked, averting his eyes from that smile.

Just then he heard a strange whistling noise.

'Who's that whistling?' he asked. But he got no reply.

No sooner had he asked the question than he heard another whistle just as loud as the previous one and shortly afterwards a third whistle.

'Klaus, get up this instant! Get up, you idiot!' shouted Alexander giving him a kick in the ribs.

'Why are you kicking me, Alexander? If you do that, I'll throw you in the water and you'll drown. Just like that day we went on the trip up the River Elbe!' whined Klaus.

'I hate you, Klaus!'

'It was your fault, Alexander! I pushed you in because you kept

242

kicking me!' Crying openly now, Klaus turned his head away. He didn't want to hear what his little brother was saying.

As soon as he turned his head he saw them. Three very large green turtles. They were sitting on a rock whistling and stretching out their necks.

'So it was the turtles. I never expected them to make a noise like that,' thought Klaus. It bothered him to know that. He hadn't reckoned on finding anything unpleasant on the island.

One of the turtles fell silent.

'The big one is bound to stop now too,' he thought. And the big turtle also stopped whistling. Only the one on the highest part of the rock continued.

'That must be the oldest one,' he remarked.

'Shut up, you old devil!'

It didn't obey him at once, but then, finally, it too fell silent. Klaus sighed, relieved, and scoured the beach for his younger brother. But the beach was empty.

'You were right to go back inside, Alexander. You're better off in there. Every time you come out, we quarrel and that's a terrible thing to happen between brothers,' he said.

From on high the sun dominated the sky and once the whistling of the turtles had ceased, the sound of the waves seemed very pleasant to him. It rocked him ever more gently, growing ever further and further away . . .

MARGARETE AND
HEINRICH, TWINS

L ET US suppose that what is about to begin is a story of
some ten to twelve pages in length, and let us make that
hypothesis more specific by saying that the protagonists of
the story will be the characters whose names appear in the title, that
is, Margarete and Heinrich, twins, who at the time of the events
described – the autumn of 1934 – were living apart in two different
cities in Germany.

We used the third person plural of the past imperfect, 'they
were living', to apply to both brother and sister and to a whole
autumn. However, we are obliged to use this second paragraph to
clarify the previous statement since the death of one of them – of
Margarete, to be exact – is one of the basic premises of the
hypothesis. Let us add, then, that Margarete died at a train station
right at the beginning of the aforementioned autumn and that she
disappeared overnight, suddenly, like one of those sea birds who,
on being mortally wounded, abandon the air and plunge into the
sea for ever.

But death, even a death of the kind we are dealing with now,
cannot remain secret; if it is to be complete, it requires someone to
record it and to make it known. Let us add then a few more details
to those already set out: first, those relating to the letter sent to
Heinrich by a Bavarian judge; second, those relating to the
circumstances surrounding the reading of the said letter. And let us
do so in the verbal forms which, although inappropriate for a
hypothetical style, are much more comfortable to use.

The Bavarian judge said:

'It is my duty to inform you that your sister Margarete Wetzel
died at 00.15 on 22nd September. It would seem that she fell
beneath the wheels of a train at that moment entering the station.

We will write to you again as soon as our investigations are completed. We do not exclude the possibility that it may have been a murder.'

Circumstances and relevant facts.

Firstly, the port of Hamburg, where Heinrich was working a crane on quay number eight and, more specifically, that crane's cabin of unbreakable glass from which he could easily see the whole deck of the ship he was loading. As regards weather conditions, a rainy afternoon, the second day of October. In respect of the ineffable, an oversight, for Heinrich – who had given no importance to an apparently official letter – did not think to read it until several days after putting it into one of his overall pockets.

Having reached this point, we crave the reader's indulgence – as the old balladeers used to say – and ask you to allow the writer to forget all about the original hypothesis. Because otherwise the use of formulae, such as those used up until now, would prove unavoidable and would serve only to encumber the narrative flow. Let us, then, continue with the story, telling it as if it had really happened.

As soon as he had read the letter, Heinrich threw his head back so that it touched the steel plate at the back of the cabin. He felt his heart begin to beat wildly, frenetically pumping blood, as if wanting to spread throughout his whole body the blow it had felt on reading the judge's letter. Very soon the pain reached his knees, his lungs, his guts.

He lay exhausted and absent from the world about him, oblivious to the hard rain falling at that moment and to the other workers shouting up to him from the quay. When, at last, he emerged from his abstraction, he heard the scream of a seagull and, instinctively, began to follow its flight with his eyes. The seagull descended from the clouds and alighted on the prow of the ship he was loading. There he read the name: *Three sisters*.

Heinrich's eyes lost sight of the bird and remained fixed and amazed on the twelve letters making up the ship's name.

'I only had one sister,' he thought. The pang he felt at what seemed a cruel joke on the part of life cleared his head completely. He returned to the world.

He lowered his gaze to the quay. His workmates were gesticulating furiously, signalling to him that the cargo was secured. Why was he waiting before hoisting it up? Couldn't he see they were getting soaked? He wiped the glass of the cabin clean and did what they asked of him without thinking about it, acting out of pure inertia. Immediately afterwards he climbed down the crane ladder and went over to them.

'I have to go home,' he told them in a muffled voice, adding, 'I think I may be ill.'

But the ten men on the quay had already noticed the letter sticking out of one of his trouser pockets and they didn't believe him.

'Don't worry, Heinrich. All women are the same. You'll find another one,' remarked the foreman in a mocking tone and all the others laughed.

Those apparently consoling words were not only the fruit of a crude misunderstanding, they were also – and above all – a scornful allusion to Heinrich's lack of masculinity. The workers on the quay didn't like this circumspect, well-mannered young man who manoeuvred the crane up there, above them. He wasn't the right sort of person to work in a port. They needed real men in the port, the sort who went out afterwards and spent all their money in the St Pauli brothels.

He ignored the provocative remark, left the quay and, after changing his clothes, crossed an iron walkway onto the main road. He was not thinking about anything. He simply made the screams of the seagulls flying overhead echoes of his own inner scream.

Heinrich had spent three long years working in Hamburg but he had not made a single friend, neither amongst the people of the port nor in his neighbourhood. He hadn't in fact needed them, because far from seeming a burden to him, the solitude that had appeared in his life when he arrived there had seemed almost a relief, a liberation, and also because the correspondence he maintained with his sister helped him through any difficult times.

That day, however, while he waited for the bus, he regretted that his life had come to this and he searched every corner of his memory for a name, a face. Letting himself be carried along by his imagination, he saw himself in the living room of that 'friend's' house, with a cup of coffee before him, talking about Margarete, telling him how she had been his only sister and, for years, since they were orphaned, had been all the family he had, and that she was a girl of twenty-four, with very blonde hair and a very different personality from his, happy, always happy, a great party-goer, and you know what, she had a real weakness for raincoats, for umbrellas too, you can't imagine how well she dressed and once, at a time when we were rather comfortably off, we went to spend a fortnight in a village on the French Riviera and she said, yes, Heinrich, it is a pretty village, but a place with no rain cannot help but be vulgar and after that we had an argument about the habits of seagulls . . . and, from the window of the bus, Heinrich watched the seagulls circling over the jetties, looking for food amongst the rotten wood and scrap iron. These were different seagulls. There was no name in his memory. There was no friend.

He got off the bus and ran home. He needed to hide, to flee the people filling the streets that afternoon, sheltered from the rain, milling around by shop windows or in cinema foyers. Without exception, they all seemed stupid, hateful: stupid because they knew nothing of Margarete's death; hateful because he knew that not one of them was prepared to share his misfortune.

Heinrich spent more than an hour lying face down on his bed. Then, feeling a little calmer, he rummaged around in the drawers and collected together all the objects that spoke to him of his sister: the photographs, a little box containing a lock of her hair, the fancy notebook she had given him when they made their trip to the South of France. Lined up on the table, the objects formed a little shrine.

'How come you didn't see the train, Margarete?' he asked,

sitting down at the table. And the ceremony begun with that question lasted until dawn.

But the shrine brought him no consolation. On the contrary, it made the void he could feel inside him grow ever larger. The objects refused to speak of the good times that the Wetzels, brother and sister, had spent together; they spoke solely and vociferously of Margarete's absence.

He was thinking of bringing the ceremony to a close when he noticed that there was something missing from the objects on the table. Something fundamental perhaps: the dress Margarete had forgotten to take with her after her last visit. He kept it in the wardrobe in his bedroom.

'I'll put it on,' he thought.

After all they were twins. For a long time the two of them had been almost impossible to tell apart. Then why try to make do with objects when he already carried a great part of Margarete within himself?

While he walked down the corridor it didn't occur to him that what he was about to do would change his life completely. His intention was simply to reclaim his sister from death, but only for a moment, just until the ceremony was over. Afterwards everything would return to normal.

But the transformation was made as soon as the dress touched his skin, in the same way fairy godmothers in children's stories – with just one touch of their wand, in an instant – change an ugly house into a palace. Because right at that moment, when he looked in the mirror and saw a woman remarkably like Margarete, Heinrich finally understood. Suddenly, all the circumstances of his life made sense, both the unease that had accompanied him in his native city and the solitude he had experienced later. Even his hatred for the world of the port had an explanation now.

Heinrich felt proud, prouder than he had ever felt. He had spent years like the boy lost in the woods, his body covered in scratches, shouting and shouting without anyone ever hearing him. But there would be no more scratches, no more shouting. He had found the path that would lead him out of the woods, he could see where they ended, he could see the open, friendly landscape that awaited him.

'From now on we will be one and the same person, Margarete,' he murmured.

These were, of course, words uttered out of the depths of insomnia and exhaustion, but they were, nonetheless, a true reflection of what Heinrich was feeling. From that day forwards, he would be a woman.

'I will never forget you, dear sister,' he added. And with that promise his earlier decision was sealed.

He sat down again at the table and wrote two notes. In the first, which he signed as Margarete, he informed the director of the port of the death of Heinrich Wetzel and begged him to send her any outstanding wages due to her brother. The second note was a list of all the things, beginning with lipstick, that he would have to buy the following day.

Before going to bed, he stopped by the window. The city was still sleeping, but there were already signs that day was dawning: the rays of light slicing through the clouds, the yellow reflection of the sun in the windows of the tallest buildings. It would not be long now before the alarm clocks in the bedrooms of all the houses would begin to sound. After that, everyone – men and women, young and old – would rush out into the street.

He sighed. For the first time in his life, he felt a desire to mingle with other people.

Such was the joy this change had brought to his life that not even a shadow of a doubt crossed his mind. He trusted in the future, or rather, he imagined it as radiant. He was convinced that Margarete's spirit would act as a guide who – like a fairy godmother – would always take him to beautiful places, to welcoming houses where he would find good friends.

It seemed, moreover, that this future in which he had placed his trust was ready to go along with him, that it wanted to give him everything he had dreamed of. One day, he went for a stroll through the city streets and ended up dancing at a party held in a mansion full of magnificent rooms; on another, he went to a pub and got an invitation to spend the weekend at a country house; on yet another day, he received an affectionate letter.

His diary, until then empty, grew fuller by the day and was soon crammed with names and telephone numbers. Barely a month after the day that he had first tried on his sister's dress, he was accepted at the Atropos, one of the best private clubs in the St Pauli district. Sometimes he even got up on stage and sang.

One day, while he was at the Atropos, he was introduced to Walter, a forty-year-old teacher. He was tall with very dark hair and eyes and he wore a red silk neckerchief.

'Would you like to share a bottle of champagne with me?' asked Walter.

'I'd be delighted, though I don't usually,' replied Heinrich.

'I'm so pleased I met you. I feel happier than I have for a long time. Really.'

Walter's dark eyes smiled.

Heinrich spent two days unable to get that smile out of his mind. On the third day, Walter phoned him. On the fourth, while they were walking in a park, they decided to embark on a stable relationship.

For Heinrich it was the happiest period of his life. Walter was his first love and, perhaps because of that, it was a love outside of time, exclusive, a love that absorbed his whole being. Nothing existed beyond those dark eyes.

'So how's life treating you?' Walter asked him one day, after writing a dedication to him in the book he had just published through the university. They were dining at the D'Angleterre, drinking French champagne.

'Very well indeed, since I met you.'

'I know that but what else, what's your life like?'

And Heinrich replied: 'Like that of a character in a novel.'

'Good for you! Novels are much more fun than essays,' laughed Walter, pointing to his book.

But Heinrich was mistaken. His life was very far from being a long novel, composed of fifteen, twenty or forty chapters. Instead it was but a brief story that was hurtling towards its denouement. And this was perhaps his own fault because by then, absorbed as he was in his love affair, he had utterly forgotten that only sister of his, Margarete, thus calling down on himself – according to the harsh law that fairy tales apply to people who fail to keep their promises – an exemplary punishment at the hand of fate.

The cloud, the same cloud that wrapped about him and on which he had built his life, began to evaporate one night after a play he had gone to with Walter. Walking through the silent streets, they were making their equally silent way home, when suddenly a long whistle cut across the whole city.

'The train,' commented Walter and went on walking.

But Heinrich remained rooted to the pavement and a shudder ran through his whole body. That penetrating whistle was just a signal, a message with a rather anodyne meaning; but for him it was a song, a piece of dark, powerful music.

'Why have you stopped?' asked Walter coming over to him.

'I want to hear it a second time,' he replied faintly.

And that second whistle came, filling Heinrich's eyes with tears.

'Whatever's wrong? Why are you crying?' said Walter, frightened. He took Heinrich's face in his hands.

'It's nothing. It's just that suddenly I remembered something sad,' and, saying that, he buried his face in his friend's chest.

Then, once he had pulled himself together, Heinrich linked what had happened with the circumstances surrounding the death of his sister.

'That's why it affected me so deeply. Because it made me remember my sister. I haven't thought about her for ages. It won't happen again,' he added.

But that eminently sensible way of explaining the facts – even Walter agreed with him and recounted several similar cases – proved inadequate.

For, very soon, Heinrich had acquired the habit of spending all night walking the city streets, like a sleepwalker, with no other aim but that of hearing the train whistle, again and again. And he performed that ritual every night, not caring what or whom he had to leave to do so. Whether he was at a party or at Walter's house, he always had to leave in the end. He could not resist the pull of that song.

The joy of those first days no longer glittered through Heinrich's life. He grew taciturn.

'It's true. I'm going through a bad patch,' he confessed one day when Walter came to visit him. He no longer went to the Atropos.

'And what about my house? You don't even go there any more. Can't you bear to be with me either?'

'I will come, but later on, once I've got myself out of this hole.'

'Have you met someone else?' said Walter lowering his eyes.

'No, that isn't it. I just need to be alone.'

Walter wept, but in vain. Heinrich's decision was absolute.

Winter came and the city grew even more desolate. When night fell, the drunks at the station seemed the only creatures alive in the city. Some, most, drank and got into brawls on the platforms; others tried to pick up the only woman who ever went there.

'Don't stand there looking at the train wheels. Look at us,' they would say to her.

But Heinrich didn't even hear them. He was waiting for the trains to arrive, waiting to hear the whistles blow; he did this punctiliously, drawing ever nearer. His whole life depended on it.

Shortly before Christmas, he received an official letter. The Bavarian judge wrote to tell him that Margarete's death could not possibly have been murder.

'Therefore,' he stated, 'we must assume that she committed suicide.'

Heinrich tore up the letter and threw it in the wastepaper bin. He didn't need that fact confirmed. Then, perhaps for the last time, he headed for the station.

I, Jean Baptiste Hargous

I, JEAN Baptiste Hargous, a soldier since my thirteenth year, left my native city of Nancy on the fifth day of December in the Year of Our Lord eight hundred and sixty-seven and went off to fight against the Norman army under the blue and white flag of Lorraine. For the Normans had sacked both Blois and Orléans, cities with which we had the closest of ties, and Count Lothaire, lord of the realm and of our lives, a man of little patience, decided against remaining within the shelter of our city walls. And so, as I have said, on the fifth day of December we left, being in number two thousand men and seven hundred horses.

But it soon became clear that either Our Lord had chosen not to enlighten the Count or the Count had chosen not to listen to Him, for it was a bitterly cold winter; the winds were icy, the rains flooded the roads and the snows covered the roofs of houses and the tops of trees. And although we prayed for the sun to come out again and for the sky above our heads to grow brighter and milder, the winter refused to relent and instead treated us ever more harshly.

After some ten days, when we were already far from the borders of our beloved land of Lorraine, and having lost along the way some forty men and more than twenty horses to sickness or ill fortune, we received the first news of our enemies, the Normans, from the lips of pilgrims.

'They are cruel and powerful,' they told us. 'They'll kill you the way dogs kill crows, and then they'll burn your flag.'

And as we were weary and in a strange land, spirits fell, especially amongst the younger soldiers, and everyone longed to turn back. But Count Lothaire was either unaware of our wishes or else, knowing of them, chose not to grant them, for he ordered that we continue onwards and march to the battlefield. He laughed as he said this, as if he were certain of victory and could already see the red blood of Norman soldiers spilled on the snow. But no one else saw what he did and the further along the road we marched, the greater the impression our enemies' reputation made on us. Women came to their windows when we passed and, with heartfelt sighs, begged us to withdraw; some came out of their houses and pleaded with the captains not to lead so many young soldiers to certain death. And when we stopped to rest at a monastery, the monks looked at us as if we were lambs on their way to the slaughterhouse and they prayed for our souls as if we had already died.

But Our Lord God never truly deserts us and even in the midst of the greatest misfortune He is able to offer us a little happiness and, in His great bounty, that is what He did for me that winter. For He gave me a good and loyal friend: Pierre de Broc.

I saw him for the first time in the guest quarters of the monastery of Saint Denis one night when I was unable to sleep. Pierre was alone in the empty room, sitting next to the burned-out fire playing the rebec and singing, and such was his skill in those two arts, it seemed a shame that, given the men's weariness and the great cold, there was no one else there to hear him.

'Why are you singing? Why aren't you sleeping, like all the other soldiers?' I asked him.

'Because I'm afraid,' he answered.

'So am I. I can't sleep either,' I in turn confessed.

'Then let's sing together.'

'We're afraid because we're so young. Not because we're cowards.'

'How old are you?'

'Seventeen I think.'

'So am I.'

We embraced in that empty room and then found much consolation in the songs of our beloved land of Lorraine.

There are those who are friends for only a moment, friends

with whom we share our food, and friends who appear at our side only in times of prosperity and joy. But the friendship between Pierre de Broc and I, Jean Baptiste Hargous, was different, for from that first moment on we became brothers and companions on the road and companions too in misfortune and in weariness, we always comforted and consoled each other and hoped never to be parted.

Forty days after we left Nancy, when the winter was at its height and the fields were deep in snow, we reached a village called Aumont. A Jew fleeing Orléans spoke to one of the captains and told him that the Norman army was less than fifteen leagues away and that, despite the bad weather, a man on horseback could easily reach them in an afternoon. Count Lothaire ordered us to set up camp and sent a scout on ahead to spy on the Normans. The count wanted to know how many men were in their army, how many horses they had and how confident they were of their strength. The scout galloped off, his horse's hooves kicking up a cloud of white snow, and Pierre and I sat down in the tent to play the rebec and to sing.

But one day passed, then two, then three and the scout did not return and when a week had gone by we all gave him up for dead. And it was then that the head cook spoke out, saying that he refused to believe what he heard. He said that the scout had not died but deserted and he accused the scout chosen by Count Lothaire from amongst his best men of being a traitor and a coward and that was when a captain, a friend of the other man, slew the cook with his sword. The more experienced soldiers protested at so severe a punishment and time soon proved them right for from that day on the food grew steadily worse.

The second scout sent by Count Lothaire returned two days later. I didn't see him with my own eyes, nor did Pierre, but those who did said he rode into camp bearing all the marks of sickness and of death. He was pale, his eyes glazed and flies buzzed about his head, in itself remarkable in such a severe winter. And that second scout was of no use to Count Lothaire either for he talked only nonsense, like a man in the grip of fever. Then the Count called us all together and asked for three volunteers, saying he would bestow many privileges and favours on anyone managing to find out anything about the Norman army.

A captain, the one who had killed the head cook, and two other soldiers declared themselves willing and left at once. But our spirits did not lift because of that and the first desertions took place that day as soon as the scouts had left. Some said it was twenty men and others that there were many more and that at least a hundred horses had gone missing from the stables.

The captain and his two soldiers took their time returning and some ten days passed before we saw them riding back along the edge of the wood and we were all surprised to see how they laughed and joked and larked about amongst themselves as if they were children.

'They've gone mad, Jean Baptiste,' Pierre whispered in my ear.

'But what is it that the scouts see?' I asked.

'They see the Normans, Jean Baptiste.'

'So it's true what the women in Aumont told us.'

The women in Aumont had told us that the Normans kept wild animals in cages and tamed them like dogs and that anyone seeing them would never again forget them for they were big as cows but with the hooves of horses and the heads of wolves, and that if we ever went into battle we would be devoured by those monsters.

'God have mercy on us, Jean Baptiste,' sighed Pierre.

We were just on our way back to the tent to get Pierre's rebec when a soldier, old and lame, who was always following us around and was angry with us because we never wanted his company, suddenly threw a bird at us just as one might throw a stone and the bird brushed both our chests, first Pierre's then mine. The bird had yellow wings and was dead from the cold, its eyes tight shut, and the fact that it had touched us seemed to us an omen of great evil.

Count Lothaire shut himself up in his tent to think and all the soldiers prayed to Our Lord God to make him see that the only way open to us now was retreat and that it was time for the sons of Lorraine to return to their beloved land. But the Count was not even considering retreat, he was seeking a new scout. And that was how he came to choose Guillaume, a bastard child from the village of Aumont who was always hanging round the camp, for the Count thought that the Normans would never suspect a nine-year-old child. And Guillaume accepted the order with great joy, because he wanted to be a soldier and because the Count promised him a fistful of silver in exchange for the news that none of his other scouts had yet managed to bring him.

He left laughing and quite without fear, having enjoyed to the full the party some soldiers had insisted on holding in his honour. Pierre and I joined in the party too because we felt that our fate was somehow in his hands. And we prayed to Our Lord God to guide the steps of that child and bring him to the cages where the Normans kept the cows with the heads of wolves and the hooves of horses. Because one thing was certain, no soldier would want to go into battle against such monsters and then the Count would be forced to give in and allow the retreat.

Meanwhile the winter continued. Many soldiers fell ill. Others stole horses and deserted.

Guillaume returned after about a fortnight and did so wearing the same joyful expression he had worn when he left. And when he went over to our master Lothaire's tent, every soldier in the camp followed behind him.

'This time we will get news of the Normans,' I said to Pierre. But when Guillaume climbed onto a cart and began to shout out tales of what he had seen in the enemy camp, we all looked at each other in amazement, for we understood nothing of what he said. He was not speaking in our language, nor even in Latin. And when our master Lothaire began asking him questions, the child looked as amazed as we did. He did not understand what he was asked.

'Do you know what language he's speaking, Jean Baptiste?' Pierre asked sadly.

'No, I don't.'

'He's speaking in Norman. In a matter of only a fortnight, he's forgotten his own language and learned theirs. They are much more powerful than we thought, Jean Baptiste. They must have an army of at least twenty thousand men.'

'But Pierre, children are very quick. They have a great capacity for learning new words.'

But we could not continue our conversation because out of the murmuring that followed Guillaume's words there emerged first one shout, then another and another and very soon there were a thousand soldiers from Lorraine shouting and a thousand running towards the horses, pushing and shoving each other, for there were not enough horses to go round.

'Let us fly too, Pierre,' I said to my friend.

'The rebec, Jean Baptiste, I left it in the tent!' he exclaimed, running off.

'Pierre!' I shouted.

I wanted to tell him to forget about the rebec, to keep out of the way of that crazed mob. Then, right before my eyes, he slipped in the mud and fell beneath the hooves of a horse. Another three horses trampled over him and a few dozen soldiers followed.

'Pierre!' I shouted again. But he was already dead.

I started to cry, unable to move from where I stood, lacking even the will to stop the lame soldier, the one who had always trailed around after us, from coming up to me and throwing me down in the mud. For I, Jean Baptiste Hargous, wanted to die as my friend, Pierre de Broc, had died, with my skull smashed in by a horse.

How to plagiarise

ALLOW ME, dear friends, to begin this explanation with a description of a dream and do not be concerned that, in doing so, I postpone for a while considerations more directly relevant to the exercise of plagiarism, for it will not be an unfruitful digression, indeed it will serve to set us off along the right track and, or at least so I hope, give pleasure to all. You should know, moreover, that this dream was the origin and basis of the change that has taken place in me; it is because of this dream that today I support opinions and tendencies which, until recently, I despised and disapproved of. For, as you know, before today I was always resolutely opposed to plagiarism.

One night I had a bad dream in which I saw myself in the midst of a wild forest, dense and inhospitable. Since the forest was plunged in the most utter darkness and beasts of every kind swarmed on all sides, I believed I would end my days there and I was exceedingly afraid.

Nevertheless, not allowing myself to succumb to despair, I tried to find a way out and, having walked some distance through the matted undergrowth, I reached the foot of a hill where the valley covered by the forest ended. And truly my efforts were not in vain for at the top of that hill I saw clear signs of the presence of the star that gives us our light, a sight that restored me to calm. My heart told me that if I managed to reach that luminous place I would be safe.

Guided by that hope, I began the ascent, leaving behind me the gloom of the forest. But when I reached the top, I was amazed, there was no sign of life anywhere to be seen, not a single plant growing in that sterile soil. And once more I felt lost and helpless, unable to decide which direction to take. And I was still in that state of distress, sitting on a rock with my head in my hands, when someone came up to me.

'Take pity on me, whoever you are,' I said.

He stood looking at me, but said not a word, as if he were dumb.

'What are you? A shadow or a man of flesh and blood?' I asked.

And only then did he answer:

'I am not a man though once I was. My parents came into the world in Urdax in Navarra. As regards my time on earth, you should know that after living in Salamanca and various other places, I settled in the village of Sara in accordance with the wishes of my dear master Bertrand de Echaus, and that there I lived out the eighty-eight years granted me by Our Lord God.'

I was speechless, wide-eyed as much with joy as with amazement.

'Then you must be Pedro Daquerre Azpilcueta, the rector who became famous under the pen name "Axular"! Our most illustrious master, our highest authority, the greatest of all Basque writers! I'm so pleased now that I read you. You are my teacher and my best-loved author. Help me, please. Look how lost and vulnerable I am in this desert. Kind and wise Master, save me from these desperate straits in which I find myself!'

'First, I must show you something,' he said and set off walking up a much steeper hill than the previous one, towards an even higher peak. Trusting in him, I followed.

When we reached the second peak, I saw that we were on an island, lost in the immensity of the sea. It was very small and there was no sign of life there. A black ship was approaching the shore.

'How tiny and cramped it is!' I said, my heart troubled. 'And how lonely!' I added.

The Master nodded.

'All the other common tongues and languages of the world have intermingled and are related amongst themselves. But Basque, *euskera*, is unique and different from any other language. That's why it's so lonely.'

When I heard those words I realised that the island was not like

260

the islands of Sardinia or Sicily but made of quite a different material. Incredible though it may seem, the geographical feature I was looking at was none other than my own language. But it seemed to me that the Master had more to tell me and I left the confusion of thoughts going round and round in my head for later consideration.

'Once, this was a place of delights, whereas now it is dead and arid. That's why the island seems so tiny and cramped to you. Nevertheless, if as many books had been written in *euskera* as have been written in French or in any other language for that matter, it would be as rich and perfect as they are and if that is not the case it is the speakers of *euskera* themselves who are to blame, not the island.'

The Angelic Doctor from Euskal Herria seemed to have grown melancholy and for a while I said nothing in order not to distress him further. But I saw that the black ship was drawing ever closer to the shore and as it got nearer I could even make out the different groups of people standing on the deck. I could not keep back a question that demanded to be asked.

'What ship is that, Master? And who are those people travelling in her?'

Before replying, he sighed.

'That ship is like the *Grand Saint Antoine* that reached the port of Marseilles.'

'I know nothing about such a ship, Master,' I confessed.

'*Grand Saint Antoine* was the name of the ship that brought the plague to Marseilles.'

'Who are those people then?' I asked alarmed.

'Do you see the ones standing in the bows?' he asked.

'Yes, I see them. And very happy they look too! They're waving flags and cheering as if they wanted to drink a joyful toast to the island.'

'Well, don't you believe them. In truth I say they are hypocrites and everything they do is done only for the sake of appearances.

They talk at great length but as to actions . . . you'll never see them do a thing. They create heavy loads impossible to bear and place them on the shoulders of the man next to them, whilst they never lift a finger. Everything they do is for show. One will sport engravings or mottos pinned to his attire; another will embellish the façade of his house with an inscription stolen from the island; the next, for his part, will want his name to figure first when it comes to signing a petition. But it's all hot air. Their words, like Master Adam's counterfeit money, serve only to deceive.'

'And those making up the group behind them? Who are they?'

'You mean the ones cradling accounts books in their arms?'

'Yes, Master.'

'They are the banausians, my son. They are people of great greed and stupidity, devoid of any spiritual aspirations. They are constantly drawing up accounts and know better than anyone how to make a profit from the island. Indeed I tell you they are much to be feared because – like all those of their ilk – it suits them perfectly that the island should remain just as it is, tiny and cramped. If the island came to enjoy a stronger position, it would be much harder for them to balance their books.'

The more I discovered about what the future held for the island, the more I felt my breath desert me. Even so, I could not remain silent. There was still much for me to learn and that impelled me to go on asking questions.

'And those standing by the ship's mast?' I asked.

'Those of a yellowish complexion?'

'Yes, Master, they are the ones I mean.'

'They are coming to the island to see if there are any meadows here. If there are and they find them, they will immediately sow them with the seeds of tares and other pernicious weeds. They cannot live without sowing bad seeds amongst the wheat. Wherever there is some sterile, miserable argument going on, wherever they see the chance to spread anger and enmity, you will find them gathered there in the name of the people or of their newspaper.'

'And those who have climbed up the mast? Why do they grimace so?'

'They have not climbed up the mast, they are roped to it. If they weren't, they would be carried off by the wind, as if they were balloons. For you should know that they belong to the family of the conceited, they are puffed-up as toads. They believe themselves to be sublime and by constantly mocking the island and attacking it, consider their sublimity proven. But they are not sublime, they are mean-minded and foul. They believe they are bold but they only dare attack the island because they see how scrawny and weak it is. Were that not the case, they would simply seek out some pond near the Court and stay there.'

This time it was my turn to sigh.

'I'm going to ask you one last question, Master, for there are many people travelling on the ship and I do not wish to tire you. Tell me, who are the ones in the stern? The ones at the other end of the boat, crying and lamenting.'

'Being, as I am, a shadow, I know nothing of fatigue. You, on the other hand, do. I see that you cannot bear much more and that your strength is failing and so, once I have told you about those last travellers, I will say no more. The people you see there are the "sad ones". Like petty lovers, they offer the island only their griefs, with which they merely make the situation worse. Like Icarus' father, they whisper in the ear of the person who is falling: you're on the road to ruin; they cast despairing looks at the person for whom things are going well and who is on the way up, letting him know that do what he may, it will all be in vain. Were the island to end up in their hands, Gethsemane would be a joyous place by comparison.'

We both stayed there for a while, not saying anything, looking out at the black ship. Then he took me by the hand and led me down the hill, to one of the few green spots remaining on the island. The ground was covered by tall grasses and scattered all around were figtrees heavy with fruit.

'Master, don't go yet,' I begged, seeing that he let go of my hand.

'What do you want from me? Some solution?' he said, reading my thoughts. I nodded.

'I told you before: If as many books had been written in *euskera* as in . . .'

'But there are so few writers, Master! And anyway none are of your stature.'

The Master plucked a fig from the tree and offered it to me. He remained thoughtful while I ate it.

'And what about plagiarists? Aren't there any of them?' he asked.

'I'm not sure I know what you mean, Master,' I said.

'What I'm asking is, is there no one who, out of great respect for some particularly fine writer, adopts his style of writing? In my time that was how nearly all books came into being.'

It seemed to me that before going on I had to clear up a few points.

'I don't think so, sir,' I began. 'Moreover, things have changed a lot since your day. Ever since the eighteenth century, people have taken a very dim view of plagiarism. It's considered as bad as stealing. Nowadays, the work of a writer has to give the impression of being created out of nothing. In other words, the work has to be original.' He looked at me hard as if struggling to understand. Then, producing a dish from somewhere, he began to pick figs.

After a while, as he went from tree to tree, he said: 'That's no good at all. In my view, plagiarism has many advantages over the labour of creation. It is much easier to carry out and less hard work. You can finish twenty works of plagiarism in the time it takes to produce one creative work. And because the qualities of the original serve as a guide and an aid, you often get very fine results, which is not always the case with creative texts. The idea that it is theft is most unfortunate, since it deprives us of the best tool we have to give life to the island.'

Although apparently annoyed, he took great care placing the figs on the dish. I, meanwhile, remained silent. I did not want to distract him from the subject occupying his thoughts.

'A rector shouldn't really say such things but . . . what if the robbery were committed with some skill?' he asked, coming over to me again. A furtive smile flickered across his face.

'Commit plagiarisms without revealing them for what they are? Is that what you mean, Master?' I said, startled.

'Exactly.'

'But to do that you would need a method, and besides . . .'

He placed a hand on my shoulder.

'My son, answer me honestly!' he said. 'Do you love this island?'

'Very much, Master,' I replied rather warily.

'And would you be prepared to run risks and put yourself in danger for it?'

Given the way he looked at me, it was impossible for me to say no.

'Then go out into the world and devise that method. Let the new generations learn to carry out with confidence new works of plagiarism! Let the island bring forth new books!'

Saying that, he placed in my hands the dish full of figs. Then he stepped into a cloud that had descended to our level and disappeared from view. I opened my eyes and woke up.

Although I could see the familiar sight of the mountains of Obaba through my window, it took me time to realise that I was in my bedroom. Everything there, pictures, clothes, books, seemed strange to me, because their reality was not potent enough to dispel the dream. Even with my eyes open, I was still standing with the author of *Gero*, now on the top of that hill looking down on the island, now on the plain amongst the fig trees. Once I was fully awake I remembered:

'I promised him I would come up with a method for plagiarists!'

I found it very hard returning to the world with that promise and I longed to go back to sleep. However, unease had taken hold of my heart and gradually my head began to clear. I felt I would be incapable of devising such a method and that, even if I were, no one would listen. Besides I had not given my word to just anyone, but to Axular himself, the Angelic Doctor of Euskal Herria. And that thought made me so nervous that, when I took a bite of fig, it went down the wrong way.

Then I thought: 'A plagiarist must select texts with a clear plot. That will be the first rule of my method.'

Feeling surprised, but nonetheless pleased with the idea that had arisen so unexpectedly, I picked up a notebook from the bedside table and wrote it down, adding:

> In other words, one must choose stories or novels whose plots can be summed up in a few facts or events. For that reason, models such as Robbe Grillet or Faulkner are unsuitable for the plagiarist, because in the works of writers such as these, the story is the least important thing. Writers like Saki, Buzzati or even Hemingway, on the other hand, can be highly recommended. In general terms, the more ancient the model chosen, the better for the plagiarist: you could use a thousand stories from those collected in *The Arabian Nights* but not one from some avant-garde anthology.

I studied what I had written. It wasn't bad and it occurred to me that perhaps it would not be as difficult to come up with a method as I had supposed.

And to celebrate my bold discovery, I raised another fig to my lips and ate it very carefully.

'In order to plagiarise one must discard all rare books,' I thought then, feeling even more surprised than when I had had the first idea. Without knowing why, I was more inspired that morning than ever before. But, of course, however surprised I was, I could not let such an opportunity slip. So I picked up the notebook again and set to writing a commentary on the second rule:

> The plagiarist should never consider using a rare book which has not been translated into his own language, for example, the novel his parents bought for him in a bookshop in Red Square on their trip to Moscow, not even if his friend the polyglot prepares an attractive synopsis of its plot. Because, after all, what does he know about the latest in Russian literature? And what if his parents, in all innocence, have happened upon someone about to become a dissident? Then what would happen? After a couple of years, that someone will be proclaimed by the mass media and then even university students will know by heart the plots of every novel he ever wrote. And, of course, if that happened, the plagiarised work would be placed in grave danger.
>
> No, the plagiarist should not employ sly stratagems to achieve his ends. He should not direct his feet to far-flung neighbourhoods or dark alleyways as if he were some shabby thief, rather he must stroll in the broad light of day through the open spaces of the very centre of the metropolis. He must head for Boulevard Balzac or Hardy Gardens or Hoffmannstrasse or Piazza Pirandello . . . in other words, he must choose his models from amongst writers who are household names. And don't worry. No one will ever know. Because, as with archangels, all anyone ever knows about the classics are their names and their faces.

I had now established two rules for my method and, feeling a little calmer, I sat for a while looking out at the mountains of Obaba, watching the comings and goings of the people working in the fields. I would have got up to have a cup of coffee, as I usually did, but I was afraid to leave my bed. If I did, inspiration might leave me too. Where were all these ideas coming from? What did I know about plagiarism? Something strange was happening.

Then I asked myself: 'Where did those figs come from?' Figs were not even in season in Obaba.

I picked up the white dish and, having examined it, all my doubts vanished. For it was clear that the fruits so neatly placed there were the very ones picked by Axular on the island.

At last I saw things clearly, I understood everything that had happened. I had not had that dream purely by chance, but according to the express wish of the Master, because he needed someone to spread the good news about plagiarism. And I realised too that the figs on the plate were no ordinary figs, those figs were full of wisdom and, as they had already begun to, they would teach me how to plagiarise.

I meditated for a while on what had happened, amazed at the powers disposed of by those who dwell on Mount Parnassus. But the notebook was still by my side reminding me of the task I had promised to undertake. With that thought, I picked up my pen and prepared myself to write rule three.

An example will explain better than any dissertation how to resolve the problem of time and space. Let's suppose that we have to plagiarise a story that takes place in Arabia or in the Middle Ages and that its two protagonists – who are embroiled in an argument over a camel – are Ibu al Farsi and Ali Rayol. Right, the plagiarist should take the story in its entirety and set it – let's say – in modern-day England. So the protagonists become, for example, Anthony Northmore and Philip Stevens and, instead of a camel, the cause of the argument between them can be a car. As you can easily imagine, these changes will bring in their train a thousand more so as to render the plot completely unrecognisable to anyone.

Having discovered the origin of my inspiration, there was now nothing to prevent me from getting out of bed, and I went down to the kitchen to make some coffee. By then a lot of people were out and about in the village and the good mornings and goodbyes they exchanged floated up to my house. The sun was driving away the few clouds in the sky. Shortly afterwards, a knock on the door announced the arrival of the newspaper. Yes, the wheel of life was still ceaselessly turning and I felt happier than I had for a long time.

A few hours later, I poured out my second cup of coffee, ate three figs one after the other and was ready to transcribe the final rule.

'The preparation of a good defence is of vital importance to the plagiarist,' I began and added to that statement the following lines:

There is a possibility that despite following the preceding four rules point by point, a plagiarist may have his plagiarism uncovered. Anyone can have a stroke of bad luck. This is especially true amongst minority cultures where, since there is little space, relations – especially literary ones – tend to be rife with intrigue, malice and hatred.

However, that stroke of bad luck need not necessarily prove prejudicial to the plagiarist; on the contrary, he may emerge strengthened from his enemy's nets. But three conditions must be satisfied if this is to happen: firstly, he must leave scattered throughout the work 'traces' of the text he has taken as his model; secondly, he must find out a little about metaliterature; thirdly, he must make a name for himself. If he fulfils these three requirements, he will have built his own Praetorian guard.

Let's suppose – to explain the first two rules of the defence – that the plagiarist has used for his purposes a story by Kipling and has done so by moving the story far ahead in time and setting it in the environs of the planet Uranus. To fulfil the first rule, it is vital then that the plagiarist call the astronaut Kim.

'May I ask you a rather impertinent question now?' a journalist will say to him a few days after his book has been published. 'It seems that the story you tell in your book bears a remarkable resemblance to a story by the writer Pikling. Some have even used the term "plagiarism". What do you have to say to that?'

'The writer's name is Kipling, not Pikling,' the plagiarist will begin with great dignity, adding, with just a hint of scorn in his smile: 'If my accusers were true readers and, instead of sharpening their claws, had read the whole of Kipling's work, they would immediately realise that my work is nothing more nor less than a homage to that great writer. That is precisely why I call the astronaut Kim. For that is the title of a work written by that charming imperialist. To be honest, it doesn't strike me as a particularly difficult reference to pick up. But, as I said before, these accusers of mine do not even have a clear idea of what reading involves.'

'Correct me if I'm wrong, but didn't I hear you use the expression "charming imperialist"? With respect, those two words together do sound slightly odd to me . . .' the journalist will start in on his attack again, from another front this time. However, the plagiarist will not let him continue along that road and, deploying the second rule for the defence, he will launch a further attack on the enemy.

'Moreover, I must say that these hairsplitters intent on discrediting others are very backward when it comes to literary theory. They've probably never even heard of metaliterature . . .'

'I have heard something about it, but I don't quite remember . . .'

'Well, briefly, all the term means is that there's nothing new under the sun, not even in literature. All those ideas the Romantics had . . .'

'Ah, yes, love and all that . . .'

'Well, no, or rather yes, their concept of love too, but I was referring to their literary ideas; the Romantics considered a work of art to be the product of a special and unique personality, and other such nonsense . . .'

'And metaliterature?'

'Well, as I said, we writers don't create anything new, we're all continually writing the same stories. As people often say, all the good stories have been written already, and if a story hasn't been written, it's a sign that it isn't any good. The world today is nothing but a vast Alexandria and we who live in it merely write commentaries on what has already been created, nothing more. The Romantic dream burst long ago.'

'Why write at all then? If all the good stories have already been written . . .'

'Because, in the words of someone whose name escapes me, people forget. And we, the new writers, merely serve to remind them of the stories. That's all.'

From everything that has been said up to now, it is clear that the respectability of the plagiarist would thus be placed beyond doubt. But just in case – bearing in mind that no one believes a complete unknown – he would be wise to have fulfilled the requirements of rule number three for the defence. In other words, he should make a name for himself. Because if his name is known and talked about, all the aforementioned reasons will take on extraordinary force and significance.

And, however arduous it may seem at first, there is no need to be intimidated by the task of making a name for oneself. Because, given the quantity of newspapers and the sheer volume of cheap chitchat – whether such and such a politician did or did not say something, whether the arrangements for the Carnival are satisfactory or unsatisfactory, whether the problems of traffic or trafficking have been resolved – getting your name into the public eye every week – answering surveys, signing petitions, etc. – will be a cinch for the plagiarist.

By the time I had written the last lines of the method, the sun was at its highest point and the smoke from the chimneys of Obaba told me it was lunch time. However, having eaten all those figs, I was not in the least hungry and I decided instead to put the method into practice right there and then. I needed to demonstrate the efficacy of the method with an example. So I went to the library and chose a story with a clear plot from a book that had gone through dozens of editions. Before nightfall I had finished and written out a fair copy of the plagiarised story that follows: 'The crevasse.'

May wise Axular's wishes be fulfilled.

THE CREVASSE

THE SHADOW of death passed over Camp One when Sherpa Tamng arrived with the news that Philippe Auguste Bloy had fallen down a crevasse. The usual bustle and laughter of supper ceased abruptly and cups of tea, still steaming, were left forgotten in the snow. Not one of the expedition members dared ask for details, no one said anything. Fearing they had not understood him, the sherpa repeated the news. The ice had swallowed up Philippe Auguste, the crevasse seemed very deep.

At last the man who was leading the expedition asked: 'Couldn't you have got him out, Tamng?' The man's name was Mathias Reimz, a native of Geneva, a man who merited an entry in every encyclopaedia on mountaineering for his ascent of Dhaugaliri.

The sherpa shook his head.

'*Chiiso*, Mister Reimz. Almost night,' he said.

It was a weighty enough reason. As soon as night fell, the cold – *chiiso* – was intense, the temperature around Lhotse could drop to forty below zero, a temperature that could in itself prove fatal to a climber but which also destabilised the great slabs of ice on the mountain. At night new crevasses opened up, whilst other older ones closed over for ever. Rescue was almost impossible.

'What did you leave as a marker, Tamng?'

Turning round, the sherpa showed his back. The missing rucksack in red nylon was the marker, securely fixed at the top of the crevasse with pitons.

'Was he alive?'

'Don't know, Mister Reimz.'

Everyone assumed that the sole aim of these questions was to begin preparations for the rescue party that would leave at first

273

light the following day. To their surprise, Mathias Reimz began clipping on his crampons and calling for a torch and some ropes. The man from Geneva intended setting out immediately.

'*Lemu mindu!*' shouted the old sherpa making gestures of surprise. He did not approve of that decision, which seemed to him suicidal.

'The moon will help me, Gyalzen,' replied Reimz looking up at the sky. The moon was nearly full. Its light illuminated the newly fallen snow, making it seem even paler.

Then, addressing his companions, he declared that he would not accept anyone's help. He would go completely alone. He was the one who should risk his life, it was his duty.

Mathias Reimz and Philippe Auguste Bloy worked together at the ski resorts around Geneva and that was how the Europeans on the expedition understood the decision, as the result of the close ties formed during their long acquaintance. Less well-informed, the sherpas attributed it to his position as leader, as the man responsible for the group.

When the orange shadow of Reimz's anorak disappeared into the snow and the night, a murmur of admiration arose in Camp One. It was an admirable thing to do, to put one's own life at risk to save that of another. Some spoke of the power of friendship and the heart, others, of the spirit shown by mountaineers, their daring and their sense of solidarity. Old Gyalzen waved his white prayer shawl in the air: may good fortune go with him, may great Vishnu protect him.

No one suspected the truth. It occurred to no one that the decision might have its roots in hatred.

Philippe Auguste Bloy's broken leg ached as did the deep cut he had sustained in one side. But even so he was falling asleep; the drowsiness brought on by the cold in the crevasse was stronger than pain, stronger than his will. He couldn't keep his eyes open.

He could already feel the warmth that always precedes the gentle death of mountaineers.

He was lying down on the ice, absorbed in his private struggle, trying to distinguish the darkness of the crevasse from the darkness of sleep, and so he failed to notice the ropes thrown from above when they landed on his boots. Nor did he see the man who, having lowered himself down on them, was now kneeling beside him.

When the man shone the torch on him, Philippe Auguste Bloy sat up with a shout. The light had startled him.

Then he exclaimed: 'Don't shine the torch in my face, Tamng!' and smiled at his reaction. He felt safe.

He heard someone say: 'It's me, Mathias.' The voice sounded threatening.

Philippe Auguste tilted his head to one side to avoid the glare of the torch. But the beam followed his movement and continued to dazzle him.

'Why have you come?' he asked at last.

The deep voice of Mathias Reimz echoed round the crevasse. He spoke very slowly, like a man who is very tired.

'I want to talk to you as a friend, Phil. And what I have to tell you may seem ridiculous. But don't laugh. Consider that before you is a man who has suffered greatly.'

Philippe Auguste put himself on guard. Behind that statement he heard the hiss of the serpent.

'Vera and I first met when we were very young,' Mathias went on. 'We must have been about fifteen; in fact, she was fifteen and I was sixteen. And she wasn't a pretty girl then. She was even rather ugly. Too tall for her age and very bony. But despite that I fell in love with her the moment I saw her. I remember I felt like crying and for a moment everything seemed bathed in violet light. That will seem odd to you, but it's true, I saw everything that colour. The sky was violet, the mountains were violet, and the rain was violet too. I don't know, maybe falling in love changes the sensitivity of the eyes. And now it's almost the same. The feelings I had when I was sixteen are still there. They didn't even disappear when we got married and you know what they say about marriage putting an end to love. Well, not in my case. I'm still in love with her, I carry her always in my heart. And that's how I managed to climb Dhaugaliri, because I was thinking about her, that's the only reason.'

The silence that followed his words emphasised the solitude of the crevasse.

'We've never been to bed together, Math!' Philippe Auguste shouted suddenly. His words resounded round the four frozen walls.

Mathias gave a short laugh.

'I almost went crazy when they showed me your photos, Phil. Vera and you holding hands at the Ambassador Hotel in Munich on the sixteenth and seventeenth of March. Or at the Tivoli in Zurich on the tenth and eleventh of April. Or in Apartments Trummer in Geneva itself on the twelfth, thirteenth and fourteenth of May. And at Lake Villiers in Lausanne, for a whole week, just when I was preparing for this expedition.'

Philippe Auguste's mouth went dry. The muscles in his face, grown stiff with cold, twitched.

'Math!' he cried, 'you're making too much out of things that have no importance whatsoever.

But no one heard him. The single eye of the torch was staring pitilessly at him.

'I've had many doubts, Phil. I'm not a murderer. I felt really bad every time I thought about killing you. I was on the point of trying it in Kathmandu. And when we landed in Lukla. But those places are sacred to me, Phil, and I didn't want to stain them with your blood. Now, though, the Mountain has judged you for me, and that's why you're here, because it has handed down its own sentence to you. Whether it will take away your life, I don't know. You may live until morning and the rest of the group will rescue you. But I don't think so, Phil. I have the feeling you're going to stay in this crevasse for ever. That's why I came, so that you wouldn't leave this world without knowing how much I hate you.'

'Get me out of here, Math!' Philippe Auguste's bottom lip was trembling.

'It's not up to me, Phil. As I said, the Mountain will decide.'

Philippe Auguste breathed deeply. He had to accept his fate. His voice filled with scorn.

'You think you're better than everyone else, Math. An exemplary mountaineer, an exemplary husband, an exemplary friend. But you're nothing but a pathetic clown. No one who really knows you can stand you!'

Too late. Mathias Reimz was already pulling himself up on the ropes.

'Vera will cry for me! She wouldn't for you!' shouted Philippe Auguste as loudly as he could.

The crevasse was plunged into darkness once more.

The excitement of the visit roused Philippe Auguste's body. His heart beat strongly now and the blood that had been about to freeze in his veins flowed easily into his muscles. Suddenly, perhaps because his brain was also working better, he remembered that mountaineers never take with them the ropes they use to descend into crevasses. They were a dead weight, an unnecessary burden on the journey back to camp.

'What if Mathias . . .,' he thought. He was gripped by hope.

He got up and felt around in the dark. It was only a moment but so intense that it made him laugh out loud with joy. There were the three ropes which, by force of habit, Mathias Reimz had left behind him.

Philippe Auguste's wounds made him groan with pain, but he knew that a greater suffering, the worst of all, awaited him at the bottom of the crevasse. Tightening his lips against the pain, Philippe

Auguste took hold of the ropes and began to climb, slowly, trying not to bump against the frozen walls. He used the narrower places to rest, forming a bridge with his back and his good leg. An hour later, he had managed to climb the first ten yards.

When he had climbed some eighteen yards, an avalanche of snow threw him off balance crushing him against a hard lump on the wall. Philippe Auguste felt the blow on the same side he had the cut and the pain filled his eyes with tears. For a moment he thought of the gentle death awaiting him at the bottom of the crevasse. But hope was still there in his heart and it whispered a 'perhaps' to him that he could not ignore. After all, he was lucky. Fate had given him a chance. He had no right to doubt it. Besides, the fall of snow indicated that the mouth of the crevasse must be very near.

Half an hour later, the walls of the crevasse became first grey then white. Philippe Auguste considered that, in throwing him against the wall, Fate had wanted to put him to the test, and that this, at last, was his reward.

'The sky!' he gasped. And it was indeed the rosy sky of dawn. A new day was breaking over Nepal.

The sun was shining on the snow. Ahead of him, towards the north, rose the mighty form of Lhotse. To his right, across the frozen valley, was the zigzagging path down to Camp One.

Philippe Auguste felt his lungs revive as he breathed in the clean air of morning. He opened his arms to the vastness and, raising his eyes to the blue sky, mumbled a few words of thanks to the Mountain.

He was still in that position when a strange feeling troubled him. It seemed to him that the arms he had stretched out had bent again, against his will, and were embracing him. But who was embracing him?

He looked down to see what was happening and a grimace of terror contorted his face. Mathias Reimz stood in front of him. He was smiling mockingly.

'It's not nice to cheat, Phil,' he heard him say just before he felt the shove. And, for an instant, as he fell towards the bottom of the crevasse, Philippe Auguste Bloy thought he understood the meaning of those last hours of his life.

Everything – the visit, leaving behind the ropes – had been a premeditated plan of torture: Mathias Reimz had not even wanted to spare him the pain of unfounded hope.

A RHINE WINE

H
OW ABOUT leaving the martini that's on the timetable for another day?' suggested the uncle from
Montevideo, laying aside his papers and getting up from
his leather armchair. The story reading session on the verandah was
over.

'That depends on what you have to offer in its place,' we joked.

'I can offer you a delicious Rhine wine that I have in my cellar.
Hearing that story about Klaus Hanhn made me feel like opening a
bottle. How about it? Shall I put it to cool in my *fontefrida*?'

The *fontefrida* was my uncle's name for the well inside the
house, next to the kitchen.

'For my part, I'd be delighted. The truth is I've never drunk
Rhine wine in my life,' I said.

'You've never drunk it and yet you write about it in your story!
The nerve of the boy!' said my uncle, laughing and shaking his
head.

'You're back to being nineteenth-century man again!
Experience and originality and, if possible, two or three adulterous
affairs per novel. So much for your new-found faith! I bet even the
story you plagiarised was from the nineteenth century!'

'Now that you mention it,' my friend broke in, 'what writer
did you base yourself on for the story about the crevasse, uncle?
You never told us.'

My uncle walked over to the door like a child ostentatiously
feigning indifference. He knew the stories he'd read had impressed us.

'Not a word! The programme states that any questions and
comments must wait until the second cognac of the afternoon. So
until then you have only two options: silence or small talk. Now go
and sit down at the table in the garden. The wine will only take five
minutes to cool.'

'As the honourable Mr Fig-eater wishes,' I said, getting up.

'The table will be in the shade won't it?' asked my friend looking out of the window. The temperature outside was hovering around the 95° mark the radio had forecast.

'It's underneath the magnolia tree in the corner. But, come to think of it, perhaps I'm being too trusting putting it there. I can hardly expect you to behave like pale nineteenth-century maidens. If you like, I'll come over in a minute and pull it out into the full blaze of modernity.'

'Oh, very droll,' we both said as we went outside.

The 'modernity' of which my uncle spoke filled the whole garden. One was aware of nothing else, just its intense heat and light. Only the monotonous song of the crickets interrupted the general stupor imposed on Obaba by that Sunday's heat.

My friend and I hurried off in search of the magnolia tree and then, seated comfortably in the centre of its shade, we settled down to make small talk, as required by the programme. Our conversation, which began with predictable remarks about the oppressive heat and the drought, drifted off onto thoughts about the unusual tree sheltering us.

'You only ever find magnolia trees in the gardens of houses built by rich Spanish emigrants returned from South America,' my friend remarked.

'They must bring them back as a souvenir. It's the same with palm trees.'

'As a souvenir? I'm not so sure about that. I can't imagine one of those rich men looking out at his garden and feeling nostalgic for his days in Panama or Venezuela.'

'Why else would they bring them?'

'Because they needed a symbol of the wealth they'd accumulated out there. They couldn't come back to their village and set themselves up in a normal house. They needed to show their fellow countrymen that they had triumphed, that it had been worth while emigrating.'

'Well, I don't know, you may be right . . .'

'How odd. I thought young people today were always so certain about everything,' my uncle said, interrupting us. He was carrying the tray with the aperitif. 'Rhine wine, small glasses, Spanish olives, anchovies from Bermeo . . .' he recited as he placed one thing after another on the table. 'Well, what do you think?'

'You may belong to the nineteenth century, uncle, but one must concede that there are some things you do very well.'

'Is the wine good?' he asked when we'd tried it.

'Very good and very cool.'

'Well, I'm glad,' he said, sitting down opposite us, a suspicious look in his eye. 'And may one know what you were talking about?'

'Don't look at us like that, uncle, we've been very good. Not a single word about literature has passed our lips. Cross my heart.'

'What were you talking about then, if you don't mind my asking?'

My friend said that he didn't mind in the least and repeated our discussion about the magnolia tree.

'Not a bad subject,' my uncle said, thoughtfully.

'What do you think, uncle?'

'I don't know much about it, to be honest, because I bought the house exactly as it is now, garden and all. But I do know that those first-generation emigrants, the ones who left their village for the first time and headed off to South America, were genuinely dazzled by the landscape and by the people they found there. And that later, when they returned home, they always tried to bring something back with them from that world.'

'So you agree with me, then, that they brought the magnolias and the palmtrees with them as souvenirs, to have something to look at when they felt nostalgic for South America,' I said.

'No, that's not what I mean. I don't think they brought anything with them as a souvenir. There's no sadness when you return home, but there is a desire to show people things. Let me explain what I mean. The man who built this house . . .'

'His name was Tellería, wasn't it?' I said.

'That's right, José Tellería. He sailed across the ocean and within ten years he was a rich man. I think he owned every textile shop in Montevideo. And when he came back to Obaba after those ten years, he brought with him a kind of sample book of everything he'd seen in Uruguay. He didn't just bring the seeds of these trees here, he also brought masses of animals: parrots, lorikeets, monkeys . . .'

'Monkeys too? I didn't know that,' I said.

'Didn't you? They were really famous around these parts. Because of course at that time no one in Obaba had ever seen a monkey, not even in photographs. They hadn't seen such brightly coloured birds before either but in the end they were just birds with wings and beaks, and so rather less amazing. But the monkeys, looking for all the world like hairy children . . . what's more, one of those monkeys, Alberto, a chimpanzee that Tellería used to dress up in a vest and baggy trousers, used to work in a circus in Montevideo and he could turn somersaults and knew all kinds of tricks. The people who came to see the monkey wet themselves laughing and I don't mean to be vulgar, for that was literally what happened. They would stand around the garden fence and after watching for a few minutes, would have to rush off and relieve themselves. But in the end, Alberto and his companions became so famous that Tellería had to keep them indoors.'

'Why did he have to keep them indoors?' my friend asked, exchanging a knowing look with me. I was slower on the uptake than him, however, and had not yet made the connection between Tellería's chimpanzee and a certain monkey from Montevideo I had first heard mentioned in a motorway café, and so I failed to understand his message. I needed a few more minutes in order – as Gautier would have said – to hear the steps of the dancer drawing near.

'He had to keep them indoors because the house was becoming a place of pilgrimage,' my uncle explained. 'Hundreds of people must have come to see the monkeys and wet themselves laughing. At first Tellería was happy, delighted to see how much everyone enjoyed his South American sample book. But after about three months he got fed up with all the hooha and from then on he only exhibited them on Obaba feast days.'

'Did you ever see them, uncle?' asked my friend.

'More or less. I did see the monkeys, but I was very young. The fact is I haven't told you the story as I remember it but as a friend of mine from Montevideo remembered it.'

'Oh yes, and who was he?' my friend asked insistently.

'Samuel Tellería Uribe, the rich man's son. Samuel emigrated to South America too, not to make his fortune like his father, but in search of adventure, with the idea of exploring Amazonas. He was one of the group of people I knew in Montevideo who used to get together at the Café Real and that's when he told me the story. I'd almost completely forgotten it until now.'

My friend turned round and looked at me again. *Did I realise what was happening?* Yes, at last I did, I was beginning to hear the dancer's steps. *Montevideo, Monkey, Amazonas* . . . those three words all pointed to the same person.

'Where does Samuel live now? In Dublin?' my friend asked.

My uncle looked at him wide-eyed.

'Well, yes, he does actually. That's how I come to be living in this house. Because Samuel sold it to me when he got married to Laura, an Irish girl. But how do you know that?'

'Aren't you expecting a visit from him, uncle?' we asked.

'He's always saying he'll come, but I haven't had a letter from him in ages. But what's all this about? Why have you both got that odd expression on your faces?'

We didn't have an odd expression on our faces. We were just smiling.

'Now, dear uncle, you really are going to be astonished. Your friend Samuel Tellería Uribe . . .'

But we didn't have time to finish the sentence. Before we could do so, the dancer gave his final steps and jumped onto the glass. Twice in fact.

We heard a car approaching the house and, shortly afterwards, a red Lancia drove into the garden and two men got out.

'Ismael *and* Mr Smith!' said my friend and I in amazement.

'Samuel!' exclaimed my uncle, even more amazed. And getting up from the table, he went over to embrace his old friend.

Samuel Tellería Uribe

WHAT DID he want to do first? Would he like to see the house? Hadn't he got any luggage? Did he still remember Obaba after all these years? What should they do then, go indoors or drink a little white wine first? How come he'd turned up in that young man's car. . . ? My uncle's questions piled up around him, bogged him down. Being a man accustomed to programmes and ceremonies, unexpected visits upset him.

'I can see his heart beating from here. It's jumping up and down in his chest like a young chick in a box,' I whispered to my friend.

'And what about Mr Smith? Have you seen the state he's in?'

The old man, all six foot five of him, kept bending towards my uncle, turning his hat round and round in his hands and ceaselessly nodding his white head. He barely had time to reply to all my uncle's questions. He seemed more embarrassed than upset.

'Why don't we give them a hand? If they carry on like this, they'll both go under,' my friend said. We left the shade of the magnolia tree and stepped out into the sun.

But Ismael beat us to it. He was the one to interrupt the animated conversation between the two men. Addressing my uncle, he began in honeyed tones to explain:

'I was driving along in my car when I saw him lying on his back in an apple orchard. In fact I got out of the car because I was worried. I thought something had happened to him. But not at all. He was just calmly, deeply asleep. And when he told me he was born here, I gave him a lift.'

'You did well,' said my uncle.

'Yes, many thanks. It was very kind of you,' said Mr Smith. 'There were no taxis about and so I lay down to sleep on the grass. But anyway . . .'

'You should have come with us!' we said. But it would seem he

286

remembered nothing of the previous night, and he looked mystified.

'Don't you recognise us?' asked my friend. 'We talked to you yesterday.'

Mr Smith looked down at his hat. And then, in contrite tones, said:

'I drank a lot yesterday. Too much. It's just as well Laura Sligo stayed in Dublin.'

'Why didn't she come? I would love to have met her again!'

Now it was my uncle's turn to ask a question. He clearly wanted to change the subject.

'Pottery!'

'Pottery?'

'Laura Sligo is always learning something. At the moment it's pottery. And she told me that she didn't want to miss her classes and that, well, she preferred to stay at home. She's like that, a very stubborn woman.' We all smiled, including Ismael.

'So, do you want to see the house where you were born or not?' asked my uncle.

He was calmer now, but he wanted to be alone with his visitor.

'Lead on!' said Mr Smith, putting on his hat. And the two of them walked back down the path to the door of the house.

Watching them move off, my friend and I considered the minor mystery we had stumbled upon twelve hours before to have been solved. Now we knew who he was, that Mr Smith we had met in the motorway café. He was Samuel Tellería Uribe, the son of a rich emigrant from Obaba; a determined man who had left first for Amazonas and then for Dublin. He was a good sort, he had class. My friend and I were pleased to have met him.

But the dancer had brought us not only the white-haired old man, he had also brought us Ismael and his presence in the garden soon began to feel distinctly uncomfortable. Leaning on the hood of his red Lancia he was looking at us out of the corner of his eye, smiling, mocking our curiosity.

The smile said: 'You want to know what sort of a person I am, don't you?'

'Yes, we do,' our look in turn replied. 'But that's not all we want to know. We'd like to know what lies behind this mania of yours for lizards. And don't flatter yourself, don't imagine you impress us. Maybe last night on the road you frightened us a little, because we were tired and didn't expect to see you there with a lizard in your hands. But not now. It's daylight now and the song of the crickets has a very calming effect. You can begin when you like, we're ready to hear your story.'

The three of us sat down in the shade of the magnolia tree and poured some wine into the small glasses. Ismael – in even more honeyed tones than usual – asked if we wanted a cigarette.

'It was you I saw yesterday, wasn't it? In a car, at about three in the morning, coming round the bend near the quarry, I mean. It was, wasn't it?' he asked once we'd lit our cigarettes. He was no slouch when it came to interpreting glances.

'Yes, it was,' we confessed. 'And if you don't mind, we'd like to know a bit about what we thought we saw there.'

'What do you mean?'

He leaned back and waited. His mouth twisted a little as he inhaled the smoke from his cigarette.

I didn't beat about the bush, I fired a question straight at him: 'What were you doing there holding a lizard?'

'Ah, so that's it. So you saw me,' he laughed. The situation seemed to amuse him. 'Naturally. Of course you did,' he went on. 'That's why you drove past me at top speed, because you wanted to get away from there as fast as possible. Yes, I know what you thought . . .'

He fell silent for a moment. Again he inhaled smoke from his cigarette and again his lips twisted.

'You think I'm sick, that I went mad after that business with Albino María. You think my obsession with lizards dates from then, and that's why I'm always messing around with the nasty creatures . . .'

'What we want to know is what you use them for,' I broke in.

'What for? Haven't you guessed? Why, to do to others what I did to Albino María. Is that clear enough?'

We let him laugh. After a pause, he leaned a little towards us and went on:

'If you don't mind my saying, you're the ones who are mad, not me. Because you'd have to be completely mad to swallow that story about lizards. Who else would believe they can crawl into your ear and then eat your brains? Only children and madmen . . .'

He paused for a moment to catch his breath and looked at us smugly. He thought he had won.

'Doctors believe it too, not just children and madmen,' my friend put in. 'The species *Lacerta viridis* can damage the brain and cause idiocy. Or at any rate, that's what it says in the books. And I'll tell you another thing. What we saw last night wasn't at all normal. There's nothing normal about coming across a person holding a lizard at three in the morning on a lonely road.'

Ismael changed his expression and tried a new approach. But it wasn't the cautious one you'd expect in someone who had just been put in his place by a specialist on the subject, by a doctor. On the contrary, Ismael began to speak like someone who, having listened to a patent ignoramus, feels like showing off.

'I could speak at length about *Lacerta viridis*,' he began, 'but the subject is too complex to deal with in a few minutes. All I will say is that the *Lacerta viridis* indigenous to our country bears no resemblance whatsoever to that of South America. The only thing they have in common is their name. But, anyway, there's no point in pursuing that topic now. I would prefer to clear up the other matter. You say it's not normal to come across someone holding a lizard, and you're right. Unfortunately it isn't normal. The normal thing is simply to run over any lizard we find lying defenceless on the road; just drive over it with your car and squash it. That's why we are as we are.'

I recalled the half-wild Ismael of my primary school days and I couldn't get over my amazement. It was true what the old primary school photo had said. Life certainly is full of changes. In my uncle's garden, Ismael was holding forth like a professor, with authority and rhetorical style. My friend and I didn't know how best to resist his reasoning.

'But why do you still trap lizards? You still haven't explained that.'

'I don't trap them, I collect them. To save them, of course.'

'To save them?'

But this time we were only pretending to be amazed. We hadn't forgotten the remark Ismael had made about the seascape hanging on the wall of his pub, and you didn't have to be a genius to grasp what he meant by 'saving' them. My friend and I began to feel ridiculous.

'I belong to a society,' Ismael began, by way of explanation. 'We look after endangered species. I look after lizards. They're in a very bad way. A lot of them are dying from the insecticides farmers use. The one last night was very sick. I took it back to the hut, but I don't know . . . I don't know if it will survive.'

'You've got a hut?' my friend asked.

'Yes, right here, next to the church. It's like a little hospital. And do you know who looks after everything when I'm working?'

We shook our heads.

'Albino María. He really loves lizards. Even more than I do. And I give him a little money for the work he does.'

He was looking at me and smiling as he spoke. But I felt incapable of saying anything. I was speechless.

Fortunately, at that point my uncle interrupted the conversation.

'Are you all right out there?' he called to us from the door to the house.

'Fine! The shade from this tree is wonderful!' Naturally it was Ismael who replied.

'We'll have to change the programme. Samuel has just got into the bath. How do you feel about having lunch at half past two?'

'Whatever suits you best, uncle. We're in no hurry.'

I wasn't telling the truth, for my one desire at that moment was to be somewhere else, but . . . how can you avoid lying when the truth is impossible to explain? My uncle could never imagine the conversation taking place at that table.

'We can go and see the hut if you like,' Ismael suggested. 'If we go via the colonnade by the church we can be there in less than five minutes.' We had no alternative but to accept.

'This is the same way we came the day they took that photo of us, do you remember?' I said to Ismael as we went up the hill. My tone was conciliatory. Deep down I wanted to excuse myself for the injustice we had done him. He was not a nice person, but neither was he someone with an unhealthy obsession with lizards.

He said only: 'Yes, you're right.' He had put on his dark glasses by then.

Ilobate, Muino, Pepane, Arbe, Legarra, Zumargain, Etxeberi, Ostatu, Motse . . . we walked past the houses we had seen so often in our childhood and reached the stone steps. They were just the same as in the photo: old, serious, full of cracks.

'I stood here, on the top step. Albino María stood there, right next to me,' said Ismael, standing on one corner of the third step and mopping with a white handkerchief at the sweat brought on by the climb.

It was a mocking insinuation aimed exclusively at me: 'Why don't you say now that Albino María went mad because of me?' that was what those words meant.

'What are you two doing up there? It's getting late!' called my friend from the shade of the church cemetery. He understood how uncomfortable I felt being alone with Ismael.

'We're coming. But don't worry, we're nearly there.'

The hut was behind the church, in the middle of a field surrounded by barbed wire. Built of white-painted cement, it was about thirty feet by nine in area and about nine feet high. The small windows were covered with wire netting. The iron door was painted green.

'The hut is divided into two sections. In one I keep the lizards that have nearly recovered. In the other I keep the ones that are still sick,' Ismael told us once we had gone through the gate in the fence.

'And what happens then? What do you do with the lizards once they're completely cured?' asked my friend.

'I look for a clean river and release them near there,' replied Ismael taking out the key to the hut from his pocket.

We smelled the stench the moment he opened the door. It was really disgusting, sickening.

'Oh, the smell!' said Ismael when he saw us covering our mouths and noses. 'It's not very pleasant, is it? I don't even notice it any more. What do you think? A lovely sight, eh?' he added, taking off his sunglasses.

No, it wasn't a lovely sight. It looked more like a warehouse for storing rotting vegetables and apples and not even the leafy branches placed in one corner modified that impression. Moreover, it was horribly hot inside.

'Where are they?' asked my friend, like me looking at the floor.

'Don't look at the floor. Look at the walls,' said Ismael.

There they were, clinging to the cement walls. I saw five on the left wall, three on the right and one more on the ceiling. Their throats puffed in and out. From time to time they opened their disproportionately large mouths and out flicked a black thread, their tongue.

'I've seen enough, I'm going outside,' I said. My desire to throw up was getting stronger by the minute.

'Wait a moment, let's go and see the cages in the other part.'

I flatly refused. I went out into the field and my friend followed.

'Well, I don't find them disgusting,' said Ismael, coming over to us. He put on his sunglasses again. 'Nature is an absolute unity, a totality, and that's why I love all animals. Lizards, for example, remind me of birds, because I know that they're almost the same thing. You mustn't forget that the first bird was born of a lizard. I know you don't feel the same, but . . .'

'No, we don't feel the same,' my friend broke in, heading for the fence. His stomach was churning too.

'Let me just shut the door and I'll come with you. I have to pick up my car from the garden.'

'Any moment now he'll start spouting about theology,' my friend whispered. He was rather angry. It had been a dirty trick taking us to that place just before lunch.

Fortunately, Ismael didn't persist in explaining his concept of nature and we walked back in complete silence. We reached my uncle's house just as the clock was striking half past two.

'Here ends the story of the lizard. Try using a bit less imagination next time,' Ismael said from the window of his red Lancia.

'We'll try.'

He reversed out of the garden. A few seconds later he had disappeared from view.

'At last!' said my friend. We didn't go back into the house straight away. We wanted to get a bit of fresh air and forget the disgust provoked in us by the stench of the lizards.

'Oh well, there's nothing we can do!' said my friend, thinking out loud. 'It seems we did go a bit overboard with our hypotheses. But it doesn't matter, it's good to make a fool of yourself once in a while. I think we let ourselves get carried away by our passion for stories. And anyway, basically, we were right. There is something a bit sinister about Ismael.'

'I quite agree,' I said. But I felt distinctly depressed.

'Martini time!' called my uncle from the living room window.

'The more I see of your uncle, the more I like him. A couple of minutes with him and we'll have forgotten all about the lizards.'

'Yes, you're right. It'll be a really good lunch. And I'm sure Mr Smith will have some interesting stories to tell.'

We were not mistaken. Lunch with the two ex-emigrants flowed by on a wave of jokes and anecdotes, and my friend and I could only marvel – once again – at how full our elders' lives seemed to have been.

Around five o'clock – returning once more to the programme – with our cognac and coffee before us, we settled down to talking about literature: what exactly was originality, where did plagiarism start and end, what should the function of art be? . . . and that was the moment Mr Smith chose, as he put it, to give us a surprise.

'Ah, my friend,' he said to my uncle, 'my opinions are not as strict and severe as your own. I'm also in favour of intertextuality. I agree with these young men.'

'Really? I don't believe it!'

'Well, it's true. And I'm going to give you the proof right now.'

Our eyes lit up. Mr Smith's tape recorder was on the table.

'Wait a second,' I said. 'If you record the story on there, you'll erase the one about Amazonas. Uncle, have you got a blank tape?'

'Yes, I have,' he replied, a little puzzled, for we hadn't yet told him about the previous night's adventures.

'Don't worry! One side of the tape is still blank,' said Mr Smith to reassure us. And he began to recount in English, with a Dublin accent, a story entitled *Wei Lie Deshang, a fantasia on the theme of Marco Polo*. The time has come, then, to insert yet another parenthesis, because I find it impossible to continue my search for the last word without first transcribing this story. I did my best to make the translation a good one. Now let's see the result.

WEI LIE DESHANG

A fantasia on the theme of Marco Polo

WEI LIE DESHANG was not like the other servants at the palace that Aga Kubalai, the latest governor of the city of Kiang'Si, had had built on a small island in the bay, and he never resigned himself to his fate. Whilst the others complained about their lot, he reflected in silence; whilst their eyes flowed with tears, his eyes, full of hatred, remained coldly watchful.

By the time he was twenty, after five years working in the palace abattoir, he felt his desire for vengeance might drive him mad, for he saw the head of Aga Kubalai on that of every animal he butchered, images that went on to fill his dreams. But he had a strong character and he went on hating, went on searching for the path that would lead him to fulfill the promise which, in the name of his parents, he had made when he was fifteen, the moment he first set foot on the island. Aga Kubalai must die and Kiang'Si, the city that had accepted him as governor, must be destroyed.

Ten years later, when he was thirty, he heard talk of a new religion preached by a beggar called Mohammed, and he saw at last the path he had sought for so long. It was a dangerous path and difficult to forge, particularly in its early stages, because it required him to escape from the city nearly every night and return before the sky was lit by the first star of morning. But he preferred to risk dying at the hands of the guards to dying, like certain snakes, poisoned by his own hatred.

It took him three years to achieve his objective. Then, sure that no one could stop him, he decided to leave the island for ever and go to the mountains of Annam. There lived the men who would believe in him and who, later, would be the instruments of his vengeance. The days of Kiang'Si were numbered.

One moonless night, along a path that crossed the governor's hunting wood, linking the abattoir with a small beach on the island, Wei Lie Deshang set off on his last journey. It was his usual route, the same one he had taken on each and every one of his night-time escapes and he arrived without mishap at the rock where he moored the sampan he had bought three years ago in the city. A moment later, he was rowing towards the coast.

Kiang'Si, the most prosperous city on the Cathay Sea, was situated on a wide bay, built on the gentle hills that overlooked the beach. Beautiful by day, it was even lovelier by night when, by the light of the torches that lit it, the buildings seemed weightless, a succession of shining, red roofs. By night, Kiang'Si did not look like a city; it looked like a flock of birds about to alight on the sea.

But Wei Lie Deshang felt utterly indifferent to the beauty and kept his eyes fixed on the waves as he rowed. Once out in the bay, he steered the sampan towards the city's great pagoda.

He disembarked near a flight of steps crowded with cripples and beggars and headed for the place where, for the last eighteen years, his god Siddartha had awaited him. He had not set foot in the temple since the day he had been taken to the island.

The gigantic image was covered with orange flowers. Beside it Wei Lie Deshang seemed but an insignificant man.

As soon as he had knelt down he heard a voice inside him say: 'What do you want, servant?' Siddartha was speaking to him in the voice of a harsh father.

'I know I look like a servant,' replied Wei Lie Deshang in humble prayer, 'but I come from a family of soldiers and the blood in my veins is still that of a soldier.'

'So why are you not a soldier?'

'Because my family rebelled against Aga Kubalai, the foreign governor. The punishment for them was death. For me, for I was only a child then, the humiliation of being a servant.'

Wei Lie Deshang closed his eyes and fell silent. It hurt him to remember all that had happened at the time of the rebellion. Why

had the city of Kiang'Si surrendered to a man like Aga Kubalai? No
one had wanted to hear his family's call to arms, no one had wanted
to struggle against the new regime. Not the merchants, not the
priests, not even the captains in the army. But that betrayal would
not go unpunished.

'Now I want to avenge myself, Father,' continued Wei Lie
Deshang, prostrating himself before his god. 'Everything is ready.
All I need now is your blessing.' But Siddartha would not agree to
his plea. His voice grew even harsher.

'Tell me first,' he heard the voice inside him say, 'why you
became a thief and a murderer. In three years you have killed more
than thirty merchants.'

'I needed their gold, Father.'

'And why in that house in To'she do you keep a long list of
names and numbers?'

'They are the names of all the traitors of this city, Father. And
the numbers indicate the places where those traitors live.'

'You should not avenge yourself, servant. Hatred cannot put
an end to hatred; only love can do that. That is an ancient law.'

'I want to kill those who broke another ancient law and
allowed a foreigner to rule in Kiang'Si.'

'Silence, servant!' the mighty Siddartha's voice changed, he
grew angry. 'Remove these malignant desires from your heart. Go
back to the island and confess your sins.'

'Why do you speak now with the voice of Aga Kubalai?'
shouted Wei Lie Deshang, standing up.

'Do not speak thus to your god!'

'You're a traitor too!' exclaimed Wei Lie Deshang retreating to
the temple exit. He was perplexed. 'I'll burn this temple down,
Siddartha!'

He ran out of the pagoda and did not stop until he had reached
the house which he had bought, three years before, in the To'she
district. He had just lost the protection of his god, but gazing upon
the stolen golden bezants and on the parchments covered in names

and numbers was enough to make him forget. That night, for the first time in many weeks, he smoked opium and saw, with all the detail and clarity of a vision, the end of that path he had imagined on the day he first heard talk of the beggar Mohammed. Kiang'Si would pay for its treachery: his vengeance would be terrible.

The following morning, dressed as a merchant now, he set off on his journey to the mountainous region of Annam, mingling with real merchants and following their noisy caravan of carts and horses. But very soon, as soon as they were away from Kiang'Si, he left the group and – asking in the villages through which he passed – he began to recruit the people he would need in order to carry out his plans. From one place, where he saw that the houses were solidly built, he would recruit carpenters and stonemasons; from the next place, young girls and cooks. His gold opened all doors.

Fifteen days later, with his journey at an end, having reached the mountains of Annam, the former servant Wei Lie Deshang chose a small valley, the one that of all others seemed most hidden and solitary. Then, he began giving orders.

'Build five palaces,' he told the carpenters and stonemasons. 'Make of the whole valley a beautiful garden complete with streams and fountains,' he told the gardeners. 'Watch over the young girls and the cattle and let no intruder near,' he told the mercenaries.

After listening attentively, the whole group – made up of more than five hundred people – scattered throughout the valley and began to put up tents. 'Your sorrow must be very great,' said one old mercenary, coming up to him. 'I never saw anyone who, being rich and capable of finding happiness amongst others, chose instead the seclusion and solitude you have chosen now.'

The fraternal feelings shown by the old mercenary touched Wei Lie Deshang.

'I see you are a noble man, and from now on I want you to be my lieutenant. But this is not what you think. The paradise I am going to build in this valley is not intended for me, but for the Annamites who live in this region.'

The mercenary did not understand the meaning of those words, but he remained silent.

'What do you know of the Annamites?' Wei Lie Deshang asked, looking up at the high, craggy mountains surrounding the valley.

'Only that they are excellent warriors and are unrivalled as hunters of tigers.'

'Yes, that's what I heard in the kitchens of Kiang'Si. And that they are like children, innocent and credulous.'

'Siddartha would be pleased with them. More than he is with me!' laughed the mercenary.

'The Annamites don't believe in Siddartha, but in a beggar called Mohammed. That's why I want to transform this valley, to give them the paradise their prophet promised them.'

'Well, if that is your desire, they shall have it.'

The old mercenary gave a half-smile. Then, returning to the other mercenaries, he hurried them to their posts.

The people who had followed Wei Lie Deshang worked for a year, raising palaces and towers, planting rosebushes and lotus trees, building fountains with four jets from which flowed water, milk, honey and wine. Then, once the work was over, they received their promised reward in golden bezants and returned to their houses. Only the young girls and the mercenaries remained in the valley.

The moment to approach an Annamite village had arrived.

'Choose ten men and follow me,' Wei Lie Deshang said to the old mercenary.

'Are we going in search of our first Annamite?' asked the mercenary.

Wei Lie Deshang nodded gravely.

'Don't worry, everything will go well,' said the mercenary encouragingly. But the grave expression lingered on Wei Lie

Deshang's face. He was about to face the final test. The days that followed would decide the success or failure of his years of struggle.

They walked for three hours through dense forests, keeping a close eye out for tigers and contrasting that wild landscape with the delightful valley they had just left. Towards midday they found a path and Wei Lie Deshang ordered his men to find a place to lie in ambush.

'We'll wait here for an Annamite to pass by,' he told them. Then he gave them the orders they were to follow when that happened.

They did not have long to wait, for that path was very close to a village of hunters. They saw the man approach carrying his bow and arrows on his back.

When he drew level with them, they raised their swords and ten mercenaries knocked him to the ground.

'Die!' they cried. But they did not kill him. Instead they had him inhale a narcotic that rendered him unconscious.

Once back in the valley and still following Wei Lie Deshang's orders, they left the sleeping Annamite by a fountain surrounded by rosetrees. By then, it was evening and the sky seemed to be composed of tiny fragments of blue crystal. The north wind ruffled the petals of the flowers.

Wei Lie Deshang and the old mercenary stationed themselves at a window in the main palace to watch over the Annamite's sleep.

Just before nightfall, the Annamite regained consciousness. He got up from the ground and looked at each of the four sides of the valley with their groves of trees, their fountains and palaces. Then, leaning over the fountain, he plunged his hand first into the milk and then into the honey. He did not need to know any more; bursting with happiness, he raised his arms to heaven and began singing hymns of praise.

A smile lit up Wei Lie Deshang's face. After all his efforts, time had proved him right. The Annamite believed himself to be in the paradise promised him by the beggar Mohammed.

'Bring him to my presence,' he said to the mercenary. Both of them were dressed all in white.

Believing himself to be before the prophet, the hunter prostrated himself on the ground as soon as he entered the hall of the main palace.

'*La ilaha ila Ala,*' Wei Lie Deshang said to him. He had not forgotten what he had learned in the kitchens of Aga Kubalai.

The hunter nodded, trembling, and called him Mohammed. Then he thanked him for the death he had chosen to give him.

'I did not deserve it, Lord, just as I did not deserve paradise, for I have been a sinner.'

'Mohammed does not see you as a sinner and welcomes you to paradise. Now enjoy the reward I have chosen to give you.'

Through the window of the palace could be seen a sky full of stars. But Wei Lie Deshang saw only the star that pointed to Kiang'Si.

'Kiang'Si,' he thought, 'the first grain of sand measuring out your time has fallen.'

'What shall we do now?' asked the old mercenary once the Annamite had been led to another palace full of young girls.

'I want two hundred more men like him.'

'It will take me a month.'

'I can wait,' replied Wei Lie Deshang.

But the old mercenary did not need that much time. After only fifteen days, there was already a large group of Annamites in the palaces and the gardens, laughing and singing and, when night fell, lying with the young girls.

Every evening they murmured: 'Allah, beloved God, we thank you with all our heart.' Not one of them suspected the truth.

Sometimes an angel came to them and asked them to go and see Mohammed, their good prophet.

'Fear not,' Wei Lie Deshang told them when he saw how they

trembled, 'you have committed no sin and I will not take away your happiness.' He would talk to them of a city on earth, Kiang'Si, filled with iniquity and disrespect for Allah.

'They deserve to be punished, Father,' the Annamites would say.

Then Wei Lie Deshang showed them the name of a sinner in Kiang'Si. Next to the name was a drawing which – having been copied from the numbers on his parchments – indicated the place where the sinner lived.

'You will be the bearers of the divine punishment of Allah. This angel will guide you once you are outside paradise. Prepare your arrows with the poison you used to employ to kill tigers. May the will of Allah be done.'

The old mercenary, the angel, nodded. He would accompany them to the city, he would bring them back to paradise once they had carried out the punishment. Relieved that the sin to be punished was not theirs, the Annamites expressed a desire to leave as soon as possible.

'Tonight you will sleep in my palace,' said Wei Lie Deshang, 'and early tomorrow morning, when you wake, you will look about you and you will see the path that will lead you to Kiang'Si.'

'May the will of Allah be done,' that was the maxim constantly repeated by the Annamites. And the divine will was always done. Death, the most terrible of punishments, spread throughout the city of Kiang'Si: a judge and his whole family; five captains in Aga Kubalai's army; three merchants, all were found at the door of their houses slain by poisoned arrows.

The Annamites returned from Kiang'Si laughing, happy that they had been able to punish the sinners who scorned Allah.

Six months later, when the whole city was in a state of terror, a patrol captured two Annamites during the tremendous confusion that ensued after Siddartha's pagoda had been set on fire. The captain of the patrol carried the news to the governor's island.

The mighty Aga Kubalai was greatly relieved when he heard

the captain's words and he ordered the two men to be brought to him, for he burned with desire to see the faces of the murderers. He wanted to know where they came from, who had sent them, why they were attacking him.

And he gave another order too:

'Seek out all the merchants and lords of the city and bring them to me. Let them hear the confessions of the murderers too.'

Aga Kubalai was concerned about the rumours that cast doubt on his abilities as governor and he wanted to show them his first triumph.

They all gathered in the cellar of the palace, the merchants, the great lords, the Annamite assassins. And the executioner began the torture.

'Who sent you?' asked Aga Kubalai after the first cries of agony from the Annamites.

'Mohammed, our prophet,' replied the Annamites.

'Where are you from?'

'From paradise.'

The governor made a sign to the executioner and the torture grew bloodier, more agonising.

'Now tell me the truth. Who sent you?' he asked when the executioner had finished his work.

'Mohammed, our prophet!' cried the two prisoners.

One of the merchants observing the scene went over to the Annamites and wiped away the blood.

'I'll give you money, a lot of money. Tell us who your chief is,' he said in a gentle voice.

'Allah is our one true God,' said one of the Annamites weakly. The other was already dead.

Aga Kubalai was gesticulating like a madman. He threatened the executioner. But it was all in vain, for shortly afterwards the second Annamite also fell silent for ever.

The disquiet amongst those gathered in the cellar grew even more intense with the arrival of the palace guard.

'Lord Governor,' said the guard, bowing his head. 'Your eldest son has died. With a poisoned arrow through his heart.'

Those who had been present at the torture exchanged glances. Aga Kubalai covered his face with his hands. Then, in groups, they all hurried back to their houses.

X AND Y

'**I**T LOOKS like the story about the lizard has kept you pretty busy,' our uncle said when we'd told him all about the Ismael affair. By then it was half past eight at night and the three of us were sitting in the library. Exhausted after his night spent on the grass, Mr Smith had retired to his room once he'd told us his Wei Lie Deshang story.

'It certainly has. It's kept us busy and made us look pretty foolish,' we admitted.

'How could it be otherwise, boys?' said my uncle with an exaggerated sigh.

'What do you mean, uncle?'

'What I mean is, that it couldn't have turned out otherwise, given the weakness of your literary theories. For what happened to you has nothing to do with your alleged desire to get to the bottom of things, nor, indeed even less so, with the great powers of imagination you believe you possess. All that is involved here is your mistaken interpretation of the little story about lizards.'

'You're being very strict and severe, my friend,' Mr Smith would have said had he been there.

'Explain yourself, uncle,' we said.

'It's obvious! You both consider literature to be a game without any practical use. And believing that, you were incapable of unearthing the clue hidden in the story your parents used to tell you. Because, if we look at it closely, what is the moral of the story? What does it tell children? What do you think it says to children? Well, it tells them that it can be very dangerous to go to sleep on the grass and that they should be very careful. "If you fall asleep, a lizard will come along and crawl into your ear," the mother tells the child. But what is the mother really worried about? What is the real danger? The lizard? Of course not! Not at all!'

'What can it be then? Snakes?' my friend said.

'Snakes are a possibility. But not just snakes. It could be the dampness of the grass, or a mad dog, or a maniac, anything. There could be many dangers, so many that listing them one by one to the child would be absurd. That's the whole *raison d'être* of the fable of the lizard because it sums up, in the form of a metaphor, every possible danger. Bear in mind too that the lizard is like a small dragon and in traditional stories dragons are always a symbol of evil. So everything in the fable fits, it's very logical.'

'What is less logical, uncle, is what you said before, about how, for us, literature is just a game. But we'd best leave that argument for another time. Returning to the subject, uncle, tell me something, why a lizard and not a snake? I think a snake would be a much more suitable protagonist.'

'What do you want? Do you want me to give you a literature class, is that it?' asked my uncle with his most provocative of smiles.

'We're used to it, uncle. Don't you worry about us,' I replied. The literary gatherings in his house usually ended with him delivering a vehement lecture.

'You may well both be used to it, but you never take a blind bit of notice of me. You least of all, nephew. Since to you I'm just a relic from the nineteenth century . . .'

'Get on with it, uncle. We can see how pleased you are with our "mistaken" interpretation of the story. But do get to the point, it's getting late.'

'Late? Surely you're not leaving tonight.'

'I'm afraid so. Don't forget he's a doctor. He has to go to work tomorrow.'

'I've no option but to go back, but you could stay. I can get the train,' said my friend.

'If there is one, of course.'

'Oh, there is one. There's one I sometimes catch and that leaves quite soon. I can tell you the exact time right now,' said my uncle, opening a drawer and pulling out a timetable. 'It's at nine fifteen,' he told us.

'Well, if you don't mind going back on the train, I'll take you to the station and you can catch that one. If we leave the house at nine, that'll give us plenty of time.'

'Fine.'

'The fact is it would suit me if you stayed,' said my uncle, looking at me. 'As you know, I haven't got a car, and what with Samuel being here . . .'

'Don't worry, uncle. I'll play taxi driver and take you anywhere you want. You ought to get some benefit out of having a modern nephew like me.'

'That's settled, then. Now on with the literature class,' said my friend.

'Where were we?'

'We were discussing why it was a lizard and not a snake?'

'Ah, yes. Well, I think that mothers in those days were very sensible, and were very careful when it came to frightening their children. They needed to frighten them but only a little, not so much that they would be utterly terrified by the story and develop a listless, cowardly attitude towards life. And from that point of view, the lizard was much more suitable. Because, thanks to some sort of instinct, the child understands that the danger is not a serious one. He'll follow his mother's advice but he'll do it just in case, without giving much importance to the matter.'

'We obviously weren't blessed with that instinct,' I remarked.

'Perhaps it isn't a question of instinct,' said my friend. 'Maybe the child reads the expression on his mother's face or in her voice or in her gestures, and so understands that what she's telling him isn't so very important. If the mother were to mention a snake, his reading would be quite different.'

'Yes, that's an interesting point. You can't tell a story about snakes without feeling some sort of repulsion or anxiety. Maybe you're right.'

'But some lizards are dangerous. The *Lacerta viridis* for example,' I said.

'I don't think so, nephew. As Ismael told you, the lizards in this country are harmless. And so, by the way, are those in England. You only have to think of that poor lizard Bill whom Lewis Carroll's Alice met. He's the saddest creature in the whole book.'

'I don't remember him,' I confessed.

'Neither do I,' said my friend.

'Wait. I'll show you.'

My uncle went over to the bookshelves and, after searching first one shelf then another, he returned holding the book.

'Look, there he is.'

The illustration showed some animals, a rabbit and a rat amongst them, holding down a small, contrite lizard and forcing him to drink brandy.

'They want to get him drunk against his will. A real unfortunate, our Bill.'

'You can say that again, uncle.'

The illustrations were delightful and we would like to have looked at them all. But the uncle from Montevideo was a very impatient teacher. The lesson must go on.

'Anyway, getting back to the subject of your mistaken interpretation of the story, you were really groping in the dark. Far more than one would have expected from two lovers of literature,' he said adopting his strict and severe tone again. 'Because, on reflection, the lizard story could also be interpreted from your point of view. I mean, it's possible to understand it using that "intertextuality" you're so keen on.'

'Do go on, worthy uncle, you're speaking like Solomon himself.'

'Laugh if you want to, nephew. But what, for example, do you make of this lullaby: "Never fall asleep in the woods, my dear; for a hunter might find you and take you for a hare".'

'It's obviously about the same thing. Which just goes to show that this preoccupation mothers have with losing their children must be very widespread,' said my friend.

'And there's more. For example, what about the character of Sacamantecas? Or have you forgotten what they used to tell us when we were children? "Never go out alone at night or Sacamantecas will carry you off".'

'I certainly do remember. He appeared in all my nightmares,' said my friend.

My uncle's eyes were shining.

'Well, do I have a surprise for you! What do you think of this: all those stories were invented in the nineteenth century!'

'That I can't swallow, uncle,' I replied. 'I can go along with you as far as the universality of the theme is concerned, and I accept that the lizard may be nothing but a variation on that theme, but as for it all starting in the nineteenth century, that I really can't believe. With all due respect, it seems a bit of an exaggeration to me.'

'All right, fine, I agree I've gone too far. Maybe not every single one of the stories arose in the nineteenth century, after all there have always been mothers. But what I meant was that it was precisely in the nineteenth century that there was a boom in such stories, that was when they were developed and became popular. And that, dear nephew, is the truth.'

'And why was that? What happened to make mothers more than normally preoccupied? Tell us quickly, uncle. If you don't, I'll miss my train!'

'The train! Exactly!'

My uncle was very excited.

'What about the train?'

'Will you give me three minutes to tell you?'

'It's a quarter to nine. You've got until nine o'clock.'

'Right, listen carefully. The railway arrived here in the mid-nineteenth century and it represented an enormous change, a change we can't even imagine now. Remember that the only form of transport until then had been the horse, every journey and all transportation involved horses. Right, so there everyone is with their personal quadruped at home when suddenly there's this contraption that can reach speeds of up to eighty miles an hour. It frightened people and many of them refused to get on and travel in it. And those who did, that is, those who were brave and bold enough to get on the train, had a terrible time. First, they all felt sick. Second, they would look out of the window and be unable to see the landscape or it would look all fuzzy, like a blurred photograph.'

'Really? I don't believe it!' I exclaimed.

'Oh I do,' affirmed my friend. 'We have to bear in mind that our eyes get used to speed the minute they're open. But that wouldn't have been the case in those days. Not as regards the first generation of train travellers. Their eyes wouldn't have been adapted to it.'

'This history of the train says exactly the same thing,' said my uncle, who had got to his feet again to show us another fat book.

'We've only got ten minutes, uncle. We haven't got time to read the whole book,' I said.

'Then I'll go on. Well, as I was saying, the train was a real shock for those people. And so it wasn't long before rumours began to spread; that the machine signalled the imminent arrival of the end of the world, that it caused some disease or other . . . that sort of thing. That was the prevailing mood when someone had the happy idea to ask this question: "How is it that it goes so fast?" Answer: "Because they grease its wheels with a special oil." "Really? And how do they get that special oil?" "How? Nothing simpler, by melting down little children. They capture any children they find wandering about here and take them to England. And there they melt them down in huge pots and . . ." '

'That's what they said?'

'Yes, that's what they said. It was the start of the industrial age and a lot of children must have gone missing while their parents were working in the factories. People just linked the two facts. And they were so convinced by that story that they took it out on the stations and started setting fire to them. Look at this photograph . . .'

My uncle opened the thick book containing the history of the train and showed us a photograph of a station burned to the ground. At the bottom of the photograph was written: 'Martorell station after being set on fire by the women of the village.'

'The women, not the men.'

'Exactly. It was the mothers.'

'But, uncle, how, if I may be so bold, do you link this business about the train with the story about the lizard?'

'Intertextuality, nephew, intertextuality.'

'Be more precise, please.'

'By the shortest route, nephew. What did we say before? We reached the conclusion that the story about the lizard and the story about Sacamantecas were one and the same, right? That they were two stories whose one aim was to protect children. Now tell me: what does the word "Sacamantecas" mean?'

My friend got in before me: 'Someone who extracts fat or oil.'

'We could extend that definition and say: "someone who extracts the fat or oil needed to grease the wheels of a train".'

'Are you sure?'

'Of course I am. Because Sacamantecas was a murderer who became famous just around the time the train arrived on the scene. As far as I know he didn't dedicate himself to killing children, in fact his victims were all very old. But, of course, the mothers didn't pick up on that fact. All they knew was that their children might disappear. That was their great fear. And the character of Sacamantecas grew out of that fear.'

'Not a murderer of old people, but a stealer of children.'

'Exactly. A typically nineteenth-century story, as I said before.'

'A beautiful lecture, uncle.'

'Thank you, nephew. And let's hope you show greater lucidity next time. You've both got more than enough imagination, but you don't reflect enough.'

'That's just what Ismael said.'

'Well, it's not surprising. Fancy making an accusation like that. And all because of a childish story that not even children entirely believe.'

'At least it served some purpose. Having heard your lecture, I'll get on the train in quite a different frame of mind,' said my friend, getting up.

'What time is it?'

'Almost nine o'clock, uncle. We have to go.'

'Come on then. I'll walk you to the car.'

The garden was not as it had been at midday. The monotonous song of the crickets had been silenced and a very fragile white moon was now making its way across the sky. It was the quietest moment of the day.

The farewells between my uncle and my friend took longer than expected and when we set off for the station it was already a few minutes past nine.

'How many bends are there from here to the station?' asked my friend.

'Not many. It's a very straight, flat stretch of road. I think we'll get there in time. But be warned, I'm going to have to drive very fast.'

'As you wish. I commend my soul to your skill.'

'It hasn't been a bad weekend, has it?'

'It certainly hasn't. And in the end all the unknown factors were explained.'

'The X and the Y.'

'The X of Mr Smith and the Y of Ismael.'

'But how odd that two such different unknowns should end up in the same equation!'

'That's life!' exclaimed my friend with the theatricality he always gave to such phrases.

But the speed I had to drive at did not favour conversation and we travelled the rest of the way in silence, listening to music on the radio. We reached the station with just two minutes to spare before the train left.

'Well, that's that. Back to work tomorrow,' my friend said with a sigh as we sat down on a bench on the platform.

'There wasn't any sign on Ismael's hut, was there?' I said. The image of that repellent hospital for lizards had just resurfaced in my mind.

'Why mention that now?' he asked, looking me in the eye.

'Oh, nothing. I was just remembering what Ismael told us. About him belonging to a special society and all that.'

My friend looked bemused.

'Don't you remember? He said he was a member of a society for the protection of animals. But what intrigues me now is that there wasn't some special sign on the hut. I don't know. It seems logical that there would be something, don't you think?'

'What are you trying to say? That the second unknown hasn't yet been fully explained? Weren't you listening to your uncle? Ismael himself explained it all in graphic detail.'

The station loudspeakers announced the arrival of the train. I didn't have time to go into subtleties.

'All right, all right. But I'd still like to find out about that sign.'

'What possible importance can it have? Even if Ismael did lie to us, so what?' cried my friend, embracing me warmly. 'Promise me one thing. That you won't go and see if that wretched hut has got a sign on it or not! I know you too well and I'm sure that's what you intend doing.'

'Here's the train,' I said.

I must confess that most of my life has been dogged by obsessions and that never, not even as a child, have I been able to muster the strength of mind to expel from my head those harmful, disagreeable 'tenants'. Any idea, however strange, can settle in my mind and live there, for as long as it likes.

My friend had asked me not to go to the hut and part of me demanded the same thing: that I abandon that story once and for all and go to bed.

But it was no use. The idea was inside my head and refused to leave. I had no option but to go to the hut and find out if there was a sign or not.

I returned to Obaba at the same speed at which I had driven to the station a quarter of an hour before and, passing my uncle's house, I parked the car next to the stone steps by the church.

Before going on, I had a moment's hesitation. Did I really want to go to the hut? Why was I still suspicious of Ismael? Did I perhaps hate him? In the end, as my friend had said, what importance could a sign possibly have?

They were all worthwhile considerations but none of them could hold me back. That evil tenant had made himself master of the house. He was the guide and instigator of my actions.

'I know what brought me here,' I thought as I walked through the colonnade by the church. 'It was the parallelism between the lizard story and the story about Sacamantecas. That's what set me on the trail. And my sixth sense tells me that I should go carefully, that I should not forget that Sacamentecas was a murderer.'

My original intention was to go as far as the barbed wire fence and have a look from there. But as soon as I reached that point, I realised that was impossible. The moon gave very little light and the hut was engulfed in the darkness of night. If I wanted to find out if there was a sign or not, I would have to go closer.

'I'll have to jump over the fence,' I thought. A moment later I was standing by the hut.

'There's no sign here,' I deduced after running my hands over the surface of the door. Then I heard a noise. It came from inside the hut.

'Who's there?'

I didn't have time to run away. The door flew open and a thin figure appeared on the threshold. It was Ismael.

For some moments neither of us moved.

'Would you mind telling me what you're doing here?' shouted Ismael when he'd recovered from his surprise.

I tried to say something but I couldn't utter a word. I was dumbstruck.

'What's wrong with you? Have you gone mad?'

He grabbed me by my shirt and shook me.

'You'd better not hit me,' I warned.

He didn't hit me, instead he gave me a shove and pushed me into the hut. My hands touched the rotting vegetation on the floor.

'Since you're so interested in finding out what happens in this hut, you can have the whole night to do just that!'

He let out a curse and shut the door. I heard the key turn in the lock.

'Open the door!' I shouted, getting up and going over to one of the useless little windows. But my efforts were in vain. Ismael had left by the outer door and was striding away. When you're angry, you feel only your anger: you see nothing, hear nothing, smell nothing. The fire burning inside monopolises all your senses and prevents you establishing any relation with your surroundings. But that moment passes, the fire goes out and the surroundings, ignored until then, begin to make themselves felt with a strange intensity. They seem to have become bigger, stronger, more painful. You have never before been so intensely aware of sights, sounds, smells. If you had any strength left, you would get angry and start shouting again. But you have none and must resign yourself to your suffering.

That was the process I went through in that hut. At first I was very agitated, yelling and raining down curses on Ismael, or blaming myself for having acted as I did. But the worst came later, when I began to comprehend my situation.

I was sickened by the stench given off by the lizards and my anxiety only grew every time I heard the muffled crunching noise they made as they munched on the rotting vegetation.

'I can't stay here!' I said to myself each time my eyes caught sight of the silhouette of the lizards clinging to the wall. But there was no point whining like a child. I had to stay there.

Standing up by one of the windows, I tried again and again to forget that filthy prison. I absorbed myself in contemplation of the moon shining in the sky and wondered why it was yellow. Why did it change colour? Through what process did I receive its light?

why did it have such an influence on the cultivation of vegetables? And when I had exhausted the subject, I scoured the corners of my mind for another. And when that too was exhausted, I relived journeys I had made throughout the world or distracted myself with sexual fantasies.

But trying to forget the presence of the lizards was an impossible task.

I spent two or three hours locked in that battle, until I could no longer stand the pain gripping my knees and I decided to sit down.

'But I won't go to sleep!' I exclaimed to cheer myself up.

I knew I would be unable to resist though. No, I couldn't stay awake, I would sleep and once I was asleep a lizard would come along and crawl into my ear and then . . . but how could I think such nonsense? Or didn't I trust what my uncle had said? Wasn't Bill – the poor lizard – the kindest and most unfortunate of all the animals to appear in Lewis Carroll's books? Was I perhaps in South America? No, I was in Obaba. And the lizards of Obaba had nothing to do with any kind of irreversible mental pathology.

The unease these reflections produced in me kept me awake for another two hours. Then I fell asleep.

'Didn't you have anywhere better to sleep? You should have come to my house! We've got loads of beds at home, at least ten,' I heard someone say.

Albino María was leaning over me. He was smiling at me affectionately, saliva drooling from his open mouth.

'That's very kind of you, but it doesn't matter now!' I said, hurriedly getting up. But he was too deaf to understand anything I said and gave only a snorting laugh.

'Aren't they pretty?' he said then, picking up a lizard and placing it in his hand. 'So green,' he added. I was already at the door of the hut.

'Yes, they certainly are very pretty. But I have to go now, Albino María. Sorry I can't stay.' And without another word, I raced off towards the fence.

'Come back any time you like!' shouted Albino María from the doorway.

THE TORCH

I WANTED to find a word to finish the book with. I mean I wanted to find one word, but it couldn't be just any word, it had to be a word that was both definitive and all-encompassing. I mean, to put it another way, that I wanted to be another Joubert, that he and I shared the same goal: 's'il est un homme tourmenté par la maudite ambition de mettre tout un livre dans une page, toute une page dans une phrase, cette phrase dans un mot, c'est moi.' Yes, that man was Joubert and, as I have just said, I wanted to be another Joubert.

I felt tired and disillusioned, old before my time, and when I sat down in front of a blank sheet of paper, I would weep. I mean that I found the invention and putting together of sentences was becoming ever more difficult, a torment, the cause of great suffering, which is why, as I said before, I kept dreaming about Joubert.

But I couldn't find that last word. I would look out of the window, I would watch the waves of the sea rising and breaking and I would ask the waves for an answer, but it was no use. Then I asked the stars in the sky and it was the same. I asked other people and that was even worse. I mean they were no help at all, they always ended up leaving me alone again in front of the blank page. And then I would think to myself: Why don't you tell the story of the journey you made to Obaba? Maybe in recounting the events of that weekend you'll find the wretched word. I mean that I screwed up my courage and set off in search of the word, since it clearly had no intention of coming to me. That's what I mean, more or less.

But the task I had set myself turned out to take longer than I thought. I mean recounting what happened on my journey was not the brief, pleasant pastime I had at first supposed, quite the contrary. The days passed and I made no progress. The last word was nowhere to be found. And I would say to myself: All right, it hasn't turned up today, but maybe it will tomorrow. Don't worry about it. Instead of worrying, why not write down that story about Baghdad? And so I did. I mean I devoted all my time to recording the things that had happened on that journey and, in the process, months and even years went by. And what I really wanted kept being left to one side, kept being left farther and farther behind. Some nights Joubert would appear to me in my bedroom and call me to account. Why do you turn away from your true work like a sick dog from a bone? I do not spurn it, master, but there is another story I have to write down first, the one an old man told me at a village fiesta; Laura Sligo, that was the name, the character's name I mean, not the old man's. No, no, no! Joubert would say to me, don't deceive yourself, the problem is that you can't do it, the problem is that you're just like a lot of other writers of today, you're just the same as them, you're identical or similar or comparable. And with that, Joubert would go, leaving me sad. I mean no one enjoys hearing the truth.

For the fact is that I did keep putting off my real work until the next day, again and again, and that was my downfall. Because now it's too late, because now I never will find the final, definitive, all-encompassing word. And that's why I could be likened to those pilgrims who went off in the hope of seeing the sea but died without even setting foot on the beach. For I too am dead, at least according to my uncle. Dead without ever having found the last word. That's why I mentioned the story about the pilgrimage and the beach. I'm not sure if I made myself clear.

But perhaps I'm going too fast, which is utterly ridiculous. I mean it makes me laugh to think that the reason I have to go fast now is that I went too slowly before. I have very little time, in other words, and I'm going much too fast. Or at least that's what they tell me, my friend and my uncle that is. I don't really know why they say that, but they're probably right. We mustn't forget that my friend is a doctor, which is important. But, anyway, as I was saying, I go much too fast and get confused. But now I'll explain properly. I'll explain the reasons for my impotence, the reason why I never will find the last word and all that.

Well, what happened was that, some months after my visit to Obaba, the people at home said to me: You're going deaf, you know. Me, deaf? I don't think so, I said, going on with my work. Because at that time, as I said before, I was engaged in writing down all the things that had happened on the journey to Obaba. But they didn't agree: You *are* going deaf. If anyone talks to you on your right side, you don't hear a thing. You should go to the doctor. And so I went. You've got a pierced eardrum, said my friend, the doctor. I mean that the doctor is my friend and it was he who told me that.

My friend – the doctor, right? – looked at me hard and said: Has your head felt strange at all? Any headaches? Do you sleep well? Of course I do. Why do you ask? I asked. And my friend looked away, embarrassed.

I did feel a little worried that day, but not much. I went on with my work. I mean I was translating a story entitled *Wei Lie Deshang* and had no time to think about anything else. And anyway, to tell the truth, I didn't really understand my friend's question. After all what did it matter if I was a little deaf?

My worries, my real worries, began later, a month later. I mean my friends began to hate me, not much, but a little. What happened was that we were all eating and drinking in a restaurant, when they suddenly burst out laughing. What are you laughing at? I asked. And they replied: What's wrong, 'Mr I – mean'? Didn't you enjoy the joke? What joke? I said, getting angry. And anyway why have you started calling me 'Mr I – mean'? Don't you know my real name? That was no way to talk to one's friends, of course, and it was then that they began to hate me, not much, but a little, as I said before.

Then, since my friends didn't want me around anymore, I decided to leave for Obaba and go to my uncle's house. And I spent hours and hours there reading and reading. One day my uncle asked: Why are you reading so many children's books? Are you thinking of writing an essay on children's literature? No, not at all, I replied, I'm reading them because I like them. Children's books are really fantastic, uncle. Are they? he asked, looking puzzled. Yes, they are, I said. For example, this one I'm reading at the moment is all about a mouse. It seems that this mouse, whose name is Timmy Willie, lives in a vegetable garden in a little village and what do you think happens? Well, one day he climbs into a basket to eat some peas and he goes to sleep there. I mean he just sort of drops off. And the owner of the vegetable garden comes along, lifts the basket onto his shoulder and goes off to the city to sell the peas. And all this time Timmy Willie is inside oblivious to everything and then, I'm sorry, uncle, but I have to laugh. And I burst out laughing. But I stopped at once when I saw the tears in my uncle's eyes. I mean it's not nice to laugh in front of someone when they're feeling sad, not nice at all.

Even so, even though he was sad, my uncle looked after me well, very well, I've absolutely no complaints on that score. He brought me orange juice in bed every morning and even a newspaper. I didn't fancy it though. I mean I'd drink the orange juice at once, but I didn't touch the newspaper. I preferred to continue the adventures of Timmy Willie. Put that book down now, nephew, and read the articles in the paper, he'd beg me. And because I love my uncle very much, I made an effort to please him. But it was all in vain. It was a real struggle for me to understand what was in the newspaper, especially the sports pages, that was the hardest bit, much harder than the political reports.

And that's why I started going out. You see, my uncle wouldn't give up, he kept going on about the newspaper, which I found both objectionable and in bad taste. So I'd go out instead and meet up with Albino María, spend all day with him and go back to his house to sleep, because there are lots of beds in Albino María's house, at least ten.

Then one day my uncle got really angry with me and he phoned my friend, the doctor I mean, and the two of them got hold of me and bundled me into a car. Then we drove and drove until at last we came to a big house, and all the people there were dressed in white. In fact everything in the house was very white, it was almost frightening. And then they led me to a room lined with cork and my uncle said: Forgive me, nephew, but it's for your own good. Putting it in terms that you can understand, what's happened is that a lizard has got inside your head. And we have to get rid of that lizard, because it's making you very ill.

A lizard making me ill? I replied. That's not possible, uncle. Lizards are so lovely and green. But I regretted my words the moment they were out of my mouth. I mean I saw the tears in my uncle's eyes.

Then my friend said to my uncle: I'm more to blame than you are. I didn't realise he was being serious, I thought the business about Ismael was just another of his literary games, a bit like playing at being detectives. And, like a fool, I went along with it.

My dear friend, I said, you're not a fool. Anyway, as far as I'm concerned, you can leave the lizard where it is. It doesn't bother me. And we chatted on like that for a while and then they shaved off my hair and they hurt me, hurt me really badly. I mean they clamped some iron things on my head and I screamed blue murder.

That was five days ago, I think, yes, five days and the three of us were happy as larks afterwards. I mean the pain stopped and we all felt really glad, especially my uncle. You're your old self again, he cried. And then, even more loudly, he said: The torch burns as long as the flame lives! The fact is he was behaving like a madman.

But now we're back again to how it was before. My uncle isn't happy any more. Yesterday he came to me and said: 'Nephew, write down what you told me about Joubert, make that your final text. And do it as soon as possible, because you're dying.'

'Me? Dying?' I replied. 'What do you mean? I think you're wrong about that, uncle.'

'What I mean is that before, your head was like a flaming torch,' explained my uncle, 'but that torch is burning lower by the minute.'

I didn't say anything at the time but I really think my uncle is going mad. My head has always been round, it's never been anything like a torch. And anyway I can't remember a thing about this Joubert person and I don't know what to write. I get bored sitting here in the library. Just as well there are some flies in here. I mean later on I can go fishing with Albino María and they'll come in really handy then, these flies I'm catching now.

BY WAY OF
AN AUTOBIOGRAPHY

I'VE HEARD it said that, like folk tales, the Game of the Goose represents a particular view of life, that it is a description of the tasks and the days we are allotted on this earth, a description and a metaphor.

What this view of life is can be seen by anyone familiar with the board and the rules of the game, for both the board and the rules show that, basically, life is a journey full of difficulties in which Chance and Free Will intervene in equal measure, a journey in which, despite those difficulties, and as long as the dice – or the fates – fall pretty much in our favour, it is possible to advance and safely reach that final pond where the Great Mother Goose awaits us.

The player just setting out on his journey can hope for nothing better than for his counter to land on one of the squares bearing a goose, because that player can then jump from goose to goose and so keep advancing.

There is nothing worse, on the other hand, than to land on squares like number forty-two, the maze, or fifty-two, the prison, or fifty-eight, bearing a skull. Landing on any of those squares means a delay or even the postponement or abandonment of the journey.

I should say, in passing, that it is not insignificant that the game-metaphor of which I speak revolves around the goose and not some other animal. And that's because the goose can walk on the earth, swim in water and fly through the air, which is why tradition has chosen it to symbolise wisdom, accomplishment, perfection.

The message of the game, therefore, is at once simple and

difficult to grasp. It is to do things as well as possible, day by day, goose by goose; only such continuity can guarantee ultimate wisdom and perfection.

But let's go back to the beginning and remember that the Game of the Goose can also be the description of a life, for example, the life of a Basque writer born in 1951.

And, of course, one notices coincidences the moment one looks at the board. Because a modern-day Basque writer, that is a writer who began writing in *euskera* some time in the seventies, bears a striking resemblance to that adolescent who appears on the first of the sixty-three squares on the board and who has as his only baggage a bundle.

Those of us who are just beginning to be translated into other languages, set off with very little baggage. We looked into our bundle and found only five, at most ten, books written in the language we were trying to write in. I read Gabriel Aresti when I was twenty; three years later, by the time I was twenty-three, I had read all the Basque literature that the dictator had not managed to burn.

This does not mean – as has so often been said – that we had no tradition, unless one is using the word 'tradition' in some ancient, obsolete sense. Because, as we know, nowadays, in the middle of the twentieth century – and this is one of the characteristics of the modern age – the whole of the literary past, be it from Arabia, China or Europe is at our disposal; in shops, in libraries, everywhere. Thus any writer is free to create his own tradition. He can read *The Arabian Nights* one day and *Moby Dick* or Kafka's *Metamorphosis* the next . . . and those works, the spirit that they communicate, will immediately pass into his own life and work as a writer.

These days nothing can be said to be peculiar to one place or person. The world is everywhere and Euskal Herria is no longer just Euskal Herria but – as Celso Emilio Ferreiro would have said – 'the place where the world takes the name of Euskal Herria'.

So I would never say that we present-day Basque writers lack a tradition; I would say that what we lacked was an antecedent, that we lacked books from which we could learn to write in our own language. Tom Thumb never passed our way and so we had no trail of breadcrumbs to lead us back home.

This is a matter of some importance, and one which, as many will have guessed, has to do with literary language. Because, naturally, to write is an artificial act and that artifice, which is literary language, is something that develops over time and through the labours of many people, adapting itself to the expressive needs of each age.

One of the consequences of those labours is, to give one example, the invisibility of certain words. When a reader reads a novel with a lot of dialogue, he probably doesn't even see the constant repetition in the text of 'he said', 'he replied' and 'he retorted'. The words are there but the same thing happens with them as happens with the trees on his favourite walk: he has read the words so many times, he doesn't even notice them.

Writing in *euskera*, I have no problems with 'he said' (*esan*) or with 'he replied' (*erantzun*) but I begin to have problems with 'he retorted' (*arrapostu*) because this word is not familiar to the reader, because it's a tree he recognises but which, nonetheless, he has never seen on this particular walk. So the Basque writer knows that his reader will stop at that word, that it will be a stumbling block.

I would say that the first duty of literary language is to be unobtrusive. And that's our weak point, because we lack antecedents, there are not enough books to create the habit of reading in Basque. And in the sixties we had an even harder time.

However, like every adolescent artist, the young Basque writer had enough energy to cover the first squares of the journey almost without noticing what he was doing, without realising what he had got himself into. Moreover, he felt he had a lot of things to say. Pío Baroja had not said it all.

Under that first impulse, the adolescent who set out on his

journey with his bundle over his shoulder got at least as far as square number nine, as far as the second goose: he published the odd story (I did in the anthology *Euskal Literatura*, 1972), the odd short novel (*Ziutateaz*, 1976) and even the odd book of poems (*Etiopia*, 1978).

But that brief experience only served to make him realise the limitations of his baggage. He immediately felt like the boy on square ten who is shown sailing in a little paper boat. The moment of uncertainty had arrived.

Nevertheless, quite a lot of us survived the paper boat test and managed to get past square ten, trying, in the first instance, to reach square twenty-four, the one showing a hare reading a book, and then square forty-three, where a venerable old man is doing the same as the hare: reading a book and taking the air.

These squares are now within our reach. To put it another way, we now have a literary market which, amongst other things, enables writers like myself to live off the royalties from such works as *Bi anai* (1984) and *Obabakoak* (1988).

The leap – from square ten to square forty-three – has been possible thanks to the help of various geese along the way. Gabriel Aresti, whom I mentioned before, was one of them, Luis Mitxelena another. They both worked so that we, the younger writers, would have a common literary language, the so-called *euskera batua*, so that we could exchange our bundle for a decent suitcase.

The journey continues and I think most of us believe that things will turn out well.

There are still fears though. I look at the board and I see square fifty-two, the prison; I see square fifty-eight, the skull; I see, right on square sixty-two, the one before Great Mother Goose's pond, a sinister man dressed in green and wearing a top hat . . . and I feel uneasy.

But we will keep trying, we will keep writing. The reason the board is there is for us to continue playing.

BERNARDO ATXAGA